Rainbow Reflections

Book 1:
A Kind of Magic

Ryder Rowan Phoenix

Special thanks to Eli for all the help with bringing this story to life, especially with figuring out the science behind the magic!
I also want to thank Raven, my parents, Alexia, Mr. Bay, and the White Dragon Martial Arts community for supporting me and who I am.
Thank you to Eli, Alex, and Hope for beta reading and editing.

Thank you to my fiancé, Blake, for supporting me in revamping this book to make it the best it can be!
…and for listening to me talk nonstop about my characters…

Idis
Storemble Ocean
Asali
Laal Sea
Estfel
Sea of Ryū
Kuokoa Islands
Galia
Ire
Balask Ocean
Teskra Sea
Churning Sea
Balask Ocean
Marsh Sea
Nederria
Treeland
Sutris Ocean
Talamh Glas

No Land
Idis
Storemble Ocean
Asali
Kòngdi
Kingdoms of Estfel
Khaaleé Jameen
Kòngdi
Kita No Ki
Xuĕ Yù
Lóng Zhī Guó
Alstraizia
Vudalaind
Tateey
Seibu No Ki
Rokkī
Shùmù Zhī Dì
Fènghuáng Chéng
Cladell
Pakshee Bhoomi
Dveep
Jangal
Galia
Sanmyaku
Căihóng Zhī Dì
Urula Lurrazia
Laal Sea
Vhel Dveep
Aakaash Parvat
Sea of Ryū
Ritterando
Truduw
Acer
Diem
Pann
Galia
Kuokoa Islands
Nuru
Kanzi
Harq Al'ard
Mamlakat Alsahra'
Dulif
Belix
Irĕ Empire
Ke Ka'aka
Mlima wa T'ai
Zahoor
Nasbeli
Ayg
Nrast
Neu
Tierra de Palmeras
Lua Pele
Visiwa Vitano
Sahra' Jafa.
'Sin Tarayih
Suhra' Alnakhil
Regden
Olpy
Dayl
Emex
Ba'a
Visiwa Vitatu
Mamlik 'Alramal
Aro
Reque
Enby
Gyn
Tierra de Fuego
Islas de la Estrella
Balask Ocean
Kidokezo cha Ardhi
Teskra Sea
Rio
Ze
Rinte
Xy'rs
X'es
Churning Sea
Balask Ocean
Andro
Gray
Triii
Plaats van Bomen
Nidawi Taigi
Alia
Marsh Sea
North Treeland
West Treeland
East Treeland
Wandle
Donoma
Plaats van Maneschijn
South Treeland
Loch Mór
Talamh an Tintri
Talamh Spiorad
Vacant Land
Sutris Ocean
Plaats van Sneeuw
Treeland
Talamh Ceo
Gan Talamh
Nederria
Talamh Glas

Caihong Academy of Magic

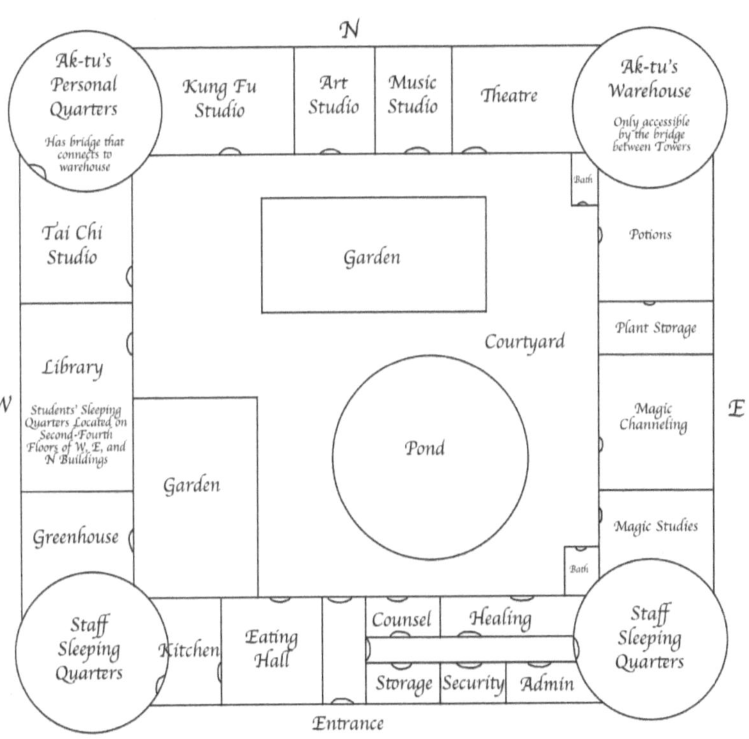

School Schedule

Time	Moonday	Trizday	Waddaday	Thorsday	Freday
7-8am	Breakfast	Breakfast	Breakfast	Breakfast	Breakfast
8-9am	Magic Studies 1	Magic Studies 2	Magic Studies 3	Magic Studies 4	Drawing/Painting
9-10am	Magic Channeling 1	Magic Channeling 2	Magic Channeling 3	Magic Channeling 4	Cooking
10-11am	Plants 1	Plants 2	Plants 3	Plants 4	Writing
11-12pm	Potions 1	Potions 2	Potions 3	Potions 4	Fashion
12-1pm	Lunch	Lunch	Lunch	Lunch	Lunch
1-2pm	Kung Fu 1A	Kung Fu 2A	Kung Fu 3A	Kung Fu 4A	Choir
2-3pm	Kung Fu 1B	Kung Fu 2B	Kung Fu 3B	Kung Fu 4B	Band
3-4pm	Tai Chi 1A	Tai Chi 2A	Tai Chi 3A	Tai Chi 4A	Theatre
4-5pm	Tai Chi 1B	Tai Chi 2B	Tai Chi 3B	Tai Chi 4B	Theatre
5-6pm	Dinner	Dinner	Dinner	Dinner	Dinner

Ak-tu Caihong

(hyahk-two sigh-honn)

Zynivus Zephyr Caihong

(zinn-ih-vis zeh-fur sigh-honn)

Ren Arashi Caihong

(renn ah-rah-she sigh-honn)

sarala Kiran

(sar-rah-lah key-run)

Jabali Kenyada

(juh-ball-lee Ken-yah-duh)

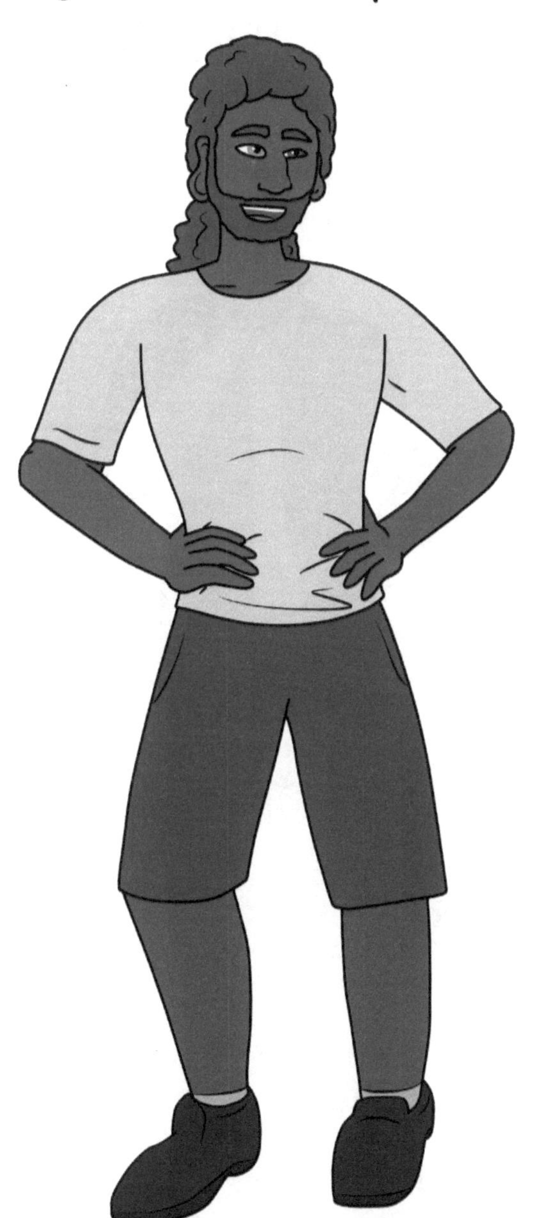

Cypress "C3"
Celyn Clay
(sigh-press see-three kell-linn klay)

Mamo "Mint" Kaheka
(mah-mo mint kah-he-kuh)

Khurshid Jihan

(Khorr-shidd gee-hunn)

Fern Oakley

(fern oak-lee)

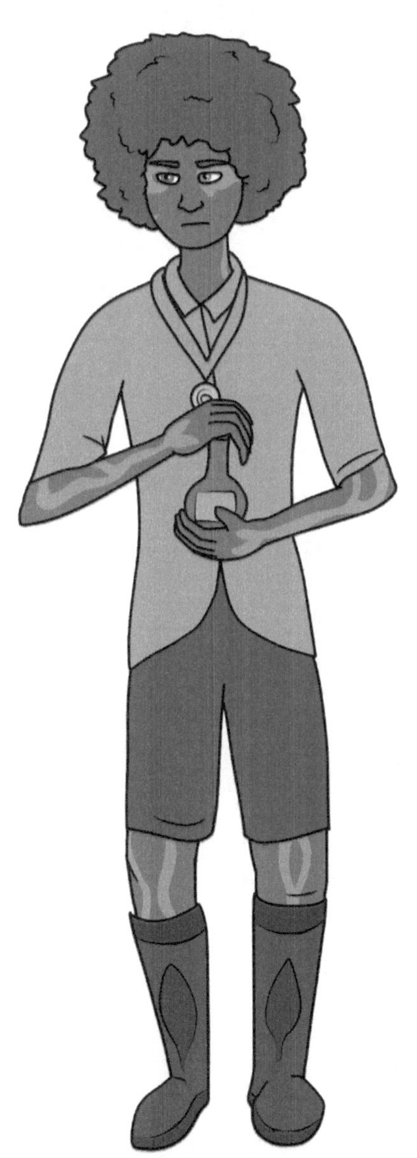

Aster Sundale
(ast-terr sun-day-ull)

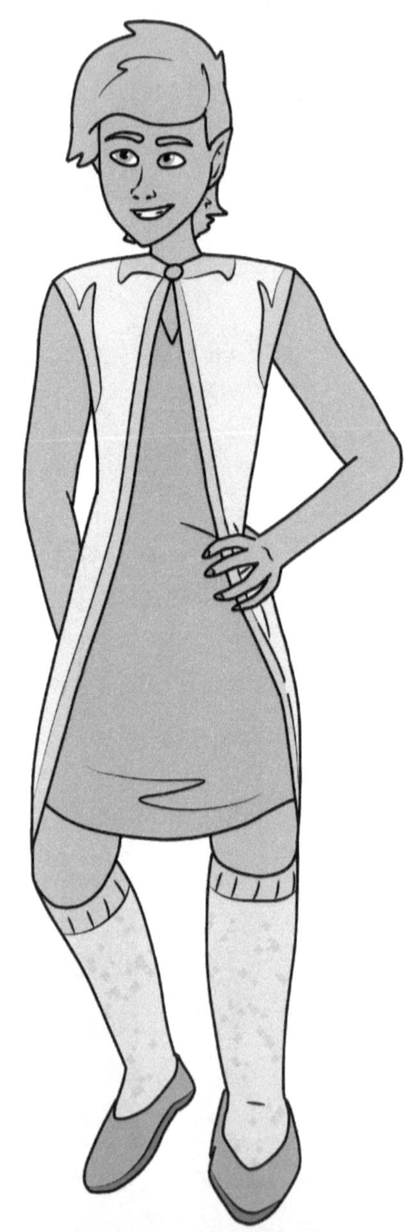

Chaocat
(kay-oh-cat)

Chaocat

(kay-oh-cat)

CHAPTER 1: THUNDERBOLT AND LIGHTNING

Lightning flashed across the sky, forking in all directions. Thunder rumbled after it, audible over the pounding sound of rain as it slammed the ground. The sky was thick with black clouds, the full moon hidden far behind them.

Ak-tu stumbled to his feet in a daze, his vision blurry and his ears rattling. All he could smell was salt—the salt of the ocean smashing around him. The moment he stood, he staggered back a few steps, a small wave of nausea passing over him. He held his arms out, but still felt off-balance. Legs giving way beneath him, he fell back to the stony ground.

He did not know if he could go on. His whole body was aching, his chest felt as if it was being stabbed with each breath he took. How could he ever get to his feet again if he couldn't breathe properly? Breathing was the life force, the one thing he could not go days or even minutes without. If he couldn't breathe —if breathing was a pain…how was he ever going to make it?

The wind whipped his indigo hair around, first behind him and then flicking about his face. It was the annoyance of his hair dancing across his closed eyes that made him come to his senses.

I'm not done yet, he thought fiercely.

Ak-tu's violet eyes opened and he got to his feet, almost without hesitation this time. He brushed his hair out of his face, so only the ends of his thick unibrow tickled his forehead. He then went against the wailing wind and lashing rain, his hair and mustache blowing behind him.

He couldn't quite remember what had happened to him. The storm had arrived out of nowhere, surrounding the little island he was upon. But he hadn't been alone…

"Chaocat!" he breathed, and his steps quickened despite his chest still aching.

He had come to the island to meet with Chaocat. The two had to be on the island for a specific purpose...hadn't they been meeting for something—some*one*, perhaps? But then the storm had struck, sending the two in opposite directions, preventing them from achieving their goal.

Ak-tu remembered the searing pain of his head being slammed against the ground. This couldn't be just any storm—it was a magical one, perhaps even a spiritual one.

I have to find Chaocat, he thought numbly. *We have to get out of here at once! If there are spirits around...*

He did not finish that thought, and pressed onwards. The thunder and lightning continued to cause chaos in the clouds, the rain hitting harder by the minute. After what seemed like ages of forcing his weary legs forward, one step at a time, each breath rattling like a maraca, he finally made it to the center of the island—the highest point.

He glanced on each side of him, his angular eyes flicking over brittle trees scattered about, waves smashing against the black-sanded shores, and a river that now threatened to consume a good chunk of the island.

{*Chaocat, where are you?*} Ak-tu's eyes flicked to and fro more desperately, his breathing becoming shallow and sharp once more. He didn't see any spirits yet, but that didn't mean they weren't already here...

"Chaocat!" he shouted pointlessly in the ruckus, hardly able to hear his own voice. "CHAOCAT!"

But no matter how much he looked around, he could see nothing beyond the forces of the storm. Chaocat wasn't there.

It's not a tiny island, said a small but doubtful voice in Ak-tu's head. *They've got to be around here somewhere.*

But what about the river? Another voice replied to the first, full of raw emotion. *If they landed in that...well, they might not have survived...*

Trembling, Ak-tu's knees collapsed beneath him, and he covered his face with his hands. He could not have lost Chaocat... they *had* to be alive!

"I will find you," he promised quietly, removing his hands from his face and looking around once more. "No matter how long it takes, I will find you, Chaocat..."

Ak-tu sat in a more comfortable lotus position on the ground and closed his eyes. Taking several deep breaths, he attempted to ignore the sharp pain that came with them, focusing on relaxing as best as he could.

Maybe I can find them with my magic... I just have to imagine them...then I'll find them!

He willed his stiff muscles to relax, his frigid fingers to unclench. Taking one more deep breath, he imagined a small red cat in his mind's eye, wearing a crescent moon necklace. His hair touched his face and the back of his neck as the wind continued to roar, reminding him of Chaocat's bushy tail tickling his nose.

Let me find Chaocat...let me see them! Ak-tu thought, over and over. *Please, I need to find Chaocat!*

But nothing changed in the storm around him, and Ak-tu groaned lightly and opened his eyes.

"Did my magic block off?" he muttered in a croaky voice he could not hear, his hands clenching into fists. "Am I too weak right now? I can't have lost my magic..."

Ak-tu closed his eyes once more, taking another raspy breath. *Where is Chaocat? Show me where Chaocat is! Show me where anyone is! Please!*

He reached his energy outwards, feeling for any vibration of magic, searching for any sign of life...

Opening his eyes, he clambered to his feet. He had felt something, near the ancient trees. It was a buzzing spark of qi, warm like fire and fluid like water, as light as the sky and as real as the earth, thrumming through his blood like a heartbeat. He wasn't alone!

Ak-tu went as quickly as his knotted feet could carry him, though they wanted to scream. He stumbled down the small slope towards the leafless trees. The plants weren't faring too well in the storm. Though they had clearly been a part of the island for a very long time, they had never been part of a magical storm before. Lots of rough-barked branches broke off, while other trees had snapped in half completely, too stiff to withstand the elements.

Ak-tu scrambled over the fallen trees, reaching out with his energy once again. For a moment, he did not feel anything but the cold wind slapping his tattered robe around his ankles. Then, he detected the other energy, merely feet away. Ak-tu opened his eyes and headed towards a hollowed-out stump several meters from him.

"Chaocat?" Ak-tu called loudly, hoping his voice could be heard now that he was nearby.

But he received no response—or maybe he did, and he just couldn't hear it.

Hoping it was Chaocat, Ak-tu knelt beside the stump and looked through the hole towards the bottom. What he saw was definitely not Chaocat.

A baby was lying under the wood, their eyes closed as they slept. Ak-tu had no idea how any infant was able to sleep during a raging storm. He looked away from the stump, then glanced back, but the baby was still there. He wasn't hallucinating then—at least, as far as he knew.

He had no idea where the child had come from, as the island lay uninhabited. Even animals did not live upon it; only some creatures remained for a few days before moving on. But as Ak-tu continued to stare, he felt a sense that he knew this newborn. He didn't know how he could; he didn't remember any babies on his travels. But there was something about this infant…

He reached out for the baby, and as soon as his hands closed around them, they started to cry. Their cries were lost in the storm, but Ak-tu could detect their turmoil nonetheless. It somehow hurt more than his sharp breaths or gnarled feet.

"It'll be okay," he soothed quietly as he wrapped the child in his soaked robe. "I'll protect you."

At the low murmuring of his voice, or perhaps because of being lifted, the baby opened their eyes. Ak-tu could sense some sort of bond between them. The baby closed their eyes again and cried, Ak-tu pulling them even closer, reacting as instinctively as any parent would.

He frowned, his foggy mind starting to clear. How could he have forgotten what had happened—what had caused the storm, the big blast, maybe even the baby?

Ak-tu shook his head. It didn't matter now. *All that matters is I find a way off of this island and protect this baby.*

Ak-tu held the infant closer to his aching chest as he clambered to the center of the island again, the pain in his body leaving bit by bit as he had something else to focus on—something else to live for. The lightning was no longer flashing, the thunder had stopped, and the rain was ebbing. The storm was at its end.

"Well, little one, you're going to need a name," Ak-tu murmured. "How do you like Arashi? It's quite fitting, given the circumstances of your birth in a storm."

The baby opened their eyes and stared up at him.

"Yes, we need something more," Ak-tu said softly, sitting down in a lotus position. "Oh—how about Ren, or Lotus?"

The child let out a soft cry; whether of delight or fear, he did not know.

"Ren Arashi Caihong it is, then," Ak-tu whispered. "I promise to protect you with my life, little one…" He looked up and stared at the vast ocean around them, which had finally calmed down. "I better see if I can contact Jabali to get us out of here…though that's going to take more magic, and I'm not sure I've got it in me right now…"

The baby made another small noise and reached out a hand towards him. Ak-tu grasped the tiny hand with his fingers, and could again feel that bond—the bond of parent and child.

Ak-tu smiled and brought the infant closer, shielding them from the air, as if the salt would sting their eyes or bite at their skin. But his smile soon turned into a frown as he realized the responsibility now put onto him, as he recalled what had happened.

Contacting his friend was the least of their worries…

CHAPTER 2: ON THE PROWL

"Gooooood morning!"

Zynivus flung the door open as she shouted, grinning from ear to ear. She gripped the edges of the doorframe and rocked back and forth on her feet. A moment later, a second call rang through the tower, bouncing off the stone walls.

"Good morning, Zyn!"

It was her sister, Ren. The siblings—or twins, as they liked to refer to themselves as—called out greetings every single day. Ever since Zyn read in a book that it was good practice to greet the spirits and nature each morning, she had adopted the practice for fun. Ren quickly picked up on it too. Zyn couldn't remember a time where she and Ren *didn't* scream greetings first-thing in the morning.

Once Zyn received Ren's acknowledgement, she dashed down the stone steps, already dressed in her usual fashion: a striped shirt, baggy pants, and a bright orange robe depicting golden sun patterns. Her scarlet hair was spiky and short, parted to the left— just like her sister and father wore their hair. Unlike her purple-eyed family, only her left eye was violet; her right eye was emerald.

She reached her sister's room on the floor beneath her bedroom. Ren's door was already open, and Ren herself sat in the middle of the lavender-painted room, matching the walls with her purple hair and robe. The window was wide, allowing a soft breeze to blow through and rustle the many potted plants. Plants hung from the ceiling, sat on the wide desk on one side of the room, stood in large pots on the wooden floor, and even hung outside the window. Sweet floral scents meshed with the earthy soil, reminding Zyn of traveling through a jungle whenever she entered her twin's room. Though there were plants seemingly everywhere, the room did not feel as cluttered as a forest, and instead felt airy and light.

"Meditating again?" Zyn asked as soon as she entered.

Ren didn't turn to face her sister. She was sitting in the lotus position on the ground, her back to the door and her palms facing upwards. Zyn knew without looking that her violet eyes would be closed behind her rectangular glasses. Zyn jumped into a seated position beside her and saw that she was correct.

"I can never understand how you just sit there like that," Zyn commented after a moment.

Ren opened one eye to glance sidelong at her, a smile dancing on her lips. "It's meditation, Zyn, not torture."

"It's torture if you can't sit still," Zyn chuckled, springing to her feet.

Ren opened both of her angular eyes and looked up at Zyn. "Maybe if you put in the effort, you'd be able to do it too," she suggested.

"Nah, it's too boring," Zyn said with a shrug, grinning.

Ren snorted in amusement and got to her feet as well. She brushed off her sports shorts, ran a hand through her parted hair, and beamed.

"Well, happy birthday, Zyn!" she said joyfully. "What's it feel like being fourteen? Finally have your magic?"

"Only one way to find out!" Zyn exclaimed, and she punched the air in front of her, concentrating on the magic within her.

But nothing happened.

"Um...how do you do magic again?" Zyn asked Ren.

Ren had discovered her magic at eleven, though most people summoned their magic at thirteen or fourteen. Zyn waited eagerly for thirteen, but her magic had still been absent. She tried to summon it several times the past year, but figured she'd have to wait for her fourteenth birthday on July 28.

"You just need to reach inside you and bring it forward," Ren said simply.

Zyn stared at her. "But...*how?*"

There was a knock on the door, and the two looked up to see a man in a rainbow tank top. He had indigo hair reaching just past his shoulders, parted to the left like the twins. A unibrow sat above his neon violet eyes, and his mustache appeared as two long strands that hung past his squarish chin.

"I should've known you'd be in here," Ak-tu said to Zyn, entering the room with a wide grin on his face. "Happy birthday!"

"Dad, how do I do magic?" Zyn asked her father, running over to him.

Ak-tu chuckled at the abrupt question. "You need to relax, reach inside yourself, and let it flow out. You can't try forcing it."

She crossed her arms over her chest and grunted, "You two need to work on your explanation skills." *{And he opened a school!}* Zyn grumbled telepathically to Ren.

Ren snorted in laughter, then said, "We're trying, you know!"

Ak-tu raised one end of his unibrow at Zyn. "If you can say it to Ren, you can say it to me."

Zyn stuck out her tongue at him. "Then work on your teaching skills, Mr. Caihong!"

They all laughed for a moment, then Ak-tu said, "You'll learn soon enough. After all, assessments are next week. I'm so excited you'll be taking magic classes this year!"

"What—did you get tired of teaching us about math and history?" Zyn scoffed playfully.

"Very," Ak-tu said blandly, before he smiled and placed his hands on both of their shoulders. "I've dreamed of this day ever since I had plans of building this school. Now that you both have your magic, you can finally learn!"

"Um—hello—I don't have any magic still!" Zyn said, waving her hands around.

"You'll have it," Ak-tu said plainly.

"Then tell me how to summon it!" Zyn insisted.

"I already did. If you can't summon it by next week, I'll have you do the magic assessments," Ak-tu told her.

Zyn sighed in exasperation. This was *just* like her father, making her wait for things when she couldn't figure them out on her own!

"Let's go have breakfast!" Ak-tu said, and he left the room.

Zyn waited for his footsteps to fade away, then turned to Ren, her hands clenching into fists at her sides as her body tensed.

"You *have* to help me summon my magic before the assessments next week!" she said, her heart beating quickly.

"But the magic assessments are there to help you and all the other students summon their magic in the first place," Ren pointed out. "They aren't *real* tests, you know."

"I guess not, but…I don't want to do them if I don't have to," Zyn muttered. "Please help me!"

"You know I will!" Ren said. She tapped her pointed chin for a moment, then exclaimed, "I have an idea!"

"What is it?" Zyn asked eagerly.

"Come join me for a meditation session!"

Zyn groaned inwardly, but followed Ren to the center of her plant-filled room. She sat down beside her sister, facing the window.

"Straighten your back and close your eyes," Ren instructed. "Once you're relaxed, I'll give you a guided meditation, to let you journey inwards to discover your magic."

Zyn nodded, doing as she said. She kept her eyes closed in as relaxed a way as possible, breathing as slowly as she could. All she could smell were stinky flowers that made her nose twitch and itch. Holding back a sneeze, she forced herself to concentrate on Ren's soft voice.

"Focus on your breath…good…that keeps you from being distracted…"

The moment Ren said the word, Zyn automatically began thinking of other things. Her mind swirled in a distracted frenzy, jumping from magic to the games they'd play that day to the cool-looking fog outside to wondering what type of magic she had to pondering if plants could help her discover her magic. She no longer paid much attention to Ren.

"There's a large pond in the clearing," Ren said gently, as Zyn finally managed to focus on her medium voice again. "Its surface is so still, so shiny. You walk towards the pond…the grass is light and springy underfoot. You stop at the pond and look down at your reflection."

Zyn imagined this to the best of her ability, but her reflection seemed to be very shimmery or nonexistent.

"Your reflection stares back at you, then lifts her hand. One of the four elements is floating in her palm, showing you your inner magic. Embrace it."

Zyn tried to picture the choppy reflection of herself doing as Ren said, but she didn't know which element she'd have—fire or air?

"You feel the magic moving through your body, coursing through your fingertips," Ren persisted. "You feel an energy within. *This* is your magic."

Zyn felt energy within, but she didn't know if it was actually magic or just her normal energy. Frowning as she considered this, she soon stopped listening to Ren once more, her mind flitting about.

"Now jump up and punch the air!" Ren yowled fiercely, waking Zyn from her stupor.

She jolted in surprise, then hopped to her feet and punched the air like Ren had ordered. But nothing happened.

"I was hoping that would work!" Ren grumbled in dismay. "Did you feel anything at all?"

Zyn sighed and shook her head. "It was kinda hard to focus," she muttered, sneezing as her nose couldn't take the floral scents any longer.

"I'm sorry, Zyn, I can't think of what else you can do," Ren admitted. "I found my magic by meditating. Hmm…we can always try researching more books, but I'm not sure if we'll be able to get away with looking up magic books. Aster always finds a way to stop us."

"We'll just have to go to the Library at night, when Aster's not snooping around," Zyn said, wondering why she hadn't thought of that before. She and Ren had tried many times to get their hands on magic books, but Ak-tu was strict about keeping any knowledge of magic from their clutch until they were attending school.

Ren bit her bottom lip. "I don't want to get in trouble. You know we're not supposed to look at those books. Besides, Aster locks the Library every night."

Zyn sighed and played with a string on her robe, lowering her gaze. "Then what am I supposed to do? If meditation and punching the air doesn't work…"

"You have to keep trying," Ren said firmly. "You're new to meditation, so if you want to give it another go later tonight, maybe once you're more worn out and relaxed, we can. And we can try again tomorrow morning, and every day until you find your magic."

Zyn fidgeted uneasily. "But what if I don't have it by the time the magic assessments are here?"

"That could be a good thing," Ren pointed out. "The assessments teach you how to summon magic. That's why they exist!"

Zyn sighed again and reverted to telepathy. *{I just don't want to take these assessments…}*

{I know.} Ren replied by thoughts, her voice echoing lightly in Zyn's head. *{But they can't be all that bad, if they're used every year on new students.}*

{It's not so much that, it's…performing magic in front of everyone.} Zyn thought lamely, tugging the string absentmindedly.

"But you love acting! Just think of it as an acting performance!" Ren pointed out, beaming at Zyn.

{No, it's not like an acting performance, not if I don't have time to prepare or know what I'm supposed to be doing.} Zyn replied dimly, mouthing the words as she thought them. *{I don't want to do those assessments. I just want my magic to come.}*

{It will.} Ren promised. "Let's go get some breakfast," she said aloud, ending their telepathic conversation.

Zyn sighed and got to her feet, following Ren down the tower stairs, the air warm around them. They passed the bathroom on the second floor and reached the family room on the ground floor.

This room was painted blue, and even the rugs covering the wooden floor were azure. Two tables were against the right wall, where tall windows overlooked the forest beyond the school. To the left was a couch and an armchair, sky blue in color. The couch faced a fireplace, while the armchair sat next to a bookshelf. Above the stone fireplace was a large picture of Ak-tu and the twins when they were younger. Several more pictures of the family hung on the walls, making the room feel warm and welcoming.

The siblings crossed the room and made it to the front door of the tower. Zyn opened the door and they slipped into the Tai Chi Studio, which was empty at the moment. After all, school was out for the summer break, meaning that Zyn and Ren had free run of the entire school. Zyn locked the door behind them (out of habit, since it wasn't necessary to lock the door without any students around), then the sisters hurried from the classroom to the Court-yard outside.

Two large gardens were situated in the Courtyard, with one in the north (to their left) and the other next to the western wall (in front of them). A huge pond lay in the southeastern corner (diago-nally to their left). The southern building straight ahead held the Eating Hall, Entrance Hall, and office rooms.

As the sisters made their way across the sunlit Courtyard though, they stopped in their tracks. Ak-tu had flung the Eating Hall door open, and was now sprinting across the stone ground, his baggy pants billowing. He entered through the next door over, which opened up to the Entrance Hall.

"Where's Dad going?" Ren asked, baffled.

"Let's go find out!" Zyn said eagerly, quivering in excitement.

The two hurried after their father, sliding to a halt just outside the door that led to the Entrance Hall. Zyn wished there was a window in the door for them to peer through, or a window in the hall itself, but there was nothing. She therefore turned the knob quietly, opening the door at the slowest pace she could manage.

Ak-tu was at the front of the hall, where the two glass double-doors sat. These doors were typically locked at all times, so no-body could enter or exit the school. But at the moment, they were wide open. Ak-tu stood in the doorway, a teenager in the grass across from him. A small stone statue sat on the ground beside the teen, its appearance that of a frog with fangs. Zyn couldn't get a good look at them from the angle she was at, since she didn't want to open the door too far.

"…your name?" Ak-tu was asking the teen.

But the teenager did not answer him, Zyn's heart picking up speed as she was tempted to lean in closer.

"Do you want to come inside? I'm not going to hurt you. I'm the founder of this school, and I won't allow any harm to come to you while you're here."

After a moment, the teen nodded. As Ak-tu turned around to reenter the hall, Zyn closed the door hurriedly, leaving it open just a crack so it wouldn't make noise when it shut. The sisters could hear Ak-tu and the teenager walk across the hall, their footsteps echoing in the empty space. Zyn hoped they weren't about to go to the Courtyard, otherwise they'd run right into the twins.

Luckily, they opened the door that led to another hall, this one smaller. The second hall held the doors that led to the Healing, Counseling, and Admin rooms. They would likely sit in one of the offices.

{Come on!} Zyn said to Ren.

Ren nodded beside her.

Pushing the door open once more, Zyn entered the hall and tiptoed to the door sitting on the left wall. She waited a long moment, then opened the door slowly and listened for footsteps. Unable to hear anything, so she poked her head through and looked down the hall. Ak-tu and the teen had vanished.

{Where do you think they went?} Zyn asked, nearly muttering the words aloud.

{Definitely not the Healing room or Storage room.} Ren replied. *{I doubt he'd take them to the Security Office, either. They're just a kid, after all, not a threat. So probably the Counseling Office or Admin Office.}*

Zyn pricked her ears, angling her head to the first door on their left, which led to the Counseling Office. She couldn't hear any voices coming from within.

{Let's try the Admin Office.} Zyn decided.

The sisters crept down the hall, keeping their footsteps as light as feathers. Once they were a few paces away from the Admin Office, they paused in their tracks, lingering just outside the door. Zyn could hear soft murmurs, but she couldn't determine what was being said, even as she closed her eyes to concentrate. She inched closer as slowly as she could, hoping she wouldn't stir the stuffy air too much.

{Can you hear anything they're saying?} Zyn asked Ren irritably.

Ren frowned beside her, focusing on the open doorway meters away. *{A bit…it's kind of muffled. It sounds like Dad's asking them where their parents are.}*

{Wouldn't be the first time a family camping trip's gone wrong.} Zyn said, trying not to chuckle aloud.

Over the years, several people arrived at the school, losing their way in the thick forest and unable to find their families. Ak-tu would always help the strangers locate their group, and they'd be on their way.

Ren's frown grew deeper on her freckled face. *{It sounds like… they don't have a family.}* She cocked her head to listen better.

Zyn blinked in surprise, shifting closer to the door. But her sister held her arm up to block her advance. Instead, Ren tiptoed ever nearer, her bare feet silent as they crossed the hard wooden floor. But before she could tell Zyn anything else, a new thought entered Zyn's mind.

{Zyn, Ren, get in here.}

It was Ak-tu. He knew they were there.

CHAPTER 3: LIAR

Sarala glanced towards the open door as two people shuffled in. Her golden eyes narrowed over her hooked nose, and she appeared hawk-like as she stared them down. Had they been outside the Admin Office the whole time? Why were they suddenly coming in?

"These are my children," the school founder told Sarala calmly, sitting across from her at a wide desk.

The first person had brown skin and spiky orange hair. Their eyes were mismatched, and did not complement the bright orange robe they were wearing. In fact, none of what they were wearing seemed to go together. The stripy gray shirt with the heavily-patterned robe, and the baggy red pants—it was all a big clash. This person did not look anything like the teacher behind the desk, or the person beside them.

The second person had thick purple hair, rectangular glasses, and angular eyes. They looked more like the school founder, though there were notable differences. Their freckled face was pretty—and Sarala did not think that of too many people.

"They are both orphans I took in," the teacher went on, rubbing his thumb and pointer finger over one of his long mustache strands.

Sarala flicked her gaze to him. *"And?"* she grumbled. "Just because I said I lived alone doesn't mean I'm an orphan."

"But you and I both know that you are," he said simply.

"Who do you even think you are, claiming to know who I am after barely meeting me?" Sarala hissed.

"I told you," he said patiently. "I am Ak-tu Caihong, the founder of this school, and the father of two orphaned children. I've been around the world. I've met all sorts of people. I know you're an orphan—or a runaway child."

"I'm not a child!" Sarala protested crossly.

Ak-tu smiled at her. "But you *are* an orphan."

She huffed impatiently and slumped back in her chair. Staring down at her dirty brown pants underneath her tattered yellow robe, she could feel the twigs poking into her tan skin and the small bits of leaves in her dark brown hair. It was no wonder Ak-tu saw right through her. What else was he supposed to think when a dirty teenager emerged from the thick forest, clearly lost for months—or years?

"Why did you come to this school?" Ak-tu pressed after a moment of silence.

Sarala didn't answer.

"If you've been living in the wild and know how to get by on your own, then you'd have no need to come to civilization for something like food or water, surely?" Ak-tu continued. "Not to mention, the lands here are bountiful in fruits, vegetables, and rivers."

Sarala clenched her jaw and made no reply.

"I will ask only once more," Ak-tu said, his features hardening a bit as he leaned closer. "Why did you come to this school?"

She took a deep breath, then queried, "What school is this?"

Ak-tu frowned. "The Caihong Academy of Magic."

Sarala searched her memory. It sounded familiar, but it wasn't exact. "Can you write it down?"

Ak-tu continued frowning at her, but did as she asked. He scrawled several words across a piece of paper in front of him, and handed it to her.

Sarala read the words with a bit of difficulty; she wasn't the best when it came to reading or writing. "*Kay*-hong!" she said triumphantly, tapping the paper.

"No, it's *Sigh*-hong," Ak-tu pointed out. "It's Asalian."

"I've always read it as *Kay*-hong," she explained. "It's not like I had anyone to tell me how to pronounce it." *Not when I got that pamphlet…not when I was abandoned…*

Ak-tu nodded his understanding. "So you are familiar with my school? You were actively searching for it?"

Sarala clenched her jaw again. She didn't know how to respond to that. Of course she had heard of the academy, and she had indeed been looking for it over the past few months or year.

She took a deep breath, then let it go and nodded.

"Why?" Ak-tu pressed.

"Can't you just leave me be, Ock-too?" she snapped, a knot twisting in her stomach as red flashed through her mind.

Ak-tu looked a bit annoyed at this. "*Hyahk*-too. It's pronounced with a sharp *hyahk!* sound."

She shrugged. "Sorry."

He stared at her through his bright violet eyes, searching her for a long moment. "I prefer to know who my students are before taking them in. But I see you are determined to learn, if you've been searching for my school. So I will let you stay."

She stared at him.

"It's what you want, is it not? A magical education? It's why you came all this way?"

Sarala nodded once.

"Then you will have it," he said simply.

"But...I'm..." She clenched her jaw. "I don't have any money."

"You don't need to have money," Ak-tu told her quietly. "But I'd prefer if you didn't scream about it to the other students—that you got in for free. While magical high schools aren't as expensive as magical universities, it's still not cheap. If you really want to be here, you must agree not to tell any other students. Ren and Zynivus—my daughters—are the only exceptions."

Sarala nodded again.

Ak-tu smiled. "Well, then...if you agree to not tell others how you got in, I will admit you to the school."

"Of course," Sarala said at once.

"Good, very good," Ak-tu said with a nod. "I'll just need you to fill out some paperwork. It's the standard forms all students have to fill out," he added, when seeing Sarala grow tense.

"Fine," she uttered.

Ak-tu grabbed the mirror that was lying flat on the desk in front of him, tapped its glass surface, and it no longer reflected the ceiling. It showed a screen with different buttons. He pressed on one, and it opened up to what looked like a document.

"To move things along quicker, I'll just fill it out for you," Ak-tu told her, tapping on a box. "I do need your signature at the bottom afterwards. Now...what is your full name?"

Sarala's heartbeat quickened. *If I give my full name…they could track me down, couldn't they? They could return me to that orphanage… What if this is all just a trap to send me back? I'll just have to make it up…* "Sarala Kiran," she said, hoping none of them would notice the small hesitation.

Ak-tu nodded and tapped a keyboard on the mirror's screen. "Birthday? Do you know your birthday?"

"Um…April…6. Yes, April 6."

"The year?"

"Um…39."

"So you're fifteen," Ak-tu said, adding that in the form.

He continued through the document, only pausing to have Sarala demonstrate she had magical ability. When she said she had earth magic, he handed her a stone and told her to prove it. She smashed the stone in her hands, making it crumble to dust. Ak-tu added that to the form and pressed on, until they were done.

When it came to the section on family history, Ak-tu wrote that Sarala had a rich uncle from Idis who passed away and left all of his money to Sarala, his only known relative. He "left" her enough money to pay for her magic education.

"I just need you to sign here," Ak-tu told her, turning the mirror and pointing at the bottom of the document.

"And there's…no magic attached to this signature?" she asked hesitantly.

Ak-tu shook his head.

After a long moment, Sarala used her finger to scribble in the box on the screen. Ak-tu then swiveled the mirror back around, Sarala able to feel a light breeze as he moved.

"You're almost all set up," he told her. "We just need to take a photo of you for your ID card, and give you a key to your new room."

"A photo?" Sarala questioned. She felt her dirty face and frowned. "Can I at least get cleaned up?"

"Of course," Ak-tu replied. "Ren, Zyn—you two help Sarala, then bring her back here for the photo."

Sarala turned to face the two teenagers. They looked to be about a year younger than her, though they all stood at about the same height. She got to her feet and approached the sisters slowly, eyeing them warily.

Which one is which? Sarala wondered.

But the orange-haired twin wearing the patterned robe quickly thrust her hand out and exclaimed, "Hi, I'm Zyn!"

Sarala stared at her for a long moment. *That was easy. So Zyn is the one with the crazy robe…and the letter Z is in crazy, plus a crazy letter in general, right? So Zyn is the crazy one. Hopefully I don't get their names mixed up now…*

Ren glanced at her sister, her mouth twitching like she was about to speak before settling back into an amused smirk. Zyn lowered her hand with a small chuckle. Sarala raised an eyebrow, wondering if she had missed something.

"Come on, Sarala!" Ren said, once the odd exchange seemed to be over.

Ren twirled on the spot and led the way from the room. Zyn motioned for Sarala to follow, then took up the rear. Ren brought them to a long room of beds and cabinets, the scent of mint strong. They then went through another door, stepping into the warm outdoor air.

A pond shimmered in front of her, and a garden lay several meters beyond. Sarala stared up at the three tan walls around her, feeling suddenly trapped between the stone structures. There were four towers, one in each corner of the wide square Courtyard. Heart beating rapidly, she almost missed Ren's words.

"The bathroom is right there," Ren said, pointing to her right.

Sarala shook herself from her stupor, then nodded and entered the small building with Ren at her heel. The bathroom looked like a hut against the southeastern tower and eastern building. As soon as she walked through the door, the light flickered on. She stared up at the metal rods, which were filled with fire magic and enchanted to shine light when movement was detected. Sarala only knew this because of her experience breaking into shops to steal food during closed hours.

She moved to the mirror against one wall, taking in her reflection. She was dirty; there was no other way to put it. Next to Ren, she looked like the ugliest person to exist. Bits of twigs and leaves clung to her robe and hair. She pulled these out as best as she could, but her hair was still a tangled mess.

"Whatever," she muttered.

"Here, let me try," Ren said.

She leaned forward and took the twigs out of Sarala's hair. Her hands were so gentle against Sarala's scalp, and she soon found her eyes half-closing in relaxation. She missed the feeling of fingers running through her hair.

"I think I got most of them," Ren said a few minutes later, stepping back to observe the back of Sarala's head. "It looks much better!"

"It's fine if you didn't get it all," Sarala said simply. "It feels better anyway."

She turned the sink on and splashed cool water over her face, removing the dirt and sweat after a few rough scrubs. Ren handed her a bamboo paper towel from a roll hanging on the wall, and she wiped the remaining water off.

"That'll have to do," she muttered.

"We'll get you more cleaned up later, but you're definitely photo-worthy!" Ren said, beaming at her.

Sarala shrugged in response, then led the way from the bathroom. Zyn stood outside, clearly bored as she tapped her foot impatiently against the cobblestone ground.

"Took you long enough!" she said, rolling her eyes. "Come on!"

Zyn led the way back to the Admin Office, practically running. Ak-tu waited for them to reenter, still holding the square-shaped mirror at the ready.

"Stand against that wall," Ak-tu told Sarala, signaling to a blank spot of the yellow wall near the door.

Sarala did as he told her, and he lifted the mirror to be level with his face. After a few seconds, he nodded that he was done, then returned to his desk.

Another silent minute passed as he tapped a few more things, then there was a rumbling noise. Sarala searched the room, her heartbeat quickening once more. But she had no need to worry—it was just her ID card printing out.

Ak-tu picked up the card from a small bin, where it had landed underneath the rumbling machine on a back desk. He handed it to Sarala. It was made of bamboo, and had her picture on the surface. Her name, date of birth, pronouns, and elemental magic were listed on it.

"This ID card is used to check out books from the Library," Ak-tu told her. "But you can also use it outside the school. It gives you an official identity, so nobody will question your background. Well, they can of course question your past, but to be enrolled in a magic academy shows that your family had enough money to send you. So nobody should assume you're an orphan who couldn't afford to go to school."

Sarala's jaw clenched. That wasn't true. There were many orphans whose parents left them lots of money, enough to give them a magical education just like her supposed "uncle" had. The orphanage she'd been at also held many fundraising programs, for the specific purpose of sending orphans to school if they never gained a family. Sarala would have had the same opportunity—if she had stuck around.

"This is your room key," Ak-tu went on, passing her a rigid key. "Student rooms are located on the second, third, and fourth floors of the western, eastern, and northern buildings. I will show you where your room is."

Sarala stared up at Ak-tu for a long moment. "Why are you doing all of this for me?"

Ak-tu smiled at her. "Why would I not?" he merely questioned in response.

She frowned. "But…why let me in for free? I thought I'd at least have to…test…or prove my worth or…"

"You are worthy," Ak-tu said simply.

Just then, a loud noise came from the printer in the corner of the room. Ak-tu glanced over at it and rolled his eyes.

"That thing always breaks down," he muttered.

"You should get a new one," Zyn piped up.

"That *is* a new one, and it's already suffered after issuing two ID cards!" Ak-tu sighed, then turned back to Sarala with a smile. "Printers are a bit ridiculous."

Sarala merely stared at him.

He put a hand on her shoulder and led her from the stuffy room, the twins following a bit hesitantly. "Well, Sarala Kiran, you are officially a student of the Caihong Academy of Magic. School will start very soon, and you'll be able to learn all the magic you want. This is your home now!"

Sarala's eyes glazed over and her breath seemed to stop. *Home,* she thought tonelessly. *My home now…*

CHAPTER 4: LONG AWAY

Ak-tu sat alone in the Admin Office shortly after showing Sarala to her new room. He tapped her filled-out form on the mirror, moving it to a folder labeled for new students. The only other form in that folder so far was Ren's, though Zyn's had mostly been filled out. All Ak-tu needed was her magic type and signature, then he could print her ID card—if the printer decided to work.

He sighed and leaned back in the hard chair, then got to his feet and paced the room a few times. As he walked, his arms lifted up, then pushed to the side, as if he was deflecting strikes towards his head. He circled them continuously, moving his torso up and down as he connected his arms to his body. But all of this was instinctive and unfocused; he was instead concentrated on his thoughts.

She was looking for this school...but why? Why this one? Did she know I'd take her in? Was she expecting that? And she gave me a fake last name... What is her true identity? What is she hiding? Is she a danger? No...I don't think so...not after I felt that... But I'll have to keep an eye on her...

Shaking Sarala from his mind, he stopped his pacing and lowered his arms. He walked to the window behind the desk and printer, peering at the forest. Trees stretched tall to the sky, their foliage a variety of colors: green was the most common, but red and blue could also be seen. Orange and purple flowers lay nestled among the bushes, some shaped like hanging bells and others like mini serpents wrapped around branches. Ak-tu watched a wad of yellow squishy moss drag itself across the grass and dirt, squelching quietly the whole way. He snorted in amusement and turned back to the desk, picking up the mirror once more as a new face came to his mind.

He tapped one of the buttons, which opened up to a list of contacts. As this was the school mirror and not his personal one, it had a long list of teachers, cooks, parents, students, and a few government contacts from the state of Pann. After a bit of scrolling, he finally reached his friend's name and selected it.

A dark-skinned person appeared on the glass, grinning widely up at Ak-tu from beneath his bushy blue beard. He had curly hair that fell to his shoulders, almost at the same length as Ak-tu's own hair. His eyes sparkled like sapphires—his right eye lighter than his left. The mirror buzzed lightly as it attempted to reach his friend's mirror. Ak-tu was just wondering if the connection would be lost when the still image of the man suddenly changed.

"YO!" the man called cheerfully, waving a large hand as he appeared in real time, dressed in a sky blue shirt that matched his right eye. "Ak-tu! How's it goin'?"

"Jabali!" Ak-tu grinned, plopping on the top of the desk with a light thud. "It's fine enough here. How about you? How's the shop?"

"Busy, busy, as usual this time o' the day," Jabali chuckled, setting his mirror against something so he could use both of his hands to shuffle through paperwork on the desk in front of him. "Gotta look through some job applications. Are 'em kids of yours ready t'work for me yet?"

Ak-tu snorted, raking a hand through his hair. "Nope, not yet. Remember, they still don't know about you."

"Mmhmm, thought as much," Jabali said, glancing around his cluttered desk. After picking up a green mug and a book, he found a pen and used it to scrawl something on the paper in front of him. "When d'ya plan on tellin' them, eh? Or are they never gonna know I exist?"

Ak-tu frowned. "I'll probably tell them soon," he said slowly. "I don't like keeping things from them… But I'm also waiting for them to learn about magic and spirits before I bring up some of this stuff…"

"Fair enough," Jabali said with a shrug, crunching up another paper and tossing it into the mess on his desk.

Ak-tu raised one side of his unibrow. "You need help cleaning all that up?"

"Eh, I'll get it later," Jabali said with a wave of his hand.

"If you say so," Ak-tu said doubtfully.

"I'm sure ya didn't just call me up to comment on my messy workspace," Jabali grunted, glancing back up at Ak-tu. "What's on your mind?"

"I just saw some crawling moss and thought of you," Ak-tu replied.

It was Jabali's turn to raise a thick eyebrow at that. "You saw some moss 'n thought of *me*? Rude."

Ak-tu chuckled and leaned back on the desk. "I dunno, it just reminded me of that time when—"

"Jabali!" a faint shout sounded.

Jabali sighed and got to his feet, uttering, "Hold tha' thought."

He ran out of the mirror's sight, likely to help his employees. Ak-tu lay back entirely on the desk, holding the mirror above his head. He scanned Jabali's workspace again: stacks of paper, three or four books, a mug containing steaming coffee, another mug (which said, "World's Okayest Boss") containing pens and pencils, a few candy wrappers (most unwrapped), a half-eaten muffin on a napkin, a set of reading glasses sitting on top of their case, several potted plants (one looked like it had spilled recently, judging by the soil on the table)... Beyond the desk were boxes of all sizes, some stacked all the way to the ceiling. The walls could hardly be seen beneath the clutter.

Ak-tu sighed and shifted his position on the desk, the hard wood becoming uncomfortable for his spine. He hopped off and returned to the window, looking for the crawling moss again. But it was nowhere to be seen. His eyes glazed over as he remembered the time that he and Jabali had camped in an area full of crawling moss. Jabali had squealed in delight and quickly patted the squishy plant, declaring that he'd take one home. But the moss had scurried away before he could catch any. Ak-tu had then charged after one, using his air magic to pull a wad of moss back and give it to his friend. As far as he knew, Jabali still had the moss just outside his house, along with the many other plants on his property.

"Ren's going to love meeting you," Ak-tu uttered under his breath, smiling lightly as he thought of his daughter.

"Wha'?"

Ak-tu blinked in surprise, glancing down at the mirror he still held to see that Jabali had returned. "Oh—I just said that Ren would love to meet you, one day. She loves plants just as much as you do!"

"Good on her," Jabali said, returning to his paperwork. "I'm sorry, Ak-tu, but I'm a lil' busy at the moment. We just got a catering order, 'n these new employees ain't the best at keeping their heads in stress. D'ya need to talk to me about anything important?"

Ak-tu was about to say no, when he stopped himself. "Actually…something strange *did* happen today…"

He quickly recounted Sarala's appearance, being sure not to skip over the fact that she had lied about her name. Jabali listened carefully, eyeing Ak-tu the whole time and ignoring the papers waiting for him.

"Well, why'd ya let her in the school?"

"Because she's an orphan with nowhere to go, and likely running from a dark past," Ak-tu said instantly.

"And not runnin' from a criminal? Or the gov?" Jabali pressed.

Ak-tu shrugged indifferently. "Only time will tell… But there's…something else…"

"What?"

"I…felt…a connection to her," Ak-tu murmured, his eyes glazing over. "Like what I felt with both of my kids…that…special bond…that they are *meant* to be here…that we're *meant* to be in each other's lives."

Jabali gazed at Ak-tu for a long moment, then grunted, "You're gonna adopt her, aren't ya?"

Ak-tu blinked. "No! Well…not yet. I mean…I guess I sorta did when I set her up here? I mean, I'm sorta her guardian now, in a way, but… No, I don't intend to *actually* adopt her, though I'd be open to the idea in the future if there *is* something here and she *wants* to be adopted. I just…haven't felt that strange calling sensation in a long time… Not since I got Zyn at that orphanage."

Jabali shrugged. "You do wha' ya wanna do, Ak-tu. But be sure you're not takin' on too much."

Ak-tu snorted. "Too much? I can handle too much. I raised twin babies on my own, after all! Now *that* was too much, but I managed it!"

As he said the words, his thoughts went back in time. He was sitting in a rowboat, two babies on the wooden floor, bundled in blankets between supplies. Ak-tu looked up to the other side of the boat, smiling as he imagined Jabali sitting on the bench across from him. But Jabali faded from sight, and Ak-tu was pulled from the memory.

"Sater to Ak-tu! Ya listening?" Jabali was grumbling in annoyance.

"Hmm?"

"Why d'ya zone out so much?" his friend huffed. "I was sayin' you've got no idea wha' her past is, and ya don't know how much trouble she might bring ya. Whatever bond ya feel, let it come naturally, and keep your guard up."

"I will," promised Ak-tu.

"Well, if ya don't have any other news for me, I'ma get back to my shop," Jabali said, already pulling a new piece of paper out and jotting down notes.

"That's all on my end," Ak-tu replied, glancing out the window again to watch a butterfly flutter by. "Anything you want to say?"

"It's Zyn's birthday today, ain't it? I'll send ya some money for her."

Ak-tu sighed and said in exasperation, "Jabali, there's no need, my kids don't know you and—"

"Nonsense! I know of 'em, and that's good enough for me to get them birthday presents. Get Zyn something good, or save it up for a special occasion. See ya later!"

"Jabali, please don't—"

But Jabali had hung up the call, the mirror reflecting Ak-tu's dismayed face back at him. Ak-tu rolled his eyes and lowered his mirror, returning his gaze to the forest as movement caught his attention. He ignored the dinging noise the mirror made as he received a notification (likely Jabali's sent money).

Ak-tu pressed himself closer to the window until his nose was almost touching the glass and his breath fogged it. Something small had scuttled through the bushes, moving more like an animal than a plant.

Could it be—

The figure shifted and left the shadowy undergrowth, allowing

Ak-tu to see it better. It was just a tiny bluish gray elephog—an animal the size of a hog with the head of an elephant.

Ak-tu shook his head and turned away. "Why did I think it was them? It's been years… I better get some breakfast in me before I forget to eat again…"

He placed the mirror on the desk and headed for the office door. He was just about to exit when he had the feeling that something was watching him. Swiveling on the balls of his feet, he gazed out the window again. The elephog was gone, and nothing else stood outside.

"You're just being silly now," he scolded himself. "This is what happens when you don't eat!"

Ak-tu exited the Admin Office, shutting the door behind him.

CHAPTER 5: DEEPER AND DEEPER INSIDE

Ren and Zyn didn't see much of Sarala over the next few days. She mostly stayed in her room, only appearing for mealtimes in the Eating Hall. She'd sit alone, and, though the sisters wanted to spend time with someone else their age, Ak-tu told them to leave her alone while she adjusted to being in a new environment.

The sisters therefore returned to their new hobby of trying to summon Zyn's magic. The days continued to pass with no success, though Ren tried hard with the guided meditations she provided Zyn. Ak-tu wouldn't give anymore tips, not even to Ren, and merely told Zyn she'd have to wait for the assessment week—which luckily wasn't too far away.

It was soon August 3. Most of the students would be arriving that Moonday, a week before school began. First-years often arrived on that first day, to do the assessments at the beginning of the week and have more time to summon their magic. Of course, the assessments lasted the whole week, so students who couldn't arrive to the school on the first day would have multiple chances to test their magic.

Ren moved to her open window, brushing past her plants. She stared out at the Courtyard below, breathing in the damp morning air. The teachers were bustling about, getting ready to greet the students in the Entrance Hall. As breakfast was already over, students would be arriving any minute.

She got dressed in her purple robe, then went down to the family room. Zyn was pacing back and forth, her robe (bright blue with swirling waves) whirling about so much that it made Ren dizzy watching her.

"It'll be okay, Zyn," Ren said gently.

Zyn stopped in her tracks, but only for a moment. "Oh, hi, Ren!" she said in an unusually high voice.

"Still nothing?" Ren asked.

"I've been trying," Zyn muttered, staring at the ground as she continued pacing anxiously.

A loud shrieking noise suddenly filled the room. Ren jumped in surprise, then relaxed as she saw it was just the family mirror, lying on one of the round tables next to the window. Zyn hurried over to it and tapped the screen, which showed a still image of Ak-tu doing what looked like a peace sign (but was actually a two-finger eye strike). As soon as Zyn answered, Ak-tu's face filled the mirror and he spoke.

"It's time for the assessments!" he said, an excited energy shining in his eyes.

"We're coming," Zyn croaked out.

Ak-tu nodded, then ended the call. The mirror returned to its appearance of a regular mirror, reflecting the wooden ceiling.

"Let's go," Zyn said.

"I'll do the assessments too, Zyn," Ren told her sister. "That way, you don't have to go at it alone!"

Zyn nodded, but did not make any other reply.

They hurried to the center of the Courtyard, where a group of ten teenagers stood before Ak-tu and one of the other teachers, Khurshid Jihan. Most of the soon-to-be-students looked to be about thirteen, the standard age magic would make its first appearance.

"Welcome, everyone," Ak-tu said, as Ren and Zyn took their places at the back of the group. "We hope you will be our new first-year students this year. But before we can take you in, you will have to pass a magic assessment. We have to make sure you have your magic before you enroll in this magic school, after all.

"There's no need to be nervous for these assessments! We aren't testing how powerful your magic is, or how well-controlled. We don't care how your magic takes its form, just so long as it does. If you can summon your magic, you have nothing to worry about.

"If you find that you don't have your magic by the end of the assessments today, you are welcome to return each day this week (including Saterday) until you find it. If you are unable to summon your magic, I am sorry to say that you will be unable to attend school this year. Any questions?"

The students shook their heads or remained quiet. Ren peered around at them curiously, taking in their faces and wondering which of these students she'd befriend. She saw with some surprise that Sarala was in the group too, despite proving she had magic already.

"We'll be doing this one person at a time," Ak-tu continued. "As I said, we don't know how powerful your magic might be or how it might take its form. To prevent injuries, I'm going to ask that you all take a seat in the lovely garden behind me. Mr. Jihan here will let you know when it's your turn to come out. We will start with the three simple tests. By the third test, students typically have their magic. If not, you will have to wait until all students are done with these first assessments, so we can move to the next location afterwards. Now, who'd like to go first?"

Ren shot her hand up in the air. *Might as well show everyone there's nothing to be scared of!*

"Ren Caihong," Ak-tu said with a nod and smile of approval. "Stay here. Everyone else, follow Mr. Jihan to the garden."

The teens walked away, some glancing curiously over their shoulders. Zyn stared at her for a long moment, then left too. Soon enough, Ren was alone with Ak-tu in the center of the Courtyard.

"Dad—can I do *all* of the assessments?" she asked, clasping her hands together.

Ak-tu frowned. "But you already have your magic. There's no need."

Ren nodded. "I know, but…if Zyn doesn't pass the first test, I want her to see what the other tests are. That way, she knows what to expect! After all, those other students might pass the very first assessment, and then Zyn wouldn't be able to see the other assessments."

Ak-tu smiled. "That's very thoughtful of you, Ren. Very well. If you want to act this out, then be sure not to use your magic."

Ren nodded again, beaming at her father.

"The first test is to move your whole body and think of pushing your magic out of you. You can punch or kick the air, stomp your feet, jump around, dance…whatever you can think of to get your magic coursing through you."

As he said this, he acted everything out—punching, kicking, stomping, jumping, dancing… Ren snorted at the silly movements, wondering what the other teens might be thinking. She waited for him to settle down before raising her hand, as if she was already in class.

"But why don't we just use wands?" she asked. "Isn't that why we've got wands—to help us bring our magic forward?"

Ak-tu smiled. "We will most certainly use wands soon. But we can't have students using wands to test their magic. A wand is very personal, and there's no sense giving it to someone who doesn't have their magic yet. Eventually, you will become advanced enough with your magic to have no need for a wand, and you'll be using your body anyway."

Ren nodded her understanding. Of course, she'd seen Ak-tu use only his hands plenty of times to perform all kinds of magic. She couldn't think of a time when he'd used a wand.

"Now, go ahead and give it a *try*," Ak-tu said, winking.

Ren took a deep breath, then tensed her body. If her body was tense, her magic wouldn't flow as easily. She punched the air, and was glad to see nothing happen. She stomped the ground and danced around, doing as many physical movements she could think of. Hopefully, one of these actions would work with Zyn, or even the other teens watching.

"The second test is probably the most effective test," Ak-tu pressed on, after the first test went on long enough. "You see those big cauldrons behind you?"

Ren glanced over her shoulder. The rough-looking cauldrons only ever came out for the assessments. There were four in total, each labelled with a different element.

"Each of those elements—as you can see from the fire in the red cauldron—are in the designated cauldrons," Ak-tu went on. "It is sometimes helpful for the student to see the element itself first, and try to control it from there."

Ren approached the red cauldron first. She might as well play with the other elements, as she'd have to be careful with the air cauldron. Standing in front of it, Ren could feel the heat of the dancing flames, as warm as lying on a sandy beach in the summer. She punched and kicked the air several times, but, of course, nothing happened.

She approached the next cauldron in line, which was yellow. She peeked inside, but saw nothing. Remembering that the cauldron had "Air" written on it, she didn't know what she expected to see. Ren stepped back and punched the air, keeping her body tense again. She didn't even feel the slightest hint of a breeze, which meant she successfully managed to *not* do magic.

She then moved to the green "Earth" cauldron. Inside were stones of various sizes and colors. She focused on them, then did a large sweeping motion with her arms, as if she was trying to lift them out. After a moment of waving her arms about, she moved to the blue "Water" cauldron.

Ren focused on the still water inside, able to see her reflection staring back up at her, calm and collected. She once again hit the air, as if she was controlling the water within. After a few seconds, she turned back to Ak-tu.

"The last test is a guided meditation," he said in a low voice, though it was quite unlikely that the students would hear him from so far away. "I'd rather get on with the others, so if you could just go ahead and summon your air magic…"

"Yep!" Ren said.

She turned back to the cauldrons, acting like she was retrying each of them. When she got to the yellow cauldron, she took a deep breath and relaxed her body. She then twirled around on the spot, and wind swirled around her, a cool breeze rushing through her hair and nearly knocking her glasses off.

"Excellent!" Ak-tu cheered. "You may sit in the garden to watch whenever Zyn comes out."

Ren nodded and skipped away to the garden, her feet light as they touched the warm ground. The other students had been watching her with wide eyes, and they clapped when she arrived.

"It was nothing," she said, blushing at the attention.

"Who's next?" Khurshid asked the students in a deep voice.

Before the words had left his mouth, Zyn hurried away. It was clear she just wanted to get it over with. Zyn was soon attempting a bunch of punching and hopping motions. But it seemed that she was having no luck with the first assessment, Ren's heart sinking to see her twin struggling.

Ak-tu was then pointing the cauldrons out to Zyn. Zyn approached the fire cauldron first, just like Ren. The fire remained undisturbed, neither growing nor shrinking in size. Zyn moved to the air cauldron, but nothing seemed to happen there. She turned to her dad with a shrug, but Ak-tu pointed to the other cauldrons.

{Come on, Zyn!} Ren thought. *{You got this!}*

{But I don't have earth or water magic.} Zyn replied, as she stared at the earth cauldron. *{My sun sign is fire and my moon sign is air.}*

{You never know! Maybe we got your moon sign wrong?} Ren suggested. *{It's worth a try!}*

Zyn tried the other two cauldrons without any luck, her shoulders slumping as she faced her father again. Ak-tu was clearly trying to cheer her up, his arms moving in wide arcs as if waving encouragement to her. He signaled her to sit down on the ground for the meditation.

{I'm totally going to fail this.} Zyn sent the thought to Ren.

Ren shook her head. *{No, don't think that, otherwise you* will! *Just focus your attention inwards, and remember to relax!}*

After the short meditation, in which Zyn was clearly fidgeting, Ak-tu ordered Zyn to try the cauldrons again. But nothing happened, and she returned to the garden with slumped shoulders, her knees seeming ready to buckle beneath her.

"I still don't have it," she muttered glumly, looking like a plant withering beneath the sun.

"Don't give up, Zyn! There are still other tests to shake that magic out of you!" Ren said firmly.

"Yeah…" Zyn murmured, staring at her feet.

The other students tested quickly compared to Zyn. While most had to use the cauldrons or even meditation to summon their magic, Sarala managed to stomp the ground and break a stone with earth magic on her first attempt. Each of the ten students tested successfully, and Ak-tu dismissed them to see Fern and Aster (the other two teachers) in the Admin Office for their IDs and room keys.

Ak-tu then approached Ren and Zyn, who remained in the

shade of the garden. "Zyn, as you're the only one who still doesn't have any magic, I'm going to have you try these tests again tomorrow," he said. "There's no point in setting up the other assessments for one student. I'm sure you'll have it tomorrow."

Zyn nodded, too dejected to speak.

But no matter how many times she tried that week, "tomorrow" never came. Fewer first-years showed up for the assessments as the week went on, and each student successfully summoned their magic. Ak-tu continued to push off the final assessments, since there was "no point" in doing them if it was only Zyn who needed them.

Finally, Saterday arrived, the last day for assessments. Only one other student had shown up for the assessment alongside Zyn. Ren sat in the garden with Khurshid and the other student, biting her bottom lip nervously as she watched Zyn from afar.

"Dad *has* to let Zyn try out the other assessments," she murmured to Khurshid. "Right?"

"Of course he will," Khurshid replied calmly, straightening the golden sash tied around his waist. "He just doesn't want to let it come to the final tests."

"Why?" Ren asked.

But Khurshid didn't answer. Ren gazed up at the blind man, staring into his pale eyes as she willed him to say more. She soon dropped her eyes to his yellow shirt and then to his baggy brown pants as she realized he would be giving away nothing more.

A few moments later, Zyn returned to the garden, having failed all three of the simple assessments once more. She hung her head, tears in her eyes and her lip quivering.

{*Oh, Zyn!*} Ren reached forward to hug her sister. {*You'll get your magic! I know you will! It's just...really deep inside of you. But you'll get it to come out! There are still more assessments, remember!*}

Zyn didn't make any reply. She sat on the ground, and Ren joined her, though the stone was hot to the touch and threatened to burn her hands. They watched the last student, a redheaded boy wearing a formal black robe, step forward to take his assessments.

After several minutes passed, the student failed each of his tests too. Ak-tu brought the student over to the others. Though he hadn't passed the tests, the boy looked much less bothered by the fact than Zyn. He kept his up-turned nose in the air, glancing curiously at the garden and school around him. He shoved his left sleeve up his arm, though it was already tucked in a golden ring at his elbow to keep it up.

"We will move onto the next set of assessments," Ak-tu said, his gaze lingering on the red-eyed Zyn for a moment. "Follow me."

"Where are we going?" Ren asked, as they headed for the southern building.

Ak-tu led them to a large, square stone on the ground outside the building. There were four of these platforms around the school, one for each building. They were placed directly beneath the doors of the upper floors. These stones used air magic to move up and down the walls, pausing at the door that the student commanded it to. Ak-tu originally had staircases installed at the school, but quickly dislodged them when a disabled student joined the school. The rising platforms were the perfect solution, and railings would appear to keep students from falling off.

Ren followed her father onto the elevator, which shifted slightly as they clambered onto it. In the time Ren and Zyn had been at the school, they had never been allowed to go on the second or third floors of the southern building. The other three buildings only contained student rooms on these floors, but their father never said what was in the southern building.

"This is where we set up lessons sometimes," Ak-tu said mildly. "*Challenging* lessons."

Ren bit her bottom lip nervously, wondering what Ak-tu could possibly have waiting for the two teens.

Once they were each on the elevator, Ak-tu commanded it to rise. Railings shot up on all sides of them, then the rock slab moved up in the air. It stopped at the second door, and the front railing moved down to allow them passage. Ak-tu pulled open the door and signaled for the students to walk in ahead of him. Khurshid trailed behind them, then Ak-tu entered and closed the door.

They were plunged into darkness for a moment, at least until Ren's eyes adjusted. Both thin and heavy curtains had been pulled across each of the windows, which only allowed small amounts of light in, or blocked it out entirely. The room smelled of dust and wood, making Ren's nose twitch.

An obstacle course stood in front of them, stretching the entire floor. There were lots of random objects strewn about haphazardly: desks, chairs, wardrobes... Other objects were harder to distinguish in the dim lighting, only noticeable by the blackness of their forms.

"This next assessment isn't going to be easy," Ak-tu warned Zyn and the other teen. "In fact, if either of you would like to turn back now, I will not think badly of you. This obstacle course is intended to *scare* the magic out of you. If you would like to try for your magic again next year, you may let me know now."

Zyn shook her head fiercely. "There's no way I'm giving up!" she growled.

"I'm not quitting, either," said the redhead. "I'm already fifteen. I cannot afford to put my magic education on hold any longer."

Ren shifted nervously. She was certainly glad *she* didn't have to take this assessment. But she was still worried about Zyn. What if Zyn didn't pass this test, either? Would the sisters be unable to attend magical classes *again*?

Ren frowned. Was she regretting her decision to wait for Zyn to have her magic? Would Zyn be angry with her if she decided to go ahead with enrollment, even if it meant Zyn would have to wait another year?

But we do everything together, Ren told herself, making sure her thoughts could not be heard by anyone else. *I promised Zyn I'd wait for her...so that's just what I'll have to do. Even if it means waiting another year.... I've already waited two school years, so what's one more?*

"I'm going to ask everyone to get in this room behind me," Ak-tu said, signaling to what looked like a hut in the left corner of the room. "You can watch from there. If anything heads your way, it will bounce off the wall due to the enchantments I put up."

"What would be headed our way?" Ren asked.

"You'll see," Ak-tu replied. "Cypress, you'll go first."

The other student scowled. "I told you to call me C3."

"Apologies," Ak-tu said, a small smile on his lips. "C3, you can go first. You're going to make it to the other side of the course

when I give the signal. You will have to avoid the enchantments…
or otherwise use your magic to get them out of the way."

C3 nodded to this.

Khurshid then led Ren and Zyn into the small hut. Ak-tu entered after them, and they were practically sitting shoulder-to-shoulder, Ren feeling claustrophobic in the stuffy space. They stared out at C3 through the window in the wall.

"Go!" Ak-tu said, clapping his hands.

At once, the whole room was alive! Objects jumped around and blocked C3's path. Large boxes crashed down on him ("Don't worry, they're empty and made of paper," Ak-tu said when Ren gasped). Scary apparitions flickered. C3 did not flinch as these randomly popped up with loud screams.

He kept going, moving so quickly for appearing to be such a formal and studious person. He slid under and hopped over objects, ignoring the illusions. Just before he reached the end, another fake figure, bigger than the other apparitions, loomed in front of him. C3 lifted his hand, sending wind at the creature.

"Stop!" Ak-tu called, clapping his hands again. The room instantly fell still.

C3 got to his feet and brushed off his robe. He then turned and walked back to Ak-tu, who had left the hut so quickly that Ren hadn't even noticed he'd gone.

"You have air magic," Ak-tu said as he approached the boy.

"Really? I couldn't tell," C3 replied sarcastically.

Ak-tu did not seem offended by this. He instead asked, "How long have you known?"

"Known what?" C3 asked.

"I could see you were holding back from using your magic," Ak-tu said. "Why?"

C3 seemed a bit annoyed by this accusation. He paused as he pondered what to say, then muttered, "I am sorry to have lied. The truth was that I indeed made a small swirl of air in the cauldron outside. I just did not want to say anything, as I desired to go through each of the tests. I wanted to see if this school would indeed be a worthy one for my education, as the reviews on the airnet say."

"I'm happy to hear you are taking your education seriously,"

Ak-tu said. "I ask that you do not perform more…experiments… unless specifically instructed to do so."

"Understood, Mr. Caihong," C3 said.

"You may follow Mr. Jihan to the Admin Office for your ID and room keys. Your parents are here?"

C3 nodded. "All three of them, Mr. Caihong."

"Mr. Jihan will let them know the good news of your enrollment."

Khurshid and C3 then left the building. Bright sunlight blinded them for a moment, and it took Ren's eyes even longer to adjust to the dim room after the door closed behind them. The darkness seemed to consume them more than before.

"Zyn?" Ak-tu called softly. "Are you ready?"

"Of course," Zyn said, her voice high and full of tension.

"You may take your place here, and wait for me to say go," Ak-tu instructed.

Zyn left the small hut and stood where Ak-tu directed her. Ak-tu then entered the hut again, which had much more space now that two people had left. Ren glanced at her father nervously, her heart thrumming in her throat. Ak-tu clapped his hands loudly, the sound as loud as a firecracker in the silence.

Zyn hurried to and fro, trying to get across obstacles as they hurled at her. More illusions seemed to appear for her than they did for C3, almost as if Ak-tu was desperate to scare Zyn's magic out of her. There were screaming griffins and roaring tigers, soaring birds and writhing serpents. But Zyn had to dodge each of these illusions, as nothing happened when she tried to punch the air. She soon reached the other side of the floor.

"I failed!" she cried out, crumbling to her knees at the far end as Ak-tu clapped the enchantments away once more.

Ak-tu led the way to Zyn, Ren close behind him, her heart still fluttering. Zyn remained on the floor, her legs sprawled out awkwardly and her face buried in her hands.

"You didn't fail," Ak-tu said firmly, placing his hand on her shoulder.

"But I did!" Zyn wailed. "I didn't pass *any* of the tests! I still don't have my magic!"

"You haven't finished the assessments yet. Get to your feet,

Zynivus," Ak-tu said gruffly.

"There's another assessment?" Zyn asked, astonished as she removed her hands from her tear-stricken face.

"Yes," Ak-tu said. "We'll be going upstairs for the final test."

"Is there another obstacle course up there?" Zyn asked, sprinting to the door with a new energy coursing through her.

"Not exactly," Ak-tu replied.

Ren glanced up at Ak-tu, her heartbeat unable to slow down. But her father did not look her way. The two hastily followed Zyn to the elevator outside, blinking dazedly in the bright light.

"Third floor!" Zyn yelped.

The front railing appeared and the platform went up. Once the railing was gone, Zyn opened the door of the third floor and scampered inside, clearly eager to summon her magic at any cost. But she soon paused in the doorway. Ren peered over her shoulder and quickly saw why.

This room had a tall ceiling, taking up what would have been the third *and* fourth floors in the other three buildings. This was due to the raised platform in the center of the room.

"You will be fighting," Ak-tu told Zyn calmly, ushering her into the room. "Your magic will spring out of you as a defense mechanism. That is how magic operates in animals, and it's how magic operated in humans until the spirits taught us to control it. Get on that platform."

Zyn gawked at her father. He nudged her forward, and she stumbled almost blindly to the platform. Ak-tu glanced back at Ren.

"I want you to stay right next to the platform, in case she falls off. Do try your best to catch her, will you?" he added.

Ren nodded, a lump in her throat. *Why have a raised platform in the first place? Why not lower it, have level ground?*

Zyn scrambled up onto the platform, which wasn't placed too high off the ground. It seemed to rock as she got on it, and she threw her arms out on either side of her to catch her balance, gasping lightly in surprise.

Really? A rocking platform? Why? Ren groaned, clasping her hands together so tightly that her nails bit into her skin.

Ak-tu took up his position opposite Zyn, on the far side of the platform. He pulled something small out of thin air; Ren realized that he had teleported a hair tie to his hand. He quickly had his hair in a tight top knot, his bangs no longer in his vision. He then untied the black sash around his waist and took off his blue robe, tossing the robe lightly to the side. He tucked his long green tank top into his baggy pants, then retied the sash. Ren tried to swallow the lump again; her father was serious about this match, acting like he was about to do martial arts for rigorous hours.

Ak-tu fell still. The minutes passed slowly. It was as if Ak-tu was hoping that Zyn would show signs of magic and they wouldn't have to do the final assessment.

"Are you ready, Zyn?" Ak-tu asked at last.

Zyn took a moment to respond. Then, she nodded, straightening her robe.

"I'm going to attack. You can attack me in return. Or you can try to evade. I'm obviously going easy on you, seeing as you have no combative experience. Just try to stay on the platform, and re-member to summon your magic. If you are in a high state of pan-ic, your magic should come forward."

Ren snorted lightly at that. *Zyn's been panicking this entire time, and she still doesn't have any magic! We're just going to have to wait until next year, when she's older and her magic comes out....*

"Three...two...one!"

Ak-tu sprang at Zyn, who jumped out of the way in fright. Ak-tu sent gusts of wind at her, trying to knock her off the platform with punches and palm strikes. Zyn stumbled about, off-balance and trying to dodge the magic. Ak-tu then started throwing water at her, the water appearing from his fingertips.

Zyn was doing much better than Ren thought she would. She had half-expected Zyn to fall off by now. But the girl was fierce, and she stayed low to keep her balance as she scrambled around the platform.

"You're doing great, Zyn!" Ak-tu called, panting. "Feel any-thing yet?"

"Maybe?" Zyn called back, also panting but not as winded as Ak-tu.

"Good, force that magic out of you!" Ak-tu said, before he

lunged towards Zyn again with a clumsy air strike.

Magic took a lot of effort, especially if using more advanced magic or the entire body to summon it. Ak-tu was getting close to his limit.

"Zyn! Look out!" Ren cried.

Zyn nearly fell off the platform after being struck by a wave of water from behind. She managed to cling on, and Ak-tu allowed her to drag herself back up.

"Anything?" Ak-tu called hopefully. "We can end this if your magic comes out."

"Come on, Zyn," whispered Ren.

Zyn did not reply to Ak-tu's words. It was clear that she still had yet to feel her magic, otherwise she would have happily thrown it forward. Ak-tu therefore attacked again, thrusting his feet out as he threw kicks.

Zyn continued to dodge. Suddenly, she was on the edge of the platform, her arms waving madly. Ren gasped, lifting her hands to her mouth. But she had no need to worry, as a gust of air pushed Zyn forward and kept her upright.

"You did it!" Ren screamed joyfully, hopping up and down.

"You have air magic too!" Ak-tu cried happily.

Zyn stared at her father for a moment, her mismatched eyes wide. She then gaped at her hands, in awe of the magic she had finally brought forth.

"Excellent work today, Zyn!" Ak-tu said, staggering over to hug his daughter, sweat dripping down his sienna skin. "I'm so proud of you. I knew we'd get there in the end."

Zyn did not reply.

A loud knock sounded on Ren's door that night, and she lifted her head groggily. She pushed herself out of bed and moved to the door, leaving her glasses on the nightstand. She opened it to see a blurry Zyn standing there, wearing stripy pajamas.

"Zyn, what are you doing here? It's the middle of the night," Ren groaned, rubbing the sleep from her eyes.

Zyn entered and turned towards Ren. "That didn't feel like my magic," she murmured. "I didn't feel any different when I did it."

"Magic is a part of you," Ren pointed out. "You don't *have* to feel anything."

"But...I should have felt something, right?" Zyn mumbled, starting to pace in circles around Ren's rug. "Especially the first time? I can see it becoming more natural over time, that you don't pay attention to it after a while. But shouldn't I have felt...I dunno...energy going through me or something? Like you and Dad are always saying?"

"You're just overthinking this," Ren said shortly. "Come on, Zyn, it's the middle of the night. We can talk more about this tomorrow."

"Ren...did you...did you send that air wave?" Zyn asked hesitantly, stopping in her tracks to look up at her sister.

"Of course not," she said.

"Then why can't I feel my own magic?" Zyn pressed.

"I don't know," Ren replied.

"You're lying," Zyn muttered darkly.

"No, I'm not," Ren hissed, her voice starting to rise.

Zyn flailed her hands about, signaling Ren to be quiet, despite their father's room being all the way on the sixth floor. "Look—I *know* you're lying. You wouldn't be this scared if you weren't!"

"Fine, I'm lying!" Ren moaned, plopping onto the floor. "But what was I supposed to do? If you don't have magic, then we don't get to go to school again. We've already missed one year—two, if you're counting me getting my magic early. Besides, I can't make you go another year without magic, thinking you're...some sort of...failure."

Ren shook her head, rubbing at her closed eyes. "I had to do something, Zyn. I know your magic will come soon, I just know it! But it's not fair if you miss a whole year simply because it didn't come *today*. What if it comes tomorrow, or even next month? We'd have to sit out a whole year just because your magic came a little late."

Ren removed her hands from her face and peered up at Zyn through teary eyes. "I'm sorry to have lied, and to have...cheated. But we just *can't* sit out another year!"

Zyn stared at her quietly, her body stiff.

"You're...you're not going to tell Dad, are you?" Ren whispered.

Zyn remained motionless, then muttered, "No. I'm not going to tell *anyone*."

Ren reached forward and hugged Zyn. "Oh, thank you!" she whispered.

Zyn sighed in her grasp. "Yeah, well, it's as you said… My magic will probably come any day now. That's no reason to miss a whole year of school."

Ren pulled away and nodded. "I'm so sorry, Zyn."

"Well…I'm going back to bed," Zyn grunted, pulling out of Ren's hold. "We've got that first-year meeting tomorrow…."

Ren nodded, remembering Ak-tu had announced the meeting to all of the first-years after Zyn's assessment. "Okay, Zyn. Good night!"

She opened the door and let her sister out. Ren then returned to her bed, feeling a bit light-headed.

Was Zyn angry with her? What would happen if Zyn's magic *didn't* come soon? Did Ren set her sister up for failure?

CHAPTER 6: GOOD COMPANY

Zyn woke up earlier than usual that Sunday. She rolled up to her feet, as she'd been sleeping on the wooden floor. She called out a quick greeting, but received nothing in response. Ren was probably still asleep, considering Zyn had kept her up the previous night. Zyn shrugged and got dressed in a scarlet robe with balls of fire patterned on it. She then went down the stairs to the family room. Soon after, a loud bell rang through the school at 7, signaling that breakfast was being served for the next hour.

Zyn didn't know if she'd be able to handle eating anything. What if Ak-tu found out that Ren had used her magic to get Zyn enrolled? How was Zyn going to perform any type of magic if she didn't have it? Would she fail her classes? Would she be forced to wait another year? And what would Ren choose? Would she really wait for her twin to catch up, or move on without her?

In seemingly no time, Ren was in the family room. Ren looked tired, and her messy hair was messier than usual. She smiled half-heartedly at Zyn, who did not find it in her to return the greeting. The sisters left the tower, locking it behind them, and made their way across the Courtyard to the Eating Hall.

"Well…it's the big day!" Ren said as they entered. "We're finally going to get started with school!"

"Yeah," Zyn replied absentmindedly.

There were quite a few people in the hall already, lining up at the counter on the right side of the room. The students slid trays along the counter, grabbing food as the cooks bustled about in the background. All Zyn could hear was chatter, and she covered her ears and closed her eyes to block the sounds out.

But then all she could smell was food: crispy bread, savory tofu scramble, sweet chocolate and berries from baked muffins… Zyn groaned and shook her head, deciding to breathe from her mouth instead.

"Come on, Zyn," Ren said, pulling her sister's arm to lead her away from the door.

The sisters headed to the counter, Ren grabbing some toast for both of them. They sat down at a table on the edge of the chattery room, but Zyn couldn't find it in her to eat the bread. After several minutes, she got to her feet and left the Eating Hall without a word. She had barely taken two steps when Ren was at her side.

"Are you still worried about your magic?" Ren asked.

Zyn nodded, pacing in small circles beside the garden. {What if I can't summon it the whole semester? What if Dad kicks me out of school?} She asked all of this telepathically, unable to form the words aloud.

The two had to step aside as more people arrived for breakfast. Sarala was among the students, keeping her distance from the others. She glanced sidelong at Zyn and Ren, but didn't make any sort of greeting as she went, though Ren had waved.

"What's with her anyway?" Zyn muttered, focusing on Sarala to distract herself.

"She's just…you know…the loner type," Ren said aloud, before she switched to telepathy. {I'll help you with your magic, okay? I'll perform the magic for you, at least until you get yours.}

{But what if that doesn't happen?} Zyn asked, feeling an anxious knot in her stomach.

{It will.} Ren replied firmly. {It's only a matter of days, maybe a month at most. In the meantime, I'll do the magic for you.}

Zyn sighed. So she was going to be cheating in school from the start. She glanced at Ren, then nodded once.

Ak-tu's voice suddenly rang through the school. "First-year students, head to the Magic Studies classroom when the bell rings again. I expect to see all of you there by 8. As for the rest of you, welcome back to school!"

Zyn fidgeted uneasily. "I think I'll just head to the classroom now."

"I'll go with you," Ren said at once.

The sisters therefore crossed the Courtyard again, this time reaching the eastern wall where the Magic Studies classroom sat. The scent of books filled the air, though there were only desks within. The desks were set up in neat rows, while two large tables lay on either end of the room, one in the front and one in the back. There weren't any decorations along the red-painted walls, only a clock.

Ak-tu and Khurshid were already in the classroom, talking in low voices at the front desk. Ak-tu was dressed in his usual blue robe with the black sash, wearing a tank top beneath. Khurshid wore his collared shirt with the gold sash, which matched the long stripes going down the sides of his pants. Khurshid angled his large nose towards the twins as they entered.

"You're early," Ak-tu said, smiling at his children as he straightened up.

"We like to be punctual!" Ren said with a shrug.

"So what are we doing in class today?" Zyn asked, curiosity making the knot in her stomach loosen a bit. "Should I even call this a class?"

Ak-tu signaled to the table at the back of the room, which contained plenty of sticks. "All first-years will be choosing a wand!"

"Ooo!" Zyn let out a delighted noise and hurried for the table, but Ak-tu snatched the end of her robe and held her back. "Hey!"

"You can't choose before everyone else gets here," Ak-tu pointed out in amusement.

Zyn huffed in annoyance. "I wasn't going to choose. I just wanted to *look*. There are so many wands!"

"You'll get your chance," Khurshid said calmly, running a hand over his buzzcut head. "But we first need to go over the school rules, schedule, and all that."

Zyn sighed. "Fine," she muttered, slumping down in a chair at the front of the class. "Is it time yet?"

Ak-tu glanced at the clock on the wall above the front desk. "7:58," he read. "One more minute, and the minute-bell will sound before the final bell."

The words had hardly left his mouth when the minute-bell rang. It was different from the first bell they'd heard that morning. It was short and sharp, whereas the first bell (and the final bell that rang seconds later at 8) sounded like a drawn-out echo.

Zyn counted the first-years as they entered. There were nineteen students, which meant that there were twenty-one first-years altogether when including herself and Ren. It seemed the first-year group would be smaller than usual that year, as Zyn was quite certain the other years had more students.

"Welcome to the school, everyone," Ak-tu said warmly once they had each taken their seats. "As you should know, I am Ak-tu Caihong, and this is Khurshid Jihan. I'm going to go through my list to make sure you're all here. Just raise your hand when I call your name."

He picked up a mirror from the desk and opened the attendance sheet. "Abhainn, Midnight? Caihong and Caihong, I know you're here. Clay, Cypress? Sorry—C3?"

The redheaded boy, who was sitting right behind Zyn, raised his hand and said, "I am present."

"Dattem, Ayl? Eenzaam, Zijdezacht?" Ak-tu continued down the list, looking up after saying each name to make note of the different faces. "Fubhuki, Kumo? Gatin, Ro-nael? Hajar-Ramliun, Alqamar? Jay, Cyan and Ebony and Scarlet? Triplets, are you?"

"Yes," three voices from the very back replied, each in different tones.

"Fascinating!" Ak-tu continued. "Kilima, Ash? Kiran, Sarala? Niebla, Rosa? Paanee-chamak, Tulasee? Ravford, Beanna? Retsel, Meadow? Rulek, Mernao? Senzakou, Raimugi? And finally, Wuolf, Frost? Good, everyone's here!"

Ak-tu set the mirror on the desk and went on. "Everyone got their school rules when receiving their room keys and IDs, yes? Does anyone have any questions about them?"

"It was very self-explanatory," C3 spoke up.

Ak-tu gazed around the room, but nobody else said anything. "Very well, but I'd still like to highlight a few of the rules.

"While you are here, you are not to leave the school, unless one of your parents comes for you. If you suffer an injury, you will see the healer on site, Fern Oakley. Ms. Oakley's Healing room is in the entrance building, near the Admin Office. It's labeled on the map handouts you all received.

"I also want to point out that magic is not allowed outside of classes for first-years during the first month of school. We don't want to have any accidents here, so please, do not use your magic unsupervised. Once you *are* allowed to use your magic, we ask that you only do it for schoolwork.

"All food is served in the Eating Hall at specific time slots, with 7-8 being breakfast, 12-1 being lunch, and 5-6 being dinner. You are welcome to hang out in the Eating Hall as long as you'd like—so long as you're not missing class, of course—but food will no longer be served after those times. If you have a food allergy, please let us know.

"As you have already been told and undoubtedly noticed, we have rising platforms instead of stairs. These elevators just need to be told where to go. Please do not order them to go up and down for the fun of it; playing with the elevators will result in an automatic referral. So please be courteous to the other students and wait your turn.

"Finally, should you need any assistance, whether it be for homework or problems with other students, you can always come to any of the teachers. We do not have specific offices, but you can find us if you ask a frogoyle. For those that don't know, a frogoyle is a small statue that looks like a frog with fangs. They're all around the school, and can guide you to any teacher—they are essentially helpers to both teachers and students. You can also go to the Counseling Office, especially if you're having trouble in classes or with your mental health. A frogoyle is always stationed there to help you set up an appointment. Any questions?"

C3 raised his hand so quickly, that Zyn could feel the wind on her neck. She wondered if he used air magic unknowingly.

"Yes, C3?"

"Are there spirits at this school? When looking at the reviews on the air-net of this place, I saw that there had been sightings of a few spirits. I wanted to verify if this was true or not. Are these frogoyles you mention spirits?"

Ak-tu frowned. "Spirits live around us on a daily basis. You might see them, especially when you're living in the middle of the forest. The frogoyles are not spirits, though they *are* enchanted by spirit magic. Now—"

"But do any spirits *work* here?" C3 pressed.

"Why would you ask that?" Khurshid inquired.

"The reviews mentioned that some of the teachers had purple eyes, and—"

"*I* have purple eyes, and that does not make *me* a spirit," Ak-tu pointed out. "The purple eyes thing is merely a myth."

"Eye color makes no difference," Khurshid added. "Especially to me."

Zyn rolled her eyes. {*C3's gonna be that annoying nerd, isn't he?*} She heard Ren chuckle softly beside her.

"Now—"

"Oh!" C3 interrupted Ak-tu again. "I have one more question."

"Yes?" Ak-tu asked patiently, while Khurshid looked a bit exasperated.

"Do spirits eat food?" C3 queried. "And if so, what kind of food do they eat? Are they carnivores, like the lions I've read about? Or are they herbivores, like us? Would they eat processed food, or only natural food?"

Ak-tu stared at C3 for a long moment, then said, "That was more than one question. Anyhow, I hope you aren't intending on looking for a spirit and feeding it. Spirits don't have to eat, like we do. Spirits *can* eat if they want to, and they can eat whatever they want at that. Most are herbivores, simply due to it being easier to eat plants that aren't fully alive like animals are.

"*Now...*" He paused significantly here, clearly waiting for C3 to interrupt again. "...we will tell you about the school schedule you'll be following. You will be enrolled in the same classes, apart from your choice of elective classes."

Khurshid took over the conversation as Ak-tu reached for a wooden water bottle. "You start off Moonday morning with Magic Studies, Magic Channeling, Plants, and Potions. After lunch, you'll go to two Kung Fu classes. The first choice of elective are the two Tai Chi classes, which are after Kung Fu. You can otherwise choose two Art classes; all Art classes are on Freday, and upper-year students are in these classes as well. First-years otherwise only have classes on Moonday. Second-years have class on Trizday, third-years on Waddaday, and fourth-years on Thorsday.

"Magic Studies is the study of magic, obviously. Magic Channeling goes into how to use your magic and will be hands-on. Plants and Potions are very similar, as you study plants that you'll be using in the potions you brew.

"Kung Fu is all about self-defense, and magic will later be added in, as magic is primarily a defense mechanism. Tai Chi is another fighting art, but goes more slowly than the explosive Kung Fu. If you have a disability that prevents you from doing Kung Fu (even with adjustments), you will be enrolled in Tai Chi instead—though I believe all of you here are fine with doing Kung Fu. Magic martial arts is reserved for high-ranking students. Any questions?"

The room was quiet, so Khurshid pressed on. "Now, take out your mirrors, or come to the front for a piece of paper. You will write down your name and which two elective classes you want to take. You can take as many electives as you'd like."

Only Sarala went to the front for paper, as the other students pulled out their mirrors. Zyn glanced over at Ren, who held the family mirror out between their desks, so they could both use it.

"Like I said, Tai Chi already has two classes to it. If you want to take Tai Chi, you don't have to worry about taking any other classes."

Ren instantly tapped the mirror several times, writing out "Tai Chi" in the writing app. Shrugging, Zyn told her telepathically to add it for her as well. She wasn't too keen on the idea of moving slowly, but if Tai Chi was slow and meditative, maybe it would help her find her magic.

"The Art classes we offer here are Drawing and Painting (which is one class), Cooking, Writing, Fashion, Choir, Band, and Theatre (which is two hours long, as opposed to every other class being one hour).

"Once you have written your electives, send them to Mr. Caihong with the air-mail button. His air-mail address is aktu-caihong/caihong-academy/net. If you wrote it down, you can just turn in your piece of paper."

Zyn glanced at the classes Ren had put down for herself. It turned out that she wanted to take all of the Art classes.

Zyn grinned and muttered, "Same."

Ren nodded and added Zyn's name to the air-mail message, before sending it off.

"Any questions?" Khurshid asked again.

Nobody said anything.

"I will get these schedules made up for you," Ak-tu said, tapping his mirror. He took the piece of paper from Sarala, who sat at the far end of the classroom. Then, he hurried out the door, calling over his shoulder, "I'll be back soon!"

Khurshid therefore took over the class. "Now, as I said, you're all going to be taking the Magic Channeling class. This class will teach you how to use objects, specifically wands, to channel your magic and control the elements. You will earn a certification at the end of the year if you pass this class, so you are legally allowed to use magic with an object."

"What do you mean, legally allowed?" Sarala asked.

"People are not allowed to use their magic if they have no control over it," Khurshid explained. "Of course, you can play around and test it out, but you cannot use magic at work, for example. This could cause injuries. Having an object channeling certification is crucial to anyone using magic outside of their homes.

"You will be earning certifications for each class, so long as you pass them. This tells your future employers how much magical education you've received in a particular subject. After the first year, you are not required to take all classes. You can choose which classes to go into. Most students end up leaving after two years, especially as third- and fourth-year students require a teacher's permission to get into the advanced classes.

"Now, you will be choosing your wand. On the back table over there, we have lots of wands. Very few are made of the same wood. This is because each wood has a different property. You can read the slip with each wand to see what properties that wood has, and choose based off of that. Or you can choose the wand if it feels 'right' to you. Please do not choose a favorite tree or color. You will be working with your wand throughout the year, so you want to have one that you truly connect with. Please, no fighting over the wands!" Khurshid added, as each of the students zoomed to the back of the room.

"This is so cool!" Zyn said to Ren, inspecting the wands at one side of the table.

"I know, right?" Ren replied, reaching for a wand and twirling it in her fingers as she read the small paper attached to it. "Hmm...this one's holly. Represents energy, positivity, and protection."

"You're gonna choose based on the qualities, aren't you?" Zyn scoffed.

"Of course," Ren said.

"Isn't Dad's wand made from holly?"

Ren nodded in reply, setting down the holly wand and reaching for another one.

Zyn grabbed one at random and looked at it. It was smooth and bland, somehow more bland than the other wands there. She shrugged and moved on.

Sarala soon made it to their end of the table, then reached for a wand. Ren took this moment to try talking to the other girl again.

"Which one did you get?" Ren asked her brightly.

Sarala looked down at the tag. "Sumac. Grounding and protection," she said simply.

"Sounds like a good one," Zyn said, joining in.

Sarala shrugged, leaving a small silence.

"Ooh, I like this one," Ren said, snatching up a wand that was pale on one end and darker on the other. "It's viburnum, which represents focus, relaxation, and deep breathing."

"That's definitely yours," Zyn remarked.

"I quite agree!"

"Can you move out of the way?" a loud voice asked suddenly.

They each looked up in surprise. C3 was standing next to them, looking annoyed.

"You're in the way," he said to Zyn.

Zyn glared at the boy with a raised eyebrow. "No need to be so rude," she muttered, as she stepped aside a bit reluctantly.

C3 ignored her and went for a wand on the far corner, which had been out of his reach when Zyn was standing by the table. It looked like the label termed it as hazel.

"You still have to choose a wand," Ren told Zyn. "Go on!"

Zyn couldn't find a wand that spoke to her, though. Most of the students had found their wands, until it was just her left. Getting the feeling that she was holding up the class, Zyn finally snatched a bent brownish-red wand, which was labeled as hazel and represented balance. Scowling that she might have just chosen the same wand as C3, Zyn returned to her seat.

"Everyone got their wands?" Khurshid asked cheerfully.

"Yep!"

"I hope so."

"Yes, Mr. Jihan."

"Good. Now you're going to make the wands more personal to you," Ak-tu said, entering the classroom and signaling for the students to return to their seats. "Lots of people choose to carve symbols into their wands, but you can add things like vines, flowers, leaves, feathers, crystals, and other charms. You can also paint yours if you'd like. You'll find all the supplies you need in that cabinet over there. Once you have personalized your wand, come to me to verify your schedule is correct, then you may leave."

Zyn had no idea what to add to her wand. She glanced at the mass of students huddled around the cabinet Ak-tu had pointed to, and decided to ponder while she waited at her desk. Yet she zoned out, imagining going on adventures with a wand at her side, guiding her way like a light in the dark.

She was still in deep thought by the time the crowd cleared. She only snapped out of her thoughts when she heard C3's annoying voice telling Ak-tu that he was done. Zyn glanced at the clock and saw that it hadn't even been five minutes since Ak-tu's instructions! She peered closer at C3's wand and saw that he had merely added three scratch marks near the bottom.

"Pfft, that's so boring," Zyn said, pointing it out to Ren.

But Ren was not beside her. She was at the cabinet, grabbing supplies. Zyn hastily jumped to her feet to join her sister.

Zyn and Ren returned to their seats with a small handful of interesting supplies and some carving tools. Sarala moved to sit down on Zyn's other side.

"Haven't started yet?" Sarala grunted.

Ren looked surprised but delighted to see her joining them. "I have ideas!" she replied.

"I still don't know what to do," Zyn muttered, wishing her daydreams had showed her what her wand looked like being decorated.

Sarala held up her wand. "Do you think it's fine if I just leave it like this?"

"You haven't done anything to it," Zyn pointed out.

"No, but it doesn't look like some twig, does it? It has elegant curves perfectly measured out around its base. Why do we need to decorate them, anyway?" Sarala asked irritably.

"If you lose your wand, you'd know what to look for," Ren explained. "Or if someone finds it, they'd have an easier time knowing who it belongs to."

"I guess," Sarala said.

"Here—take this!" Ren said, handing her a purple crystal.

"Don't you want it?" Sarala asked, narrowing her eyes.

Ren shrugged. "You need it more than I do."

"Does it do anything?"

"It's agate, which helps stabilize you," Ren said. "Not that you need stability right now, but you know, in the future, if you happen to be unbalanced or—I mean—well…you know, if you're stressed out or something, not saying that you're unbalanced…" She blushed as she stumbled over her words and fell silent.

"I'll take it," Sarala grunted.

She tied the crystal around the top of her wand. Once done, she got to her feet and approached Ak-tu. She had to wait for her schedule, as more students had finished with their wands.

"What *are* you doing with your wand?" Zyn asked Ren.

Ren didn't respond right away, as she focused on attaching a fluffy white feather to the base of the wand. "Well, since I have air magic, and Dad does, and you probably will too…I thought it'd be a nice touch to include a feather," she whispered. "And these charms represent *us*!"

Zyn watched as Ren attached a pale blue crescent moon and a golden sun charm just above the feather. Zyn smiled.

"I think I'm done!" Ren said, eyeing her wand proudly.

"Not you too!" Zyn groaned. "Hold on, let me put something together real quick."

She grabbed a small vine and twirled it around the wand. But it didn't feel like enough. She frowned and glanced over at Ren's wand, then smiled as she had an idea. She used a carving tool to draw a sun and a crescent moon at the top of her wand.

"Ooh, I like it!" Ren said.

"It still isn't done though," Zyn said, observing it. "It needs more carvings on the bottom to balance it out. Ooo, I have an idea!"

She started at the base, etching a tree standing on a rock. She then moved up the wand, adding what she hoped looked like raindrops, fire, and clouds.

"The four elements?" Ren guessed.

Zyn nodded eagerly. "This wood is about balance, after all, and you can't have balance without all four elements! Or without the sun and moon."

"I like how it starts with the ground, then goes to the sky with the sun and moon," remarked Ren.

"Yeah, kinda cool."

"Are you done now, then?"

"Yep!" she said with a nod. She looked around the classroom and saw that she and Ren were the last students there. "Whoops."

"Don't worry about it," Ren chuckled. "It's not like we have anything else to do for the rest of the day."

They made their way to their father, showing him their wands and explaining the purpose behind them. Ak-tu nodded to their words, beaming.

"Excellent work," he praised. "I'm glad to see you have both taken my past lessons to heart."

"Past lessons? You mean all the math and history?" Zyn teased.

"He means the philosophical lessons of balance and living naturally," Ren scoffed.

"Yeah, yeah, I know," Zyn chuckled.

Ak-tu laughed, then said, "Well, I'm happy regardless. Learn these lessons early, kids. Now…you know you enrolled in every Art class, right?"

Zyn and Ren nodded.

"You sure you want to take on so much?" Ak-tu asked.

"Of course!" Zyn replied. "It'll be fun!" *And Art doesn't require magic—at least as far as I know.*

Ak-tu smiled. "Okay. Here are your schedules."

He passed them identical schedules, and the sisters grinned at one another.

"Yee! I can't wait for classes!" Zyn exclaimed, hopping in the air.

They were almost to the door when Ak-tu stopped them. "I almost forgot! Sarala will be staying in the empty bedroom above your room, Zyn."

Zyn and Ren exchanged a glance. "Why?" they asked in unison.

"She asked if she could have a room change," Ak-tu said with a shrug. "She didn't want to be around so many people. I told her the only free room was in our tower."

"That's not true. There's plenty of space, and not that many students," Zyn pointed out. "The rooms in the northern building are probably full of dust, they're never used!"

Ak-tu shrugged again. "All the more reason not to use them! That's actually where most of the extra supplies are kept, rather than actual beds," he chuckled. Then, he said seriously, "If she wants a room change, then I might as well keep a closer eye on her. We don't know anything about her, after all…"

"Do you think she's trying to cause trouble?" Ren asked, sounding dismayed.

"Possibly. Or maybe she's just uncomfortable with all of the students being around now. Anyhow, go ahead and show her to her new room. She already has the key to her room, but I'm not giving her a key to the tower. She'll have to depend on one of us to get in."

Zyn and Ren nodded.

"Go on, then! You have the rest of the day to get to know her better," Ak-tu said, waving them off.

Zyn and Ren hurried from the room. They didn't have to look far for Sarala. She was standing outside the Tai Chi Studio, beside the stone elevator that led to the upper floors of the western building. She seemed a bit uncertain, but nodded to Zyn and Ren as they came bounding over.

"Mr. Caihong told me I'm taking a room in the tower now," she said shortly.

Ren nodded eagerly. "Yes, we'll show you! Come on!"

"Do you have all of your stuff?" Zyn asked her.

Sarala shrugged in reply. "All I have are my wand and…just my wand."

"Oh, did Dad not get you any new clothes?" Ren asked in surprise.

"He offered," Sarala muttered.

"And you didn't take him up on it?" Zyn queried.

"He's already given me so much," Sarala grumbled.

"Well, you can borrow some of my clothes!" Ren said cheerfully, entering the Tai Chi Studio and walking over to the tower door. "And Zyn wouldn't mind sharing, either. She has so many robes!"

Zyn opened her mouth to protest, but noted that was true. Her wardrobe mostly contained heavily-patterned robes, for many different occasions.

"No, thanks," Sarala grumbled, glancing sidelong at Zyn as Ren unlocked the door.

"But you have to wear something besides what you're wearing now!" Ren objected.

"No thanks to taking clothes from Zyn," Sarala clarified. "I'll take some of your clothes…if you really want to give them to me."

"Of course!" Ren said.

She led the way into the family room and to the spiral stairs across from the door. She darted up, Zyn and Sarala following. Ren stopped on the second floor to tell Sarala it contained the bathroom, then stopped on the third floor to go into her room. After about ten minutes, the trio came out carrying bundles of soft clothes for Sarala. They then went up to the fourth floor, Zyn announcing it was her bedroom, before they went to the fifth floor. They opened the door and led Sarala into the plain bedroom, which was painted yellow.

"Here's your new room!" Ren said, dumping the clothes she'd been carrying onto the bed. "It doesn't get used too often. Actually, I don't think it's ever been used."

"Besides that one time when Aster's room caught fire," Zyn pointed out.

Sarala raised an eyebrow at that. "How…?"

"It's a long story," Ren chuckled.

"What about your dad? Where does he sleep?"

"On the sixth floor," Ren replied.

"He likes to go up and down the stairs for exercise purposes or something," Zyn added. "Though I swear I've heard wind in the tower before, as if he was riding a bunch of air down…"

"Well, make yourself at home!" Ren said brightly.

"If you need anything, we'll be downstairs," Zyn said.

"We'd love to get to know you more!" Ren added.

Sarala grunted and lowered her eyes to the floor.

"I think that's everything?" Ren questioned, glancing at Zyn.

"I think so. Yep! No—wait! Be warned that I scream every morning!" Zyn said delightfully, as she and Ren left the room.

Sarala stared after them, looking bewildered.

"She's totally going to hate you for that," Ren muttered to Zyn as they went back down the stairs.

Zyn shrugged carelessly. "You can't please everyone!"

CHAPTER 7: AS IT BEGAN

"Gooooooooood morning!"

Zyn poked her head out of her room, throwing her arms out on either side of her. She was dressed in a bright blue robe with dark blue birds scattered across its smooth surface. Underneath the robe, she wore a green-and-blue striped shirt and black pants with green stripes down the back.

"It's the first day of school!" Zyn called, her voice echoing off the stone walls of the tower. "Wake up and get ready for a great day!"

"Why can't you let us *sleep*?" Sarala's annoyed voice screamed down to her. "It's the crack of dawn!"

"It's only 7!" Zyn replied loudly. "Or—almost 7!"

"I don't care what time it is!" Sarala growled in return.

"Now, kids, stop your howling!" came a gruff voice one level down—it was Ren pretending to be Ak-tu. "Let people sleep if they want to."

Zyn snorted in laughter. "Oh, come *on*, Ren! Let me have some fun! It's not like Dad's here to actually scold me, after all."

Ren bounded up the stairs, appearing around the turn with a grin on her face and dressed in a simple pink robe. "Yeah, I know, Zyn! But I just couldn't resist!" she teased. "Not that Dad sounds like that anyway."

"Yeah, if anything, he'd get in on the joke!" Zyn looked at the stairs spiraling up towards Sarala's room and yowled as loudly as she could, "COME ON, SLEEPYHEAD!"

"UGH!"

Zyn and Ren walked down the steps to the first floor. Ren went to sit on the rug in front of the empty fireplace, while Zyn jumped onto the couch behind her.

"I can't wait for class!" Zyn said, fidgeting excitedly.

"I can see that," Ren chuckled, closing her eyes. "Do you mind keeping it down, though? I want to meditate for at least five minutes!"

Zyn shrugged quietly in response and hopped off the couch again, placing one hand on her hip as she scanned the tower room in a bored fashion. Sniffing the air, she could detect a trace of something fruity; it seemed Ak-tu had eaten breakfast in the tower that morning.

A bit later, Sarala came dragging her feet down the stairs. She was dressed in a new yellow robe, one that Ren had seldom worn before. She would have appeared nice in the new outfit if it wasn't for the annoyed look on her face and the dark marks under her golden eyes.

Maybe I shouldn't have woken her up... Eh, what am I thinking? Of course I had to wake her up, otherwise she'd miss breakfast! The bell will sound any minute now anyway.

"What's the first class again?" Sarala grumbled.

Zyn put her pointer finger to her lips, then pointed at Ren over the couch with her other hand. Sarala scowled and crossed her arms, leaning against the entranceway to the stairs.

"Why can't she just do that in her room?" Sarala whispered.

"Because she wants to do it near the fireplace," Zyn mouthed to her.

"Why?" Sarala hissed.

Zyn thought about that for a moment. *Why is she doing it by the fireplace?* "I don't know!" she whispered back honestly.

"You two are ridiculous," Sarala muttered loudly.

"I heard that!" Ren said, opening one eye and looking back at Sarala. She smiled playfully at the other girl, then hopped to her feet. "Well, that'll have to do! I lost concentration when you two had your hissing match. Let's see what's for breakfast!"

The three therefore left the tower, Zyn digging around in her pockets for the tower key (she'd keep spare keys in most of her robes). Once finding it, she locked the door and hurried after Ren and Sarala, as the two walked on without her.

They crossed the Tai Chi Studio and Courtyard until they reached the Eating Hall. There weren't too many students at breakfast yet, as the bell had just rung. The three made their way through the many wooden tables to reach the food counter near the Kitchen door. The usual aromas of savory and sweet filled the air, but this time, the smells didn't bother Zyn.

The cooks always made a variety of good food. There were blueberry muffins, cinnamon rolls, plain and chocolate chip pancakes, peanut spread toast, fruit bowls, cereal, teas and blends of multiple flavors, hot cocoa, and plain water.

"Do you ever wonder how the cooks have time to make all this food?" Zyn asked Ren, grabbing three bamboo trays from the clean stack on one side of the counter.

Ren took a tray from Zyn and replied, "Well, there *are* six of them."

She led the way, sliding her tray down the scratched-up counter and reaching for some pancakes.

"Do you think they use magic to make it go by faster?" Zyn wondered.

"I would, if I knew how," Sarala commented.

Zyn collected food unconsciously, thinking back to a time that she and Ren had been cooking with their father. The family had been traveling (as was usual in the good ol' days), and they were low on food supplies. They only had flour, a few spices, some mangoes, and a handful of blueberries. Instead of eating the fruit by itself, the twins voted on making a mango blueberry bread. Aktu had used his air magic to make the bread rise, and Zyn recalled how she had wanted to do magical cooking for at least a month afterwards.

Smiling at the memory, Zyn trailed Ren and Sarala to a nearby table and sat down to eat. But it tasted nowhere near as savory or sweet as the mango blueberry bread she'd made with her family.

As they ate, more people trickled in, until the Eating Hall was completely full. Chatter filled the air again, pulling Zyn from different memories of the places the Caihong family had traveled to before the school's creation. She scowled at the annoying people, then realized that she had finished eating while she'd been reminiscing. Standing up, she placed her pointed shoe on the bench.

"Hey, Ren, do you think we'll ever travel again?"

"Of course we will," Ren said, raising an eyebrow in question and appearing much like their father. "We go on vacations every summer."

"Yeah, but…I mean traveling like we used to do, just going around the world and never being tied down, or only staying at the little house for a few months before traveling again!" Zyn explained, tripping over her words as she spoke rapidly.

"Oh. Well, it's hard to do that when Dad owns a school," pointed out Ren.

Zyn's shoulders slumped. "Yeah, I guess that's true… How much time do we have left anyway?"

"Umm…school just started, so it'll be another year before we can go anywh—"

"I meant until class starts," Zyn interrupted.

Ren pulled out the squarish family mirror and said, "It's 7:35! What should we do to kill time?"

"I would have *slept*, if given the choice," Sarala muttered, glaring up at Zyn.

Zyn raised an eyebrow at her. "Sleep is for the weak," she finally said in an uninterested voice.

In the end, Zyn pulled out a deck of YAT cards from her robe. She played with Ren, until Sarala was done eating and surprisingly joined in too. The card game was fun, especially when Zyn constantly made Sarala pick up cards. They were so invested in their game, that the chatter faded around them and they almost missed the ringing bell.

"Ah! That's the minute-bell!" Ren cried. "We better go!"

"I don't have my wand though," Sarala said, her voice slightly panicked.

"Hurry up!" Zyn yowled.

The three raced out of the Eating Hall, each of them heading for the western building containing their tower.

"I'll get our wands!" Ren shouted over her shoulder. "You get to class, okay?"

Zyn nodded and changed directions, heading for the Magic Studies classroom instead. Sarala followed her, as Ren vanished into the Tai Chi Studio.

Zyn and Sarala sat down at the front of the class, saving a seat for Ren. Khurshid stood at the large desk, waiting for the students to gather. The final bell rang and Ren appeared soon after, panting heavily. She sunk into the seat beside Zyn, passing Zyn and Sarala their wands and a stack of notebooks.

"Welcome, class!" Khurshid began. "You will be in this classroom for the next two hours, for Magic Studies and Magic Channeling. Next week, Magic Channeling will be in the room over. You will report to the Greenhouse for Plants, and then to the Potions classroom. In the afternoon, you'll go to the Kung Fu Studio for Kung Fu, and those of you who are taking Tai Chi will go to the Tai Chi Studio.

"I'm going to have my mirror call out your names for attendance, to make sure we've got everyone here for the first day. Please say 'here' when you hear your name."

He pulled out his mirror and ordered it to read out the attendance. It called out their names in a bland voice, its surface lighting up each time it spoke. Everyone was there, so he put the mirror away to start class.

"In Magic Studies, we will be going over the types of magic and how to determine a person's magic. In Magic Channeling, we will be going over common uses for magic and why we use objects for channeling. We won't be doing any actual channeling until next week.

"Now, I am blind, but that doesn't mean you can't ask questions. Just knock on the desk to get my attention. If I seemed not to have noticed, you may interrupt—but only if your question is important, please. Any questions so far?"

Nobody moved, as if afraid that any small movement or sound would catch Khurshid's attention.

"Very well. Let's begin. If you'd like to take notes, you can do so. I don't mind if you use your mirror or your notebooks, just so long as you're paying attention."

Khurshid paced slowly at the front of the class as he lectured them about the different types of magic. There was elemental magic (which everyone knew of), natural magic, enchantment magic, and spirit magic.

Elemental magic was what every living animal had in them, and was said to be the source of life itself. The elements consisted of earth, water, fire, and air. People typically channeled their magic through an object (like a wand, as only plants could channel magic), but could also use actions (like martial arts or dancing) to control it.

Natural magic was found in nature, specifically plants and crystals. This magic could be used to help a person's own magic be more powerful (especially when added to potions), heal body or mind, and more.

Khurshid didn't spend much time on enchantment or spirit magics, saying they'd learn more about those types of magics at the higher levels. Enchantment magic made objects do certain things, while spirit magic was said to be that of imagination.

Zyn wished Khurshid would go into the magic types more, as Ak-tu didn't even tell his children much about them, despite using advanced magic often.

The rest of the class was spent looking up astrological birth charts in textbooks. After all, the placement of the sun and moon in somebody's chart determined their type of magic. If someone was born during the day, their sun sign would determine their magic; if born at night, it would be their moon sign. If a person was born at dawn or dusk, it could swing either way.

Studying birth charts took a lot of concentration, that the class was quickly over before the students realized it. Khurshid assigned them homework to figure out their personal birth charts, which would be due the following week. Zyn groaned at the idea of receiving homework already, but at least Khurshid told them they were allowed to use the air-net for pointers.

In Magic Channeling, Khurshid briefly explained that objects helped a person channel their magic. People used plant magic through wands to help their own magic come out and be stronger than if they were trying to channel on their own. Zyn hoped that this would mean she'd be able to summon her magic when it came to using a wand, but Khurshid strictly told each student not to try practicing any magic until the following week—so Zyn would still have to wait.

Once a person mastered using their wand (or other wooden object, like a staff or stick), they moved onto using their entire bodies to summon their magic. The most advanced wielders got away with using only their hands.

C3 asked so many questions in this class, that they had little time to go over how magic could be used on a day-to-day basis.

As a result, they were assigned homework of how to use each element in two daily tasks.

After Magic Channeling, the first-years hurried to the opposite side of the Courtyard where the Greenhouse was located, glad to be out of the stuffy room and stretching their legs. They had to walk through the thick garden to reach the glass doors concealed behind it, shoving poky branches and slick leaves aside.

The Greenhouse wasn't connected to the western building, due to being made entirely of thick-paneled glass instead of stone. It stood four floors high to house the many plants comfortably; this meant that there were less student rooms in the western building than the northern and eastern buildings, due to the Greenhouse taking up a large chunk of space.

The glass building was more cluttered than the gardens. There were all sorts of plants, from trees and shrubs to pulsing bushes and dancing vines. There was even a large pile of sticky pink-and-green goo. The glass windows at the top of the Greenhouse were open, allowing birds and many insects inside. Between the birds, bugs, and bushes making a racket, it was difficult to hear the teacher, Fern Oakley.

Fern was a tall woman with a bushy green afro. Her right eye was purple and her left eye was red, but it was the green vine-like tattoos covering her body that caught everyone's attention. She wore a spiral necklace over her plaid shirt; Zyn never saw her without it. Her face always looked chiseled to be a stern expression.

Most of the class was spent studying a few of the most common plants and what magical properties they had. Fern had them taking extensive notes. The students not only had to write down how to detect the plant by their four or five senses, but also sketch them to the best of their abilities. The class once again flew by with the notes and sketching. Soon enough, they were leaving the humid Greenhouse and crossing the Courtyard to return to the eastern building, where the Potions classroom lay.

Fern was teaching this class too, and she spent most of the time lecturing them on potion safety. Many of the students had fallen asleep, worn out after getting so much information in one morning. After C3 asked plenty of questions, Fern let the class go early for lunch, thankfully not assigning any homework.

"FINALLY!" Zyn yowled, as she raced across the Courtyard.

Ren snorted in amusement. "I thought you couldn't wait for classes?"

"Yeah, and it was fun until Potions, and now I'm hungry," Zyn huffed.

"It wasn't as bad as I thought it'd be," Sarala said, coming up behind them. "But, then again, I haven't been in school since the fourth grade...I think."

Zyn and Ren stared at her.

Sarala blushed and pushed past them, reaching the Eating Hall first. The room was packed when they got inside. Sarala had paused in the doorway, clearly taken aback by how full the room was when she didn't get there early. She muttered that she'd save a spot for her, Zyn, and Ren as long as they brought her food. Zyn and Ren therefore went to the long line at the counter.

Lunch had more of a selection than breakfast did. There were falafel wraps, bean burritos, veggie and fruit salads alike, soups of different savory flavors, dumplings, spicy noodles, rice, mashed potatoes, crispy cauliflower with sauce, apples with peanut spread, grilled fruit, sweet açaí bowls, and even fruit tarts. A few snacks were available, from salty pretzels and crackers to healthier carrots and sunflower seeds. More drinks were added to the variety of teas and blends from that morning too: fresh smoothies and fruit juices. There were even popsicles and pie slices at the ready for dessert!

Once the line finally moved, the two collected food on their trays. They got a third tray for Sarala, selecting random foods to add to it.

"She eats bread with everything, I've noticed," Ren said, grabbing a fluffy roll.

"Does she like spicy stuff?" Zyn asked, tossing on a burrito.

"Ooh, let's give her a popsicle!" Ren exclaimed, snatching one from the counter.

"Yeah, maybe that'll teach her to chill out a bit."

They grabbed three different smoothies, then looked around for Sarala. She was sitting at a table near the start of the line, reserving two seats at the benches by sticking her arms on one and her feet on the other. She sneered at anyone even looking at her. Zyn and Ren made their way to her, chuckling at the sight.

"Here's some food," Zyn said, setting down the third tray in front of her.

She eyed the bread, burrito, and popsicle. "How very…kind… of you," she murmured.

"Wanna go outside?" Zyn asked. "It's pretty warm and loud in here."

"But I had to jump at this table before someone else took it!" Sarala complained.

However, the trio went outside, entering the garden to the left. Ren, who loved spending time in the gardens, knew exactly where a bench lay hidden within the tangle of plants. The bench sat beside a willow tree, which provided shade from the bright sun above. It was only big enough for two people to sit on though, so Zyn sat on the soft grass.

They ate in silence for a while, then discussed their classes and wondered what they could expect for Kung Fu. Getting food and eating took awhile, that they did not have time to get any sort of head-start on the homework they'd been assigned. They instead walked to the Kung Fu Studio in the northern building, determined to arrive on time to their next class.

They entered the building to see it wasn't empty. Ak-tu and C3 stood off to the side, on the small bit of ground that wasn't covered in orange mats. C3 seemed to be asking Ak-tu more questions.

"I was wondering, why are humans able to eat plenty of different foods? In the few documentaries we've gotten on wildlife, it appears that other animals merely eat one or two things. Like elephants have only been seen to eat grass and a bit of fruit. But humans eat a variety of things, from fruits and vegetables to grains and beans. I suppose a bean can count as a vegetable, but I mean to say…why don't wild animals eat as many foods as *we* do? I am talking about herbivorous animals, of course, as we aren't carnivores or omnivores. Aren't these herbivores missing out on nutrition? Or are we just eating lots of food, simply due to our cultivation of plants? Do we need to eat that much food? Are there side effects of having too much nutrition?"

Ak-tu looked over at Zyn, Ren, and Sarala as they entered. He smiled at them in a bemused fashion, then replied to C3.

"We don't know much about animals, considering they tend to keep to themselves. We cannot come to any conclusions as to what sort of nutrition they might need, or how much nutrition they're gaining from the food they eat. But I admire your inquisitive mind, C3.

"Welcome, you three! Excited for class, then? I hope you didn't eat too late, or too much!" Ak-tu continued, hurrying over to them. *{Glad you came in!}* He added to Zyn and Ren telepathically.

The sisters glanced at each other and chuckled.

The minute-bell soon rang, bringing the other first-year students with it. Once the final bell rang and everyone was in, Ak-tu began the class.

"Some of you are probably wondering *why* you have to learn Kung Fu. Yes, there's the defense mechanism of magic, and Kung Fu teaches self-defense. But there is so much more to it than that. Kung Fu will get your body stronger and conditioned to handle magic. And when it comes time to channel magic with your body, martial arts will give you a stronger connection to it, making magic easier to channel. Of course, exercise is also very important, so this is our version of physical education that you'd find at other schools.

"Now, Kung Fu classes (and Tai Chi, for that matter) work in a different way from the other classes. You advance depending on your rank. What we term as Kung Fu 1, or the first-year Kung Fu class, is actually for the white, yellow, and green sashes. Kung Fu 2 is blue and purple sashes. Kung Fu 3 is brown and black sashes, and where a bit of magic comes in. Kung Fu 4 is focused entirely on magic.

"In order to move up in rank, you will each have to test. If you move more quickly than the other students, you could find yourself switching to the Kung Fu 2 class, which takes place on Trizday. Not many students advance that quickly within a year though. If you don't advance as fast as the others, that is totally fine. The average student should test for blue sash by the very end of the year, so they can start next year in the Kung Fu 2 class.

"You will need to change out of your normal clothes and into the proper uniform." Ak-tu flicked his hand and caught a white vest, baggy black pants, and a white sash that appeared out of thin air. The vest had a small black-and-white symbol on the front left, and a large one on the back—just like Ak-tu's robe. "I'd like you to get dressed in this before class starts, so we can jump right into it. Any questions?"

There weren't, so he got to work once they had all changed. Ak-tu had them practicing blocks and basic strikes for a good chunk of the class. These were mostly done in the air, until Ak-tu came around with a blocker bat or target for them to strike. They had to call out different sounds with each move, making their breath come out sharp and aggressive. The remainder of the class was spent drilling a few of the basic kicks, though they didn't have time to get through all of them.

"I thought we were supposed to be learning self-defense," Sarala muttered once the Kung Fu class was over.

"We are," Ak-tu said, hearing her. "The first two classes will be focused on learning basic strikes and kicks, then we'll be making techniques out of them. And, as I said at the beginning of the class, we'll split into groups according to rank. Mr. Jihan will be helping me out in teaching you once we have two different ranks here."

They then moved onto the next Kung Fu class, which was "Kung Fu 1B" on the schedule.

"The second Kung Fu and Tai Chi classes are the combative classes. For Kung Fu 1, we will only be doing kickboxing and grappling. Weapon sparring comes at Kung Fu 2. We will work on kickboxing one week, grappling the next, and alternate. Kickboxing is exactly what it sounds like: kicking and boxing combined. Grappling is all about ground fighting. We won't be holding matches anytime soon, but I still want you to get dressed up in the kickboxing gear."

He opened a door to one of the small rooms on the left side of the large mat, which led to a closet (the other two doors were personal training rooms). Ak-tu pulled out bags of gear, which included helmets, gloves, chest protectors, shin guards, and groin protectors. The sturdy material was made from rough plants.

As everyone put the gear on over their uniforms, Ak-tu explained the rules of kickboxing, with the most important one being that they were only allowed to strike to the chest protector.

Once everyone was dressed, Ak-tu had them pair up to practice simple drills. They started off with jab-cross back and forth, and how to block the two punches. They then did the same drill with swinging hooks to either side of the body. Finally, they learned how to do straight snap kicks off either leg, and the different ways to block kicks.

The students were exhausted and sweaty by the time class was finished. Zyn was starting to wish she hadn't signed up for Tai Chi. She watched jealously as the class cleared out after taking off their gear and wiping it down, done for the day.

{We still have two hours!} Zyn said to Ren telepathically.

{Don't worry, Zyn. Tai Chi is perfect to do after a Kung Fu warmup!} Ren replied. *{And then we can stretch after. It'll be so nice!}*

"Tai Chi class, to the Tai Chi Studio!" Ak-tu called, waving for the students to follow him outside the Kung Fu Studio.

He led the way to the familiar Tai Chi Studio, which often stood empty. Zyn and Ren trailed right behind him, chatting about the fun Kung Fu classes as they went. They knew Sarala wasn't doing Tai Chi, but when they got into the studio, they were quite surprised to see that *nobody else* had signed up.

"Umm…"

Zyn and Ren stared around, as if another student would appear out of thin air like the Kung Fu uniform Ak-tu had summoned.

Ak-tu nodded sadly. "Not many people are interested in Tai Chi—at least, not many people your age. Plenty of elderly people find Tai Chi beneficial to their old joints, but kids hardly like the sound of moving slowly and calming down."

{Jeez, if I didn't sign up, you'd be alone, Ren!}

Ren glanced sidelong at Zyn, but made no response. She instead said to Ak-tu, "Well, *I* know what kind of benefits Tai Chi gives, from better stability to a tranquil mind to stronger joints… there's just so many benefits! All of those other students are missing out."

Just then, the door opened, and C3 came in. He stared at the mostly-empty room. The Tai Chi Studio was a bit smaller than the Kung Fu Studio, only holding a large mat and no personal training rooms. There wasn't any equipment, either, as anything for Tai Chi would be stored in the Kung Fu closet. C3 blinked in surprise, then cleared his throat.

"I apologize for my tardiness," he said awkwardly. "I had to use the bathroom."

Ak-tu smiled. "You are more than welcome here. I *thought* I had more than my own children. Now, as I said in Kung Fu, Tai Chi ranks and tests work the same way. The uniform is a white top with sleeves, and a white fringe instead of a sash.

"Rather than learning techniques, you will be learning a form of self-defense movements. We have forms in Kung Fu, which are a series of techniques linked together, so it's pretty similar. But in Tai Chi, you have to move slow and low. It's a very intricate art, as you will soon see through empty-full movements, and using the body instead of just the arms or legs."

They spent the Tai Chi hour learning the stances and the beginning of the form. At the very end, they did a bit of qigong exercises to cool down. There were many types of qigong, which targeted different areas of the body but always focused on controlling the breath. Qigong was said to have great healing qualities like Tai Chi.

The second Tai Chi class was all about the combative, push hands. Since there were only three students, Ak-tu got to jump in the mix to drill with them. Push hands was all about feeling the opponent's energy, and redirecting or deflecting their attacks. Zyn found it very difficult, more so than Tai Chi's slow movements. It was restraining in that they had to stand in place, and, if they lifted their foot and stumbled back, they automatically lost the point.

Once class was over, the bell rang for dinner. Zyn, Ren, and C3 were bone-weary at this point, and they were slow to get changed back into their normal clothing. By the time the trio reached the Eating Hall, there was a long line again.

"Look—there's Sarala!" Zyn said, pointing.

Sarala was at the head of the line. Zyn led the way over to her, ignoring C3's complaints behind her that the sisters were cutting.

"How was Tai Chi?" Sarala asked as they approached.

"Eh," Zyn grunted with a shrug. "It's way harder than it looks."

"It's fun though!" Ren said, her purple eyes lighting up as she grabbed an açaí bowl.

"I was trying to work on that astrology homework," Sarala muttered. "But…I didn't get very far."

"We still have a week," Zyn pointed out, snatching a bean patty sandwich.

"I know, but…" She shrugged and fell silent.

Zyn frowned, then asked Sarala, "Where did you go, if not back to the tower? After all, you don't have the key—though we easily could have opened the door for you if you came with us."

"I didn't want to get stuck going to Tai Chi," Sarala said, adding a bread roll to her tray.

Zyn snorted in laughter. "Wow, you *really* don't want to take it, do you?"

She made a small grunting noise in reply.

The three finished grabbing their food and went to sit down at a table by the door. They ate and chatted about their first day of classes for a while, then decided to do homework together the following day. After eating, they went back to the tower.

"I'm glad to see you're opening up, Sarala," Ren said, as they stopped outside the tower door to unlock it.

Sarala stared at the ground and made no reply. Once the door opened, she hurried inside and went up the stairs. Zyn and Ren remained by the door, frowning after her.

"I think you scared her off," Zyn noted dryly.

Ren looked concerned. "Did I say something wrong?"

Zyn shrugged. "I dunno. Well, I'm tired. I think I'm going to bed. Do you think we could try to summon my magic tomorrow?"

The door opened behind them and Ak-tu came in. Zyn immediately tensed. Did her father hear her? Did he now know that Zyn still had yet to summon her magic?

"Oh, you just want to jump right into learning magic, don't you?" Ak-tu chuckled. "I'm afraid you'll have to follow the rules, just like every other student. No magic outside class for the first month!"

Zyn laughed lightly, acting like she wasn't on high alert. "Sorry, Dad, I'm just so excited to learn!"

Ak-tu ruffled her hair, making it lose some of its spiky look. "I'm very happy to hear," he said proudly.

Zyn pushed Ak-tu's hand away. "I'm going to bed now. See you tomorrow!"

She bounded to the spiral staircase, before Ak-tu or Ren could reply. She soon slipped inside her room and closed the door quietly behind her, her heart racing. Going to the hammock in the center of the room, she collapsed on it, her mind and body too weary to think or move.

Her room used to have a bed in it, until one of the students broke their bed. Zyn offered to give up her bed to the student, and instead got a hammock (she still didn't know why her father allowed this, considering there were many empty rooms with extra beds). When Zyn didn't feel like sleeping in the hammock, she would simply lay on a blanket on the floor. She didn't care much where she slept.

Her room was painted orange. There were lots of posters across the walls, depicting different regions of the world: Galia's thick rainforests, sandy deserts of Sin Tarayib, a volcano in Mlima wa Tai, palm trees in Lua Pele, tall peaks in Fènghuáng Chéng, a mountain range with a brilliant sunset in Aakaash Parvat...

Above the wardrobe was a large board with photos of the Caihong family in different locations: the beach, a water park, a thick jungle, tall mountains, even a huge bowling competition! Zyn often woke up to the sight of adventurous memories.

There were a few shelves around the room. Some held sticks and stones, while others had enchanted souvenirs from around the world. Books sat on one shelf, most of them full of fantasy adventures—adventures that Zyn missed taking.

Zyn focused on the posters, paintings, souvenirs, and books, trying to calm down or focus on memories of traveling. *Dad doesn't know… Dad doesn't know…*

She repeated the phrase in her head, reassuring herself until she fell into a dreamless sleep.

CHAPTER 8: LOST OPPORTUNITY

Sarala wanted to pummel Zyn the next morning, as her wakeup call rang through the tower yet again. Why did that girl have to be so annoying? She groaned and got to her feet, throwing the soft blankets off her and stomping loudly to the door.

"Shut UP!" she growled fiercely.

"No!" Zyn replied.

Sarala crossed her arms over chest angrily. "Why do you even bother?"

"I always greet the spirits and nature each day!"

Sarala snorted at that. "Spirits, *really*? Spirits don't exist! And even if they did, I'm sure they're not deaf, so *stop your screaming*!"

Zyn made no response, so Sarala clambered back into her bed. She had just pulled the blanket back over her and closed her eyes when the bell rang through the school. She sighed loudly and got to her feet, figuring there was no point in missing breakfast just to sleep in a bit.

"Why does breakfast have to be so early?" she complained as she entered the family room minutes later.

Zyn and Ren were already there. Zyn was dressed in a green robe with golden flowers, and Ren wore a simple blue robe and sweatpants.

"Because there are classes to be had," Ren pointed out. "If we had breakfast later, we'd have to have lunch at 1. Who eats lunch at 1?"

"Yeah, I'd rather eat lunch at 11," Zyn commented.

Ren rolled her eyes. "Come on, let's go eat!"

"So we're doing that homework today, right?" Sarala asked as they made their way across the cool Courtyard, the sky cloudy above.

Ren nodded eagerly. "I can't wait to plot out my birth chart! I mean, I've looked it up on the air-net plenty of times before—"

Sarala stared at her. "Wait—Mr. Jihan said we can use the air-net to help us, right? So can't we just…find the whole chart and copy it down?"

Zyn shrugged, opening the door to the Eating Hall, the smell of burnt toast hitting their noses at once. "I don't think he meant we could *completely* take it. That'd be plagiarism, after all. But we can definitely use it to help us out!"

Sarala frowned as they made their way over to a semi-long line. "I don't have a mirror though. I don't even know much about air-net…"

"You can just borrow our mirror," Ren told her. "Zyn and I already share the family mirror."

She huffed in annoyance at the thought of having to rely on others, then reached for a blueberry muffin as the line moved. The three soon had their trays loaded with food and went to a table. They ate with small talk, then finished and set their dirty trays on the trashcan by the door. They exited the Eating Hall as the bell sounded for the second-years to get to their first class. Ignoring this, Sarala and Zyn trailed the skipping Ren to the Library.

"I thought we were going to get our charts off the air-net?" Sarala asked.

"Shush!" Zyn hissed back.

The Library was vast, with red-painted walls that were mostly covered by bookshelves. There were aisles upon aisles of shelves, some squished together that there was little space to move between the hundreds of books. Right upon entering, there were a few tables and chairs, which allowed students to do their work; however, even the tables were so close together in the cramped space. Windows lined the back wall, allowing Sarala to see specks of dust floating in the light streaming through.

"What're we in here for?" Sarala grumbled. "Let's just get the charts off the air-net."

"But then you're not learning anything, silly!" Ren replied.

"I don't *want* to learn it," Sarala muttered.

Ren ignored her and went up to a large desk off to the side, which was practically pushed against a shelf. Leaning against this desk was a blonde man in a pink floral dress. He glanced over at them as they approached, his orange eyes lighting up.

"Ren! Zyn!" he greeted them, smiling.

Sarala huffed lightly in annoyance. It was as if she didn't exist. *But it's not like I even know that guy,* she reminded herself. *Why would he bother greeting me?*

"Hey, Aster!" Zyn said.

"That's 'Mr. Sundale' to you kids," Aster said in a pretend-stern voice. "What can I do for you?"

"We need to figure out our birth charts," Ren told him. "Can you help us?"

Aster's eyes seemed to light up even more. He clapped his hands together and nodded several times. "Of course, of course! I'd be delighted to help! I love doing birth charts—and astrology!"

Ren winked over her shoulder at Sarala. Sarala scowled in return. She had half-a-mind to turn and walk out from the Library; Ren seemed to sense this and asked, "Can we start with Sarala's chart?"

Aster nodded, grabbing several pieces of paper from inside the desk. He then rummaged in the drawers, making a lot of rattling noises until he pulled out several books on astrology and birth charts.

"What's your birthday, place of birth, and time of birth?" Aster asked, glancing up at her as he crouched over a book.

Sarala stiffened. *Is this a trick? Are they trying to find out more about my background?* she wondered.

"April 6, 39," she muttered.

Aster scrawled that across the top of one sheet of paper, then asked, "Place and time of birth?"

"I don't know," she said flatly.

Aster blinked up at her. "You have to know, otherwise we can't do this birth chart for you. The place of birth determines how the planets were lined up according to your location on Sater, and—"

"I guess I'll be failing this assignment, then," Sarala uttered, crossing her arms over her chest. "But didn't Mr. Jihan say we only needed to chart the sun and moon sign, anyway? And...what's

Sater?"

The others stared at her. Then, Aster said, "Sater is our *planet*."

Sarala blushed. *How was I supposed to know that?*

"Yeah, I think that's what Khurshid said—about what we needed to chart," Zyn replied after a small moment of silence. "Charting a full birth chart on your own...that'd take weeks or months..."

Ren flicked her sister. "It would *not*!"

"Yeah, it would!"

"Girls, calm down," Aster said with a sigh. He looked over at Sarala. "Well, we know your sun sign is in alignment with fire. Is that your elemental magic?"

Sarala shook her head. "I have earth."

"So you were born at night, with a moon in the earth sign," Aster said simply. "There are only three signs that represent earth, so we just need to figure out what that would be..."

He opened one of his books and handed it to her. "This book tells you the combination of your astrological sun and moon signs. See here? That's your sun sign. This page is one of the moon signs in earth combined with that fire sun sign. Read all of the moon signs in earth, and choose whichever one fits your personality best."

Sarala read the first description of a fire sun sign with an earth moon sign. She frowned and went to the next passage.

"That's an air sign next," Ren told her, pointing at the title of the section. "And the next one is water, and the one after that is fire. There's the second earth sign!"

Sarala read the next passage, feeling confused over these different signs. All she knew was that there were twelve astrological signs that were associated with a particular element. She had no idea what they were called or why she'd need to know anything about them. This second passage sounded a bit like her personality though, so she told Aster, who wrote it down.

"We still can't figure out the exact placement, and finding when the moon was in this earth sign during that particular year will be a bit tricky," Aster told her. "But I'll figure out something worthy enough for your birth chart!"

Sarala didn't care.

They spent the whole day in the Library, taking a break for lunch and returning soon after. Aster only had to leave once to help a student find a book, but otherwise remained with them. As it was only the second day of school, most of the students didn't need the Library just yet.

Sarala's birth chart took the longest, as they had to figure out the moon's position. Zyn, who had a fire sun sign and an air moon sign, also didn't know her exact birthplace, but was able to get her chart made sooner due to knowing the exact signs and her time of birth.

Ren, who also knew her information, only took a long time to get through because she wanted to know the placement for all of the other planets. At this point, Sarala decided to leave, getting a headache from being cooped up in a dusty room, and having a hard time reading.

She went to the Courtyard for a breath of fresh air. It was almost dinnertime, and the bell would be ringing soon. She would head to the Eating Hall in a bit, so she wouldn't be stuck at the end of a long line.

That's when something caught her eye. Frowning, her body tensed. She tiptoed towards the northern garden, where she had seen the small movement. Though she hadn't seen it fully, the movement did not seem to be human.

It's probably just a bird, she thought to herself. She had seen plenty of bird movements during her time in the wild, which would always frighten her. She often mistook the birds as some sort of monster lurking in the bushes, stalking her. Most times, it had just been birds, or perhaps a squirrel. *It's definitely just a bird.*

But Sarala relied a lot on instinct, and even though she knew it was just a bird and that she was safe at the school, she still had to check it out. Therefore, she crept forward until reaching the garden, her heartbeat louder in her ears as she approached the undergrowth where she'd seen the movement.

There was nothing there. Sarala scanned the bushes and trees for several long moments, her ears pricked and her whole body on alert. Yet she couldn't sense anything; she couldn't even detect any danger. She allowed her body to relax.

Just a bird. I knew it, she thought irritably.

However, as she turned her back on the garden, she felt that she had missed something. She frowned and looked over her shoulder, as if expecting the bird to suddenly appear. The garden was still empty.

Calm down, she scolded herself. *You're too jumpy.*

She shook herself and headed for the Eating Hall. Uncertain why she sensed something was wrong, she just knew she'd feel much better inside. She had hardly taken two steps when she felt like she was being watched.

Sarala swiveled swiftly on the spot, staring at the trees once more. *There!* She saw the bushes move, though there was no wind to stir them, the cloud-scudded sky as still as the buildings below it.

Rushing to the plants, she did not care if her footsteps were loud on the stone. She was out in the open, after all, and whatever had been watching her would surely know that she'd seen it. The bell rang, and, as students started streaming into the Courtyard from all around the school, Sarala vanished into the prickly bushes.

She shifted leaves aside, her gold eyes scanning the darkest areas of the garden. As it was only August, the sun still stayed out in the evening, providing her with enough light to see by. But she still saw nothing.

After searching the entire garden for the next ten minutes, totally forgetting about dinner, she decided to give up. She sensed that whatever had been watching her before was now gone. Sighing and stumbling out of the garden, she suddenly saw a small object on the ground, catching the rays of soft sunlight managing to poke through the clouds.

Sarala bent down to pick it up. It was a mirror shard. She frowned as she inspected it, but there was nothing sinister about it. It was literally just a broken piece of glass.

Not knowing what to do with it, she put it in her robe pocket and remembered about dinner. She hurried to the Eating Hall, and sighed in annoyance as she saw the long line upon entering the loud space.

Before she could make her way to the end of the line, she felt a tugging on her arm. Whirling around, her fist ready to punch her attacker, she barely managed to stop herself in time.

"Whoa, don't hit me! It's me—Ren!"

"Why'd you sneak up on me?" Sarala sneered, dropping her fist.

"I didn't sneak up on you. Didn't you hear me calling your name?" Ren asked, her hands held up in front of her to protect herself.

"No," Sarala said bluntly. "What do you want?"

"I was just asking you where you were. We didn't see you when we came in," Ren pointed out, lowering her arms.

"I didn't realize I had to tell you my every movement," Sarala uttered, glaring at the girl.

Ren bit her bottom lip, looking worried.

"I was just in the garden," Sarala went on.

"But why'd you come late to dinner? Didn't you hear the bell?" Zyn asked, walking over from the table she had been sitting at paces away.

Sarala glared at her. "Obviously."

"Then why are you late?" Zyn pressed.

I can't tell them what I saw…they'll think I'm crazy! But then again…who—or what—would just show up and drop a mirror shard? Maybe I should tell them… What if this is some sort of security issue?

"Sarala?"

She snapped her gaze to Ren, then looked around the Eating Hall. There were too many people nearby. She grabbed Ren's arm and pulled her outside, where they were less likely to be overheard. Zyn trailed after them curiously.

"What is it?" Ren asked, once the door to the Eating Hall closed behind them.

"I saw something in the garden," Sarala told her in a low voice. "Well, I didn't *see* anything, but it felt like I was being watched. I went to look, but whatever it was left."

"Oh, that's probably one of Dad's frogoyles," Zyn said, chuckling. "They usually just stay still and sit on the walls high up, or stay in certain areas like Counseling. They only 'turn on' if they detect movement—like when you showed up, and it alerted Dad, since there's some outside the school too."

Sarala frowned, remembering how the statue's eyes lit up violet when she had approached the school. "Those things are creepy…"

Zyn shrugged in response.

"Do you think it was a frogoyle you saw?" Ren asked Sarala.

She thought about that for a long moment, then shook her head. "It…didn't move like stone? I thought it was a bird, since it was so fast. And it wasn't low to the ground, but in the air."

"That doesn't sound like a frogoyle," Ren commented.

"It could be if it was jumping," Zyn objected.

"Well, would a frogoyle drop *this*?" Sarala asked, pulling out the mirror shard.

The sisters stared at it blankly, then Ren queried, "How do you know it dropped this?"

"What else would drop it in the garden?" Sarala grumbled. "A student?"

"If they broke their mirror by mistake, then yes," Zyn said.

Sarala sighed. "Should I tell your dad?" she grunted.

Zyn shrugged. "If you want to. But if something weird got in the school, the frogoyles would have told Dad already."

"Where would he be?" Sarala asked.

"Having dinner, like the rest of us," Ren said. "Come on!"

She led the way in the opposite direction from the Eating Hall, towards the northern wall. They went through the door next to the Kung Fu Studio, which was labeled as the Art Studio.

This room was long, and smelled of paper and paint. A few wooden desks sat in the front of the class and large canvas stands stood at the back. Ak-tu was currently standing in front of one, a plate of food on a table beside him as he painted on a canvas. He glanced up at them as they entered.

"What're you three up to?" he inquired.

"Sarala has something to tell you," Ren said.

Sarala quickly recounted her story. Ak-tu seemed a lot more concerned about it than Ren and Zyn, but did not interrupt. He took the mirror shard from her and inspected it closely. Finally, he spoke.

"Thank you for bringing this to my attention," he said seriously. "I will check in with the frogoyles, and with Khurshid."

"Do you know what might have dropped this, then?" Sarala asked curiously.

Ak-tu pursed his lips, then murmured mysteriously, "I have ideas." He shook his head. "Make sure you get some dinner. If you see anything else, be sure to alert me. And if you come across any more objects, do *not* pick them up."

Sarala frowned, narrowing her eyes in suspicion. *What's with that mirror shard? Am I not safe here, either?*

CHAPTER 9: COMING SOON

Ak-tu turned the rigid mirror shard over in his fingers, trying to inspect every centimeter of it. He was now alone in the Art Studio, his painting of a waterfall forgotten and his dinner cold. He looked up as the door opened again. Khurshid and Fern entered, shortly followed by Aster.

"Why'd you call us all here?" Aster asked. "I was in the middle of dinner!"

"It's important," Ak-tu said.

"Oh, is it your painting? How's it coming along?" Aster queried, bounding forward to take a look at it.

Ak-tu rolled his eyes. "It's definitely not the painting. It seems one of our students was being watched by a spirit earlier."

His words had an instant effect: Aster froze, Fern frowned, and Khurshid looked alarmed.

"I want the security upped," Ak-tu went on. "The frogoyles are going to be awake every day and night now. But I also want the grounds to be checked regularly for any objects."

"Objects?" Fern asked, her frown growing deeper.

Ak-tu nodded and showed them the mirror shard. "The spirit left this behind. We were lucky Sarala saw it. I don't know how a spirit could get past the enchantments, but I'm more interested in *why*. And why would it leave this mirror shard?"

He shook his head and looked over at Fern and Aster. "Could you two make sure there aren't any other objects in the garden that Sarala might have overlooked?"

Fern nodded and left, dragging Aster behind her. Ak-tu waited a moment for them to go, even though they had closed the door behind them. He then turned to Khurshid.

"You know more about that mirror shard, don't you?" Khurshid asked.

"Possibly," Ak-tu said, thinking back to his adventures before the school's creation. "But it's impossible to know for sure if I can't use my own magic on this mirror. It's protected, quite heavily. Which makes me wonder if it's the same spirit who dropped a shard before, or a different one. Last time, that spirit made no attempt to hide who was behind the dropped mirror shards. People would pick up a mirror shard and stare at their reflection, then get teleported to the big mirror that the shard belonged to. Last time, it was in a cave. This time…who knows?"

"Sarala was lucky not to have stared at it, then," Khurshid murmured.

"Quite," Ak-tu agreed. "We cannot risk having more mirror shards turn up. I'll try to figure out where this came from, and who it was meant to teleport—if it's the same spirit we're dealing with."

"Why would that spirit come here?" Khurshid asked.

"When we came across the spirit before, they were stealing people to make weapons for it," Ak-tu said.

"But none of the students—none of the teachers—know how to do that."

Ak-tu nodded. "Well, I'll just have to figure out what the spirit wants…and who it even is."

"If you need any help, just let me know," Khurshid told Ak-tu. "You know I've got your back…even if I can't see it."

Ak-tu smiled up at his tall friend. "Thank you, Khurshid."

Khurshid grunted and left the Art Studio as well. Ak-tu was now alone with the mirror shard, which he still held between his thumb and pointer finger.

He raised it to eye level and inspected it, keeping his eyes darting about its edges. He couldn't allow his eyes to fall still, and they definitely could not look at his own reflection. If he was teleported out of the school… He couldn't think of that.

He continued to turn it over in his fingers, trying to feel its magic. Closing his eyes, he reached out with his own magic, but knew it'd be no use. The shard was too heavily protected, disarming any magic that might be used against it.

Ak-tu opened his eyes and frowned. The hair on the back of his neck was prickling, and a shiver went down his spine. He had the feeling that he was being watched.

But as he scanned the room around him, and checked the mirror shard again, he could see nothing. He closed his eyes and reached out with his energy once more, but he was still quite alone.

You're watching me from the other side of that mirror, he realized. *Well, I'm not going to give you anything to look at.*

Ak-tu stuffed the mirror shard in his robe pocket, refusing to allow the spirit to see what was going on. He then pulled out his personal mirror from his opposite pocket and held it up. He tapped his passcode in (736996), then opened his contact list of five people: the family mirror for the kids, Jabali, Khurshid, Fern, and Aster. Selecting Jabali's name, he stared down at the still image of the man's face as he waited for the mirrors to connect. It luckily didn't take long.

"Yo, Ak-tu!" Jabali's loud voice boomed from the mirror as he appeared in real time, his bushy hair tied back in a tail.

"Hey, Jabali," Ak-tu said. "I'm not interrupting anything, am I?"

Jabali shook his head, setting his mirror down as he bustled around his kitchen island. "Just doin' some cookin'!" he called as he disappeared from the frame, stooping down to grab something. "Ya interrupted me more on tha' last call, y'know."

Ak-tu snorted. "That's true."

"What's up?" Jabali asked, reappearing with a metal pot in his hands.

"What are you making?" Ak-tu asked curiously.

Jabali raised a thick eyebrow. "Seriously? Ya called me to ask me for my dinner plans?"

"No, I—"

"Gonna make me some spicy tomato-potato soup!" Jabali declared. "Now why you botherin' me?"

Ak-tu rolled his eyes and sat on the floor, positioning himself more comfortably as he quickly told Jabali about the mirror shard. Jabali placed the pot on the counter and did not move again as he listened to Ak-tu.

"Ya think it's the same spirit?" Jabali queried when he had finished.

Ak-tu shrugged, shoving his bangs from his eyes. "I'm not sure. I thought that spirit would've learned their lesson… Listen, do you think you can come by tonight, to take a look at the enchantments? I don't know how a spirit could've gotten in, but—"

"Sure thing! But ya better feed me good when I get there!" Jabali chuckled, reaching for the mirror. "See ya in an hour!"

He hung up the call before Ak-tu could say anything. Shaking his head in amused exasperation, Ak-tu exited the Art Studio and headed for the Eating Hall to get food for Jabali (forgetting his own plate as he went).

Within minutes, he had a bowl for his friend, asking the cooks to keep it in one of the warm ovens for the next hour. Ak-tu then went to the Entrance Hall, where he practiced martial arts while he waited. He did a few jumping kicks, using his air magic to propel him higher and allow him to land softly on the hardwood floor. Wanting to test his body connection, he assumed a low square stance and turned his waist as he scooped his arms in blocking motions. By the time Jabali showed up outside the glass doors, Ak-tu had moved onto doing a tiny section of a form, trying to get the body connection down.

Jabali tapped on the door with his knuckles; though it had been a light knock, the whole glass rattled like it was about to shatter. Wincing, Jabali stopped at once and smiled in at Ak-tu.

Ak-tu rushed forward to unlock and open the door, then stepped out to join the tall man in the cool night air. Jabali stood at about six feet, and his broad-shouldered frame only made Ak-tu look even tinier in comparison. He was dressed in a pale green shirt and dark blue shorts.

"That was fast," Ak-tu commented.

Jabali shrugged. "I can move really fast when I needa."

"Oh, I know," Ak-tu said. "Do you want to eat first, or check the enchantments?"

"I'll look first," Jabali said. "Can't have any other spirits gettin' in, now can we?"

Ak-tu shook his head in agreement. "No, we can't. Thanks for coming so quickly, though. You really didn't have to do that."

Jabali shrugged again and started walking around the stone building, heading for the southwestern tower to move clockwise around the school's perimeter. Ak-tu trailed after him quietly. Crickets chirped and plants groaned, setting a peaceful tone to the summer evening. The sun set beyond the clouds, the sky turning a deep blue within mere minutes.

"So the year start off fine apart from a potential spirit?" Jabali asked, staring up at the school the entire time as he walked.

"Yes," Ak-tu said. "Zyn has air magic, just like Ren and me."

"Great, now y'all can blast me backwards," Jabali huffed. "Why couldn't one of ya be an earth magician, eh?"

They turned the corner and walked along the perimeter of the western wall, behind the Greenhouse, their footsteps padding softly against the grass and dirt.

"I was concerned Zyn wouldn't get her magic, actually," Ak-tu murmured, gazing at the trees opposite them. "It took her trying all of the assessments—even fighting me. She didn't gain it until the very end, after I already pushed myself almost to my limits."

"Do ya think she actually got it, then?" Jabali grumbled.

Ak-tu paused in his tracks with a frown. "Why wouldn't she have it?"

"Cuz Ren coulda made her have air magic, if they both have the same magic," Jabali pointed out, moving on around the Caihong family tower to the northern wall.

Ak-tu hurried after him, nearly stumbling over his feet as he considered this. "But…my kids wouldn't do that. Much less Ren! She wouldn't lie about something so serious, especially if it could hurt Zyn."

Jabali shrugged, still staring up at the building. Ak-tu looked up too, but none of the lights were on in the tower. His kids were likely asleep by now.

"Ren wouldn't lie," he repeated under his breath. He shook his head and ran after Jabali again, not realizing he'd been falling behind as he walked slowly. "I suppose I can look into it a little more, but I'm sure Zyn has her magic," he said as he walked alongside the broad man once more.

"If ya say so," Jabali said, walking next to the eastern building. "Anyway, I ain't seein' any holes in your enchantments. The school looks as safe as it always does. There's a nice big purple shield all the way 'round it. I mean, I can't see the *top* o' the dome from out here, but there ain't any cracks or holes. And I'll check the top when we're in the Courtyard."

Ak-tu frowned, slowing his pace again as they returned to the front of the school. "That's so odd…"

Jabali gazed down at Ak-tu for a long moment, slowing down as well. "I'll check when we go in," he repeated.

Ak-tu nodded. "Please do, and thank you."

"You're lucky I can see spirit magic," grumbled Jabali. "Wanna appoint me as your security guard yet?"

Ak-tu snorted, flinging open the door to the Entrance Hall so rapidly that the glass shook. "I already offered that to you years ago! It's not my fault if you were running too many businesses to come."

"Eh, I just didn't want ya havin' to tell your kids abou' me before you were ready," he said as he entered.

"I appreciate that," Ak-tu murmured, locking the door with a quick click. "This way!"

Jabali trailed Ak-tu through the empty Entrance Hall, eyeing the blank walls. "Ya really gotta add some decor in here, y'know."

"Well, this hall is tiny and nobody really comes through here," stated Ak-tu. "Anyway, we're already here."

He opened the door to the Courtyard. The area was illuminated by curved lampposts; the metal lanterns glowed orange due to the fire magic within them. The pond reflected the shimmering light; Ak-tu wondered if it also mirrored the spirit magic shield around the school. He looked over to Jabali in question.

"Yep, tha' shield sure be goin' strong," Jabali said with a nod, staring up at the night sky. "Bright violet, almost as neon as your eyes."

Ak-tu nodded. "That's a relief," he murmured. "But that still doesn't answer how a spirit got in…"

"Maybe it wasn't a spirit?"

"But I could *feel* something watching me on the other side of that mirror, I could *tell* something was wrong with that mirror shard," Ak-tu insisted.

Jabali frowned. "Well, maybe there *is* a spirit on the other side of tha' mirror. But it might notta been a spirit tha' dropped it in the Courtyard. Maybe it was tha' Sarala."

"Sarala?" Ak-tu queried in surprise.

Jabali nodded. "Ya said yourself, you don't know who she

might be runnin' from or wha' secrets she might be hiding. So wha' if she brought the mirror shard into the school?"

"But she seemed alarmed by it too," Ak-tu pointed out skeptically.

"Maybe she was. Maybe it was somethin' tha' she didn't realize she had on her, then she brought it to ya. Or maybe she planted it on ya so some spirit can spy on ya."

Ak-tu frowned and ran his fingers over his mustache strand as he contemplated this. "I dunno," he mumbled. "I don't think this is Sarala's doing…or that she knew anything about it…"

"Well, I guess ya better just keep an eye on her," Jabali said. "Now where's tha' food at? I'm starving!"

Ak-tu straightened up. "Right! This way!"

He took off running several paces to his left, to the Eating Hall door. Jabali grumbled something sarcastically behind him, but as Ak-tu pulled open the door, he could hear Jabali's loud footsteps stomping against the stone ground. Ak-tu rushed inside and darted around the empty tables, nearly smashing his hip into one corner. He soon made it to the other side of the Eating Hall near the edge of the counter, laughing as Jabali caught up seconds later.

"Why ya always runnin' off?" Jabali scoffed, unable to hold back a broad grin.

Ak-tu winked up at him. "I may run off, but I'll always wait for ya!"

Jabali raised his eyes to the ceiling.

Ak-tu signaled for Jabali to follow him behind the counter, where a door lay to the Kitchen. The cooks had finished cleaning up by now, and the room lay dark. There were two long islands in the center of the room, and multiple metal fridges lined the walls. Against another wall was a long sink, where many trays were placed on a rack to dry overnight. Pots and pans were scattered along the marble counters, and a variety of spoons hung from the ceiling.

"There should still be a bowl in the oven," Ak-tu said.

"Which one?" asked Jabali, scanning the row of ovens on the far wall.

"This one!" Ak-tu said, opening the door of the oven nearest the door that led into the southwestern tower, where the cooks were quartered. He pulled out the bowl and passed it over. "Hope it's as good as that soup you were going to make!"

Jabali took the bowl, sniffing at the food Ak-tu had selected: a chickpea curry with bits of potato, carrots, rice, and extra chili flakes. "Mmm, smells tasty! Your cooks are too good to 'em students here. Tha's a lotta chili flakes, though."

"I know you like things hot," Ak-tu said with a shrug.

Jabali stared at him for a long moment, then burst out laughing. Ak-tu raised one side of his unibrow, confused by the action. But before he knew it, he found himself chortling too. Eventually, both men calmed down enough for Ak-tu to grab Jabali a shell-shaped spoon from the ceiling to try the curry.

"This is *good*!" Jabali praised. "You oughta give your cooks to me!"

"You run a coffee shop," Ak-tu stated bluntly.

"Eh, I can open a restaurant; I've done so before," Jabali said.

"I'll think about it," teased Ak-tu.

"Then I'll hire ya too," Jabali said. "Ya still know how to cook, right?"

Ak-tu snorted, reaching up for another spoon (this one more of a ladle than a spoon), passing it to Jabali and taking Jabali's spoon instead. He dipped it in the curry and tried a bit. It was on the cooler side since it'd been sitting for a moment, but the flavor was intense and hot, causing his tongue to burn and his throat to swell. Turning away, he coughed and choked over the chili flakes, Jabali laughing the entire time.

When Ak-tu finally recovered, he sputtered, "*Yes*, I know how to cook, obviously! You taught me, after all. But no, I will *never* cook something this hot again! GAH!" He coughed again, then said, "Anyhow, I can't help you with a restaurant. I have a school to run."

"Do ya even wanna be running this place?" Jabali queried, all traces of laughter gone as he scrutinized Ak-tu closely.

"What do you mean?"

"It's just...ya never wanted a magic school," Jabali said, setting the bowl of curry down on the counter beside him.

"Maybe not, but it's what I ended up with," Ak-tu said, shifting his weight to one leg and placing a hand on his hip.

"Don't ya wanna travel again?"

"Of course I do, but…it's not going to happen anytime soon. At least, not long-term traveling like I'm used to," Ak-tu said with a shrug. "Traveling over the summer is enough for me, and it seems to be enough for the kids. But the school is where our lives are now."

"If ya say so," Jabali murmured, grabbing the ladle and scooping more curry into his mouth. "But I dunno if this life really suits ya."

Ak-tu frowned at the comment, but did not know what to say in return. He therefore walked past Jabali to the counter, grabbing a pot and pushing a button on the side to turn it on. The metal object was filled with fire magic, and it seemed to have just been re-enchanted by one of the cooks judging by the fast pace it was heating up. Then, he grabbed some almond blend from a bamboo carton in the nearby fridge, and took a sack of chocolate from the pantry in the island.

"Making hot cocoa?" Jabali asked; his tone sounded like he was smirking.

"Yes," Ak-tu stated.

"It's summer."

"And?"

"It's *hot* out."

"And?"

"It's hot in here."

"You ate something hot," Ak-tu pointed out. "Why can't I have a hot drink?"

Jabali seemed disappointed when Ak-tu turned around after adding the blend and chocolate to the pot. He returned to his bowl of curry, the smirk gone from his face. Ak-tu frowned, wondering if he had somehow offended his friend.

Actually, knowing Jabali, I probably didn't understand some sort of joke he just made, Ak-tu reconsidered, rolling his eyes.

He grabbed a wooden spoon (shaped like a serpent) from the ceiling to mix the pot's contents, breathing in the chocolatey aroma as it melted into the blend. After a minute of stirring, he grabbed some pepper from a spice pantry, adding a bit in. By the time the hot cocoa was done, Jabali set his empty bowl on the counter.

"Well, tha' sure was tasty. Thanks for the meal, but I best be goin' home now," he said.

Ak-tu blinked in surprise, turning the pot off. "Already? I thought you'd stay longer."

"Nah, you know my visits don't last long," Jabali said. "Too risky with your kids 'round. But it was nice to see ya again. We gotta meet up soon. Properly, eh?"

"Yes!" Ak-tu agreed at once, smiling up at his friend.

He poured the hot cocoa in a mug, then led the way out of the Kitchen. They were soon walking through the glass doors and exiting the school.

"Where's your boat?" Ak-tu asked, peering at the dark forest in front of them.

"Oh, y'know me, I took a rock to get here extra fast," Jabali said.

"Then you shouldn't be going back on one after you just ate!" Ak-tu exclaimed in alarm. "You're gonna get sick!"

"I'll take it nice 'n slow, don't ya worry," Jabali said, pulling his mirror out of his shorts pocket. "I already got my jazz music ready for a chill ride back!"

Ak-tu smiled and shook his head. "Fine, fine. Just be safe out there, okay?"

"Y'*know* I'm safe," Jabali retorted. "If anyone ain't safe in these parts, it's *you*."

Ak-tu snorted. "Yeah, sure." He reached forward and hugged Jabali. "Thanks for coming by and checking the enchantments. I really appreciate it."

"Yep," Jabali said, patting his back before stepping away. "See ya soon enough!"

"See you!"

Jabali vanished into the shadowy forest, Ak-tu waving the entire time. He eventually lowered his hand and turned back to the school—but not before something caught his attention.

Snapping his gaze back to the forest, Ak-tu relaxed his body with several deep breaths. He scanned the undergrowth for a few minutes, wishing that the movement would happen again. Was it just an animal? A plant? A frogoyle? Or was it something more sinister?

"Who goes there?" Ak-tu called out, his voice bold and confident.

But nothing answered. Nothing stirred.

The crickets continued to chirp and the trees continued to whisper to each other. Ak-tu waited ten minutes...sixteen...twenty-two...

"Guess it was nothing," he uttered, opening the door at his back while keeping his gaze on the forest.

He was in the school in two steps, but everything remained calm outside. Locking the door, Ak-tu waited another two minutes before finally walking away, only looking once over his shoulder as he went down the hall.

The world was quiet.

CHAPTER 10: IN ONLY SEVEN DAYS

The remainder of the first school week went by without any other issues. Ren and Zyn had asked their father what the mirror shard was about, knowing that he was hiding something from them. Yet he wouldn't say, even after Zyn poked and prodded him with a stick, so the twins therefore focused on their homework. Freday was just as long as Moonday, but instead of being full of magic or martial arts, it was entirely focused on art.

The first class, Drawing and Painting, was taught by Ak-tu. The students learned the fundamentals of sketching different shapes and a bit with perspective. Ren and Zyn, who often drew pictures growing up, sketched entire scenes while conversing by mind instead of following Ak-tu's lecture.

The next class was Cooking, which Sarala joined them for. This was the only class that was taught by the cooks. It was also the only time students were allowed in the Kitchen. The fall semester would be focused on cooking, while the second semester would go into baking. The older students were allowed to use magic as they worked, but the first-years weren't.

The three friends worked as a team, making bean patties served with potato sticks. Since the students finished early, they got to eat the food they made as a morning snack. The first-years weren't allowed to serve any food they made until their second year (if they kept the class), once they had their food handler's certificate after the first year. Even so, the food wasn't always served, especially if a mistake was made.

Writing was next, and Ren and Zyn went to the Art Studio alone to see that their father was teaching again. It was a session about grammar, providing them with a foundation. Their homework was to edit a student paper. The class would go into writing stories and poetry later in the semester, once the basics of writing were covered.

Sarala joined them again for the fourth class, Fashion. Aster taught this class, and he tried lecturing about different clothing styles, particularly robes. He eventually gave up when he saw that nobody was paying attention. He therefore allowed the students to choose color combinations for clothing, while he went to try on different robes from the Theatre costumes and showed them off to the few interested students.

After lunch, they went to the Music Studio for Choir. The Music Studio was full of instruments, including two pianos, but the students remained in the front of the class, away from the instruments. Ak-tu was teaching both the Choir and Band classes. Most of the students who were enrolled in Choir were also doing Band, which meant an easy shift from vocal warmups to instrumental warmups.

Ren and Zyn then went to the Theatre for their final class that day, once more taught by Aster (who had more command in Theatre than the laidback Fashion class). The Theatre was on the small side, with rows of seats in front of a stage. There was a back room behind the stage, which contained the costumes and props. The students learned a few warm-up exercises for acting, how to read a script, and chose roles for the play they'd be putting on at the end of the semester. Though the class was two hours, it would be fast-paced, as they only had a few weeks to get an entire play produced.

"Ooo, tomorrow's the club day, right?" Zyn asked Ren as they stood in line for dinner that night, exhausted after a full day of classes.

Ren nodded eagerly. "Yep! We get to join as many clubs as we want!"

"Do you think we can join that boat driving club so we can get our driving certifications?"

Ren bit her bottom lip. She switched to speaking telepathically instead of aloud. *{Zyn, I don't think that's a good idea. If you still don't have your magic, you won't be able to learn. And I can't just do the magic for you. Driving a boat takes a lot of skill, and I*

*doubt I've got that kind of skill right now. Plus, if you can't do it...
well, you're not actually learning it, now are you?}*

{Yeah, you're right.} Zyn replied, sounding disappointed.
*{Well...there's always next year. Besides, there's probably going to
be so many other interesting clubs anyway!}*

She was right. The next day, there were tables strewn around
the Courtyard. Students from the upper years had set up tables
with banners hanging off them, telling the others what their club
was. Each table held a signup clipboard for students interested in
joining the club.

Ren and Zyn darted around the Courtyard, leaving Sarala behind as they explored the tables. There were clubs related to aca-
demics, like studying spirits or getting help with channeling
stronger magic. Other clubs were made for fun and hanging out,
like the game club and art club.

"Which clubs should we join?" Zyn asked, looking down at
the mirror after they'd run around the entire Courtyard, jotting
down the names of the clubs they were interested in. "I definitely
want to do that game club!"

"But it's on Freday at 2," Ren said, looking over Zyn's shoulder
to see the mirror. "We've got class."

"Ahhh," Zyn moaned. "But I wanted to do it!"

"Maybe next year?" Ren suggested.

"Fine," Zyn muttered.

"How's about that one on construction? It sounds interesting,"
Ren said, scrolling through the notes. "And it's on Trizday at 10, so
we can make it!"

"Eh, I'm not interested in it," Zyn grunted.

"But you always made little towns for your toys when we were
kids," Ren pointed out.

"Yeah...not that interested in it," Zyn repeated.

Ren snorted in amusement. They continued through the list,
debating which clubs to join, only looking up as Sarala approached.

"Have you joined any clubs, Sarala?" Ren asked the other girl.

Sarala shook her head once. "Clubs aren't my thing," she muttered.

Ren frowned. Of course that would be Sarala's response! Why

did she expect anything else? "Well, was there anything you were interested in?" she pressed.

"No," Sarala said blandly. "Well…there was a weapon club."

"Weapon club? Why don't you join it, Sarala?"

Sarala shook her head. "You have to be a blue sash in Kung Fu or Tai Chi to join. We're obviously far from it. Too bad, though… weapons are really interesting…"

"Oh…" Ren tapped her chin thoughtfully. "Do you have any hobbies? Like…before you came here?"

Ren hoped she wasn't prying too much. The few times she tried to ask about Sarala's past, the girl would become very tight-lipped and even ignore her for the rest of the day. Ren had learned to stop asking questions.

Sarala stared at her for a long moment, then said simply, "My hobby was surviving."

Ren could have slapped her hand against her forehead. She didn't know what else to say, and so remained quiet. A moment of awkward silence lasted, until Zyn broke it. It appeared she had not been paying any attention to the conversation.

"Let's do the art club!" she said, pointing to the bottom of the list. "It meets on Saterday. Let's go to that table to get more information!"

"Okay!" Ren agreed, and she hurried after Zyn once more, glad to get away from Sarala.

They soon reached a table labeled "Art Club" on a green banner. The sisters slid to a stop just before they could slam into the table. A chunky student sat behind it, looking a bit bored as they played with their curly green hair. When Ren and Zyn came over though, they perked up and smiled.

"What's this club about?" Zyn asked before Ren could finish saying, "Hello."

The person smiled at Zyn's enthusiasm. "We do art, lots and lots of art!" they said in a high voice.

"Umm…yeah…I got that much," Zyn said blandly. "But what *kinds* of art?"

"Whatever art we want," the person said promptly. "No lectures or assignments, just whatever we want to do. We do collaborations and sometimes choose monthly themes too!"

"Ooo, I'm in!" Zyn said, and she signed up at once.

Ren snorted in amusement and wrote her name on the clipboard too. She and Zyn were the only two on the list so far.

The person looked at their names and glanced up at them in surprise. "Wait—you're Mr. Caihong's kids?"

"That's right!" Ren said brightly, and she stuck out her hand. "I'm Ren Caihong."

The student took her hand and shook it quickly. "I'm Mint Kaheka."

"I'm Zyn," Zyn said bluntly.

"It's very nice to meet you," Mint said.

"You're holding up the line," said a sudden loud voice behind Ren.

She turned around to see C3 had arrived. There was no line behind her, but she was clearly in his way of the signup clipboard.

"Sorry," she said, smiling at him.

Scowling at her, he added his name to the list. He then grabbed a small pamphlet from the table and walked away.

"O-kay," Mint mumbled, their green eyes wide with panic. "That was…a bit…um…"

"He's pretty rude," Zyn told them.

"Well, hopefully he just woke up on the wrong side of the bed today," Mint murmured uneasily.

"So how long have you been in the club?" Ren queried curiously.

"Since last year, my first year. I got to take over the club since all the other students who made it left. I'm so excited! We're gonna have all kinds of fun, making art!"

"Yee!" Zyn yowled.

Ren chuckled. "I hope so. Let me just talk to Zyn for a quick moment…"

She grabbed her sister and pulled her away from the table. Once she was sure they were out of Mint's earshot, Ren muttered, "Are you sure you want to sign up for this?"

"Why not?" Zyn replied.

"We're already doing a full day of art on Freday, and we do art in our free time," Ren pointed out. "It's not exactly trying out new things, is it?"

Zyn frowned. "I guess not. But the other clubs sound boring, or they meet at times when we're in class. Besides—now we can share our art with other people!"

"But we do too much art, don't you think?"

"You can never do too much art! Besides, we've never had any art friends before," Zyn said.

Ren tapped her pointed chin. "We've never had friends before, in general, huh? Unless you count the teachers... Well, I *guess* we can do it. Mint does seem pretty fun, and the club is so small...I wouldn't want to disappoint them by taking our names off the list."

"Yeah, so let's do it!"

Ren smiled. "Okay, fine. Hey—do you think Sarala would be interested in joining?"

"You ask," Zyn said with a shrug.

Ren nodded and turned on the balls of her feet, skipping across the stone ground until she found Sarala. Sarala was now standing by the large pond, staring down at its rippling surface. She had her back to her, so Ren slowed to a walk and tiptoed the rest of the way. Once she was right behind Sarala, she launched herself forward with a loud cry.

Sarala whirled around and threw a punch at Ren. Ren moved out of the way just in time, glad she had quick reflexes; but she had felt the wind on the strike, and it felt close!

"What was that for?" Sarala snarled.

"Sorry!" Ren squeaked, her heart racing. "I just—it was—"

"Sneak up on me again, and you're dead," Sarala growled in a low voice.

"It won't happen again!" Ren promised, her body stiff and a lump forming in her throat.

Sarala continued to glare at her for a long moment, then turned and walked away. Ren watched her go in a daze. After a moment, she sighed and made her way back to Zyn, who was chatting to Mint about the Caihong family's most recent vacation to Wudawuda Hu'ha, a small island part of the Kuokoa Islands, where Mint was from.

Ren looked down at the clipboard, which only contained three names. She flicked her gaze up to Mint and asked, "Is this club generally small?"

Mint turned to her, while Zyn made a face at her for interrupting the story. "Yes," Mint said. "Last year, we had five members."

"So do you think Zyn, C3, and I will be the only other members?" Ren pressed.

"Probably," Mint said with a shrug. "Nobody wants to join an art club if they're already in art classes, after all."

Ren did her best not to exchange a guilty glance with Zyn. She merely nodded and added Sarala's name to the clipboard. "Well, now we'll have five members in the club," she said.

"Did Sarala *say* she wanted to join?" Zyn asked skeptically.

"No," Ren replied with a shrug. "But I'll see if I can get her to come, at least to the first meeting."

"That's next Saterday, right after breakfast!" Mint told them.

"She can always leave the club if she wants no part in it," Ren pointed out. "But she should try out *something*, you know?"

"I guess," Zyn muttered. "I just don't think she'll be too happy."

"She'll be happier than when I scared her right now, that's a for-sure-getter," Ren said.

"You scared her?"

"Yep."

Zyn stared at Ren. "How are you still alive?"

Ren laughed. "Quick reflexes?"

"Is this Sarala person…a downer?" Mint asked, frowning.

"She's had a rough past," Ren explained. "But she needs to learn to open up more and have fun."

"I'll be a tree before that happens," Zyn scoffed.

As Ren and Zyn headed back to the tower, Ren couldn't blame her sister for doubting her. Sarala would take ages to open up—if she ever did.

Maybe I can try talking to her later, once she's cooled off, Ren thought, humming lightly to herself as they entered the tower. *That sounds like a good plan… I just can't be too blunt about it, otherwise she'll get scared off or offended.*

She skipped up the spiral steps to the bathroom, trying to figure out what she was going to say to Sarala on the way. As Ren entered the bathroom, Zyn continued to the next floor, likely headed for her room to read or draw.

Ren closed the door behind her, the metal lights turning on as they detected her movement. She walked over to the sink, inspecting her messy-haired reflection in the mirror with a chuckle as she washed her hands.

"Well, that's one week of school done," she murmured to herself. "And it feels *great!*"

She walked over to the nearby window, which looked out on tall pines and dancing trees. Opening the glass to let in some fresh air, she took a deep breath and released it in a satisfied sigh.

"Ooh, what's that?"

Movement caught her eye, and she looked down at the shrubs. A small farm cat was walking through the grass, bushy tail held high. Ren smiled at the sight.

"So *cute!*" she squealed in a high-pitched voice, unable to help herself.

The cat stopped walking and glanced up at her curiously, then scampered into the bushes before she could get a closer look.

"You're cute!" Ren called out, laughing lightly. "Speaking of cute, I better get to watering my cute lil' plants…"

CHAPTER 11: FEELINGS, FEELINGS

When the students entered the Magic Studies classroom on Moonday, both Khurshid and Ak-tu were waiting for them.

"Please take out your birth charts," Khurshid told the class after the final bell rang. "Mr. Caihong will be looking at them for me."

Some of the students exchanged glances and hesitated to take out their mirrors or notebooks.

"We don't have all day," Khurshid said briskly, a small smile forming on his lips.

"Let's get this over with," Ak-tu said, rotating his wrist in several circular motions. "Raise your hand if you didn't do your homework because you thought a blind man wouldn't look it over."

Five people raised their hands tentatively.

"Raise your hand if you took the birth chart directly from the air-net," Ak-tu continued.

"Mr. Jihan said we could!" Mernao Rulek protested from the back of the class.

Ak-tu nodded slowly. "Yes, he said you could use the air-net as a guide—not as a way to plagiarize. But who here actually looked up how to make a birth chart on their own, without just stealing it from the air-net?"

Ren proudly raised her hand from where she sat beside Sarala. Zyn raised her hand after a moment, and Sarala followed. C3 was the only other student to join them.

Ak-tu smiled. "Next assignment, try to put a bit more effort in, will you? Plagiarism is not accepted here, whether your teacher is blind or not. Now bring me your work."

The students lined up in front of Ak-tu. Ren was first, and she showed her work off to her father eagerly. Zyn was less enthusiastic, but brightened when Ak-tu told her she did a good job. Sarala was next, holding her piece of paper a bit awkwardly. It was filled with eraser marks and folded in places.

"Well done," Ak-tu praised.

A smile danced at Sarala's lips as she returned to her seat.

Most of the class passed, so long as they did something—even if it was plagiarized. The five students who did not do their work failed their first assignment.

"Carry on with class, Mr. Jihan," Ak-tu told Khurshid. "As for the rest of you, be sure to do your own work!" he added sternly as he opened the door and left.

"Today, we'll be talking a bit about spirits," Khurshid said, drawing the class's attention back to him. "We won't go too in-depth with them, but... Well, we all have different views on spirits. I'll give you a small introduction to how this school views spirits."

"Are spirits the same as monsters?" Frost Wuolf asked loudly at the back of the room.

"Or demons?" Ayl Dattem asked in a quivering voice.

Khurshid smiled lightly. "This is exactly my point. What we call spirits here, others might call guides, ghosts, gods, creatures, demons, and monsters. It all depends on where you grew up, and what your culture believes about these spirits.

"All of these terms are referring to spirits, which are from the spirit realm. Spirits like to cross into the physical realm, which is the world we are in. Some spirits come to live in peace, while others like to cause mischief. The ones that scare or attack people are often referred to as demons and monsters. There are also spirits who just like to cause mischief for no other reason but fun, and these spirits are still looked down upon, but maybe not as much as the others. Not all spirits are 'evil' though, as there are others who seek to help people as spirit guides, whether it be answering their questions or even saving their lives. Ghosts and spirits are not the same.

"Each spirit is just like you or me. We are all different, and spirits are too. Each spirit has their own motivation for doing what they do. Therefore, they can neither be seen as pure 'good' or 'evil'—which is why we refer to them as spirits."

Sarala rolled her eyes. *There's no such thing as spirits,* she thought dismissively.

She wasn't the only one. A few students at the back of the room were muttering how they'd never seen any proof of spirits.

Khurshid frowned as he heard the whispers. "Is there a problem back there?" he asked.

The students stopped talking at once. Some of them shifted guiltily in their seats.

"You do not believe in spirits, do you?" Khurshid asked them calmly.

"Of course not," Sarala scoffed, before she could help herself. "Besides, how would you know some other realm thingy exists?"

Khurshid frowned at her, his blind eyes focused on her face; Sarala felt a shiver run down her spine.

"There is evidence of spirits, across the whole world," Khurshid said after a moment. "Spirits are even viewed as gods in some religions, typically in places where they took over at one point in history before moving on. Some spirits have even been seen to attack human settlements for destroying too much of nature, terming spirits as nature's defenders. I know that we all have different beliefs here on the matter, so I am asking that you are merely open-minded to the fact that spirits exist—since our classes revolve around this knowledge."

But I've never seen a spirit, in all the time I've been in nature, Sarala thought bitterly. *If such things existed out there, then surely I would have met one...*

It was as if Khurshid was reading her thoughts, as he added, "A spirit does not need to make themself known to *you* for them to exist.

"Now, the reason I'm bringing up spirits is because I want you all to have the same definition before we delve into the history of magic's beginnings. It was said that spirits—who hold spirit magic as their core magic—were the ones to teach humans how to use the elemental magic in every living creature (despite spirits not having control of elemental magic themselves, for the most part)."

Sarala sighed as she realized that this class was going to be a lecture praising nonexistent spirits for giving magic to humanity. She was just starting to fall asleep when the class finally came to an end.

"Before we move to the Magic Channeling classroom, I'd like you to make note that this week's homework will be researching evidence of spirits existing," Khurshid said. "You will be paraphrasing your findings in next week's class. Now, let's get to channeling some magic!"

Finally! Sarala thought, and she got to her feet eagerly.

They left the Magic Studies classroom to go to the next room over. When they entered, they saw that the purple-painted room was set up like an obstacle course. Desks, chairs, sticks, and other random objects were strewn about all over the place. There were even firm pillows painted as targets on the far side of the room. Sarala sniffed the air, detecting the faint scent of something burned—was that the result of fire magic?

"We will be working on magic now!" Khurshid said. "Or—soon. I just have to remind you of a few things before we begin...

"There're two ways of using magic. You can control the elements in your surroundings *or* you can bring your own elemental magic out. We will be doing environmental manipulation for the first semester, and using our own magic—from within us, that is—the second semester.

"When using wands, you have to tell the wand what you want it to do. The more confident you are, the better your magic will be. Any self-doubt, anxiety, or depression can cause your magic to be shaky or weak. Sometimes, your magic can even 'shut off' altogether. This is what we call a magic block. Magic blocks are nothing to be afraid of, and happen once or twice in your lifetime, typically if you're seriously ill or struggling with your mental health."

Khurshid signaled to the obstacle course, and Sarala saw the large cauldrons that had been in the Courtyard during the magic assessment week.

"All four elements are in the cauldrons already, so there's no need to conjure up anything. Gather around your elemental cauldron."

Sarala moved to the green cauldron with the "Earth" label. Three other students—Raimugi Senzakou, Ebony Jay, and Beanna Ravford—joined her. Sarala glanced at the yellow cauldron nearby, where Ren and Zyn were joined by C3 and Mernao Rulek. There were six or seven students at both the fire and water cauldrons. A buzz hung in the air, as if each student held their breath in eager anticipation.

"Now, take out your wands," Khurshid ordered. "We will have one student go at a time per cauldron. I want you to lift your element out of the cauldron, then put it back down. Remember to order your wand. Try this five times before the next person goes. If you have any questions, call me over."

Sarala glanced at the other three students a bit shyly. Raimugi, a blonde person, smiled at her. Ebony, a tall boy with dark brown hair, stood off to the side nervously. Beanna, a girl with vibrant orange hair, rolled her eyes at him and approached the cauldron first.

I think I'll just go last, Sarala thought to herself.

"Remember: You need to command your wand with confidence," Khurshid said loudly, as excited chatter started around the large classroom.

"Lift the rock!" Beanna ordered, pointing her wand at the rough stone in the cauldron. But the rock didn't move, so she repeated her command more briskly. "Lift the rock!"

Khurshid moved over to their cauldron. "Focus on the boulder, not on the wand," he told her.

Beanna frowned, then ordered, "Lift the rock!"

The stone floated out of the cauldron as Beanna moved her wand upwards. She squealed in delight, then lowered her wand, causing the rock to sink back into the cauldron. She repeated the exercise two more times, then stepped aside for the others.

Raimugi went next, and they moved their boulder on the first try, picking up Khurshid's advice. They lifted and lowered the stone all five of their turns successfully, giving a loud noise of victory each time. They then moved back to let Sarala go.

Sarala approached the cauldron with her wand out in front of her, feeling a bit uncertain. Did it matter which way her wand pointed? Was she supposed to point it at the stone first, or while she commanded it?

"Lift the stone," she said gruffly, hoping that her confident voice would mask the fact that she didn't know what she was doing.

It didn't. The stone remained where it was, in the bottom of the cauldron. Sarala frowned, then remembered what Khurshid had told Beanna. She had to focus more on the stone—on lifting it—rather than on what she was supposed to be doing with her wand.

Sarala took a deep breath and tried again, her golden eyes piercing the rock below her. "Lift!" she ordered, her lip curling back slightly.

The stone shifted a bit, but it didn't go as high as it had for Raimugi.

"Lift!" she growled, her anger starting to flare as she flicked her wand upwards.

The boulder suddenly shot out of the cauldron, flying up towards the ceiling. It smashed through the wood with a loud bang, causing each student to stop their work and stare in awe. Sarala blushed in embarrassment as the boulder fell from the air and crashed back into the cauldron. The cauldron shattered at once, the metal pieces clattering on the floor.

Khurshid swiveled his head about at all the noise, clearly trying to detect what had happened. "Who did that?" he asked in the silence that followed.

"She did!" Beanna yowled, pointing at Sarala.

Khurshid moved closer, feeling the air with his hands to detect who the offender was. He frowned and said, "Ah. Sarala Kiran. Go see Mr. Caihong, please."

Sarala knew her face was a deep shade of red by now, especially as she was holding her breath. Body stiff, she merely nodded to Khurshid's words and exited the quiet classroom, only allowing herself to breathe again once she was out. She frowned as she glanced around the Courtyard, uncertain where Ak-tu might be.

Remembering about the frogoyles, Sarala glanced around for one. It took her a minute or two, but then she saw the fanged frog statue only meters away, connected to the side of the stone wall. She stepped forward until she was standing directly beneath it.

"Um...frogoyle?" she called up to it. "I need to see Hawk-tu Caihong." *Ugh, I still can't pronounce his name!*

She stood staring at it for a long moment, but nothing happened.

"Do you know where he is?" she pressed.

The frogoyle suddenly landed on the ground in front of her with a crunchy-sounding thud that was much softer than the stone hitting the cauldron. She let out a yelp of surprise, but quickly regained control of herself. The frogoyle peered up at her through purple-shining eyes, then hopped away, the stone scraping with each hop. It headed towards the Greenhouse. Sarala hesitated only a moment, then hurried after it.

She entered the stuffy Greenhouse, but quickly lost the frogoyle in the tangle of plants. She started to panic, then realized that it didn't matter where the frogoyle went. *He's in here somewhere.*

"Mr. Caihong?" Sarala called over the loud noises of birds, bugs, and bushes. "Are you in here?"

She wandered around the ground level, calling out for Ak-tu as she went until she reached the spiral stairs leading up to the next level. After going up, she walked across the wooden planks, which went around the perimeter of the Greenhouse.

"Mr. Caihong?" she yelled again.

Ak-tu suddenly appeared in front of her, dressed in a green tank top that had easily concealed him amongst the plants. Sarala let out another yelp of surprise and stumbled back. She blushed outwardly, but only felt anger searing through her at her blunder. She should have punched the man, not jumped away in fright! Then again…she'd probably be in big trouble if she did attack. *Still would have been better than being a total coward,* she thought dismally.

"Can I help you?" Ak-tu asked brightly, flicking his wrist to create a tiny tornado in the palm of his hand.

"Um…Mr. Jihan told me to come see you."

"Is there a particular reason for this?" Ak-tu pressed patiently.

Sarala hung her head. She glanced at the wand she still held in her hand, as slumped as her shoulders. "I threw a rock into the ceiling and it broke the cauldron when it landed."

Ak-tu seemed to be glaring at her for a long, quiet moment. His unibrow always made him appear angry if he wasn't smiling. Sarala waited for the yelling to come, to hear what her punishment would be.

But then Ak-tu snorted in laughter. "You broke the cauldron?" he exclaimed.

"Yeah?" she questioned, taken aback.

"Were you angry as you did this, or too excited?" Ak-tu asked.

"I was angry," Sarala said. "I couldn't get the magic to work right the first two times, and then the third try…it…flew away."

Ak-tu shook his head, chuckling. "Ah, Sarala, you need to control anger when it comes to magic! If your emotions are too strong, it can have a bad effect. It will also take more energy out of you—not that it matters too much when you have a wand. A wand means you're wasting less energy than if you were just channeling with your body on your own. But it's still valuable to learn to control your emotions before you get too far in magic."

Sarala scowled. "I'm not an emotional person," she grumbled, her hold tightening on her wand.

"Apparently you are, otherwise there wouldn't be a hole in the ceiling," Ak-tu pointed out, smiling. "Speaking of which, I'd better go patch that up. I hope the student whose room you damaged was out at the time."

Sarala frowned. She hadn't even considered if there was anyone in the room above the classroom. She hoped she didn't accidentally knock someone out with the stone.

"Return to class, Sarala," Ak-tu told her. "I'll have that hole fixed soon. And get a new cauldron."

Sarala nodded and went down the spiral stairs. When she looked back, Ak-tu was gone. *But where did he go? There's only one staircase,* Sarala pondered.

As she reached the first floor again, she realized that Ak-tu had slid down a tree. He hopped off the slimy blue branch and hurried towards the front of the Greenhouse. Sarala snorted lightly and trailed after him at a slower pace.

By the time Sarala reached the Magic Channeling classroom again, Khurshid had moved onto a different exercise. The students were still around their cauldrons (or their rock, in the case of the three earth magicians), but now they were attempting to move their element in circular motions.

Khurshid walked over to her as she entered. "What did Mr.

Caihong say?" he asked.

"To not let my emotions get out of control," she muttered grumpily.

Khurshid chuckled. "Good advice. He's fixing the hole right now."

Sarala glanced up at the ceiling. Ak-tu saw her and waved, then set back to work. She looked at Khurshid, waiting expectantly.

"You can join the earth students again, but I want you to watch them," Khurshid told her. "You're to go last in each exercise for the remainder of class today."

"Yes, Mr. Jihan."

Sarala returned to the other students. Raimugi grinned in greeting, Beanna shot her a glare, and Ebony quickly moved away from her in fear.

"You didn't miss much," Raimugi told her. "We moved the rock side-to-side, and now we're doing a circle. It's pretty simple!"

Sarala nodded once.

She waited for the other students to do the exercise, each taking five turns again. She then lifted her wand, took a deep breath to make sure she was calm, then ordered the stone to move in a circle. It worked on her first try! She was happy to see it working—but not *too* happy—and had success on her next attempts.

The last exercise they did was moving the element to spell out their names in the air. Sarala had a bit of difficulty moving the stone to write each individual letter, and she almost misspelled her name, but it went fine otherwise.

She left the class feeling confident about her magic. As the students exited the room to go to the Greenhouse for Plants, Sarala glanced for Ren and Zyn. She saw them hanging back, and hurried over.

"I'm hopeless!" Zyn was crying out to Ren in a panicked way.

"Shush!" Ren hissed in a whisper.

Sarala frowned. "Why are you hopeless?" she asked bluntly. "Those exercises were easy."

"Zyn didn't have much control over the air, that's all," Ren said quickly. "I mean, it *is* a bit hard to see it, right?"

Zyn sighed and made no response.

Sarala glanced from one sister to the other. *They're hiding something,* she thought. As they crossed the hot Courtyard quietly, she could have sworn they were whispering to one another. But whenever she looked at them, they weren't moving their lips at all —which only made her more suspicious.

Yet she did not press the issue as the students went through Plants and Potions. They were too busy sketching out plants and mixing their first "potion" (which was actually cooking a soup as practice for real potions) to speak much.

The bell rang for the end of Potions class. Sarala grabbed her wand from the table and got to her feet, glad that they could go to lunch now. But before Ren and Zyn could join her, there was a loud bang, a splashing noise, and a yelp of pain. Sarala whirled around to see what had happened.

"Whoops. Sorry," C3 said indifferently, and he rushed from the room.

Sarala glared after him, then looked over at Ren and Zyn. Zyn was on the floor, next to a knocked-over cauldron. Large soup stains covered her robe, which was steaming. Ren was helping Zyn take off the burning robe. Sarala hurried over to pick up the fallen cauldron, though it was a bit pointless considering it had already lost its contents.

"Are you okay?" Sarala asked Zyn.

Zyn crossed her arms over her chest, appearing suddenly small without her crazy robe. "Yeah," she muttered. "I don't think I got burned."

"I just got a little burned," Ren said, showing Sarala her forearm, where the soup had splashed her. "No biggie!"

At that moment, Fern crossed over to them. She handed Ren a small vial and said, "Cover the burns with that. They'll be gone in two days. I'll clean up here."

Ren nodded and opened the vial, taking out a sticky purple substance. She spread it out on her forearm with a little difficulty, then offered it to Zyn. But Zyn shook her head, keeping her arms around herself.

"Should we get some food?" Sarala asked, as Ren pocketed the vial.

"Yeah, I'm starving!" Ren said. "Come on, Zyn!"

But Zyn didn't move.

"What's wrong? You didn't get burned, did you?" Ren asked, looking at her sister in concern. "Did the cauldron hit you?"

"I'm fine!" Zyn said in a bit of a high voice.

She grabbed her soaked robe and made to put it back on, but Ren stopped her.

"You can't wear that! It's covered in hot soup!"

"But—"

"You don't *always* have to wear a crazy robe, you know," Sarala jeered.

Zyn looked a bit hurt by this. "I know, but…I just…"

"We have Kung Fu after lunch. It's not like you'd be wearing your robe in that class, either," Sarala pointed out.

Zyn shifted uncomfortably. "I just…don't like to wear this shirt…by itself."

"Why?" Sarala asked, peering at the stripy shirt.

"It's a bit…revealing," Zyn said uneasily.

Sarala remembered how Zyn always had her shirt only halfway buttoned, leaving the top and bottom open. She always assumed it was because the robe made her hot. Why Zyn thought it was "revealing" made no sense to her though. Many people would walk around without shirts on (especially in the summer), so having a half-buttoned shirt was no different in her eyes. It wasn't the most professional, but as long as she was wearing clothes, what was the big deal?

"Just button up your shirt, then," Ren scoffed playfully.

Zyn stood stiffly for a moment, then lowered her arms. She quickly buttoned her shirt the rest of the way, but still appeared uneasy.

Sarala rolled her eyes. "Can we get going? I bet we're the last ones to get food!"

She turned on her heel and went across the Courtyard, the sun hot on her back. Behind her, the twins were muttering in low voices, and she remembered how they were keeping something from her. She pricked her ears to listen in.

"But it feels so…weird and…awkward," Zyn was saying.

"You're just used to wearing your robes all the time, that's all," Ren chuckled.

"But…"

"Don't worry about it! Let people see you for once!"

Zyn made no reply as they finally reached the Eating Hall. Sarala opened the door. There was indeed a line, but it wasn't as long as she thought it'd be. They'd apparently taken some time to arrive, that the start of the line was already seated.

"Let's eat outside," Sarala said abruptly, once they got their trays of food.

"Okay! It *is* a nice day!" Ren said cheerfully. "And then Zyn's robe can dry out a bit in the sun."

The three therefore left the crowded Eating Hall and went out to the bench in the nearby garden. Zyn sat on the ground, still in a bad mood, her whole body tense. She put her soup-covered robe on the grass beside her, in a patch of sunlight streaming through the plants. Sarala and Ren took the bench, but Sarala didn't bother touching her food.

"What's going on with you two? What happened in Magic Channeling? I know it wasn't me. I didn't throw the rock at you," she added, trying to sound light-hearted rather than accusing.

"Nothing," Ren said, pushing her glasses up her small nose.

"Then why's Zyn being so quiet for once?" Sarala asked, signaling to the girl on the ground. "This isn't like her at all! Surely she's not *that* sad she can't wear her robe!"

Ren frowned. She seemed to fall in deep thought, as she stared over at Zyn with a concentrated look on her face. After several minutes passed, Sarala wondering if she should just drop it or investigate the sisters further on her own, Ren spoke.

"Zyn doesn't have her magic yet," Ren said quietly. "But please, you can't tell *anyone*."

Sarala stared at her. "But…how can she not have magic? Didn't she pass the assessments? If she didn't have magic, she wouldn't be allowed to take classes."

"I did magic for her, at the very end, on the very last assessment," Ren explained, shifting uneasily. "It was the only way to get her to attend school."

"You cheated."

Ren sighed at the bland statement, dropping her purple eyes and scuffing the dirt with her bare foot. "Yes…but why should Zyn have to sit out another year just because her magic didn't come soon enough? What if it comes tomorrow? It wouldn't be fair if it came a day late and she missed out again."

Sarala frowned over at Zyn. Ren made a good point, but... "What happens if her magic doesn't come?"

"It will," Ren said confidently.

"What happens if she shows no sign of magic the rest of the year?" Sarala pressed roughly. "Are you just going to keep cheating for her to pass classes?"

Ren's shoulders slumped. "What else am I supposed to do? We can hardly tell Dad. Besides, it's like I said—Zyn's magic will come. So what if it's a bit late? It'll come, and then she can do all those exercises on her own. Sure, she might have to catch up a bit, but she'll pick it all up!"

Sarala doubted that. Yet she was never one to have faith in the first place. She turned to her food, picking up her bread roll and biting into it.

"You're not going to tell, right?" Ren asked in a shaky voice, setting her angular eyes on Sarala.

"Why would I?" Sarala grunted back. "So long as you don't come running to me for help, I don't care. It's not hurting anyone if Zyn doesn't have magic—besides Zyn, of course. And maybe you, if you're having to do double the work."

Ren looked over at Zyn, her eyes growing watery. Sarala gazed in the opposite direction, not wanting to see the other girl cry. Nobody said anything else as they picked at their food in an un-appetizing way.

Way to ruin the mood, Sarala, she thought bitterly. *That's all you're good for, isn't it?*

Oh, well. It's their own fault, she argued with herself. *Zyn shouldn't be enrolled if she doesn't have magic. It's common sense. They're just going to hurt each other... Zyn better hope she gets her magic soon...*

CHAPTER 12: MISFIRE

But Zyn's magic did not come. As the weeks went on, she was getting more and more convinced that her magic simply did not exist.

Magic Channeling classes were getting difficult to keep up in, as Zyn did not have any magic to do the exercises with. She tried to take notes on each exercise, so she could do them in the future. But because she was so distracted jotting down notes, she got exercises mixed up when it was her turn, and she moved her wand in the wrong directions. Ren struggled with making "Zyn's magic" work *in*correctly, as she had to match her own magic to Zyn's mistaken wand motions. It was also taking energy out of Ren to do work for the both of them, especially as the exercises grew harder.

Plants and Potions classes also weren't getting easier. They had to start using magic to identify certain plants. If they struck a plant with a specific elemental blast, the plant would act in a particular way. The dancing dragon tree and the "regular" dancing tree were two trees that looked practically the same, but had very different properties. The air magicians had to send large gusts at the trees and note their reactions. The dancing dragon tree would curl its branches in response, while the dancing tree would shiver.

Each potion they made required a bit of elemental magic to enchant them too. Soaking and mixing plant magic made potions for specific purposes, like healing or invisibility. But in order for the potion to work once the plants were done being brewed, the students had to cast a spell on them with their wands. The wands, also containing plant magic, would mix the elemental magic into the potion with the given command, therefore assigning the potion with its specific purpose. This same method was used to make enchanted objects and technology.

Fern provided the class with their elements, as the students could only control their surroundings. Of course, as Zyn had no magic, she couldn't actually enchant any of her potions when Fern was looking—and Fern was always looking. In fact, the students had to enchant their potions directly in front of her, one by one. Ren tried to enchant Zyn's first potion for her, but Fern sensed that the magic wasn't coming from Zyn. The sisters therefore did not attempt it again, and all of Zyn's potions remained useless.

Though the Magic Studies class was all about magic throughout world history (mostly about how magic was used to progress society or otherwise conquer new territories), it was still a struggle for Zyn to get through the class. It was so lecture-heavy that it was hard to pay attention and take notes, and Zyn often found herself doodling all over her paper, even if she was still listening.

Kung Fu and Tai Chi also weren't going the best, though Zyn definitely preferred the active Kung Fu to the slow Tai Chi. Sarala had already leveled up to yellow sash, which was the second level in Kung Fu. Ren was getting close to testing, and yet Zyn still felt so behind. She didn't know why she was struggling, as she loved being active, but she couldn't keep up. Tai Chi was no different.

Art classes were no longer as fun, but Zyn was glad that magic wasn't a requirement. The advanced students could add magic to their work (to make their paintings have special effects), but the first-years weren't allowed to until the following year. The Art classes were the only classes Zyn was able to keep up in.

The only enjoyable part about school was the art club, much to Zyn's surprise. The twins dragged Sarala to the first meeting, and she liked it enough to keep going back. It was definitely relaxing to sit around and chat with other students, as they didn't have much time to speak in their classes.

Mint was very talkative and friendly, but often became anxious if the conversation steered towards schoolwork. As a second-year, they had dropped Kung Fu from their schedule. They were doing Plants and Potions, and continued the Magic Studies and Magic Channeling classes. But they held lots of self-doubt (and tended to stress eat), so their magic wasn't the best. They tried performing a simple spell of swirling water over their head, and only succeeded in dropping it on everyone.

They also got to know C3 a bit more. The redhead had moved to Galia from Talamh Glas, a country south of Galia. It had gotten too expensive to live in their region, so they became citizens of Galia. The Clay family moved around for a while, until they came across Ak-tu's school in the state of Pann. The magic academy wasn't as pricey as most magic schools, so the family settled down nearby and was able to pay for C3 to attend.

There were a few other students in the club too. The three first-years—Raimugi, Mernao, and Frost—joined them (though it sounded like Raimugi had dragged their friends, as they weren't too interested in art). There was also a second-year girl named Moon, who, like C3, was quiet and sat alone.

Zyn and Ren were currently in a club meeting in the Art Studio, Zyn sketching a scene she'd use colored pencils with later, and Ren doing a painting. Sarala hadn't joined them that Saterday morning, claiming her head hurt too much to go.

"What are you two working on?" Mint asked the sisters, glancing at them from where she sat in front of a large canvas. Mint was gender fluid, and the blue bracelet on her wrist told them that she was identifying as a girl that day.

"Just drawing a forest," Zyn replied, continuing to sketch.

"And I'm painting a waterfall," Ren said.

"Cool!" Mint said eagerly, staring down at their work. The twins were on the ground, so their art was quite easy to see. "I love your painting technique, Ren, it's so fluid!"

"Thanks, Mint!" Ren said brightly. "Yours is nice too!"

Zyn tried not to snort out loud. She'd seen a lot of Mint's paintings already. Mint literally threw paint at the canvas and claimed it was art, making up interpretations from the splotches.

Frost leaned over from where he sat at one of the nearby desks. "Your art is really nice, Ren!" he agreed.

Zyn huffed softly in annoyance. Was anyone going to compliment *her* art? *Probably not,* she thought. *Nobody ever saw me as an artist. It's always Ren and Dad, even though I do more art than them. It's just because they have more of a realistic style...and can paint....*

"What do you think of my painting, Ren?" Frost asked, holding up his small canvas for her to see.

She craned her neck to take a look. "Is that...a...um..."

"It's a pumpkin," Frost said promptly. "I thought it'd be fun to paint since the Day of Spirits is almost here."

"The Day of Spirits is almost here?" Ren repeated in alarm. "Oh yeah—it's already October!"

"You doing anything for it? It's tomorrow, so we won't be in any classes, like we were for the Tree Festival," Frost commented.

The Tree Festival celebrated the season of autumn, but it took place during the week. Though the week-long festival started on Trizday and not Moonday, the first-years were still too busy with homework to celebrate. The summer and winter festivals were much more widely-celebrated than the spring and autumn festivals anyway.

Just as there were four seasonal festivals, there were also four major holidays in each season. The Day of Spirits was the autumn holiday, honoring the spirits. Not everyone celebrated this holiday, and it depended on the culture and how people viewed spirits. Some people called this holiday the Day of Ghosts, and celebrated those loved ones lost to them. Others called it the Day of Monsters, and were quick to hide at home and not come out. For some reason, October 11 was the day that plenty of spirits (or monsters) would make themselves known to societies all over the world.

"Yeah, we'll probably do what we always do," Ren replied to Frost, signaling herself and Zyn. "We hold a meditation, go into the forest, and praise the spirits. Then we hold a feast."

"Sounds…interesting," Frost said after a small pause. "Would I be able to tag along?"

"Ooh, are you interested in spirits too?" Ren asked, her purple eyes lighting up at once.

Zyn sighed and focused on drawing her forest. She didn't feel like getting in a conversation about spirits, as she herself still didn't know what to make of them. Ak-tu had taught his daughters that the spirits existed and they were to be praised for their natural part in the world. After all, they praised nature, and spirits were a part of nature, just like plants and magic itself. But she had yet to see a real spirit, and wasn't sure what to make of them. She called her morning greeting to show her appreciation of being alive and thanking nature, but it was partly for the spirits too—though she never received greetings from any spirits.

As she expected, C3 soon joined the conversation, always interested in spirits. Zyn couldn't block out his annoying voice, and listened in.

"But what I don't understand," C3 was saying, "is why spirits come out on this day. What is so significant about October 11? Why is *that* the recorded day that spirits come out of…wherever they might have been hiding…all around Sater? Each year, I try to search for spirits on this day, but I never manage to find one."

"We haven't seen any, either," Ren told him.

"Then how do we truly know spirits exist, if there are none to be found?" C3 pressed, tapping his pen against his chin. "I know we have searched the Library for evidence, and I myself have conducted research on the subject where I could. But how do we know that spirits are real, and not some sort of illusion? Or just other animals? Or they could be creatures, as creatures are also of high intelligence like these spirits seem to be, rather than acting on instinct like animals."

Ren bit her bottom lip, clearly trying to think of what to say. Before she could respond, Frost answered.

"I think it's just a bunch of myths," he said. "I mean, has any-one here ever seen a spirit?"

"I have," Raimugi said.

Frost glanced over at his friend in surprise. The room fell quiet, and even Zyn stopped doodling. They all stared at the blonde person with keen interest.

"When I lived in Rittorando, we praised the spirits—but also feared them," Raimugi said, playing with their single braid. "The spirits lived in the forest nearby—a collection of them. They'd come out every year on October 11, as if to remind us that they still existed. We'd throw a feast in their honor, but we were all scared of them at the same time. I'm not sure why, since they never did anything to us. They were just…there."

Zyn frowned. "Did they have any powers or anything?"

"Some of my village said that they could control the weather," Raimugi commented. "So if they were angry with us, they'd make large storms that would create floods and ruin all of our crops. But that never happened when I was living there. I would've thought it was just a bunch of myths myself, if I didn't see the spirits with my own eyes."

"Interesting," Zyn murmured, flicking her pencil back and forth against the floor, a satisfying vibration spreading up her arm. "Did you happen to get any pictures or videos for us to see?"

"No," Raimugi admitted. "I didn't have a mirror at the time. And besides—the village head told us that pictures and videos were strictly prohibited around the spirits. That was one thing that'd set them off: technology. I can try drawing them, though."

And with that, Raimugi pulled out their sketchbook and began drawing. The other students all watched them curiously, apart from Moon, who was knitting a scarf absentmindedly in the corner. After a few minutes, Raimugi held up the sketchbook for them all to see.

"I'm not the best artist," they chuckled. "But this is sorta what they look like."

To Zyn, it appeared that the spirits were scribbles with horns and sharp claws.

"Interesting," Ren said.

"That looks hideous," C3 remarked, squinting at the picture. "I can't even make out its head."

Everyone ignored him. They were quite accustomed to his rude remarks by this point, and only Mint was hurt by the comments now.

The bell rang for lunch. The students quickly put away their art pieces and supplies, then hurried to the Eating Hall. Zyn and Ren took their time, knowing that there would already be a long line.

{What did you think of the spirit thing?} Zyn asked Ren telepathically, so the students still packing up wouldn't hear her.

{I believe Raimugi. Why wouldn't I?} Ren queried, glancing over at Zyn curiously.

{I dunno.}

Before Ren could say anything else, Frost suddenly approached the sisters. Zyn realized that the classroom was now empty, apart from the three of them. Birds chirped loudly outside, the only noise that seemed to exist for a moment.

"Hey, Ren," Frost said. "I was wondering if I could have a word?"

"Sure," Ren said.

Zyn and Ren waited expectantly. Frost cleared his throat,

glancing over at Zyn.

"Did you forget what you were going to say?" Ren asked brightly.

{He wants me to go.} Zyn told Ren.

{Yeah, I know, but I don't want you to.} Ren replied carelessly.

Frost ran a hand through his spiky blue hair, looking a bit annoyed as he continued staring at Zyn.

"Did I get pen marks all over my nose again?" Zyn asked Frost pointedly.

"No," Frost grunted. He glanced over at Ren. "I was wondering if you wanted to go out with me."

{Well, that's random.} Ren thought to Zyn, her chuckles echoing in Zyn's mind. *{What should I say?}*

{I don't like him.}

{I mean, he's okay. Should I give him a chance?}

{Why would you?}

{Because it's only fair to give people chances.}

{Always the optimist, aren't you?}

"Yes, I'd be happy to!" Ren said aloud to Frost.

Frost brightened up. "Great! Let's have lunch!"

He put his hand on Ren's shoulder and led her out of the Art Studio, leaving Zyn glaring after him. Zyn stuck her tongue out at Frost's back, then hurried to catch up.

{Why don't you hang out with Sarala?} Ren's thoughts reached out to Zyn as they entered the Eating Hall. *{I'll be fine with Frost, you know.}*

Zyn sighed in annoyance. She trailed after her sister to the long line, but after getting some food on her tray, she left the Eating Hall alone. She would sit at the bench in the garden where she, Ren, and Sarala typically sat at lunch.

But when she got there, she saw that she wasn't alone. Sarala was already there. She looked up as Zyn plopped down on the ground in front of her, her spine rattling uncomfortably at the jolting action.

"Where's Ren?" Sarala asked in surprise.

"Eating lunch with her new boyfriend," scoffed Zyn.

Sarala stared at her for a long minute.

"Frost," Zyn expanded. "That guy with the spiky hair who never pays attention in class."

"You have spiky hair and don't pay attention, either," Sarala pointed out.

"I pay attention! Doodling just helps me focus better," Zyn muttered. "Anyway, how's your headache?"

"It's fine," Sarala said. "My head never hurt. I just didn't feel like going to the club."

Zyn frowned. "You could have just said so. It's a club meeting, not a class. You're not required to show up."

Sarala shrugged and picked at her food. She didn't seem that hungry. Zyn wasn't feeling too hungry, either, her stomach seeming to hold a rock.

"So…ready for that assignment on Moonday?" Zyn asked Sarala. "The make-your-own-obstacle-course thing in Magic Channeling?"

Khurshid had assigned them the task of using the surrounding elements to create an obstacle course of their own. The first-years were allowed to practice their magic outside of class now too, so they could at least prepare.

"I think so," Sarala replied shortly.

"You're not one to talk much, are you?" commented Zyn in a bland voice.

"No."

Zyn sighed. "I wish Ren was here."

Sarala said nothing in response.

They ate quietly for several long minutes, the food seeming more bland than usual. Suddenly, the bushes rustled in front of them. Zyn set down her tray as Sarala got to her feet. Zyn was more curious, but Sarala was entirely tense. *Maybe it's a frogoyle,* Zyn thought. *Or maybe it's that thing that Sarala saw a few weeks ago…*

They had no need to worry, though. In the next moment, Ak-tu appeared. He was dressed in a purple tank top and baggy black pants, clearly too hot to don his typical robe.

"There you are, Zyn! I'd like to have a word with you."

Zyn froze. Did Ak-tu know that she still didn't have magic? Was he going to kick her out of the academy, and go back to homeschooling her about history and math? She remained rooted to the spot, her heart beating faster.

"I'll just…go," Sarala said a bit awkwardly.

"You don't have to," Ak-tu replied. "We're going to take a stroll around the Courtyard. Come on, Zyn."

Zyn forced her feet forward. She trailed after her father as the two left the garden. They were soon out in the warm sunshine. The wind blew lightly, spreading red and orange leaves around their feet. Within another month or two, snow would cover the stone ground and clouds would block out the sun's heat.

"What did you wanna talk about?" Zyn mumbled, hoping she didn't sound too guilty.

"Your education," Ak-tu replied, frowning slightly.

Here it comes, Zyn thought helplessly, feeling tears pricking at the edges of her eyes.

"Khurshid and Fern told me that you're struggling in classes," Ak-tu said. "I wanted to see if there was anything I could do to help you."

"Oh," Zyn murmured, letting out a small breath of relief. "I dunno," she admitted, in answer to his question.

"Are you still having a tough time connecting to your magic?" Ak-tu pressed, watching Zyn closely as they walked.

"Kinda?" Zyn replied truthfully.

"Is there anything else going on?"

"What do you mean?"

"You're not being bullied, are you?" Ak-tu asked.

"No," Zyn said.

"Are you unable to understand lessons? Are Khurshid and Fern not doing a good job teaching? Do they need to slow down, or change their methods?"

"No, it's not like that at all," Zyn objected.

"Perhaps it's because Ren has strong magic, that you feel yours is blocked off?" Ak-tu continued.

Zyn frowned, a bit puzzled. "That's a weird question," she commented. "But still no."

Ak-tu shrugged. "I'm just trying to think of why you're having a hard time in classes. I thought that, perhaps with Ren being talented with her magic, you…felt your magic wasn't as good. Low self-confidence is sure to make your magic weak."

Zyn felt a surge of anger rise through her. Her lip curled back and her hands squeezed into fists at her sides. "Oh, so you're saying that I'm good-for-nothing? Useless? Just because my magic is weak when compared to Ren's?"

"No!" Ak-tu said, his eyes wide in alarm.

"Well, sorry to be such a big disappointment to you!" Zyn seethed sarcastically. "I'm glad to know that Ren's the best magician around, and I'm *nothing*!"

She stomped away from her father, glad they were so near the tower. She entered the Tai Chi Studio, unlocked the door to the tower, and stormed inside. Once in her room, she slammed the door bitterly behind her.

Zyn kicked the nearby desk angrily. A few of the objects gathered on its surface fell over. The wand rattled away, almost falling to the ground. Zyn caught it before it could go anywhere.

She lifted the wand in front of her and stared at it, long and hard. She had half-a-mind to snap the stick and be done with school. After all, she had no magic. It was no use pretending that she did. It wasn't some "magic block" that she had—why would she have a block if she was in perfect health? She might as well have told Ak-tu the truth and get pulled out of classes.

But she also didn't want to get left behind. She didn't want to go back to learning boring subjects. Even though she struggled to keep up, the magic classes were interesting. They were different. And if she dropped out, Ren would be way ahead of her by the time Zyn was able to attend.

If my magic ever comes, she thought bitterly, feeling the tears pricking at her again.

She took a few deep breaths and closed her eyes, trying to calm down. She put her focus inwards, trying to reach out for whatever small amount of magic might exist.

Come on…you have to be in here somewhere… Please, magic…come out… Come to me… Just let me have magic!

But nothing happened.

Zyn collapsed to the ground, feeling even more useless than before. Her lack of magic was a disappointment to not only her, but her family. It was a strain on Ren, who had to do magic for herself, for her sister, and even figure out how to mess up Zyn's magic when she did something incorrect.

She closed her eyes and set her head against the door, her breathing getting shallow as she started to cry. *I wish Ren never got me enrolled. I wish I wasn't even here… It's not fair for any of us! I don't get to learn magic, Ren has to do so much, and I got in over other students who would have been turned away. And now Dad will just be disappointed in me—not just for my stupid lack of magic, but for not telling him in the first place. I never should have been enrolled!*

She wiped away the tears, but couldn't stop the gasping breaths. *I'm so pathetic, just sitting here, crying over having no magic… I hate being nonmagical…I hate myself…I hate this body… Why do I have to be so useless?*

CHAPTER 13: ONE VISION

The Day of Spirits was soon upon them. Ren woke up early that Sunday morning, even before Zyn's usual wake-up call. She got dressed in a midnight blue robe and sat down in the center of her room to meditate, breathing in the scents of flowers and soil.

"Good morning!" Zyn called out shortly.

"Morning!" Ren replied, as Sarala screamed, "Shut up!"

"Watch your tone!" Ak-tu's bark came.

"Sorry, Mr. Caihong!"

Ren opened her eyes and snorted in laughter. Sarala wasn't accustomed to Ak-tu still being in the tower when they all woke up, as he was often out training. He typically only hung around the tower in the morning for special events.

Ren opened her door, but didn't see Zyn anywhere. Figuring that Zyn was looking for a specific robe to wear for the holiday, Ren went down the stairs to the family room. Ak-tu was waiting for her, dressed in a silver robe covered in black-and-white symbols.

"Good morning, Dad!" Ren said cheerfully.

"Hello, Ren!"

Ak-tu was standing by one of the tables, but he hurried over to Ren and glanced up the stairs. Ren frowned, looking at her father expectantly.

{Did Zyn talk to you last night?} Ak-tu asked her.

{No?} Ren questioned. *{Is something wrong? She didn't sound that happy this morning.}*

{I think she's…having a hard time in school.} Ak-tu told her a bit hesitantly. *{I tried to talk to her about it yesterday, but she got mad at me. I believe she thought I was comparing you two when I asked her if she was having a hard time with her magic because you have no problem with it. I thought that it could be a potential block, if she thinks her magic is weak compared to yours….}*

{Oh.} Ren said dully, not knowing how to reply.

{Khurshid and Fern told me that she's unable to do any sort of magic, actually...} Ak-tu went on, eyeing her closely. {But she did do magic in the fight assessment. Right?}

{Yes!} Ren replied at once, trying not to sound alarmed at his question. *Does he know?* she wondered, being sure to keep the thought to herself.

Ak-tu gazed at her for a long moment. {Have you seen her do magic at any other point?}

{Yes! She's done magic a few times during Magic Channeling, but she seems to be unable to do it in Potions with Fern glaring her down.} Ren said, pushing her glasses up; it wasn't a complete lie, as Fern was definitely intimidating enough to make someone too anxious to use their magic.

{And you'd tell me if you knew anything, right?} Ak-tu pressed.

A lump formed in Ren's throat, and she was glad they were speaking telepathically. {What do you mean by that? Do you think Zyn is...cheating or something?}

Ak-tu pursed his lips, shifting uneasily. {I'm not sure...but if you don't know anything, I bet it's just some sort of magic block, or low self-confidence, or something...natural...} He shook his head, his hair falling across his concerned eyes. {And you're sure Zyn hasn't talked to you about this? Maybe she's opened up to you about something she's struggling with?}

{I haven't seen her since art club, actually.}

{Did she miss dinner?} Ak-tu asked, shoving his hair out of his face.

{I'm...not sure.} Ren admitted awkwardly.

{How can you not know? You two do everything together!}

{We didn't eat together...} Ren told him, realizing she had said nothing about Frost.

{Are you two fighting?} Ak-tu asked, looking even more alarmed. {I noticed you weren't with Zyn and Sarala at lunch, either. Is this why Zyn's facing magic blocks? I don't want magic to come between you two!}

{No, it's not! I promise it's not!} Ren said hastily, biting her bottom lip. {I...just kinda...got a boyfriend now...}

{A boyfriend?} Ak-tu asked blankly, blinking several times.

{Frost Wuolf. He asked me in art club yesterday. I said yes, and we went to lunch together. Then, we had dinner together too.} As Ak-tu continued to look uneasy, she pressed on hurriedly. *{It's nothing serious, Dad! At least, I don't think it is. I just thought I'd be nice by saying yes.}*

Ak-tu put a hand on her shoulder. *{Ren, I'm very thankful that you are a kind person…but you can't just be saying yes to people if you don't actually care for them.}*

{But how would I know if I care for them if I don't give them that chance?} Ren asked seriously. *{I don't know him that well, but he wants to get to know me, so why can't I agree to that? It's not like he's a jerk. If he was, I wouldn't have said yes.}*

Zyn came down the stairs as Ak-tu tried forming a response, and their telepathic conversation broke off. Ak-tu smiled at Zyn, but Zyn kept her eyes on the ground and didn't say anything. She wasn't dressed in any robes, just her stripy long-sleeved shirt (fully buttoned) and baggy red pants.

"Hey, Zyn!" Ren said, beaming.

Zyn glanced up at her for a moment, forced a small smile, then went back to staring at the ground. An awkward silence filled the family room, the tension heavy in the air.

{Umm…do we need to talk about something?} Ren asked them at last, sticking to the telepathic conversation in case Sarala came down.

{If anyone needs to talk to me, I'm here and willing to listen!} Ak-tu said at once, glancing at Zyn.

Zyn kept her eyes firmly on her feet. *{Everything's fine. What are we doing for the holiday?}*

Ren exchanged a glance with her father. He shrugged in response, then said aloud, "We'll be doing a meditation in the forest, and give the spirits our praise."

Zyn nodded once.

{Zyn, what's wrong?} Ren asked her sister, blocking Ak-tu out.

Zyn looked over at her, an odd expression on her face. Ren couldn't figure out what might be going through her mind, especially as she did not respond. The sisters stared at each other, Ak-tu looking from one to the other. But before anything more could be said—by thoughts or out loud—Sarala entered the room.

She stared at the family, standing in a triangle with some distance between them. The tension was still as thick as fog. Sarala turned and went right back up the stairs. The Caihong family waited for her footsteps to fade away before they resumed the conversation, Ak-tu joining in once more.

{Is there something going on that I need to know about? No—I know *there is* something going on. Can you please tell me what it is?}

Ren didn't give Zyn a chance to answer. {*Zyn's just upset that I'm dating Frost now!*} She lied to Ak-tu, pushing her glasses up her nose again. {*She's mad that I abandoned her at lunch and dinner yesterday. That's all.*}

Zyn didn't argue and remained silent, leaning against the couch with her arms crossed over her chest. Ak-tu looked between the twins again, a suspicious gleam in his eyes.

Ren's head was starting to hurt and she sighed lightly. *If Zyn wants to tell Dad, it's her decision,* she thought to herself. *But I've done what I could…*

"About Frost…and dating…" Ak-tu said aloud, "I suppose I better have the sit-down talk with you two…"

Zyn snorted aloud. "I'll skip this one."

"It's important!" Ak-tu said urgently.

"I have zero interest in dating, thanks," Zyn said gruffly.

Ak-tu blinked. "Oh. Right." He turned to Ren. "Well—"

"Yes, Dad, I know," Ren said in slight exasperation. "Don't worry. Like I said, I don't think it's serious. I doubt we'll do more than hold hands—if we even get that far."

Ak-tu frowned. "I just want you two to understand that if you're not careful—"

"Bye!" Zyn said abruptly, and she hurried to the stairs.

"I'm going out for some fresh air," Ren grumbled as Zyn's footsteps faded upstairs. "I'm getting a headache…"

She turned on the balls of her feet and quickly scampered to the tower door before her father could reply. As she exited the family room, she could hear his soft sigh behind her. Ignoring this, she bounded through the Tai Chi Studio and the Courtyard alike, her feet taking her to the Entrance Hall unconsciously.

I'll just get an early start to the holiday celebration—if we're even doing that still, Ren thought as she crossed the empty hall.

Her heart sank at the prospect, and guilt seeped through her. Stopping in her tracks abruptly beside the glass doors, despair took over her mind and her breathing quickened.

Am I…ruining things? Am I ruining the family? Dad wanted me to tell him what was going on…and I lied to him…and what if I just made things worse for Zyn? What if she gets mad at me? What if—

A yowl sounded outside, and Ren was pulled from her thoughts at once.

"Was that an animal? Did it just get hurt?" she wondered. "I have to go help it!"

Yet Ren realized that she didn't have the key to the glass doors. Swiveling around, she headed for the Admin Hall, throwing open the first door on her right. Entering the lemon-scented Storage room, she clambered over boxes of cleaning supplies and bamboo paper products until she reached the window. Ren grabbed the bottom edge of the window and heaved it up, groaning lightly at the effort. Once it was open, she stumbled out into the dirt.

She had hardly taken two steps when growling croaks sounded behind her. Glancing over her shoulder, she realized that two frogoyles were hopping out the window after her!

"Dad's enchantments," she breathed, straightening up. "But I need to help that animal…"

Without giving it a second thought, Ren bolted away to the trees, her purple hair flying behind her. She crashed through prickly bushes that tore at her clothes, but she did not allow that to deter her. The yowl came again to her right, seeming to be only paces away. Slowing down, Ren swiftly turned towards the screech and jumped through the plants until she burst through a clearing.

Ren scanned the ground for any signs of a struggle—churned soil or scattered feathers, maybe blood. But the clearing was empty. Panting lightly, Ren pricked her ears and glanced around, wondering if she was missing something in the shadows.

"Hello?" she called softly, not wanting to alert the frogoyles to her position. "Is anyone out here?"

A low moan sounded behind her, and she turned about. Yet

nothing was there. She couldn't even hear the stone statues hopping through the plants, and pondered briefly if the frogoyles had lost her trail.

"Hello?" Ren called again.

She was certain something was right in front of her, but she could not see anything. Her headache growing more intense, she closed her eyes, hoping the small action would amplify her hearing.

"Where are you?" she whispered, willing the creature to make noise again. "How can I help you?"

The words had barely left her mouth when Ren suddenly collapsed. She hit the ground, writhing in pain, her entire head feeling like it was going to explode. She screamed out in agony, her hands rigid as they tried to reach for something—anything—to make it stop. But there was nothing! What was happening to her? Why wouldn't the pain end?

Then, images flashed through her mind. But they were going too fast, she couldn't make them out! As she tried to focus on them, she noticed the pain less and less.

Her mind went black…

She was floating…or was she being dragged away?

The animal, her mind thought dully, her stomach churning unpleasantly. *It tricked me…it called me in, then attacked me… It's taking me to its lair right now, isn't it?*

Ren forced her heavy eyes open, the world too bright around her. Groaning, she lifted a bone-weary hand to shield her eyes, attempting to take in her surroundings.

But it turned out she hadn't been floating or getting dragged away. She had been carried out of the forest and back to the school, right to the Healing room. She recognized the strong scents of mint and lavender, her eyes taking a long moment to adjust. When they finally did, she could make out several long beds in front of her, and cabinets lined with plants and potion vials.

Something stirred beside her, and Ren flinched in a panic. Yet she had nothing to worry about—it was just Ak-tu and Zyn, both of them hovering over the soft bed she had been placed upon.

Dizzy and confused, Ren nearly swayed and fell over. But

wasn't she already lying down? How could she fall over if she was already on her back? Groaning, she closed her eyes, willing the nauseous feeling in her stomach to go away, for the headache to retreat.

"Are you okay?" Ak-tu asked in a soft voice.

Ren moaned in response.

"The frogoyles alerted me that someone had left the school," Ak-tu murmured, stroking her hair with his hand gently. "I took off after you at once, and when I found you, you were just lying on the ground, screaming in pain…"

"What happened to you?" Zyn asked, her voice cracking in concern. "Why'd you leave the school?"

Everything was starting to come back to her, though she still felt dazed and light-headed. It took her a moment to speak.

"There was a hurt animal…" she mumbled into the pillow, keeping her eyes firmly shut. "I heard it…I wanted to help it…"

"So you went out," Ak-tu said promptly. "Did you find it?"

"No," she grunted. "I think it tricked me…sounded hurt, then attacked me…"

"That explains all the scratches," Zyn uttered nervously; Ren could feel her twin shivering beside her.

"That's from the plants," Ren murmured. "The animal—or whatever it was—attacked my head. I think? Wait…no…I just had a headache…it hurt so bad…and then I…saw things…"

"You saw things?" Ak-tu repeated in concern, his hand pausing. "What sort of things?"

Ren shook her head and buried her face in the pillow. "I'm not sure," she admitted. "They were just whizzing by before I could get a good look at them…"

Ak-tu frowned. "Zyn, go get Aster, and make sure Fern's on her way."

Zyn scampered away at once, a door slamming shut behind her. Ren winced at the loud noise, though the headache was gradually leaving her. She let out a soft sigh, trying to relax her body as the nausea also dwindled.

"How are you feeling now?" Ak-tu asked her, running his hand through her hair again.

She turned around and opened her eyes. "A little better… My

head still hurts a bit, but it's more like the type of headache you have after straining your eyes too much when reading. Not…torture-pain."

Ak-tu frowned deeply.

"Dad…what happened to me?" Ren croaked. "Could an animal have done that to me? But it doesn't make sense…my head was starting to hurt before I went outside… I don't know if there was an animal at all… Do you think I hallucinated hearing that animal in pain?"

Ak-tu shook his head, sitting on the bed beside her. "I'm not sure… It sounds like you had a vision, but I don't know where the animal might have come in. Maybe what you heard was part of your vision?"

"A vision?" Ren repeated.

Ak-tu nodded. "I've never seen it happen, but it sounds like it, from what I've read. The head hurting like it's about to burst, the collapsing, the quick images… I'm sure it was a vision."

Ren frowned. "But…visions are…"

"Visions of the future, typically as warnings of bad things to come," Ak-tu said with a slow nod.

"But how's it supposed to warn me if I don't remember any of it?" Ren asked, her heart beginning to race in panic.

"Some people reported their visions would repeat, especially before the particular event was to take place."

"Why bother warning me, though?" Ren asked in confusion. "If visions are things that come true…if there's no stopping it…"

"There is," Ak-tu said reassuringly. "Some people have had visions where they were able to figure out what the visions meant in time to stop events from happening. That's why visions are warnings."

Ren sighed. "That still doesn't help *me*."

Ak-tu frowned. "Did you hear anything, feel anything?"

"Just lots of pain and screaming," she said in a light-hearted way, the nausea now fully gone.

Ak-tu rolled his eyes. "I can see you're getting back to normal," he commented, ruffling her hair.

Ren chuckled at the action, though it increased her headache levels again.

Just then, Zyn entered the Healing room with Fern and Aster on her heels. She hurried to Ren's side and crouched beside the bed, peering up at Ren in concern. Fern approached briskly, shooing Zyn away as she bent over Ren, inspecting her quickly.

"What happened?" Fern demanded.

Ren repeated the events of her supposed "vision" to Fern and Aster. Neither of them interrupted her, and they were quiet for a long time after she spoke.

"Here, take this," Fern said abruptly, shoving a glass vial into Ren's hands. "It'll make your headache go away."

Ren nodded and drank the potion, which tasted like bark and left a dry feeling in her mouth.

"Well?" Ak-tu asked Fern and Aster.

Aster nodded slowly. "I believe Ren had a vision."

"That's what I thought," Ak-tu murmured. "But, as she said, she can't remember anything."

"You can hardly expect her to remember her very first vision," Aster said, looking at Ak-tu incredulously. "It's more of a shocker than anything, and it drains your energy. It takes a bit of getting used to before you can focus on what the vision actually is."

"Am I going to keep getting visions?" Ren asked in dismay.

Aster shrugged. "Possibly. Most people do," he said. "Sometimes, it'll just be the one vision over and over, until the event occurs—or is avoided or changed. Other times, the person will get many different visions for the rest of their lives. It just depends."

"Well…what do I do about it?"

Aster shrugged. "Just pay attention to them whenever they occur again, since it's likely you'll keep receiving them."

"But where do they come from?" Ren asked.

"Some people think it's the universe, some people think it's the spirits," Aster said vaguely. "Some people think it's their magic, or some special gift that makes them a seer."

Ren frowned. "But *you* know, don't you?"

"It doesn't really matter where they came from," Aster said slowly. "It matters that someone is looking out for you."

Ren stared at the cotton blanket, her frown growing deeper. *Was it that animal?* she pondered. *Did it give me visions? And if so, why? What's it trying to warn me about?*

Thinking of the warning made Ren suddenly recall what she'd been wondering before she had left the school.

Is the vision trying to tell me that I'm hurting this family? That I'll…break it? Ren's breathing quickened, and she flicked her eyes to Ak-tu and Zyn, who were both still watching her closely as Fern and Aster talked in low voices. *No…I'm not going to let that happen! If anything, today just proved that we're still a family, that we still love each other no matter what issues we might be going through.*

Ren grinned at the thought, causing her father and sister to both smile in return.

"I love you so much," she whispered to them.

Zyn reached forward to hug Ren, Ak-tu quickly joining in. "I love you too," they both said in unison.

Ren breathed in the sweat, dirt, and wood scents clinging to her family—the familiar scents that distinguished them. Her beam grew wider as she hugged them more tightly.

Nothing will ever *come between us…*

CHAPTER 14: HEADLONG

The Day of Spirits wasn't fun. Everyone was so worried that Ren would collapse in agonizing pain again, that they didn't dare leave the tower, remaining in the family room most of the day. Ak-tu reminded the teens that they weren't allowed to leave the school, though he didn't punish Ren for doing so, as she had a "valid reason" (even if it ended up being a false alarm).

Frost stopped by the tower a bit later in the morning, but Ak-tu turned him away, telling him that Ren was sick and they wouldn't be doing anything to celebrate the holiday. Sarala and Zyn watched him go with satisfied expressions on their faces; both of them knew Ren could do better than him.

That Sunday passed very slowly, and Sarala was quite happy to see Moonday arrive. She and Zyn walked on either side of Ren as they went to breakfast and then to Magic Studies. Frost tried to approach, but Sarala sent him a glare that stopped him in his tracks.

Sarala didn't pay much attention to Khurshid in Magic Studies, her concern for Ren turning into concern for the obstacle course challenge. She hadn't practiced over the weekend, given everything that had happened. Twirling her rough hair around her finger, she ran through the obstacle course in her mind's eye, hoping that she'd still be able to accomplish her ideas.

The first-years made to move for the Magic Channeling classroom after Magic Studies, but Khurshid stopped them.

"We'll be doing the obstacle creation outside," he told them. "Can someone help me move the cauldrons out?"

Once the cauldrons were in the Courtyard, Khurshid summoned the students forward. They clustered around him, most of them anxious about the challenge as they shifted their weight uneasily or whispered to their friends.

"As I said last week, you have to make your own obstacle

course based off of your elemental magic. Your course must run for at least two minutes. You will be demonstrating to me that you understand how to move the elements around you. Nobody needs to run through the obstacle course you create."

The students nodded to his words.

"We'll start with the earth group," Khurshid continued. "Which of you would like to go first?"

Sarala, Raimugi, and Ebony all looked over at Beanna, who took the first turn every time. She tossed her orange hair over her shoulder and moved ahead, raising her wand in front of her.

Khurshid slid forward and thrust his palms at the four cauldrons in front of him. Each cauldron moved in a different direction, until they shaped a long rectangle. He signaled to the space bordered by cauldrons.

"That's where your obstacle course must be contained. We can't have you throwing rocks into windows," he said, smiling lightly.

Sarala huffed in annoyance. She knew he was referring to her. Nobody else had caused any accidents in class. There were a few small burns amongst the fire magicians, but nothing more serious than that.

Beanna approached the obstacle course as Khurshid took out his mirror. He told the mirror to set a timer for two minutes, then started it when Beanna was ready.

The moment the timer began, Beanna swished her wand about, ordering her magic to shift the stones in the cauldron nearest her. The stones came out and landed at the start of the rectangle, where they then rose up and down with loud thuds that shook the ground, as if blocking a person from proceeding. She then made the stones stack into one large boulder, which zigzagged through the middle of the course, as if trying to crush someone. At the end, Beanna's boulder separated into multiple stones with sharp points. She flung these at the finish line, where they stabbed the ground, creating a dust cloud upon impact.

"Nicely done, Beanna, but you did that in only one minute," Khurshid told her. "I'll have to take a few points off."

Beanna looked disappointed, but said nothing as she returned to the other students. Raimugi then stepped forward to take her place, always eager to show off what they could do with their magic. They did something similar to Beanna's obstacle course, except that they made many little boulders roll across the path to trip anyone going through. Raimugi almost hit the two-minute mark, but was still short.

Sarala went next, knowing that Ebony would want to go last. Lifting her wand in front of her, she saw her obstacle course idea in her mind one last time. The moment Khurshid commanded her to go, she was ready.

"Build a wall," Sarala ordered her wand, and the stone shifted together to form a tall wall at the beginning of the obstacle course.

Once she judged enough time had passed for a person to either climb over the wall or simply go around it, she pointed her wand at the stone again.

"Shake the ground, become pebbles!"

The ground began vibrating at the same time that the wall broke apart into tiny stones. The pebbles then rolled around on the shaking ground, ready to trip anyone stumbling across. After several seconds passed, she stopped the earthquaking.

"Rise up!" she snapped briskly.

The stone ground then shot up at random points, the edges as sharp as blades. Sarala did not want to see what would happen if someone stepped in the wrong spot at the wrong time. They'd probably lose their foot—or worse!

"Make a punching wall!"

The stone stacked together into another wall near the end of the obstacle course, but this time, the structure was moving instead of being still. Some parts of the wall launched forward with a loud scraping sound, while the rest of the wall remained motionless. If Sarala had to cross her own obstacle course, she didn't know how she'd be able to do it.

She allowed the punching wall to last for several seconds, before dropping the spell entirely. Sarala then looked over at Khurshid, wondering if she had made it in the time limit. Though the mirror had been counting aloud in an automated voice, she had been too focused on her magic to listen to it.

"Excellent job, Sarala!" Khurshid said, nodding to her. "You made it just over two minutes. I also like what you did with the pebbles. Making the stone so tiny is a difficult task, and to move them all individually from there while shaking the ground is extraordinary. You are skilled to be able to pull it off."

Sarala smiled briefly before returning to the other students.

"That was so good!" Ren complimented her, as Ebony took his turn.

"I suppose it was okay," Sarala said carelessly with a shrug, though she was glowing with pride inside.

"I'd *hate* to do your obstacle course," Zyn said. "All those rocks could kill!"

"Isn't that the point of an obstacle course?" Sarala asked.

Ren and Zyn exchanged a glance.

Once the earth students were done, Khurshid called up the water students. The Courtyard was so wet afterwards, but it didn't last long. The fire students heated up the stone and made the water evaporate quickly. The air students went last.

"Should I go first?" Zyn asked Ren in a quiet voice, so only Sarala could hear. "Just to get it over with? Or do you want to go first and have more energy for yours?"

"I'll go first," Ren said. "I'm still a bit shaky from yesterday."

But she was too slow. C3 had already stepped forward. His course mostly consisted of sending large wind blasts in all directions (which was annoying, as each wave managed to toss Sarala's hair around and send shivers down her spine). Once he was done, Mernao hurried to go, swirls of air flying around the rectangle (and thankfully contained within the space).

Ren then stepped up and pulled out her wand. She made an air wall much like Sarala's in the beginning of the course, followed by mini tornados crisscrossing each other. After, she created multiple air slides, which would pick up a person and send them back to the beginning. Finally, she ended the course with a tornado—but it was under superb control, and didn't even move outside the rectangle or tug at any of the nearby garden plants. The tornado dropped with her wand.

"Excellent control!" Khurshid praised her. "Good timing, too!"

Ren beamed and returned to Sarala and Zyn at the back of the group. Zyn moved forward with her wand, as Ren lifted her own once more.

"Still nothing?" Sarala commented under her breath.

Ren shook her head in reply.

"Why don't you just tell your dad already?" Sarala asked. "It'd be better for the both of you."

But Ren shook her head again, her eyes glinting.

Zyn spoke very loudly as she waved her wand, clearly for Ren's benefit to hear her at the back of the crowd. She ordered her wand—or Ren—to make a mini tornado of air that would keep a person from advancing forward. Ren did so, then changed the air into a large wave at Zyn's command. The final move was supposed to be a wall of wind pushing the person back to the start. But Ren accidentally made the wind run in the same direction it was going, away from the gathered students and towards the end of the course instead of against them.

"That was a bit short on the clock," Khurshid told Zyn as she lowered her wand. "And that final move would have sent our imaginary person over the finish line, not send them back to the beginning."

"I know," Zyn muttered. "I just…got it wrong."

Khurshid pursed his lips. "You seemed to be taking from the air behind us too, rather than directly around you. I felt wind at the back of my neck the whole time."

Zyn's eyes widened for a moment, but she quickly masked it and said, "I thought that'd power it up more. Like winding up a toy."

Khurshid frowned thoughtfully. "That's not a bad idea, especially if your magic isn't as strong."

Zyn scowled, but made no other reply as she rejoined her sister and friend.

"Sorry," Ren hissed in a whisper.

Zyn shrugged, seeming too dejected to speak.

"Class dismissed!" Khurshid announced.

Ren raised her hand, looking alarmed. "Khur—Mr. Jihan! What about homework?"

Khurshid smiled in her direction. "The homework is the same thing. Perfect your obstacle courses for next week."

The first-years still had a few minutes before their Plants class, so they took their time crossing the cool Courtyard to the Greenhouse. Sarala hung at the very back of the group with Ren and Zyn.

"At least we have more time to get the obstacle course right, Zyn," Ren said. "We didn't practice over the weekend, but now I know what you want, so I can do it properly."

Zyn sighed. "Don't bother, Ren," she muttered. "I'll just tell Dad."

"But—"

"There's no point in hiding it," Zyn said, looking at her sister. "I'm not going to get anywhere if we keep this up."

"Ren!"

Sarala glared as Frost came running over. Raimugi and Mernao stood a bit farther away, watching their friend in dismay.

"Hey, Frost!" Ren said, wiping the frown from her freckled face quickly.

"What happened yesterday? I went to your tower, but your dad said you were sick and told me to leave. You look fine to me," Frost added, a bit suspiciously.

"It was just a *really* bad headache," Ren said brightly, pushing her glasses up. "Anyway, there'll be plenty of chances to spend time together."

Frost nodded. "That's true. But I got all dressed up for the holiday."

"Well, the Moon Festival will be here soon—and the Moonlight Dance," Ren said.

Frost grinned. "That's right! I forgot that school rule handout mentioned a winter dance. So we're going together?"

"Yep!" Ren said. "Then we can dress up and have tons of fun!"

The minute-bell rang, and the students hurried to the muggy Greenhouse. Sarala kept sending glares at Frost, wishing he'd just leave her friend alone. But Ren didn't seem to mind his hand on her shoulder as they entered the thicket of plants, nor how he kept talking about himself.

She must have all the patience in the world to put up with that arrogant idiot, Sarala thought irritably. *If that fool bragged about himself to me all day, I'd just punch him in the face. That'd mess up his looks and give him one less thing to brag about, at least...*

As was usual, the class was studying plants. They were almost halfway through the first floor of the Greenhouse, but there were still so many plants to cover. There were even bushes and flowers that grew on the trees, so they'd have to climb up to the other levels to take a look at those plants too.

The class was getting repetitive with drawing plants and listening to lectures on those plants. Though most of the class still found these sessions to be interesting, Sarala was growing bored of them. She would usually scribble a few words she heard and copy Ren's work later. But this time, she was completely distracted, watching Ren and Frost several feet away.

She shook her head and stared out the window to the forest bordering the school, forcing her thoughts to the tree walking near the glasshouse instead.

I wonder…

Sarala was eager for Kung Fu class that afternoon. She had already learned all of her yellow sash material, and she was quite confident that she'd be able to test for her green sash. She often practiced during her free days, doing more Kung Fu than homework despite the heavy workload they would receive.

Ak-tu started the class, breaking the students into two groups: white sashes and yellow sashes. The yellow sashes were gaining more members each week, as the last white sashes tested.

"Does any white sash want to test today?" Ak-tu asked the remaining white sashes.

Zyn and Ren, both still white sashes, stepped forward. "We will!" they said in unison.

"Excellent. Anyone else?" Ak-tu asked.

"I do," Sarala said boldly as she approached, straightening the yellow sash tied around her uniform vest.

Ak-tu glanced over at her in surprise. "You've only been working on the yellow sash material for a few weeks. It typically takes a few months," he told her.

"I want to test," she repeated, clenching her jaw.

Ak-tu shrugged. "Anyone has the chance to test, so long as they know all of their material. I'll test these two for now. Practice your material in the meantime."

Sarala nodded and hurried to one of the private training rooms off the large mat, leaving the door partially open so she could listen to what was happening beyond. While Ak-tu tested the twins, Khurshid—the assistant teacher in the Kung Fu classes—taught the yellow sashes their new material. Not all students had to listen to Khurshid though, and some went to train on their own. Each of the students were able to approach Ak-tu or Khurshid at any point if they had questions.

Sarala practiced her kicks and self-defense techniques for about ten minutes until Ak-tu called her name. Sweaty and panting lightly, she left the room to see that Zyn and Ren now had yellow sashes gleaming around their waists. The sisters beamed at her as the other students applauded them.

"Are you still wishing to test?" Ak-tu asked Sarala.

"Yes," she said firmly.

"Then, let's begin," Ak-tu said.

Sarala nodded and took her place on one side of the large mat, which was reserved for tests when they occurred. She bowed to Ak-tu—as was custom to open the test—then waited for him.

"Wheel kick," Ak-tu ordered.

Tests started with the current level of kicks. She performed the seven kicks required at that level, putting extra snap behind each strike like she was kicking down a door for each. Once she was done, she stood feet together to wait for the next instruction.

"First half of techniques," Ak-tu said briskly.

Sarala nodded, knowing she'd have two chances for each technique. The techniques put her in specific scenarios—such as a chokehold or an opponent trying to kick her while she was on the floor—which she had to defend against and then take down the pretend opponent.

Sarala imagined a red-clad enemy in front of her the entire time, spiking her adrenaline so she could perform the combinations hastily and with as much power as she could muster. Everything was done in the air, as Ak-tu didn't use the blocker bat or mitts like he did for the white-to-yellow tests.

"You can take a water break now, if you'd like," Ak-tu told her as she stood at the ready once more.

"I'm fine," Sarala panted heavily, sweat pouring down her skin like she had just gone swimming.

"Very well. Show me your form."

The yellow sash level was different from the white sash level in that it also had a hand form added onto the techniques and kicks. Forms were like several self-defense techniques put together, with repeated motions to have students practice the same thing continuously to master the strikes. The yellow sash form was a series of straight strikes and blocks linked together, with a few kicks.

Sarala performed it, now panting so much that she didn't know if she'd pass out. Ak-tu gave her a small break before she moved onto the second half of the techniques, for which she was grateful despite not wanting it.

After she was done with the next techniques (which had a little less power than before, her muscles now screaming at her to slow down), she showed off her six white sash level kicks. The students had to perform each kick they learned on their tests, no matter what level they were. The last kicks nearly took it out of her, though. Her lungs screeched in pain, and her breaths rattled in her chest.

"Get your kickboxing gear on," Ak-tu told her briskly. "Frost! You too. You'll be sparring Sarala."

Sarala forgot how tired she was the moment she heard Frost's name. If her body didn't feel so numb, she might have smiled at the opportunity to strike him down. Wondering briefly if Ak-tu also didn't like Frost dating Ren, she hurried to the closet.

She grabbed her sparring gear (which was kept in a pink bag with her name on it), pulling it on over her uniform and pushing past Frost as she returned to the big mat. Frost darted in and out of the closet for his gear too, looking excited that he was going to help out with the first green sash test.

No matter what Ak-tu's intentions might've been for setting up Sarala with Frost, he was a good opponent for her. Both of them were broad-shouldered and had good power behind their strikes. Sarala eyed the boy as they lined up across from each other in the center of the mat, both holding their gloved fists up at the ready.

"You two know the rules from our Kung Fu 1B class," Ak-tu said. "Hit to the chest protector only. Don't hit each other too hard. Now bow to each other and tap gloves. You have two minutes. Go!"

Sarala darted forward, lifting her left leg to throw a snap kick at Frost. He blocked the kick, but she had intended for that to happen. As her leg was cast to the side, she slammed her fist into Frost's chest. The air was knocked out of him and he staggered back.

But she didn't give him any time to recover. Ignoring Ak-tu's second rule, she pummeled Frost with punch after punch, throwing in a kick or two when she remembered. The power sent rippling vibrations up her arms and coursing through her body, encouraging her to hit even harder with the next strike and the next.

She didn't give Frost much chance to do anything but block, throwing her punches as quickly as she could. She was rapidly out of breath, but she kept forcing herself all the same. If she stepped back, she knew Frost would be upon her, throwing his own strikes —and he'd knock the remaining air out of her.

"And time!" Ak-tu called out loudly, throwing a mitt between the kickboxers.

Sarala staggered away from Frost, completely out of breath. Her chest ached so badly, she thought her lungs had been pierced. A painful stitch had formed in her side, making her wonder if she'd somehow bruised her ribs on one of Frost's blocks. The squishy mat glistened with her sweat, which might as well have been the size of the pond in the Courtyard.

"Bow to each other to close up the match," Ak-tu said.

Sarala and Frost bowed once more, tapping their gloves.

"Good job," Frost grunted.

Sarala was too weary to speak.

"Now close the test with me, Sarala." Sarala bowed to Ak-tu, who returned the action. "Gear down. And please—get a drink of water."

Sarala returned to the closet. She peeled the sweaty gloves clinging to her hands, then took off her helmet, chest protector, and groin guard. She nearly forgot to take the shin guards off, until Frost reminded her as he took off his own.

"Next time, hit lighter," he added, as she left the closet.

Sarala was soon standing before Ak-tu once more, still sweaty and breathing heavily. Ak-tu surveyed her calmly for a minute before speaking.

"You have definitely been working hard the past few weeks. I don't think I've ever held a second test so quickly. I admire your determination and hard work, but don't rush through the next level. I expect at least one month of training before you beg for another test."

I didn't beg! Sarala thought indignantly.

"You fought hard in the sparring match, but I do ask that you tone down your power a bit," Ak-tu continued. "You need to focus more on moving around and being tricky, throwing more fakes and kicks. But you did well.

"Take a step back. I've got a new sash for you," Ak-tu said, smiling.

Sarala stepped back as Ak-tu came closer. She untied her yellow sash from around her waist, almost forgetting about this part of the ceremony. She then took off the sash and folded it as neatly as she could, her fingers trembling the whole time. With the tips pointing to the right, she handed the sash to Ak-tu with both hands.

Ak-tu took the yellow sash and pocketed it in his robe, then took a green sash from a different pocket. He waited for her to bow to him again, before passing the sash to her. She tied the green sash around her waist, her hands still fumbling in her exhaustion. At long last, she had it tied. Ak-tu then bowed to her, and she quickly mirrored the action.

The other students applauded her, Ren and Zyn the loudest amongst them. Sarala grinned around at them all, proud that she had leveled up—and beat up Frost a bit along the way.

CHAPTER 15: ACTION THIS DAY

The semester pressed on, time seeming to fly once the leaves had fallen from the trees. Freezing snow fell in heavy heaps, blanketing the Courtyard in glistening white. The students wore thick winter robes, and were often seen drinking hot cocoa for each meal.

Most students were also seen with their noses in their books on a frequent basis. As test week approached, more and more students were getting anxious. Some students broke down completely and went to the Healing room to get a soothing potion from Fern in order to finish studying their notes. Others practiced their magic so much that they ended up getting weaker or even sick from overuse, causing their magic to block off temporarily.

Ren, Zyn, and Sarala studied together as often as they could. But even this was a difficult task. They still had to write essays, practice their magic, and work on their martial arts. On top of that, Ren and Zyn had to rehearse for Theatre, where the test would be putting on a show at the end of the week. Ren was no longer trying to help Zyn summon her magic, like she had been for most of the semester; she was simply too busy.

Zyn had also given up with her magic. She was now focused on remembering important names and dates for Magic Studies, and how to identify plants. If she couldn't perform magic, then she'd at least try to pass the classes that didn't require as much magic. Zyn seemed to be getting better with Kung Fu and Tai Chi too, grasping the subjects now that she no longer cared about the magic situation.

Ak-tu thankfully didn't ask either twin about Zyn's magic again, but that could've been because he was also busy grading homework and getting tests prepared.

Ren was glad to see Zyn putting more focus on her other studies, but she was still worried about her sister. The two seemed to be drifting apart, especially as they were so busy getting their work done and didn't have much time to talk.

In addition to that, Ren tried to spend at least one day with Frost, though she wasn't enjoying her time with him. The only reason she didn't break up with him was due to how much easier it'd be to go along with it in the meantime. Both of them were dealing with copious amounts of homework, and didn't need anything added onto it. There was also the upcoming Moonlight Dance, and Ren didn't want to go without a partner. A part of her hoped that she and Frost would actually get along well once they were at the dance together, and not struggling through homework. But another part of her just wanted to break up with him and be done with it.

December 14 soon arrived. The first-years trudged through the falling snow to the Magic Studies classroom for their first test after breakfast that Moonday morning.

Khurshid was waiting for them, wearing a long-sleeved robe. The students took their usual places and sat at attention, each of them anxious; some students were shivering, though Ren couldn't tell if it was due to apprehension or the frigid room.

"Good morning," Khurshid said in his calm voice. "As you know, today is your test day! You will be taking a written test. The test should not take you the entire class. I ask that, when you are done, you leave the classroom and go to the Magic Channeling room."

Each of the students nodded to his words.

"You will be taking your tests on these mirrors," Khurshid continued, motioning to a box on the front desk. "I have to listen to the tests in order to grade them. The mirrors are locked on the test only, so don't try to access the air-net or some other app to cheat. Come get a mirror, and you may begin."

The students did as he told them, grabbing a mirror from the box. They were already open on the tests. Khurshid probably had Ak-tu or one of the other teachers get the test together and the mirrors locked.

Ren got to work right away. The test only contained twenty multiple choice questions, which were fairly easy after all the studying she'd done. The last five questions were essay-based, but only required short responses. It was a simple test, and she finished it rather quickly. She clicked on the "Submit" button after making sure she'd typed her name in the box at the top. Then she put the mirror on the front desk, like a few of the other students had done, and left the room.

Ren entered the Magic Channeling classroom next door, wondering what Khurshid would have them do. More students joined her in the room, until the whole class appeared. C3 was the last one to enter, probably due to double-checking all of his answers or writing so many details.

Khurshid came in after him. "Now, for this class, we'll actually be going outside, two at a time," he told the students gathered before him. "We will be doing the obstacle course challenge again, but with a twist.

"This time, one of you will be making the obstacle course, just like how we've been practicing for the past few weeks. But then the other person will have to try to get *through* the obstacle course."

The students gasped, all of them looking over at Sarala in fear. Sarala's obstacle course had grown more brutal with each class session. None of them fancied going up against her. She seemed unbothered by the fact that everyone had inched away from her.

"You won't be going into the obstacle course totally defenseless," Khurshid went on. "You are allowed to use your wand, to summon the elements around you to help you out. You can even summon the magic from within you, if you're able to manage it. You don't have to use your wand, and can rely purely on your body to wield magic. I just want you to use magic to get across the obstacle course."

Ren raised her hand. "Mr. Jihan?"

"Yes, Ren?"

"Do we have to do both parts? Setting the obstacle course *and* getting through it?"

"No," Khurshid said. "You will only have to do one or the other. But you must use magic, no matter which one you do."

"Do we get to choose who to go with?" Sarala asked.

Khurshid smiled. "My mirror has already chosen a randomized list. The first name will be the student setting the obstacle course, and the second name will be the student going through it."

And with that, he had the mirror read out the first two names: Ebony and Frost. Khurshid then led the way from the room, back to the freezing Courtyard with the pair of chosen students. It had at least stopped snowing for the moment.

Some of the students pressed against the window to watch the duo outside. However, their breath fogged the glass quickly, that they could not see anything. Most of the students resorted to pulling their personal mirrors from their robe pockets and going over notes for Plants and Potions. Others practiced a bit more magic.

{*How am I supposed to get through this test?*} Zyn asked Ren.

Ren frowned, only having a lame suggestion to offer: {*Just try to summon your magic again?*}

Zyn shrugged beside her. {*I guess there's no harm in giving it another attempt. I haven't tried in a few days. And if magic is supposed to be a defense mechanism, it might finally be triggered!*} Zyn added, her echoing voice sounding a lot happier in Ren's mind.

{*That's the spirit! You got this!*} Ren encouraged her. {*Your magic will come in no time!*}

Frost and Ebony returned in a swirl of chilly wind, their skin tinged blue. Frost looked a bit shaken, but otherwise appeared fine for going through Ebony's obstacle course. Ebony's magic wasn't too powerful, so Frost probably had an easy time of it.

Khurshid poked his head in. "Ren and Sarala," he announced.

Ren let out a small sigh of relief; she would be the one setting the obstacle course for Sarala, not the other way around. She and Sarala exited the classroom, closing the door behind them. A shiver ran down Ren's spine, and she began trembling uncontrollably.

Stop it! she ordered herself as they took their places. *Focus on the obstacle course!*

Ren lifted her wand and commanded her wall of air to appear at the start of the obstacle course, right in front of Sarala. Yet Sarala had studied Ren's course plenty of times by now, and she merely lifted a rock wall to halt the rush of air. Sarala then scampered away, hurrying into the crisscrossing tornadoes Ren conjured up.

But Sarala got through these easily too. She lifted more stones from beneath the snow, which stopped the air in its tracks. Ren was glad that she wasn't hurting her friend, but she also wanted her obstacle course to be more challenging.

"Air slides!" she commanded sharply.

About ten different slides appeared in the air above Sarala. One of them sucked her up with a slurping sound, and Ren ordered her magic to whisk Sarala back to the beginning of the course. Yet Sarala again escaped by raising the earth beneath her and cutting off the air flow.

Ren gritted her teeth in annoyance. If her magic was so strong, why couldn't she keep Sarala from advancing? She flicked her wand, summoning the giant tornado at the end of the course. This tornado was more powerful than the small swirls of wind, and it was not so easily defeated.

Sarala lifted the earth in front of her and attempted to push it forward as a shield. But the tornado was too strong and forced her back. She then tried to make a tall earth wall, yet she only succeeded in keeping herself from advancing. Finally, Sarala pointed her wand at the ground, opened a hole, and hopped down. Ren stopped her tornado as she saw Sarala pop up on the other side, over the finish line.

"She's definitely resourceful," she muttered under her breath, not expecting Sarala to easily escape.

Ren and Sarala returned to the class, once receiving full marks from Khurshid. Ren was relieved that she wouldn't have to make it through anyone else's obstacle course, feeling worn out after creating powerful wind bursts in the bitter cold.

The rest of the students continued to be called outside, Ren still shivering in the drafty room. Zyn was getting antsy waiting around, but she wasn't summoned at all. In fact, she was soon the only student who had yet to go.

Khurshid entered the room again. "Now, we have twenty-one students here, so the odd number means one of you will have to go again, with our last student," he said. "Zyn, you will be going with Sarala. Sarala, as you have already gone through the obstacle course, you will be recreating your own for Zyn to fight through."

Ren's heart skipped a beat. Zyn's eyes widened in shock. The whole room seemed to be more frozen than the snow outside. Everyone stared at Zyn like she had just been sentenced to death. Even Sarala was horrified.

"Come on!" Khurshid said. "This is the last test!"

Ren followed Zyn and Sarala out of the classroom, crunching through the snow in a bit of a frenzy. There was no way she could let Zyn face Sarala's obstacle course alone!

{Don't do any magic for me.} Zyn told Ren, as if she knew what Ren was thinking.

{But Sarala's course is so dangerous! Did you not see those spiky stones? She'll kill you!}

{Maybe it will finally trigger my magic!} Zyn replied, glancing over her shoulder at her sister. *{It will trigger my magic!}*

Ren did not have any time to argue the point more. She watched as Zyn reached the start of the obstacle course, Sarala just behind her.

"Sarala, please tone down your obstacle course," Khurshid said. "Make it so Zyn can feel the rocks coming before they hit her, so she at least has a chance to get out of the way. Of course, Zyn," he added, turning to Zyn, "you could always use your air magic to propel you over the rocks—like you're flying."

Zyn frowned, looking doubtful.

"Ready, you two? Go!"

At once, Sarala raised a stone wall in front of Zyn. Zyn was at least expecting this after watching her menacing course several times, and she dodged around it before it slammed into her.

But then Sarala ordered the ground to shake, and some of the stone turned into pebbles that darted beneath Zyn's feet. Zyn tried to prance over them, but combined with the ice, she slipped and fell.

"Use your air magic!" Khurshid yelled out to her.

Zyn scrambled across the pebbles on all fours, her wand tucked away inside her snowflake-patterned robe. She finally managed to make it through, and Sarala stopped the vibrations, the pebbles returning into the ground.

"Remember to give Zyn a warning," Khurshid told Sarala.

Sarala nodded. She pointed her wand at different parts of the ground, commanding the earth to shake before shooting up.

When the first stone rose from the ground, it wasn't as sharp as before; in fact, it was quite blunt. Ren was relieved, but the rock would still hurt Zyn if it smashed into her.

Yet Zyn had gotten plenty of warnings and managed to get through the section of rising stones easily. She still showed no signs of magic, but at least she would survive the obstacle course.

"Punching wall!" Sarala ordered briskly.

The final challenge rose in front of Zyn just before the finish line. Punching at her, the stone soon caught her directly in the chest. It sent her flying back, the air getting knocked out of her.

"ZYN!" Ren shrieked, her hands flying to her mouth. "Are you okay?"

Zyn didn't answer, but she got to her feet after a moment.

"Use your air magic to propel you over the wall!" Khurshid shouted.

Zyn didn't show any sign that she had heard him. After all, his advice was useless. She eyed the wall from a distance for a moment, watching as it punched forward. Zyn then hurried towards it, keeping her body bladed so she wouldn't be hit squarely in the chest again. But the wall slammed her once more before she could do whatever she had been attempting.

{Zyn, try your wand again! Your life is in danger! Your magic will come! Remember when you faced Dad? Maybe it didn't come because you didn't have a wand to help you. But now you have a wand, so use it!} Ren practically screamed at Zyn through her mind.

Zyn took her wand from her robe pocket and pointed it at the wall. Running forward again, she was only struck down. She repeated the process, as if hoping her magic would suddenly leap forward, that her wand would take command to help her out.

Her magic's not coming, Ren thought to herself. *I need to do something! I have to do the magic for her, or—*

Ren turned to Khurshid, unaware that tears had been streaming down her freckled cheeks.

"You have to stop this!" Ren urged him. "Please!"

But then Zyn suddenly stepped on the punching bits of wall, and climbed up them like a staircase. She threw herself over the top of the wall and made it past the finish line. Ren stared in wide-eyed astonishment, hardly able to believe that her sister had made it through—without magic.

Sarala let the wall drop at once, and the two hurried over to Zyn, Khurshid following more slowly.

"Zyn! Are you okay?" Ren shouted, not caring that she slipped over the ice numerous times. "Zyn?"

Zyn was laying on the snow, not moving. Ren dropped beside her sister, the tears falling once more. She grabbed Zyn's shoulders with her stiff hands and turned her around, so she could see her properly. Zyn blinked up at her in a daze, her face tinted blue.

"Are you okay?" Ren choked out, dragging Zyn up into a seated position.

Zyn winced, her ragged breaths coming out as puffs of warm fog. "I…I think so. But…I didn't do any magic, did I?"

Khurshid reached them at last. "No, you did not," he said simply. "And for that, I'm afraid I can only give you a half-pass. Truthfully, I should fail you completely, but you put in hard work in a difficult course. I have to give you some credit."

Zyn hung her head.

"Why didn't you use your magic?" Khurshid inquired.

"She just felt a bit sick today," Ren lied at once. "You can't do magic properly if you're sick—if at all. Plus it's a hard test, and she was nervous for it, as anyone *should* be!"

Khurshid frowned at this. "True," he said slowly. "But even sick or anxious students who attempt magic are able to make something happen, more often than not."

"We all have bad days," Sarala grumbled, toeing the snow with her boot.

Khurshid sighed. "I suppose that's true as well," he conceded. "Well, Zyn, I ask that you work harder next semester. Go to the Greenhouse, you three. That course took longer than it should have and—"

The minute-bell rang.

"Exactly my point," Khurshid commented.

Ren helped Zyn to her feet. "Are you okay, Zyn?" she repeated. "Can you walk?"

Zyn nodded, but still seemed dazed. She leaned a bit against Ren as the trio crossed the Courtyard to get to the Greenhouse.

They barely made it when the final bell rang. The Greenhouse was much warmer than the Courtyard, the windows shut for the winter season.

Much to the class's delight, they would be taking another multiple choice test, identifying plants and the types of properties they had. The class sat down beneath different trees and used the school-owned mirrors to take their tests, while Fern paced around like a tiger to make sure they weren't cheating.

The test was more difficult than the Magic Studies test had been, especially the questions asking how to identify a plant by taste or smell. Yet Ren still thought she did a decent job. She was happy that it was another written test, so Zyn had a chance to pass.

The first-years then crossed the Courtyard to the Potions room with Fern when everyone was done. The room was frigid when they entered, especially after they had grown accustomed to the warm Greenhouse, but it would soon heat up once they lit the row of cauldrons.

"This test is a bit different from the potions we've been making all semester," Fern told the shivering students. "You will be working in pairs instead of individually. However, one of you will work alone. The recipe will be a bit simpler for the lone student. Any volunteers?"

C3 raised his hand at once.

"Very well," Fern said, nodding to him. "Two to a cauldron, with the exception of C3. There is a different recipe on each desk. Call me over once you have finished."

The students broke off to form pairs at once. Ren saw Frost headed her way, but she went to stand beside Zyn. Sarala got stuck with Frost, and it was clear she hated the fact by the way she clenched her jaw and tensed her broad shoulders. But Ren was still worried about her sister, and wanted to make sure she'd pass the test.

"Ooh, an invisibility potion," Ren said, eyeing the recipe card on the desk Zyn had chosen.

"Should be fun," Zyn commented.

"Hmm...it says that the water needs to heat up before we put any ingredients in," Ren murmured, scanning the recipe quickly.

"You go ahead and grab the ingredients from the storage room, while I heat up the water."

Zyn nodded and took the recipe with her. There was a storage room on the right side of the classroom, where many plant ingredients (and some crystals) were kept. Ren watched her go, wondering if she should use the class time to speak to Zyn privately.

No…we need to concentrate on what we're doing, she told herself. She turned on the blaze beneath the cauldron sitting beside the table. *Zyn can't afford another half-pass, or worse.*

By the time Zyn returned with the ingredients, the cauldron water was boiling. The sisters set to work. Ren read out the instructions, while Zyn prepped the ingredients. Some of the plants had to be trimmed to a certain size, while others had to be thinly-cut. The plants also had to be an exact weight, so Ren put them on her scale before adding them to the cauldron. Since Zyn was doing most of the preparation, Ren took it upon herself to stir.

The room soon smelled sweet and rancid at the same time, some potions mixing together well and others burning. A few cries sometimes stirred the pungent air, but the twins ignored this as they worked.

It was quickly apparent why they had to work in pairs for this test. The ingredients needed so much preparation and the potion required so much stirring. Ren's arm was getting tired, and she didn't look forward to doing martial arts that afternoon with a dead arm. She switched her grip and which hand was stirring so many times, but it did not help her aching muscles.

Once the potion was a purple hue, all Ren had to do was enchant it. But enchanting a potion required more than just waving a wand over it and adding elemental magic. The sisters had to come up with a rhyme for the enchantment to work—something that Fern never gave away with the recipe.

"What rhymes with 'invisible'?" Ren asked.

"Divisible?" Zyn suggested.

"Hmm…how about invisibility?"

"Tranquility, stability, humility?"

Ren scrawled out a line on the piece of paper in front of her, muttering, "Enchant this potion so that everything it touches is cloaked in invisibility. Only reverse when there is true tranquility."

Zyn shook her head. "That'll never work. What if a setting never becomes tranquil?"

Ren snorted softly. "It could be tranquil if everyone falls asleep," she pointed out.

"What if the person is having nightmares?" scoffed Zyn.

Ren was glad her sister seemed to be having fun. "Well, what do you think, then?"

Zyn bent forward, taking the pencil from Ren to scrawl something different. Ren read it upside-down as she wrote it out.

"Enchant this invisibility potion, only reversing when there is no more motion." Ren considered that for a moment, then nodded. "I like it. So if someone becomes too still, the invisibility would wear off?"

Zyn nodded. "Exactly!"

"Okay. Let's hope it works!" Ren said. She pulled out her wand and hovered it over the cauldron, then said clearly, "Enchant this invisibility potion, only reversing when there is no more motion."

A swirl of wind entered the potion, turning the purple color darker. Ren and Zyn glanced at one another, beaming. The darker a potion, the stronger it was.

Once Fern finished looking at C3's potion, Zyn called loudly for her. She approached them and looked down at the cauldron.

"Invisibility?" she asked them, and they nodded. "Hmm...it's certainly got a good coloration to it. And what was the enchantment you used?"

Ren and Zyn repeated the rhyme in unison.

Fern nodded. "You failed to say *how* the potion would work in the first place. Does it make a drinker invisible, or any object it touches? Let's test it."

Ren kicked herself mentally. She had lost points on the last potion she had made after she didn't specify the drinker from any object. She bit her bottom lip nervously, hoping they'd still pass.

Fern dipped a long ladle into the cauldron and held it up. She poured some of it onto one of her tattooed hands. Her hand turned invisible, and she moved her arm around, clearly waving her hand. She then allowed her entire body to fall still. After a few moments, her hand reappeared.

She then drank the rest of the potion in the ladle. She turned entirely invisible, vanishing on the spot! Ren and Zyn exchanged an eager glance as she reappeared a minute later.

"Excellent work, you two," Fern told them. "Who came up with the enchantment?"

Zyn raised her hand. "Me!"

"Be more specific," Fern told her. "But considering this works both ways, it's a good potion. I'll be adding it to my collection."

"So it's a pass?" Ren asked.

Fern nodded, offering them a rare smile. "I only take the best potions into my stock."

Ren cheered and hugged Zyn. "We did it!"

"Just out of curiosity," Fern said, her face becoming serious once more, "who *cast* the enchantment?"

"I did," Ren said with a frown.

Fern nodded slowly and walked away.

{Do you think she knows I can't do magic?} Zyn asked.

Ren let go of Zyn. *I can't tell them that the teachers already talked to Dad about this…can I?* She shook her head and settled on a partial truth. *{I'm sure the teachers have noticed something's been up with your magic… But who knows if they* actually *know?}*

Zyn sighed softly beside her.

They got to leave the class once they turned off the fire under their cauldron and cleaned their table, leaving the potion where it was for Fern to collect later. The twins then headed to the Eating Hall together, forcing their way through mounds of snow and whipping wind.

{Zyn, now that we're done with the class…are you doing okay? Like—for real?} Ren asked her sister. *{You were really dazed after you fell off that wall.}*

{Well, I fell down. What do you expect? I don't like heights, and while that wall wasn't too high, it was still high enough to get hurt from.}

{Did you get hurt?} Ren asked in alarm. *{Did you break a bone or anything? You could have told Fern at the start of Plants!}*

{No, I think I just have a bunch of bruises. It's no big deal.}

Ren frowned, but followed her sister into the Eating Hall, which was thankfully warm and smelled much more pleasant than the Potion classroom. The two staggered over to the counter, which didn't have a line yet since the bell hadn't rung. They gathered their food and sat down at a table near the door. A few more students arrived early, including a few from the Potions class. But Sarala still hadn't arrived, so Ren decided to push Zyn a bit more.

{*Are we…falling apart?*} Ren queried Zyn after a brief hesitation.

Zyn looked up at her. "Why would you ask that?"

Ren reverted to speaking aloud too. "I just feel like you're keeping something from me. And with all the schoolwork we've had to do lately…well, we've hardly been hanging out. I know that's my fault too, since I hang out with Frost. But still. I feel that there's this…ice…between us."

"It's Frost, you literally just said it," Zyn chuckled.

Ren snorted, then became more solemn-faced. "But, seriously…did I do something wrong?"

Zyn sighed, the smile dropping from her lips. "I just…realized something that I didn't really realize before…. And…I don't know what it means."

"What is it?" Ren asked, leaning forward. "It's…oh, Zyn, it's not something to do with *me*, is it? I'm really—"

"It is definitely not you," Zyn said flatly, holding up her hand. "Well, the Frost thing is kinda annoying, but this…this is something else. And I want to figure it out first."

"Does it have something to do with your magic? If you tell me, I can help," she offered.

But Zyn shook her head. "I don't think so. Well, maybe it does. I dunno."

Before Ren could ask anything more of her, the door banged open loudly. Snow was thrown inside with the chilly winds as Sarala entered. She saw Ren and Zyn nearby and stomped over to them, almost as if she was causing the blizzard outside herself.

"Frost made us *fail*!" she seethed, plopping down on the bench beside Zyn and shaking the whole table.

Ren gasped, her hand flying over her mouth. "He *didn't*!"

"He *did*," Sarala muttered grimly. "After all the work *I* put into that potion, he made up the stupidest rhyme and it didn't work. And he enchanted it before I could do anything. He's so useless!

You better break up with him, Ren."

Ren bit her bottom lip. "Um…what does me dating him have to do with anything?"

"Nothing," Sarala muttered. "But if I have to see Frost again, I'll punch his stupid face!"

At that precise moment, Frost had entered the Eating Hall. He heard Sarala's words, stared at Ren for a long moment, then backed out into the Courtyard.

The rest of their lunch was spoiled by Sarala's nasty mood. In an attempt to get Sarala to lighten up (and so they wouldn't be late), Ren beckoned them to follow her to the Kung Fu Studio. They got there early and changed into their uniforms, then sat on the orange mat.

Sarala seemed to be in a better mood once they were inside the studio. The trio chatted and played a few games of YAT before the minute-bell rang, bringing plenty of the first-year students with it.

Ak-tu and Khurshid entered the studio last. Each student wondered what sort of test they'd have to take for Kung Fu, especially the few who had just leveled up to yellow or green sash.

"Hello, everyone!" Ak-tu said cheerfully, pulling the door shut with a bit of wind magic. "I know you've had a busy morning taking tests. The good news is that there are no tests for this class—unless you'd like to test for the next level. Just get to work on your current level's material otherwise! Next class, we'll be doing kickboxing and grappling matches nonstop as your 'test'—but it's nothing formal that you have to win to pass. Just put in the effort, and you'll be good to go!"

"Should we try testing for green sash?" Ren asked Zyn as they got to their feet.

Zyn shrugged. "I'm not sure if I'm ready yet. I think I got the form mostly down, but I still have trouble with sliding my feet correctly. And my body hurts from Magic Channeling."

"Yeah…maybe you shouldn't test, Zyn. I'm not sure I have the balance for my kicks, either," Ren commented.

"There's no harm in trying," Ak-tu said, winking at them.

"Is that a challenge?" Zyn asked loudly, grinning.

"Is it?" Ak-tu questioned, smirking.

"I ACCEPT YOUR CHALLENGE! TEST ME!" Zyn yowled, causing everyone to wince or glare at her.

Ren snorted. "Test me too, then!"

"And me!" Sarala said.

Ak-tu glanced over at her. "You already want to test for blue?"

"Yes."

Ak-tu rolled his eyes. "Sarala, you're moving a bit fast. But…if you think you can handle it, then that's on you. Anyone else?"

A few more students agreed to test for their green sash, as none of the other green sashes had learned enough to move up to their blue sash.

Ren, Zyn, Mernao, Scarlet Jay, and Midnight Abhain stepped forward to test first. It was more convenient to test multiple students at a time, so they each bowed to Ak-tu to open up the test.

The five students were soon doing kick after kick, demonstrating techniques, and showing off their forms. Once they were done with their white sash kicks, they hurried to the closet to grab their individual sparring gear. They put the gear on and returned to the mat. Ren got to spar with Midnight, Zyn went with Mernao, and Midnight went again with Scarlet. Once the kickboxing matches were done, they geared down and returned to the mat for Ak-tu's feedback, covered in sweat and panting.

"Ren, you have good form, but you tend to lean too much into the strike," Ak-tu began. "You also need to work on the balance for your kicks. Remember that good balance comes from keeping your head upright, your eyes locked on something that's not moving, and having a slight bend in your supporting leg.

"Zynivus, your stances still need to be worked on. You are putting too much weight on your toes, which is bad for the knees. Keep more weight on your heels, and make sure your heels are pressed all the way to the ground. The heels should only come up when you're turning on the balls of your feet."

He continued to critique the others, then stepped back to observe them all for a moment. Each student was left wondering if they had done enough to pass their test. Ak-tu wouldn't allow students to continue if they were lacking the skills he was looking for at the particular level.

If Ren lacked balance and Zyn's stances weren't correct, Ren truly wondered if their father would allow them to advance to the next level. Mernao, Scarlet, and Midnight had all been at the yellow sash longer than the twins, and their Kung Fu looked better (especially Mernao, who was determined to train harder after he failed his test the previous week).

"Congratulations, you five," Ak-tu said at last. "You have all passed to the green sash level."

The students around them applauded as they took off their old yellow sashes and tied on the new green sashes Ak-tu passed out. Ren beamed at her sister, then they hugged.

"You green sashes can take a break for the remainder of class," Ak-tu said, smiling around at them. "There's no point in learning new material that you'll forget during winter break. You may watch Sarala test."

Sarala glanced over at them from the other side of the room, where she had been practicing her form, her skin already slick with sweat. Her jaw clenched, but she didn't protest to the others watching. She instead stepped forward alone, as the new green sashes moved aside. Sarala then bowed to Ak-tu to open up the blue sash test.

The green sash level added yet more kicks, new techniques, and a second form containing advanced blocks. It took the remainder of the class time for Sarala to get through the test, which included a grappling match at the end (with Raimugi, who was an excellent grappler). The bell rang for class's end, right as the grappling match stopped. Since Sarala didn't require any gear for the match, all she needed to do was put her uniform top back on over her plain black shirt and retie her green sash around her waist. Appearing a lot less winded than her last test, she waited for Ak-tu's feedback, the entire class now listening in.

"You have performed another good test," Ak-tu said. "This now marks three tests in the span of about four months. Your balance was a bit wobbly and sometimes you were striking to the incorrect levels. I would like you to pay more attention to the details. Otherwise, I will not pass you again in the future."

He was silent for a long moment, then smiled. "But congratulations, Sarala. You passed the blue sash test!"

Ren cheered loudly for her friend. {*It's so great that Sarala's a natural with Kung Fu!}*

{Yeah!} Zyn replied in amusement. *{She's so good at it!}*

They watched the sash ceremony, nobody caring that the second Kung Fu class had technically started. Once Sarala had the blue sash tied around her waist, they applauded once more. Sarala smiled a full smile—her teeth were even showing! Ren couldn't help herself and ran forward to hug her friend before Ak-tu was finished speaking to her.

"As you are now a blue sash," Ak-tu said, trying to keep the amusement from his voice, "you will be enrolled in the Kung Fu 2 classes on Trizday, starting spring semester. I expect you to take your time and work harder to earn your next sashes."

"Yes, Mr. Caihong," Sarala said, her smile dropping.

"Don't you dare stop smiling!" Ren scolded her. "You've got such a beautiful smile!"

Sarala stared at her a long moment, then laughed. But the girls couldn't chortle for too long, as they soon had to gear up for sparring.

For the next thirty minutes, Ak-tu had four kickboxing matches going at the same time. Once the two minutes were up, the next eight people would step forward to do their matches. The matches (and the stench of sweaty bodies) seemed to be never-ending.

After kickboxing was over with, they moved onto grappling matches. Ak-tu again had four matches running at once, Khurshid helping him keep an "eye" on the students. By the time the class ended, Ren felt extremely weary. She didn't know if she'd be able to do Tai Chi with how sore her muscles were.

But she, Zyn, and C3 pushed through Tai Chi, where the three tested for their green fringe together. The 24-Step was a form split in half between the white and yellow fringe levels. They only had to perform the first half to get their yellow fringe earlier in the semester, as well as four of the qigong exercises known as the Eight Brocades. At the yellow fringe level, they learned the second half of the form and the rest of the brocades. For their test, they only had to show off the last four brocades (instead of all eight, like they thought they'd need to), and the entire 24-Step. They did push hands to finish off the test (each of them had shaky arms as they attempted to push one another over), then were rewarded with their green fringes.

"Next semester, we start with learning the 40-Step!" Ak-tu announced, once they had tied their green fringes around their waists. "Now, as a bonus, you three don't have to worry about doing any other push hands matches. Go ahead and take the rest of the day off, and get ready for your Art tests on Freday."

"Thanks, Dad!" Ren said gratefully, thinking her arms would fall off by this point.

"Yeah, thanks!" Zyn cheered.

C3 looked disappointed as he left the Tai Chi Studio, but they paid no attention to him. The twins turned to the tower door, unlocking it and entering their home. Ak-tu didn't follow them in, instead walking off to the snowy Courtyard. Sarala was in the family room, sitting on the couch.

"You're back early," she remarked. "Got your green fringes?"

"Yep!" Zyn said, grinning as she held up the stringy tail of her fringe.

"So now you're green in both martial arts."

Ren nodded. "Oh, this is so exciting! We did good on our tests today, didn't we?"

Sarala shrugged. "Apart from that disastrous potion…"

"I didn't do as bad as I thought I would, either," Zyn said, smiling over at Ren. "I mean, I don't know about Magic Studies or Plants, but I felt like I did a fine job on the tests. Magic Channeling was a fail from the start, but martial arts went good! Maybe… maybe I don't need magic after all."

Ren blinked in surprise. "Is this the thing you were talking about earlier? The realization?"

Zyn shook her head. "No…but now, it might be one."

Ren frowned. "When are you going to tell me?"

"When I'm ready," Zyn replied mysteriously, and she headed for the stairs.

Ren stared after her sister. She felt that something was still off, but she couldn't quite place it. She sighed, supposing she would just have to give Zyn some space to figure out whatever it was. But at least her twin seemed to be getting back to her cheerful self again.

"What was that about?" Sarala grumbled.

"I don't know," Ren said earnestly. "But anyway, I'm glad the day's over with. Just a few more tests left on Freday, which don't require as much studying as all these magical ones!"

"At least that's only two tests for me, then. Sucks to be you, and still have seven to go."

Ren shrugged. "We signed up for all the Art classes, so now we have to deal with it. It'll be fun, though!"

"Yeah, right," Sarala muttered.

"You know, I was being serious back in Kung Fu," Ren said. When Sarala looked confused, she elaborated, "You should smile more."

"In your dreams," the other girl remarked, though there was definitely a smile dancing on the corners of her lips.

Ren rolled her eyes and sat down on the couch across from her. "Anyway, you should smile whenever you ask someone out to the dance."

Sarala stared at her. "What?"

"The Moonlight Dance," Ren said. "It's in the rules that you must have a partner to attend."

"But…" Sarala shook her head. "What?"

"It's to make sure everyone has at least one person to spend time with," Ren explained. "Dad didn't want any of the more quiet students to feel left out, so he made that rule. That way, nobody's left out!"

"What if I don't want to go?" Sarala grunted.

"But it's so much fun!" Ren protested.

"Can I *not* go?"

"I mean, it's not in the rules that you *have* to…I don't think."

"Good. I'm not going, then."

Ren grabbed Sarala's shoulders and shook her hard. "Sarala, please go! It's so much fun! There's lots of good food and dancing and music!"

"Ugh!" Sarala grumbled, scrunching up her hooked nose. "Sounds terrible—apart from the food, perhaps. Well, good night!"

And she got off the couch and hurried up the spiral stairs. Ren blinked, then shouted after her, "If I wasn't going with Frost, I'd totally make you go with me!"

"I'd like to see you try!" Sarala called back.

"What's going on?" Zyn's voice echoed.

"Zyn, take Sarala to the dance on Saterday!" Ren yelled.

"Okay!" Zyn replied. "That makes my life easier, if I don't have to find a partner!"

"It's this Saterday?" Sarala shrieked.

"You don't have a choice now!" Zyn laughed evilly. "It's the least you can do for putting me through that obstacle course of torture!"

"Yeah, Sarala, you owe her!" Ren chuckled.

"Ugh, fine! But I'm only going for five minutes!"

"Sounds good to me!" Zyn replied.

Ren snorted in amusement and leaned back on the couch. She closed her eyes and took several deep breaths, bringing her mind into a tranquil state. After a few minutes of quiet breathing, she relaxed and could feel an energy coursing through her sore body.

She was just getting into what promised to be a good meditation session when she heard a small buzzing noise. The buzzing got louder and louder, until she could no longer ignore it. She tried to acknowledge it by focusing on it for a moment, then allowing it to be part of her surroundings to block it out. But this did not work.

Ren opened her eyes, feeling a bit irritated at the interruption. Was Zyn trying to speak telepathically with her and ruin her meditation? She'd done that plenty of times in the past, and her voice would come through sounding like a distant hum in Ren's head.

But Ren realized that she was no longer in the family room, sitting on the couch. She gasped as she saw tall plants all around her, most of them red or purple in coloring. The plants consisted of the tallest mushrooms and the craziest dancing trees she'd ever seen. Looking down, she saw soft blue grass, which rustled in a light breeze.

"Where am I?" she whispered to herself.

She narrowed her eyes. There was something on the other side of the small valley she had somehow ended up in. It looked like some sort of animal moving towards her. She tilted her head, trying to figure out what it was.

"Is that *the* animal?" she mumbled.

But then the plants around her vanished, the tranquil breeze disappeared, and she found herself falling face-first to the ground.

"Oof!"

She sat up and shook her head dazedly, then rubbed at her small nose, which had smacked the floor.

"That hurt," she muttered.

Ren glanced all around the family room, but she was quite alone. There weren't any sort of mushrooms or dancing trees around her—nor any animals approaching from the distance. Even the soft floral scent she had whiffed had disappeared.

"I must have dozed off. I better just get to bed…"

Ren got to her feet, glancing around the room once more. She didn't feel tired—indeed, she felt quite awake now—but she still forced her feet to carry her to her room. Entering the purple-painted space, she instantly felt much calmer. She breathed in the plant smells, but the floral scent was not among the ones she detected.

Ren got changed into her pajamas and hopped onto her bed, forgetting that she hadn't even eaten dinner yet. She pulled the fuzzy blankets around her and waited for sleep to come as her room fell dark. But she still felt restless.

Ren sighed and got to her feet, the ceiling lights turning back on as they detected her motion. She grabbed a small watering can sitting on her desk, made sure there was water in it, then gave some to the plants around her.

That animal…what was it? Was it the one I went out to help, which might have tricked or hurt me? Is it the one that gave me that vision? Was it trying to warn me? I wish I could go back!

She returned to her bed after setting the empty can down beside her door, as a reminder to fill it with more water in the morning. Then, she sat down with her legs crossed in the lotus position, keeping her back straight.

I'll just have to meditate again!

But she could not return to that strange valley, even after quieting her mind. After trying—or not trying—for an hour, Ren gave up. She finally felt weary enough to fall asleep, and hoped that she would come across the animal in her dreams instead.

Yet her dreams were quite normal, as she plunged into the ocean with Zyn and Sarala at her side, and Ak-tu behind her…

CHAPTER 16: A HUMAN BODY

Zyn woke up quite happy on Trizday. Her dreams had been pleasant, reflecting her test victories the previous day. She could do it! She could get through school without magic!

She hurried to her desk, staring down at the wand sitting on top of it. *I wish you worked for me,* she thought a bit sadly. *And I know one day you will, once I actually get my magic. But I don't have it right now, and we can't connect yet.*

Her eyes shifted to the objects sitting on the desk beside the wand. They were mostly souvenirs from other parts of the world. Zyn smiled softly as she examined them.

These objects, on the other hand… They've already got a bit of magic in them. Not the most powerful magic, of course, since enchantments don't last forever. But what if I could use these objects instead of real magic?

There was a sudden knock on her door, and she jumped in fright. She had forgotten to scream out the morning greeting! But then again—she checked the rainbow clock on her wall—it was still rather early, even for her.

"Zyn? You up?"

Zyn frowned and opened the door to see her father standing just outside. He smiled at her as she stepped aside to let him in. He closed the door behind him, Zyn standing a bit awkwardly.

"I'd like to talk to you," Ak-tu murmured.

"About what?" Zyn asked in a snappish way; she hadn't forgotten their last one-on-one conversation.

"Your magic," Ak-tu said simply. Before Zyn could make any sort of interjection, he continued. "I spoke to both Khurshid and Fern yesterday. They said you did well on your tests—but that you didn't do any magic."

"Ren was the one who enchanted the potion," Zyn pointed out, trying to keep the concern out of her voice. "Potions can only have the one enchantment—at least, for the level we're at. You know that. She offered to do it."

Ak-tu nodded. "They only have one enchantment right now. But in the future, there will be many enchantments that go into potions. There will be more magic mixed in, during the brew rather than just at the end. I hear you're good at making potions from scratch and getting them up to the very end point, but then you have to get points taken off for being unable to enchant them properly."

"Maybe my rhyme is just off," Zyn said. "That happens a lot— even yesterday, I missed something."

But Ak-tu was shaking his head. He led Zyn to the hammock, and the two sat down, causing it to rock gently. Zyn's heartbeat was picking up speed. Ak-tu knew. He *had* to know.

"In the obstacle course challenge," Ak-tu persisted seriously, "Khurshid set you up with Sarala on purpose."

"What?" Zyn yelped indignantly.

"Shush," Ak-tu said in a quiet voice. "No need to wake up everyone else just yet. I asked Khurshid to do that. He tried to stop me, but I told him to place you in her obstacle course."

"Why?"

"Because you don't have your magic, do you?" Ak-tu asked sadly.

Zyn could have sworn her heart stopped for a moment. She was silent, not knowing what sort of reply to give, a lump forming in her throat and preventing her from speaking even if she wanted to.

"I thought that the obstacle course would help scare the magic out of you," Ak-tu went on. "But it didn't. Khurshid told me you just ran through it like a nonmagical person, and climbed up the final wall—after being hit plenty of times."

Zyn winced at the memory. She unconsciously lifted a hand to her chest, where she knew many bruises lurked—if she ever took a look at them.

Ak-tu stared at Zyn for a long moment, then dropped his eyes and sighed. "I had a feeling this would happen…"

Zyn blinked in confusion, then growled, "Wait—you knew I'd have no magic?"

"To be fair, your 'magic' didn't come in that sparring match with me during the magic assessments," Ak-tu pointed out. "It only 'showed up' at the very end, after we'd been going for so long. And after speaking with my fr—teachers, I realized that you weren't just struggling due to a minor magic block. You're struggling because you don't have magic."

"So you had the teachers test me? Keep an eye on me?" Zyn sneered.

Ak-tu dipped his head. "I didn't want to believe it, but they kept coming to me, asking if I knew how much you were struggling. I tried asking Ren about it, but she told me you *did* have magic and performed it sometimes. I realize now that she was lying..."

He glanced up at Zyn, a sadness in his violet eyes. "I wish you told me about this magic problem yourself."

Zyn scowled, trying to ignore the guilt trickling through her veins.

"I know Ren's been helping you in classes, and I'm sure you were just trying to protect her as much as she's been lying to protect you," Ak-tu went on. "But this can't keep up for the next semester."

Horror flooded through Zyn. Ak-tu was still going to make her drop school? He was going to prevent her from taking magic classes?

"But, Dad!" she cried out. "What if my magic comes today? Or tomorrow? Or even the first day of the spring term? You can't make me stop taking classes just because my magic's late! Please, Dad!"

Ak-tu shook his head. "I honestly don't know what to do," he admitted, stroking one mustache strand. "I've never had someone sneak in without magic before. Of course, there were a few kids who tried, but they never got further than the magic assessments. In fact, of those who tried to get through the assessments without magic, none of them ever attempted the final test. You were the first—the most desperate."

Zyn's lip curled back. She knew she was desperate for her magic to appear, but for Ak-tu to just say it like that...

"I don't blame you," Ak-tu said. "I would have been desperate for my own magic to appear—especially next to Ren, as she got her magic early. But, Zyn, now that we both know that I know about your magic…*is* there something holding you back? Is there anything that you can think of that'd be blocking off your magic, if you *do* have it?"

Zyn frowned. It sounded like Ak-tu still wanted to help her, to get her into the spring semester. Zyn thought about what she had mentioned to Ren the previous day, about her realization. Ren had asked if it had something to do with why she couldn't access her magic. Zyn didn't think it would be, but what if she was right?

But what if I'm wrong about…this? Zyn wondered, unable to term her realization. *What if I've got it all wrong, and it's not the reason for my magic block at all? I mean—why should it be blocking my magic in the first place? And if I don't have magic, then do I actually have a magic block? Or just no magic?*

"Is there anything at all, Zyn?" Ak-tu asked quietly, his gaze intense.

Zyn sighed. "No, Dad…not that I can think of," she muttered.

Ak-tu lowered his eyes again. "I'm afraid that, if you don't show magical ability by the spring semester…I'm going to have to remove you from classes."

Zyn snapped her gaze up to her father, her eyes wide. "But, Dad—"

"It's not fair to the other students," Ak-tu said. "I wouldn't have allowed any of them to continue if I found out they had no magic."

"But—"

"And it's not fair to your sister, making her work so hard on your behalf. And it's definitely not fair to you, when you can't learn everything and have to struggle to keep up." Ak-tu stared at Zyn for a long moment, then pulled her into a tight hug. "I'm sorry, Zyn," he whispered. "I really am. It hurts so much to have to do this."

"Then don't do it," Zyn mumbled, not returning her father's embrace as warm tears slid down her cheeks. "Don't take me out of classes. I can still learn!"

"But you can't put any of that knowledge to the test," Ak-tu pointed out, his voice sad.

Zyn pulled away. "Let me learn! Please, Dad! I've wanted this for so long. Don't take it away from me! I can still study magic and plants, and do martial arts. Why can't I keep learning?"

Ak-tu frowned thoughtfully. "I suppose you could realistically keep up the martial arts. Magic doesn't come in until the higher levels. Art would be fine too, and probably Magic Studies. But both Plants and Potions are going to require magical skill next semester, and obviously Magic Channeling will get more challenging as you shift your focus from the environment around you to the magic inside you."

"Some classes are better than none!" Zyn protested. "Do you really want to homeschool me again, teaching me useless math and the same history lessons, over and over? I don't want that!"

Ak-tu observed Zyn for a long moment, then sighed. "I suppose you can keep up the nonmagical classes," he said at last. "If you are able to summon your magic by next semester, I will allow you to continue all of your classes. If not…it's just the nonmagical classes for you."

Zyn nodded, dropping her gaze. She was glad they were at least able to compromise, that she'd be able to stay in some classes. But how was she ever going to catch up with her magic?

What if my realization does *have to do with my magic being blocked off?* she pondered again. "Dad…what if I *did* have a magic block?"

Ak-tu frowned. "We would work all winter break to clear that block, so you could summon your magic. Do you think you have a block?"

Zyn merely shrugged in reply.

"If you think you do, then please tell me," Ak-tu said. "We can work it out—together."

Zyn sighed, then glanced over at her desk. Her eyes lit up and she turned to her father. "What if I used magic, but not my own? And not anyone else's magic, either?"

Ak-tu frowned, clearly confused.

Zyn hopped off the hammock and went to her desk, picking up a cube. "My magic objects!" she explained. "If I learn to use these, could I just use them in classes?"

"No," Ak-tu said shortly, struggling to keep his balance on the swinging hammock. "That's still not using your own magic, and the enchantments will wear off the more you use them. Those objects do all sorts of things too, meaning you won't be doing the correct exercises in class. And then everyone would know you'd been cheating."

"But if you take me out of classes, everyone will know I've been cheating anyway," Zyn pointed out. "And Ren. They're… they're going to want to see us get punished, aren't they?"

Ak-tu sighed. "There will have to be some punishment, yes. I definitely don't appreciate you kids lying to me…I'll be talking to Ren about this later too."

Zyn's heartbeat quickened again. *This is all my fault! Oh, please, don't take Ren out of classes too! That wouldn't be fair to her at all, she was only trying to help!*

"I will have to think over what your punishments will be," Ak-tu said after a moment. "But if your magic comes by spring semester, I will overlook everything that happened. You were already working with Ren in Potions, and she didn't help you out in Magic Channeling. Neither of you cheated on the tests. But I will have to ask the teachers to take points off your homework assignments—for both of you."

Zyn nodded quietly.

"If the entire school ends up learning you don't have magic after all—that you and Ren cheated, and you are removed from some classes—I'm afraid the punishment will have to be more severe," Ak-tu said briskly. "And I will think more about these punishments next year."

Zyn nodded again. Then, she frowned. "Isn't telepathy magic?" she asked. "I've been able to speak to you and Ren through thoughts for years! So I *do* have magic, then, right?"

Ak-tu nodded, observing his palm as he created droplets of water and sent them spiraling into the air. "Yes, you have magic—everyone has magic. But magic will lie dormant until puberty, most times. Even so, telepathy is a different type of magic altogether, and wouldn't count as the elemental magic we're discussing right now."

Zyn opened her mouth to ask more questions, but Ak-tu pressed on before she could.

"Now, Zyn…are you sure there's nothing I can help you with? Even if you have the tiniest idea of what might be causing a magic block…"

"What causes a magic block?" Zyn asked flatly.

"Surely Khurshid's mentioned it in Magic Studies?"

"I just want to make sure," Zyn replied.

Ak-tu shrugged. "A magic block can be caused if you are suffering illness or injury, particularly the more severe they are. You're in perfect health—apart from a few bruises at the moment, I'm sure—so this shouldn't be the issue. But it can be blocked if you're undergoing a mental illness too, like depression or severe anxiety. With anxiety, your magic will typically still work, but it will be sporadic. With depression, the longer you're in depression, the more your magic will just shut off. Are you depressed, Zyn?"

"I don't think so," she said honestly. "I've had bad days this semester, but I still try to have fun."

"Hmm…well, if you're dealing with depression, then we'll need to get you out of it," Ak-tu said. "Let's say that you *are* depressed. You're not having…bad thoughts, are you?"

"No, I'm not *that* depressed, if I am," Zyn assured her father swiftly. "I like spending time with you and Ren, and learning magic despite not having it. I like to play games and do martial arts. I enjoy living! I don't think depression is the issue."

Ak-tu nodded in relief. "Well, if you think it is, then please let me know. We will get you the help you need. Can you think of anything else that might be holding you back?"

Zyn shook her head again, not even wondering about her realization.

"Very well. My door is always open, Zyn. I promise I will help you overcome whatever magic block you might be going through. Take the winter break to look inwards and find that block," Ak-tu said firmly. "Of course, it could just be that your magic really *isn't* there, and that it's not blocked off if it's nonexistent. It could come when you're closer to turning fifteen. There's no shame in being a late-bloomer. Well, Zyn…you know where to find me."

Ak-tu got to his feet and walked to Zyn's side, giving her a small hug again. He then went to the door, glanced over his shoulder at Zyn, offered her a smile, and left. Zyn sighed and plopped on the wooden floor, not bothering to yell out the morning greeting.

She walked over to her desk and rummaged around in the drawers, looking for her disc player. She didn't often use the disc player, as the family mirror played music just fine. But the mirror was currently in the family room, and she had no intention of going down the stairs to grab it.

After a bit of searching, she took out the disc player (a metal box that she had painted rainbow) and an album by her favorite band, Uneeq. She put the disc into the player and hit the "Play" button, then turned the volume down so it wouldn't disturb anyone. Once her music was playing, she walked to the door and locked it. Zyn then sat on the floor again, ready to figure out her realization.

She took a deep breath. *You can do this,* she told herself. *You just gotta be strong and believe in yourself,* she sang in her head, in time to the song.

And with that, she pulled off her pajama top and threw it far away, where she wouldn't be able to grab it and put it back on so easily. A shiver ran up her spine, but it wasn't due to the cool temperature in her room.

Her torso was entirely covered in bruises, just as she knew it'd be. They were black, blue, purple, and yellow, each of them an ugly mark. But she'd still take them any day, when compared to her body.

Her heart pounded faster than it had when Ak-tu was in her room—it thrummed in her ears and pounded in her throat. Her whole body seemed to quiver in tune to its beat. The continuous thudding drowned out the sound of the music, the comfort of the song.

No, she kept repeating in her mind, as she stared down in repulsion. *No, no, no!*

But there was no denying the sight before her eyes. Tears flooded down her cheeks, her body tensed, her hands curled into fists at her sides. She had the sudden urge to rip her chest apart, to destroy what was attached to her. Forcing her fingernails into the wooden floor, she knew she had to hold back from hurting herself.

No, no, no!

"Zyn? Are you okay?" Ren's voice called.

Zyn ignored her. In fact, she didn't even hear her.

No, no, no, no…

Zyn scraped the ground with her hands, trying to hold them in place. But she soon brought them up in front of her, in line with her chest, her fingers shaking from how much tension they held. Her eyes widened as she continued to stare down at her chest.

Another thrill of panic and repulsion coursed through her. Her chest was definitely bigger than it had been when she started the semester—wasn't it? Or was it just the way she was sitting on the ground? No—she had felt it more throughout the semester, even though she tried to deny it was there. But she couldn't dismiss its existence when she had no robe to cover her slim figure, when she was in the obstacle course with the stone hitting her chest so many times—as if to laugh that she was now burdened with this horror!

Wrapping her arms around herself, she attempted to squish her chest out of existence, her nails stabbing into her back from how tightly she was holding onto herself. She closed her eyes and clenched her jaw shut, trying to keep from screaming. All she could feel was revulsion and panic and agony and a strong sense of helplessness!

I have to do something about this! she thought, trying to pull herself together.

"Zyn?" Ren called again.

Zyn hurried to the drawer where she kept her martial arts uniforms and sashes. She grabbed her white sash and tied it tightly around her chest, feeling a bit better.

It's flat now…it's gone, she thought in relief.

She took several deep sighs, then pulled on the feathery pajama shirt she'd tossed aside, and grabbed a nearby sweater to add on top of that. She'd just have to wear extra clothes, that was all. Then nobody—not even herself—would be able to notice her chest.

But what about in the spring? she wondered. *Hardly anyone wears sweaters, especially when it gets hotter. Oh, no…what about* summer?

She shivered at the thought. Oftentimes, Ak-tu would take his daughters to the beach, where they'd each throw aside their shirts and run into the crashing waves, feeling the warm sun on their bare chests. It was very common for Galian people to be half-naked in the hot temperatures, even outside the beach. Zyn always felt uneasy seeing other half-naked people, especially if they had large chests. And now…

Now I'm going to be one of them! No…no…

Breathing shallow again, she sunk to the floor, closing her eyes. How could this be happening? She didn't ask for this! She never wanted anything but a flat chest!

A sob escaped her. She placed a hand over her mouth, trying to keep the sound from echoing. But it was no use. Once one sob was out, more just followed. She couldn't stop the salty tears streaming down her brown cheeks and into her open mouth. She couldn't stop the thought of her bare chest from entering her mind. Shaking all over, all she wanted to do was shriek her agony to the world!

"Zyn, open up!" Ren screamed, rattling the door fiercely. "What's wrong? Zyn! Zyn!"

No, no, no! Just end this! Make it stop! Make it go away! I don't want this, I never wanted this! I hate this! I HATE THIS! GO AWAY!

Zyn tore her clothes off again, throwing the sash aside. She knew she'd feel guilty later for disrespecting her uniform, but she didn't care in the moment.

"GO AWAY!" Zyn shouted.

"ZYN!" Ren cried. "ZYN! What are you doing?"

By the time Ren, Ak-tu, and Sarala crashed through the door, Zyn was lying on the ground, her arms wrapped around her bare chest. She had barely concealed her bruised body from sight before they entered.

"What's going on?" Ak-tu demanded.

Ren threw herself on the ground beside Zyn. "ZYN! What happened? What are you doing?"

"I failed," Zyn moaned, closing her eyes tightly. She didn't want to see any of them—and she definitely did not want them to see *her*. "I failed…"

"You failed what?" Ren asked urgently, shaking her sister.

Zyn rolled away from her, her body rattling with sobs. She was much too upset to speak, and she had no energy left to explain anything.

"Sarala, get Fern," Ak-tu ordered.

Zyn heard his footsteps come closer as Sarala's left, felt him crouch down next to her. Nobody spoke for a long moment, and Zyn could almost see her father and sister exchanging worried glances. She felt a hand stroking her messy hair, knowing it was Ak-tu attempting to comfort her.

"Did she try hurting herself because you said you'd take her out of classes?" Ren wailed at last, turning to Ak-tu.

"No—she was fine with it—we compromised—we—Zyn!" Ak-tu said, his stroking hand now shaking her. "What happened? You were fine when I left."

But Zyn made no response, crying too hard to say anything aloud and her mind too shattered to respond by thoughts.

"Dad, what's wrong with her?" Ren cried.

Ak-tu didn't reply.

{Zyn, what happened? Please, talk to me! Talk to Ren!} Ak-tu's voice echoed in her mind.

{I failed, I failed, I failed…} It was the only thing Zyn could manage. She didn't know where her thoughts were going, whether they went to only one family member or both—or if they simply remained in her own head.

{What did you fail?} Ren asked at once. *{What's wrong with you?}*

Zyn's mind clouded over. How could she explain any of this? Explaining it would mean she'd *have* to accept the fact that her body existed—and she wasn't prepared for that.

{What's wrong?} Ren pressed.

Zyn could make out the sound of running footsteps. Fern and Sarala had entered the room.

"Move!" Fern snapped briskly, clearly ushering Ren and Ak-tu out of the way.

Zyn soon felt the healer's hands on her bare skin. She flinched at the touch, but there was nowhere she could go. Fern pried Zyn's arms away from her chest, and Zyn screwed her eyes even tighter, the tears falling quicker. Why did Fern have to show off her body to everyone else?

"Oh, Zyn!" Ren gasped.

"Where did all these bruises come from?" Fern asked.

"My obstacle course," Sarala said meekly from the doorway.

"Hmm…she appears to be fine, then," Fern murmured, more to herself than the others. "There are no other injuries…"

"Were you trying to…to…" Ren didn't finish the sentence.

"I want it gone!" Zyn yowled, trying to squirm away from Fern. "I don't want this! I hate it! I hate my body!"

Silence met her ears. The Uneeq song continued to play softly in the background, the only sound in the room. She was tempted to open her eyes, but didn't want to make eye contact with anyone. She was more humiliated than she had ever been in her life. Her chest ached, from the bruises and even from her heart pounding so much.

"Why didn't you say anything?" Ren wailed, and she flung herself at Zyn. "This is your realization, isn't it? Your magic block? Oh, Zyn!"

"Fern, is there something we can do about this?" Ak-tu asked. "Do you have a potion that can make her chest flat?"

Fern sighed from somewhere near Zyn. "I'd have to brew one up. But you know it's illegal, Ak-tu."

"Not anything long-term," Ak-tu said quickly. "Just something that she can take for now, to keep her chest flat?"

Zyn opened her blurry eyes at last, to peer up at her father over Ren's shoulder. Ak-tu was staring at Fern, who now stood up. Sarala gazed from one to the other. Nobody was looking at Zyn.

"I suppose I could do it, but that still requires—"

"I know what it requires," Ak-tu said shortly. "We will get the permission necessary. But for now, while Zyn is figuring things out, can you give her a potion?"

Fern sighed. "Yes. But I'll only make enough for one month. You better get the necessary healer permissions if you want her to continue taking the potion."

"We will, if this is the route Zyn wants to go," Ak-tu promised.

Zyn was confused. What were they talking about? But her mind was too muddled and drained to question it any further.

"Can you heal her bruises too?" Ak-tu asked Fern.

"Easily," Fern replied.

"And the shock?"

"Who do you think you're talking to?" Fern snapped, causing Ak-tu to take a step back and lift his hands in front of him. "I'll have her healed up in no time. She'll be back in class to take her last tests on Freday."

And with that, Fern shooed Ren away from Zyn, put a sweater over Zyn's head, and picked her up like she weighed nothing. The healer then left the room, slipping Zyn a small vial.

"Drink it," she ordered as she walked down the stairs.

Zyn opened the vial with a bit of difficulty, feeling embarrassed as she was carried away. She drank the sour potion, and fell asleep before they were even out in the bitter cold.

CHAPTER 17: OUTSIDE-IN

Ak-tu and Ren sat in the herb-scented Healing room, watching Fern work on Zyn's bruised body in the middle of the room. They were silent, both of them still shaking from shock at what had happened.

{Did you know about this?} Ak-tu asked Ren at last, his eyes still on Zyn.

Ren shook her head beside him.

{Did she show any sign of being uncomfortable with her body?}

Ren shrugged.

Ak-tu sighed. *{Why didn't she tell us? We could have helped her… But now…}*

{She can't be helped?} Ren asked, staring at her father with wide eyes.

{No, she can.} Ak-tu said hastily. *{But I think she will require help that I can't give to her…}*

{You're not going to send her away, are you?}

Ak-tu stared at his daughter in surprise. *{Of course not! I wouldn't dream of it. But Fern is right in saying that we need permissions from certain healers. Zyn will need to see a therapist about this dysphoria she's facing, to be officially diagnosed and see a different healer for surgery. If she wants to undergo permanent surgery, that is….}*

{I just wish she told me.} Ren said dully. *{I would have been there for her. We would have gotten her through this… And then she wouldn't have to go through therapy or potions or surgery.}*

{Yes, she would.} Ak-tu told her. *{If she wants her chest modified, she'd have to go through therapists and healers to verify that she wants to undergo this decision.}*

{But I'd have made her see that there's nothing wrong with her body!} Ren thought confidently. *{Our bodies are gifts to us, from*

the universe, from nature. She should be thankful she has her body, and see it in a positive light.}

Ak-tu shook his head. *{It's not like that with some people.}* He spoke to her gently. *{There are plenty of transgender people out there, who praise nature and spirits, just like us. And they consider their bodies a gift too. But they are still…so uncomfortable, that they simply cannot live in their bodies until undergoing change.}*

{But it's not natural to change our bodies!} Ren protested.

{It might not be natural in some ways, but it is natural to the individual. In Zyn's case, it's natural for her to change her body. That's her path, if she chooses it—or if it chooses her. That will be the path that's natural to her.}

{But—}

{Ren, if you want to help your sister, you will be there for her and understand her perspective.} Ak-tu said sternly. *{She'll need you, now more than ever. And if you're trying to get her to love her body so much, when she's clearly beyond that point…she'll just push away from you.}*

{But why would she push away from me if I'm trying to help her see her body positively? She should love her body, and be thankful she has it!}

Ak-tu sighed. *{Ren, please don't try to push your point of view on her. I'm sure Zyn very much likes being alive and living the life she has. She told me so herself, before all of this happened. But she clearly does not feel at home in her body. It looked like she was going to try tearing her chest before we came in. Do you think telling her to love her body will help her?}*

Ren stared at her feet, and Ak-tu could see the doubt creeping into her eyes. *{I don't get why she's making a big deal about her chest. It's nowhere near as big as Sarala's, and you can hardly see it with what she wears anyway! Sure—that one day, she had to take her robe off and was all uncomfortable about it, but…why does she have to make it a big deal? It's not like we could really see her chest, even without her robe on. She's just being dramatic!}*

{That might be so, but to her, her chest is big and has to go. Think of it like this. Zyn has a…a poison in her body. This poison prevents her from being herself, being happy, and even accessing

her magic. Removing this poison would allow her to be happy—and probably reach her magic, if it was blocking the magic off. And isn't that what you want for your sister?}

Ren nodded at once. {Of course!}

{Then allow her to remove this poison, if she so desires.}

Ren sighed and sat back in her chair. {I guess it makes sense when you put it like that. But Khurshid said magic blocks come from being seriously injured or sick. Does that mean Zyn is seriously sick? What about the other transgender students here? Did their magic block off because they're transgender? Does being transgender mean you're mentally ill?}

Ak-tu shook his head at once. {Of course not! Some transgender people might be depressed due to their dysphoria or feeling trapped in a body that isn't right to them, which can then result in a magic block due to being depressed or mentally stuck. But being transgender doesn't mean you're more likely to have a magic block, or that you're mentally ill.}

Ren was quiet for a long moment, taking in his words. {Okay… I was worried something more might be wrong… But what if she gets permanent surgery, and then regrets it? Would that make her magic block off again?}

{Don't worry. She can't get any permanent surgery done until she's sixteen.} Ak-tu told her. {She'll only be able to take potions, once we get that permission from the therapist and healers. She'll have more than a year to think it through. But once she transitions, she's likely to be comfortable in her body and therefore able to access her magic no problem.}

{But did this actually cause her to have a magic block?} Ren queried, biting her bottom lip. {Because if she wasn't actually ill with anything, or didn't feel like this all the time, then wouldn't she have done something?}

{I thought you said she did manage magic sometimes?} Ak-tu asked, glancing down at her with one side of his unibrow raised.

Ren blushed and looked away.

{Don't worry, I already know by now that you were lying. I would appreciate that you're honest with me in the future. Anyhow, I'm not sure if it's a magic block. If Zyn's dysphoria has been strong, it could be the reason for her having no magic. Or she *might still have no magic, regardless of the dysphoria. Who's to know until she starts feeling more at home in her body?}*

They were silent for a while, watching as the large bruises on Zyn's body vanished slowly. Fern stood over Zyn with her hands outstretched and her eyes closed. Her hands and necklace glowed as she healed Zyn, muttering words that Ak-tu could not hear.

{Zyn was very upset when she started puberty....} Ren said a bit shyly. *{You know, when she had her first cycle.... It took her a long time to get used to it. And I think she was jealous of me because I...still have yet to have my first cycle... My chest is still flat too. Do you think something's wrong with me?}*

{No.} Ak-tu replied simply. *{Some people just take longer to develop—just like Zyn's magic.}*

{But if it's taking a long time for me to start puberty, how come I got my magic so early? And why doesn't Zyn have her magic?}

{You have a stronger connection with yourself.} Ak-tu pointed out. *{This connection allowed you to access your magic early. If Zyn has been rejecting her body from the start of puberty, then that just means she struggled to connect with her magic from the start too. Or, like I said, maybe she just has no magic yet until she gets older.}*

{Oh...right...}

They lapsed into silence again. Zyn's bruises were now entirely gone, as if they were marks erased from paper. Fern was still examining her though, as if making sure that Zyn hadn't clawed out her chest.

{Do you think Zyn still wants to be a girl?} Ren asked.

Ak-tu shrugged. *{It's up to her. There have been many girls who got their chests modified, and still identified as female. And there have been many people who chose to identify as male or nonbinary. Right now, the important thing is that Zyn feels comfortable in her own body.}*

{But she chose to be a girl.} Ren said. *{Didn't she?}*

In Galia (and in much of the world), most children grew up using they/them pronouns and having no set gender. At about three- or four-years-old, most children knew what their gender identity was. Many ended up choosing the gender "aligned" with their biological sex, though there were many transgender and gender fluid people.

Some transgender people got surgeries to align with the sex they wished to be, and there were many hormonal potions that existed too. Not every transgender person took these routes, especially if they were fine with their biological sex but still identified as a different gender (in which case they would just use the appropriate pronouns). After all, there weren't major differences between the genders, and it was up to the individual person if they felt at home in their bodies or not. Anyone could be any gender that felt right to them.

Ak-tu remembered when his daughters had chosen their genders. Ren reported that she felt very much like a girl one day. A few moments later, Zyn said she was a girl too. But Zyn had hesitated when she said it, and now…

{I'm not sure if she actually did….} He admitted to Ren. {She might have chosen whatever her twin chose. But whatever she chooses now, we'll be here for her.}

{Yeah…}

Ak-tu looked sidelong at Ren. {Your friend Mint is gender fluid. Raimugi is nonbinary. And there are plenty of trans students here. Why are you having a hard time with Zyn?}

{I'm not!} Ren said hurriedly. {I just…don't want to lose my sister.}

{You won't.} Ak-tu promised her, placing his hand on her cheek and brushing the hair gently from her eyes. {Zynivus will always be your twin.}

Ren smiled lightly.

Fern approached them. "Done having your little mind conversation?" she asked.

"How did you know?" Ren asked curiously.

"The concentrated looks, the energy in the air," Fern stated blandly. "Anyway, Zynivus is good to go. Her bruises are healed, and I made sure she didn't hurt herself anywhere else. I will make that potion and have it to you by Freday night. It takes awhile to brew."

Ak-tu got to his feet and bowed to Fern. "Thank you," he said. "I know you aren't happy about making the potion, but I think it'll keep Zyn from hurting herself. I will get her into therapy, so she can get the official permissions."

"Huh. See that you do. I don't like breaking rules," Fern said briskly. "I'll keep her in here the rest of the day, to make sure her mental state is fine. She should be back to you tonight."

"Thank you," Ak-tu repeated. "Come on, Ren. Zyn is in safe hands."

Ren reluctantly stood, staring over at Zyn. She then trailed after her father, leaving the Healing room and entering the snowy Courtyard. Ak-tu sniffed the frigid air, a shiver trickling down his spine; he could tell it was going to snow again soon.

"Do you think breakfast is over?" Ren asked.

"Let's find out," Ak-tu said. "If it is, I'll just get the cooks to throw us the leftovers. That's what I do whenever I miss meals."

Ren snorted. "Dad, you have to eat!"

"I know, but sometimes I get too caught up in my work," he chuckled.

Ren's face became serious again. "Why do you know so much about transgender people?"

Ak-tu frowned, stopping in his tracks before they reached the Eating Hall. "Transgender and gender fluid people exist all around us. It's common knowledge."

"Yeah, I know, but…how do you know what a transgender person *feels*?" Ren asked. "Are you…?"

"I've worked with plenty of transgender students here, and intersex people who did not feel in alignment with being the 'in-between' gender."

"What's even the point of having different genders if it doesn't matter?" Ren asked curiously. "I understand having male and female sexes, in order to have children. But what's the point of intersex people?"

Ak-tu signaled to the small black-and-white symbol on the front of his robe. "Yin and yang," he told her simply. "From two, we get infinite. Two combine to make the world. Light and dark allow a range of colors to exist. You can't have light without dark, up without down, right without left. And all that space in between, where the colors would exist or what's considered the middle—that's where the beauty of this world lies.

"If male people are the white part and female people are the black part, then intersex people would be the rainbow in between. And it's the same when it comes to gender, sexuality, the races of this world…. Nothing is ever just one shade of black or white. Everything and everyone has multiple colors, inside and out. That's what makes them whole, that's what makes them unique. And that's why this world is so beautiful—and rainbow-colored!"

Ren frowned thoughtfully.

Ak-tu opened his mouth, but his next words died in his throat. He was about to tell her that he had gender struggles himself—but that would mean explaining his childhood. And he wasn't ready to tell his kids about *that* just yet….

He shook his head roughly, as if to rattle the thoughts out. Glancing back at Ren, he could tell that she was still processing his words, perhaps even getting overwhelmed by everything. He placed his hand on her shoulder comfortingly.

"Come on, Ren. Everything will be okay and work itself out. It's only natural, after all. Just like yin-yang, everything is a cycle. Zyn will gain her magic and be on the up soon. Okay?"

Ren nodded, keeping her glazed eyes on the snowy ground. A long moment passed in silence, Ak-tu giving her all the time she needed to think things through. Suddenly, she gasped, startling Ak-tu and causing him to jump backwards.

"Dad—last night, I had a weird dream! I almost forgot about it, what with Zyn…"

Ak-tu acted like he was practicing his water magic, sliding around the ice as he spoke. "A weird dream? Was it like your vision?"

Ren shook her head, not even acknowledging that Ak-tu might as well be iceskating while having a serious conversation. "I don't think so? It definitely didn't hurt like one."

"Hmm… So what happened in this dream? Is that why you didn't have dinner last night?" Ak-tu asked, glad he was warming up in the chilly morning air by sliding around.

"Kind of," Ren chuckled, combing her hand through her hair. "I mostly forgot about that, to be honest."

"Ha! I'm not the only one who forgets to eat, then," Ak-tu replied, causing Ren to snort in laughter. "Let's get inside and get some food in us!"

"Yeah, good idea!"

Ak-tu led the way to the Eating Hall (still sliding on water-turned-ice), hoping that there was some hot cocoa left. He opened the door for Ren, then trailed her inside. There were plenty of students eating in the cozy room, though the cooks were putting the food away. They saw Ak-tu approaching and stopped what they were doing, quite accustomed to him coming in late for meals.

"Late again, Ak-tu?" one of the cooks chuckled.

"Yep!" Ak-tu said merrily. "We'll just take whatever's still out, then we'll be on our way."

The cooks laughed lightly and stepped back from the counter, watching as Ak-tu and Ren grabbed clean trays. The two hurriedly snatched some crumbly muffins and hot cocoa, then sat at a table. Once they were seated, Ak-tu resumed the telepathic conversation.

{So what was this dream?}

{Well, I don't know if it was a dream…or maybe it was a daydream? Or it could have been something of a vision. I don't know what to call it, actually.} Ren rambled, poking at her muffin and causing crumbs to roll off.

Ak-tu took a bite of his blueberry muffin. *{Were you not asleep when it happened?}*

{I don't think I was? I was meditating, and then I heard a buzzing noise, and then when I opened my eyes, I was in some weird valley. It wasn't like any place we went to before.}

{What did it look like?}

{There were really tall mushrooms and some wildly-dancing dancing trees.} Ren finally ate some of her own muffin, more crumbs dancing to the table. *{And there was this faint floral smell…but it wasn't like any flower I've smelled before…I don't think?}*

{Was there anything that happened in this meditation-dream?} Ak-tu pressed, leaning a bit closer to inspect Ren.

Ren bit her bottom lip. *{There was an animal, and it was heading towards me. It was too far away to see properly. Do you think it was the animal I heard outside? Do you think it's the one giving me visions?}*

Ak-tu frowned, his muffin forgotten as he ran his fingers through his hair. *{Hmm…it could be. But I'm sure if it's an animal trying to reach out to you—well, it's more likely to be a spirit than an animal or creature.}*

Ren's eyes lit up. *{A spirit? Ooh, do you think I have a spirit guide? That's so cool!}*

Ak-tu smiled lightly. *{Let's hope it's a guide… How did you feel when you saw this being? Excited? Threatened?}*

{I felt on high alert after, I guess, but…no, not threatened.}

Ak-tu sat in silence for a while, in deep thought. Ren gazed at him expectantly.

{Are you…saying anything to me, or just thinking? I'm not getting any messages.}

{Just thinking… I suppose you will have to wait to see if you meet this spirit again. If you do, please alert me at once.}

{Do you think it was something bad?} Ren asked, pausing as she made to take another bite from her muffin. *{Maybe something to do with that mirror shard Sarala found?}*

A series of images flashed through Ak-tu's mind: a mirror shard, a jagged face, a large storm… He closed his eyes for a moment. *{We cannot label something as good or bad. There is good and bad to everything. Remember, yin and yang, the natural order…}*

{I know, Dad…}

{As for the mirror shard…it is a possibility that your meditation-dream and/or visions are connected to that. We'll just have to keep an eye on everything, I suppose.}

Ren nodded, then said aloud, "I'll be sure to tell you if it happens again."

Ak-tu opened his eyes and smiled at her. "Thank you," he murmured.

The two finished their breakfast, Ak-tu swiping the muffin crumbs off the table and tossing them in the trashcan. Ak-tu then claimed he had to get back to work, leaving Ren in the Eating Hall alone. He walked outside for a moment until reaching the door that led to the Entrance Hall. Entering the Admin Hall, he headed for the Security Office.

There were several frogoyles in the room, most of them staring out the front window of the school and into the forest beyond. A few others were positioned throughout, some on tabletops and some on the floor. The eyes of the statues glowed purple as they detected his presence, but they did not move and merely awaited their master's orders.

"Just keep doing what you're doing," Ak-tu told them.

He pulled the mirror shard out of his robe pocket, which had been sitting there for months. He quickly scanned its surface, not allowing himself to look directly at it. But the shard was as plain-looking as the day he first saw it, and he couldn't detect anything watching him from the other side like he had before. Sighing, he returned it to his pocket.

"Frogoyles," he said abruptly, and they all turned towards him. "I want two of you to search the Courtyard for more mirror shards. I want another two of you to search the classrooms, Library, and Greenhouse."

Four of the frogoyles hopped away. They paused at the closed door, then one bounced up to open it. The statues were soon on their way out, closing the door behind them.

What's going on with these spirits? Ak-tu wondered, walking over to the window to gaze into the forest as well. *First, the mirror shard. Then, Ren's vision. And now, a spirit is singling her out to meet with her? What do they want?*

He reached into his opposite pocket to pull out his personal mirror. Before he really knew what he was doing, Jabali's image showed up on the glass as he called his friend. But Jabali did not answer, the mirror giving up the attempt to connect after a few minutes.

"Probably busy with his shop," Ak-tu uttered to himself. "I'll just ask him to keep an eye out for spirits later... But something is definitely going on here...."

CHAPTER 18: INNUENDO

Freday soon arrived, everyone in high spirits. Zyn was feeling much better now that the secret of her magic—and her body hatred realization—were out in the open. At first, she was embarrassed by how she had acted, but Ren and Ak-tu quickly reassured her that she didn't have to worry about it. Ak-tu then told Zyn that he had booked an appointment at the end of December for her to see a therapist in Graytor, one of the nearby cities. When Ren asked her sister if she still wanted to be a girl, she merely shrugged in response and said nothing about changing her pronouns. Ren was a bit happy to hear this, but had a feeling this would change soon—just like everything else seemed to be changing.

Ren and Zyn practically flew through their Art tests. For Drawing and Painting, they merely had to present one of their favorite art pieces from that semester to the class, and explain what technique they'd used and why they liked it. For Writing, they had to read one of their written works out loud. In the Cooking class, each student had to cook something small of their choice. As they'd been working in groups or partnerships throughout the entire semester, the cooks had them working independently for their test. For Fashion, Aster had the whole class make a new outfit for him within the hour. Choir was merely singing a favorite song, while Band was playing an instrument without any mistakes.

The last test was Theatre. The class had been working on one production for months, and the test would be performing it for the entire school to see. The class moved to the Theatre, getting dressed in costumes and prepping the music and lighting. Everything was set by 3:15, which was when the doors opened for the rest of the school to come in. Not every student showed up, but there was still a wide audience.

Ren was admittedly nervous as she saw how many people had

arrived. Though she found the class to be fun, she wasn't sure she'd like performing very much. She hurried over to Zyn, who was dressed in a bright white robe with rainbow stars plastered all over it. The robe would shine like a beacon in the darkness of the large Theatre, which was exactly the point—Zyn had the lead role.

"I'm so nervous!" Ren said, her eyes wide. "How do I deal with this? Ahh!"

Zyn chuckled. "It's okay to be nervous. It's natural! I'm pretty scared too. I still can't believe we got the lead roles."

"I know—and I think I'm regretting it!" Ren moaned, her stomach twisting uneasily.

Before Zyn could say anything else, a boy named Gray, who was the director of the production that term, stomped over to Zyn and jabbed her hard. "Make sure you don't act too crazy," he sneered.

Zyn shoved his hand away. "Yeah, yeah, I know," she muttered. She glanced at Ren, speaking telepathically. *{I know you don't want me to take my role seriously, so I'm obviously going to do the complete opposite of what you want!}*

Ren snorted.

"What's so funny?" Gray snapped. "Take your places! We're about to begin!"

Zyn stuck her tongue out at Gray's back as he left to check the other actors. The play then began, more noticeable by the lack of chatter in the seats beyond the stage rather than the clock on the back wall. Ren could hear Aster's voice beyond the curtain, and she scurried to the deepest shadows to ensure she was out of sight.

"Good evening," Aster said, and the remaining chatter died down within seconds. "We are very happy to present you with the Theatre's fall production, 'The Spirit of the Midnight Forest'! We hope you enjoy it!"

Music soon started up, and the first actors took their place on stage as the curtain opened. They were enacting the scene of a family traveling through a forest when a spirit (also known as Ren dressed in a feathery costume that glowed) suddenly jumped out at them. The family hurried away in fright as Ren also ran back into the shadows.

That wasn't so bad, she thought.

She watched as the family got to a town, not knowing who to turn to for help. It happened that the townspeople knew a person by the title of the Rainbow Spirit Seeker—Zyn.

Zyn bounded forward onto the stage, sliding across the wooden floor towards the family. She exclaimed that she was the Rainbow Spirit Seeker, who'd be happy to search for the spirit. The curtain closed briefly as the stage scenery was changed.

Gray hurried over to Zyn and whispered harshly, "Tone it down a bit! You're getting too excited!"

"Sorry," Zyn whispered back, not sounding sorry at all.

The production went well. The other actors, mostly playing as people who got terrorized by the spirit, could have used work with their acting but were otherwise right on time with their acts (unlike in some rehearsals, where they were off a beat or two).

Eventually, Zyn's character found the spirit. The spirit had been evading the Rainbow Spirit Seeker, until she worked out that a person had stolen something from the spirit. The spirit wanted the object back, and so the Rainbow Spirit Seeker was then searching the town for the object. The play ended with Zyn returning the lost object (a hat with a sun on it) to Ren, who vowed to leave the town alone.

The crowd applauded happily as the other actors joined Ren and Zyn on stage at the very end. Gray didn't look too happy, scowling at Zyn. Ren was glad she didn't get on Gray's bad side.

Once most of the audience had left the Theatre after Aster's final thank-you, Aster turned to the team.

"Zynivus didn't listen to my orders!" Gray shouted at once.

"Orders? What orders were those, Gray?" Aster asked, his orange eyes confused.

Gray was seething. "I ordered her not to act up!"

"Oh," Aster chuckled lightly. "I thought you had told her to act more lively. I do believe the play has benefited from that. The students were laughing quite a bit at the dramatic movements Zyn made."

Zyn shot Gray a triumphant look.

"However, Zyn," Aster went on, catching the glance, "you *do* need to listen to your director more. I hope for more teamwork next semester. I will be judging the performance tonight, and choosing who will be the director next term. You will know at the start of next semester. You all passed the Theatre test with great marks tonight, so I hope you're proud of yourselves!"

The students broke off into groups, some staying to chat as others left after taking off their costumes. A few, like Gray, helped pick up the props and put them in the backroom, where they were stored.

Ren and Zyn pushed the curtains aside and hopped off the stage, Ren's knees jolting at the action. However, this did not keep her from running to Ak-tu and Sarala. Frost lingered nearby with his friends, and even Mint hurried over.

"You all did such a great job!" Mint exclaimed. "And you, Ren—you were such a scary spirit!"

"I'm still surprised you two had the roles you did," Ak-tu said to his kids. "I thought you'd be dying to play the spirit, Zyn."

"I did want to at first," she admitted. "But Ren wanted it, so I didn't audition for the part. And she did great!"

Ren chuckled. "It's so much fun to act evil and scary!"

"Yeah, I'm glad that's not who you really are," Sarala said plainly.

Zyn snorted. "Imagine that!"

The whole group laughed at the thought, then Ren asked Zyn, "Are you going to put that robe back?" She had already taken off her own costume and put it away.

Zyn raised a finger to her lips. "Ssh! I was hoping I could get away with keeping it."

Ak-tu rolled his eyes. "Of *course* you were. Come on, then, let's get out of here so you can steal it successfully."

Mint darted away to chat with some of the other second-year students. Frost headed towards Ren, but, suddenly not feeling in the mood to talk to him, she merely waved and followed her dad out the door.

Ak-tu led the way into the thick snow that covered the Court-yard. The sky was heavy with clouds, but it luckily wasn't snow-ing. Only the barest of breezes blew, but it was still enough to make them shiver as they trudged towards the Tai Chi Studio.

"It was a good play," Ak-tu said. "I'm glad to see you kids having fun."

"It *was* fun!" Ren said, beaming.

"Yeah!" Zyn agreed. "I'm kinda glad this semester's over with, though."

Ren chuckled uneasily. "Yeah..." *Now we just have to help you find your magic connection before the spring semester starts...that way you can stay enrolled and we don't get punished...*

"When do we find out how we did on our tests?" Sarala asked. "And what happens if we don't pass?"

Ak-tu shrugged, opening the door to the studio and allowing the teens to walk in ahead of him. "These tests are more of preparation for the finals that will come next semester. The finals matter a lot. If you didn't do well on the tests you just took, you will have a discussion with the class's teacher next semester. The tests are merely a measure of where you are in your studies right now."

"So they don't even matter?" Zyn mumbled, pausing as she reached for the tower key in her pocket.

Ak-tu stared at the three for a long moment, then said, "No."

Ren, Zyn, and Sarala stared at him in disbelief.

"But it *does* get you working hard!" Ak-tu pointed out with a mischievous glint in his eyes. "It was worth it, right? The first semester is now over with! And hopefully, you'll all enjoy the next semester even more..."

"If I even get to do it," Zyn muttered, unlocking the door.

"You will!" Ren said firmly, clutching her twin's arm tightly. "We know what the problem is now, so we'll get you connected with your magic in no time!"

Zyn smiled at her, leading the way into the family room. "Yeah...it feels great to be taking the potion!"

"So you kids know who you're going to the Moonlight Dance with tomorrow?" Ak-tu asked them.

"Ren's making me take Sarala," Zyn said glumly.

"Why is that such a bad thing?" Sarala growled.

"Because you're no fun," Zyn replied.

"Fine! I'm not going with you! I'll find someone else!" Sarala snapped, and she stormed away towards the stairs.

"But who am I supposed to go with?" Zyn called after her.

"Not my problem!"

Ren snorted. "Zyn, you can be so blunt sometimes."

"Eh, maybe I shouldn't go," Zyn said.

"What? You have to!" Ren protested at once.

"It'll be fun," Ak-tu added. "I promise to play plenty of Uneeq music—our favorite band!"

"But I don't have a partner," Zyn pointed out. "It's in the rules, isn't it?"

"Just ask the other first-years," Ak-tu said.

"There's twenty-one of us. What happens to that extra person?" Zyn asked.

"You can ask the second-years. Or third- and fourth-years," he suggested.

Zyn scowled. "I'd rather just go alone."

Ak-tu sighed. "Either you find a partner, or I will have to find one for you—which will be anyone else who thinks they don't have a partner."

"But if there's still an odd number between the years—"

"There isn't," Ak-tu said simply. "We make sure we have an even number every year."

And he walked off to the staircase, leaving Zyn staring after him in dismay.

Ren glanced at her sister. "You better just find someone. You never know who the leftover might be."

"But what about Sarala? Does she have someone else in mind already?"

"I'll talk to her," Ren said. "I'll see if I can get her to agree to go with you…again."

"Thanks."

Ren dashed away to the stairs and went up to the fifth floor, feeling a little winded after the many steps. She knocked on the door, and Sarala opened it with an irritated scowl on her face.

"What do you want?" she grunted.

"Who are you going to the dance with, if not Zyn?"

"I don't know yet."

"Hmm…how's about one of the other earth students?" Ren suggested, entering Sarala's room.

"You're not going to shut up until I go, are you?" Sarala muttered.

"Nope!" Ren replied cheerfully. "How's about Ebony? He seems nice."

"No, thanks."

"Raimugi?"

"They're going with Mernao."

"Hmm…what about C3?"

"C3? Are you serious?" Sarala huffed, sitting on her bed. "There's no way I'd go with someone as rude as him. He's worse than Zyn."

Ren snorted. "Does that mean you're going with Zyn?"

"If she was interested in being a girl, maybe," Sarala grumbled.

"Of course she is," Ren said blankly. "She didn't say we had to call her by different pronouns now. She's still my sister."

"Huh."

"Oh—" Ren's eyes widened. "Are you saying you're only interested in girls?"

Sarala made a noncommittal noise.

"No wonder you don't want to go with any of my suggestions," Ren chuckled. "I must say, I haven't met many people who are only attracted to one gender. Most people are pansexual or bisexual. I think even asexual people are more common than unisexual people!"

"What?" Sarala asked blankly.

"Oh! Pansexual is when you're attracted to people more for personality, and gender or sex doesn't matter. Bisexual is when people have preferences, but are still interested in more than one gender or sex. Unisexual is you—only attracted to one gender or sex. And asexual is someone who's not attracted to anyone, like Dad."

Sarala grunted.

"Of course, you can be asexual but still have a romantic orientation, like panromantic. In this case, you'd be sexually attracted to nobody, but romantically attracted to any gender. Does that make sense?"

Sarala shrugged.

"Anyway, I'm panromantic myself. Gender doesn't matter, but personality is everything."

"Then why are you with Frost?" Sarala asked simply.

Ren didn't expect that. "Umm…what do you mean?"

"I'm still mad at him for the potion mess-up," Sarala growled, crossing her arms over her chest. "He's such a jerk. You can do way better than him."

"I know," Ren admitted, feeling a bit uneasy as she shifted her weight from one leg to the other. "But I wanted to be nice and give him a chance when he first asked me out. I was sorta planning on ending things after the dance tomorrow."

Sarala smirked. "Good," she muttered.

"Why?" Ren asked. "I feel like that's such a mean thing to do… like I'm just using him to go to the dance, and dumping him after. That's just…well, mean."

Sarala shrugged carelessly. "Then dump him before the dance and go with someone else."

"Like who?"

"Me."

Ren eyed Sarala a bit skeptically. "Did you just ask me out?"

"Just as a partner for a stupid dance," Sarala said, twirling her hair around her finger. "Not forever. I'm not *that* interested in you."

Ren snorted. "So you'd want to go to the dance with me, just to dump *me* after?"

"Maybe."

Ren tapped her pointed chin thoughtfully. "Well, I must admit, you're way more interesting than Frost. Okay, we'll go together."

"What about me?"

Ren swirled around to see Zyn standing just outside the room, leaning against the doorframe. "How long have you been standing there?"

"Long enough to know you betrayed me and decided to go with Sarala instead," Zyn chuckled.

"Umm…" Ren blushed, not knowing what to say.

"It's fine, I don't really care," Zyn said, waving her hand as she walked away. "I think you'd make a good couple."

Ren exchanged a glance with Sarala, feeling more heat rise to her cheeks. Sarala quickly dropped her gaze, her own face red.

"Well, um, I guess I'll go break up with Frost early," Ren said, laughing uneasily.

She hurried away down the stairs, glad that it would be dinner soon. She'd find Frost in the Eating Hall and break up with him, simple as that! And as for finding a partner for Zyn, she'd have plenty of chances during dinner.

Ren made it to the Eating Hall just before the bell rang, flavorful scents hitting her nose at once and making her stomach growl. Yet she didn't bother getting a tray and instead waited by the door. Students began showing up in small groups, until the Eating Hall was packed with bodies and loud chatter. Frost came in with Raimugi and Mernao, as usual.

"Hey, Frost!" Ren said, waving.

Frost smiled and walked over to her. "Hey."

"I just wanted to tell you that, um...well, you see...I kinda am..."

"Just spit it out," Frost said in exasperation.

"I'm...breaking up with you," Ren mumbled.

Frost stared at her for a long moment, then frowned. "Why? What about the dance tomorrow?"

Ren shrugged. "I just don't feel we have a connection," she said apologetically. "And I'm...going with someone else."

Frost snorted derisively and shoved past her, rejoining his friends. Raimugi and Mernao glanced at Ren, then grinned at her and pointed their thumbs up. Ren frowned at the delightful reaction, but she didn't have time to ponder it as Zyn and Sarala arrived.

"Did you do it yet?" Zyn asked.

"Yep!" Ren said. "And look at all these people you can ask to go with you, Zyn!"

Zyn sighed.

"How did he take it?" Sarala asked Ren, glancing over at Frost.

Ren shrugged. "He seemed more annoyed than anything. Raimugi and Mernao were happy though."

"Everyone knows you can do better than him," Sarala scoffed.

"Oh, and *you* are better?" Ren teased.

Sarala's face hardened. She stalked off towards the counter, grabbing a tray from the clean stack. Ren frowned after her.

"How do I do this, then?" Zyn asked Ren, not seeming to have noticed the strange exchange. "Do I have to go up to people one at a time?"

"Who here does not have a partner for the dance tomorrow?" a loud voice suddenly rang through the room.

The Eating Hall fell quiet as the students turned about to see who had spoken. It was C3, standing in the center of the hall on one of the table benches, where his short figure would be seen better.

"Well?" C3 demanded. "It is my understanding that we have to attend the dance with a partner. I have counted the number of students in each year, and we are at an even number overall. So we each have a partner. Raise your hand if you do not have a partner."

"Here's your chance," Ren told Zyn in an undertone.

"There's *no way* I'm going with him," Zyn muttered.

"You don't have to," Ren said. "Look—there are other people! You can go with one of them instead."

Zyn glanced at the people raising their hands. There was Frost, of course, as well as two or three third-years and a fourth-year. Zyn lit up and pointed at someone. Ren followed her gaze and saw Mint, standing awkwardly on the other side of the room with their hand limp in the air above their bushy head.

"MINT!" Zyn screamed. "WANT TO GO TO THE DANCE WITH ME?"

Mint looked terrified at being called out. But when their green eyes landed on Zyn, they seemed to relax a little. "YES!" they squealed back.

Zyn chuckled. "Well, that was easier than I expected."

Ren rolled her eyes.

The remaining people quickly partnered up, leaving C3 and Frost stuck with one another. Ren and Zyn laughed about the fact as they ate, then discussed what they were going to wear the following day. They were almost done eating when Ren realized that Sarala wasn't sitting with them. Ren frowned and got to her feet, glancing around the crowded hall.

"What are you looking for?" Zyn asked, sipping at her bowl of tangy tomato soup.

"I was wondering where Sarala got to, but I don't see her," Ren muttered. "I just thought she was being quiet…"

"Maybe she turned in early," Zyn suggested. "It's a big day tomorrow."

Ren frowned. "Maybe…but I don't think so."

"Well, I'm done eating. If you're done, we can go back to the tower and see if she's waiting for us to get in."

The sisters therefore left the Courtyard after putting their dirty trays on the trashcan by the door. They walked through the snow, their fuzzy winter robes flapping around their ankles in the light breeze. They had almost made it to the Tai Chi Studio when Ren's head started pounding.

"Zyn—" she gasped, and she reached out to grab her sister's arm quickly.

"Ren!"

But Ren did not hear Zyn's cry. She fell to the snow, screaming in pain as her head felt like it was about to explode. She was having the vision again! Or was it a different one?

She had to focus on the images flashing through her mind. What was that shiny object? Was that water rushing towards her? There was something purple… But it was happening too fast, and she couldn't remember anything else by the time the pain subsided and her eyes opened.

Staring at Zyn, her sister's face slowly coming into focus against the dark night sky, Ren realized she had ended up on the ground. Everything was quiet around them. She shifted until she was sitting up, rubbing at her aching head. The sudden silence felt unnatural.

"It was another vision, wasn't it?" Zyn mumbled, her brown skin appearing unusually pale. "Are you okay?"

"Yeah," Ren murmured, bringing her knees up so she could rest her chin on them. "I wish it didn't hurt so much. Or that I could actually *see* all the images…"

The Tai Chi Studio door banged open. The twins glanced up to see Ak-tu and Sarala hurrying towards them, kicking up snow.

"What happened?" Ak-tu demanded as he sunk down beside Ren.

"We heard you screaming from the tower," Sarala said, her golden eyes concerned.

"Another vision," Ren muttered.

"Did you see anything this time?" Ak-tu asked.

"Something shiny, something purple, and something to do with water—I think," she told him.

Ak-tu frowned, then grabbed her arm and pulled her to her feet. "Well, let's get you inside, where it's nice and warm. Come on. I'll get a headache potion from Fern."

Ren shook her head. "I still have some from the last vial she gave me," she muttered.

Ak-tu and Zyn helped her across the Courtyard, as she was a bit unsteady on her feet. Sarala went ahead of them, opening the doors and stepping aside to allow them through.

"I think I'm just going to bed," Ren said, feeling drained as she entered the warm tower. "Don't worry, Dad. I'm fine."

{Did you see that spirit again?} Ak-tu asked. *{The one from your meditation-dream?}*

Ren shook her head, then instantly regretted the action. It made her dizzy all over again. *{No, nothing.}*

Ak-tu merely nodded to her words, though he looked concerned. They all escorted Ren up the stairs and to her room, moving at a snail-like pace. Ren thanked them, then went to her desk drawer and pulled out the half-full potion vial from Fern. She drank the rest of the potion, and the pounding in her head stopped soon after.

Ren walked over to the window and stared out. "What do these visions mean? What is that spirit trying to tell me?" she whispered to herself. "And why *me*?"

CHAPTER 19: PARTY

The next day went by fast, and it was soon time to get ready for the Moonlight Dance.

Zyn hopped down the last few steps to the family room, where Sarala and Ren were playing a game of YAT. Zyn had just been playing with them, but she vanished minutes before. Sarala thought she had just gone to the bathroom, but that was clearly not the case.

Zyn was now dressed in a bright blue robe covered with white snowflakes of various designs. Underneath, she wore a stripy silver-and-white collared shirt and baggy blue pants. She had pointed blue dress shoes, the tips silver in color. To top everything off, she wore a tall hat with snowflakes hanging off it.

"I'm READY!" she shouted.

Ren looked up from where she sat at the table with Sarala, pausing as she placed her Draw 6 card down. She looked amused as she saw Zyn.

"Zyn, where did you get that hat?" she asked. "And are those Dad's pants?"

Zyn bounded over in a zigzag way, her arms out on either side of her. "Why aren't you dressed yet?" she demanded.

"It's only 5:30," Ren pointed out.

"Go get ready!" Zyn ordered. "NOW! You only have thirty minutes until it begins!"

Ren rolled her eyes. "Yes, ol' wise one," she scoffed. She looked to Sarala and chuckled, "Looks like you're saved from drawing six cards…at least, for now! We'll have to finish it later."

"Ugh, not a Draw 6!" Sarala huffed.

Ren glanced back at Zyn. "Do you mind helping Sarala get something nice to wear from the Theatre?"

Sarala froze, YAT vanishing from her mind. She thought *Ren* was going to help her! She wasn't sure she wanted Zyn flinging multi-colored robes at her.

"Sure thing!" Zyn said cheerfully. "Come on!"

The Theatre looked much different from the previous day, when Sarala had first entered it to watch the play. The chairs had vanished, leaving a wide dance floor. There were tables along the back wall, the kitchen staff hurrying about with cartfuls of food, drinks, trays, and utensils. The dusty smell that lingered the day before was now replaced by aromas of sweet and savory food, as well as pine and spruce.

The decorations themselves were coming along nicely. Fern was moving her hands about, causing mini winter trees to sprout from the floor. They stretched to the ceiling before falling still. Aster weaved silver garland around the trees, which lit up once placed. Ak-tu, meanwhile, was causing snowflakes to fill the air, and Khurshid used his air magic to cast them about.

Each person was already wearing fancy robes or dresses, except for Khurshid, who wore his typical golden robe. Ak-tu wore a green suit robe with black-and-white symbols scattered across it, a collared shirt with zigzagging green-and-blue stripes, and black dress pants. Fern donned a curvy suit with two pieces of fabric hanging down from the back; the suit itself was a vivid green with purple flowers patterned across it. Aster wore a pink-and-silver dress with long sleeves that ended in fluffy cuffs. Even the cooks were dressed in rainbow colors.

Sarala didn't have much time to look at the other decorations, like the emerald tablecloths or the blue candles strewn about the room. She had been so focused on the magic, that she nearly walked right into Zyn as they reached the stage.

"Come on!" Zyn said, hopping onto the platform.

Sarala bounded up after her, and they hurried to the backstage. A large room full of props and costumes waited for them.

"Here you go!" Zyn said cheerfully, opening a closet door full of the fanciest robes. "Have fun!"

Sarala looked at her in surprise as she turned around, preparing to leave. "You're not going to stay?"

"Why would I?"

"I need second opinions!" Sarala pointed out. "And Ren asked you to help me!"

"Oh." Zyn considered that for a moment, then said, "I just assumed she wanted me to bring you here to find an outfit of your own. I didn't think you'd want my opinion, since I dress so crazy."

"I've never dressed up for anything fancy in my life," Sarala pointed out. "I have some fashion sense, but...not much."

"Oh, okay!" Zyn chuckled. "I'll wait here, then, and give you a rating for each outfit! But try to be fast about it. We've only got thirty minutes—or less, by now."

Sarala did as she asked for the next twenty minutes. She would come out of the closet (where she got changed in private), dressed in multiple outfits, while Zyn threw out random numbers between one and ten. She had tried on various outfits of multiple colors and textures, until, at long last, she finally found the one.

She now wore a dark purple dress with long sleeves that went a bit past her wrists. Golden stars were patterned across it, but not as brightly as anything Zyn ever wore. The dress had a horizontal silver stripe across the middle, separating the tight top from the flowing bottom. Pale purple tights and winter boots could just be seen beneath. A full moon necklace completed her look.

"Perfect!" Zyn exclaimed when she exited the closet. "And that'll have to do. The dance will be starting soon!"

Almost as if Ak-tu had heard her words, his voice rang throughout the school. "The Moonlight Dance is about to begin. Please come to the Theatre to have some fun!"

"Did he make an announcement earlier to give people a chance to dress up before coming?" Sarala asked Zyn.

"Why would he?" Zyn asked, as they left the backroom and returned to the stage. "We all got an air-mail about it, and there are some posters around the student quarters for those who don't check their air-mail."

Sarala didn't have a mirror or an air-mail, nor did she see any posters if they were only put up in the student quarters.

The two jumped off the stage and hurried to the Theatre door, where Ak-tu and Aster would be checking in the students. According to Zyn, wands weren't allowed at the event, so each student would have to turn out their pockets. Wands and parties were a bad mix, a fact that Zyn liked to remind Ak-tu of leading up to the dance. When the school first opened, wands were allowed and disaster followed, something Ak-tu tried to forget.

"Let's wait for our partners out here," Zyn said, pointing to the garden nearby.

They were only waiting a few minutes when Ren came bounding over, nearly slipping on the snow. She was dressed in a purple robe with a white collared shirt beneath. The robe fell past her knees, unlike her usual robe, which was shorter. The robe looked plain, but when she turned around, there was a large full moon on the back of it. She wore black pants with thin purple stripes on the sides, and black dress shoes.

"Hey, we're matching, Sarala!" Ren chuckled, pointing at Sarala's purple dress. "I guess it's a good thing we're partners!"

Sarala held back the smile, but knew she was blushing.

"Any sign of Mint?" Zyn asked Ren.

"How should I know?"

"Good point."

"Should we go in, then?" Sarala questioned Ren.

"No, let's wait for Mint," Ren replied.

The three girls therefore stood, shivering in their dress clothes as a cold breeze swept through. They luckily weren't huddling for long, as Mint soon approached from the western building.

Mint was wearing a bright green dress with a falling leaf pattern on it, and enormous brown boots on their feet. The green bracelet on their wrist identified them as nonbinary that day. They wore a plain green jacket to cover the sleeveless dress, which simply did not go with the fancy outfit.

"How do I look?" Mint asked, twiddling their thumbs nervously.

"Great!" Ren said at once, in a slightly higher voice than usual.

Sarala and Zyn did not reply. Sarala could see that Zyn was regretting her choice of Mint.

They joined the long line, which moved quickly. Ak-tu checked them in, and the four moved off to the side, a bit uncertain about what to do now.

After a good portion of students had entered, music started blasting. Some students took to the dance floor at once, while others merely stood off to the side to eat or chat. How the students could hear one another, Sarala did not know, wincing at the booming beats. Lights danced around the room, adding to the fun and chaotic atmosphere.

"What do we do?" Sarala asked Ren loudly, hoping the girl could hear her.

"Dance!" Ren replied brightly, a shine in her eyes.

Sarala groaned. "I am *not* dancing!"

Ren laughed. "Nonsense!"

She grabbed Sarala's hand and pulled her forward. Sarala was normally steady and could hold her ground, especially in sparring matches. But Ren had swept her entirely off her feet.

"Come on!" Ren encouraged, releasing Sarala and dancing on the spot.

"I don't know how to dance!" Sarala growled, feeling flustered and embarrassed.

"It's easy, just move your body in time to the music!" Ren shouted above a particularly loud song.

Sarala groaned. She was not about to make a fool of herself. Turning away from Ren, she walked off and dropped her eyes so she wouldn't see the pained expression on Ren's face.

Why did I ask Ren to go with me? I'm such an idiot! I should have gone with Zyn, or not bothered to go at all, Sarala thought, annoyed with herself as she hurried over to one of the food tables.

She shoved through several people, barely able to avoid being hit by arms flinging about. Mint almost full-on slammed a hand into her face, as wildly as they were dancing; the students around them quickly shuffled out of the way, and even Zyn had abandoned her partner.

She finally reached the food table, and saw with no surprise that C3 stood alone. He was wearing a dark green robe instead of his typical black one, but the left sleeve was still rolled up and tucked into the golden ring at his elbow. Sarala wondered briefly why he always wore the ring, and why it reminded her of something. He also wore a plain white shirt, gray vest, and black pants underneath. It was all topped off with a dull green tie, to match the robe.

"Greetings," C3 said loudly, his voice hardly audible over the music.

She glanced around, then asked, "Where's your partner at?"

C3 shrugged. "I came with Frost, but he went to hang out with Mernao and Raimugi."

"So you're alone?"

"Basically," C3 said carelessly. "I don't mind. I'd rather be here alone, than with someone I do not speak to."

Sarala didn't know what to say, and didn't feel like shouting a response. C3 stared at her for a long moment, then signaled to the food.

"Have you tried any of this food yet? It's actually much more magic-filled than the typical food we eat."

C3 was soon pointing to each dish on the table. "That's a frosty-full (like a waffle), that's a crackling cracker (which explodes at random points), that's snowy shortbread, over there are chocolate cloud clusters, those are powdered pine pasties (which aren't actually pine trees, of course), that's gingerbread glory, and that last dish over there is blizzard beans. There's also winter wine (which is juice, not alcohol), cold crystal water (which *is* different from regular water), fizzing fire pop, and stormy smoothies."

Sarala gazed at him for several long moments, then turned and walked away. There was no way she was going to stand around at the dance with C3—especially if he was going to nerd over the different types of food.

She walked to another food table, remaining on the edge of the dancing students. The music seemed to have been turned down a bit in volume—or she was going deaf. She glanced at the crowd. There were Raimugi and Mernao, dancing energetically with each other as Frost watched on grumpily. Moon danced alone like Mint, but she was much more controlled and merely seemed to be waving her hands in the air. A bit farther away, Aster was prancing about, lifting his knees high as he hopped like a deer rather than danced. Several students watched him with large grins on their faces, clearly laughing.

Everyone was having so much fun. But was Ren? Sarala wished she hadn't left her friend, yet what was she supposed to do? She didn't know how to dance! And there were too many people, too much noise, too many aromas that made her stomach twist, and too many dazzling lights that made her dizzy.

"Sarala!"

She was surprised she even heard the yell, and glanced up to see Ren and Zyn headed her way. She forced her stiff legs to hold her in place, though all she wanted to do was run away. How could she face Ren after asking her to the dance, just to leave her dancing alone?

"Are you okay?" Ren shouted, as the music got loud again.

Zyn scowled, then grabbed Ren and Sarala, dragging them both towards the door. Fern was standing there, and opened the door to allow them outside. They weren't the only students outdoors, as a few others had gone out to take a break from the noise and heat.

"Now we can hear each other better," Zyn said.

"Are you okay?" Ren repeated to Sarala.

Sarala shrugged. "It's too much for me," she muttered, her ears pounding and her stomach still clenching.

"It's a dance," Ren said with a shrug. "It's kind of what happens."

Sarala rubbed at her forehead, hoping she wouldn't get a headache. Not knowing how to respond, she merely wanted to leave the dance behind. However, she also didn't want to do that to Ren, considering she broke up with Frost early just to go with Sarala.

"We can stay out here, if you want," Ren said.

"Yeah, we can still hear the music," Zyn pointed out. "Though *that* song sucks and I wish we couldn't," she added with a dark look towards the Theatre.

Ren snorted in laughter. "Oh, Zyn!"

"You two might as well go back in and enjoy yourselves," Sarala grunted. "I'd just get in the way." She looked up at Ren for a moment, then lowered her eyes as she muttered, "I'm sorry, Ren... But I just can't do this."

She turned and headed for the nearby garden, seeking shelter from both the cold and her friends. She clenched her jaw bitterly, wishing she was stronger.

Sarala was a bit surprised that the sisters didn't chase after her, but she was glad to see that she was alone. Finding a bench amongst the twisted trees and bare bushes, she sat down.

I'm such an idiot, she thought, again and again.

She didn't know how long she sat there for, but she suddenly realized that she wasn't alone. Pulling herself out of her head instantly, she scanned the undergrowth around her. She narrowed her eyes as she got slowly to her feet, searching behind and above her.

That's when she heard a small rustle to her right. She snapped her gaze in that direction, flicking her eyes to and fro, trying to catch any sign of movement.

There!

But she had nothing to worry about. It was just C3. The boy staggered through the bushes, eyes scanning the plants and an excited smile on his face. He looked up as he noticed Sarala standing only meters away, staring at him. His mouth quickly fell into a neutral line as he saw her.

"Oh—Sarala," he said plainly. "What are you doing out here?"

"I could ask you the same thing," she huffed. "What are you looking for?"

"Nothing," C3 said.

She cast him a skeptical look.

"Fine. I *might* have seen a spirit over here, but there is apparently nothing, as I can't find anything," C3 said, eyeing her closely. "I've been searching this garden for a while now."

Sarala frowned. This was the same garden she had seen the weird movement months before—and where she found the mirror shard. Was it possible that there was another piece of glass lying around?

"Have you seen any spirits?" C3 asked her. The corners of his lips twitched, as if he was about to smile. "Do you want to help me look?"

Sarala shook her head. "I don't believe in spirits," she muttered. "It was probably just a frogoyle you saw."

He stared at her for a long moment, frowned, then turned and walked away with slumped shoulders.

Sarala waited several long moments, making sure that he was gone, then searched the bushes. She wished there was more light. But the moonlight hardly penetrated the trees, and the lamplight around the school didn't reach the gardens.

Sarala sighed. Maybe she'd just have to come back the next

day to see if there were any glass shards. But what if it disappeared? What if a different student stumbled across it? Ak-tu had said that the shards were dangerous, that they shouldn't be picked up... Sarala frowned and decided to keep looking.

But after another thirty minutes, she was shivering so much and she couldn't feel any parts of her numb body. She gave up the search and staggered out of the garden like a rigid tree. Set on going back to the tower, she remembered that Ak-tu was at the dance too. He would have to be alerted of the potential mirror shard.

She therefore turned back towards the Theatre and entered the dance room stiffly. The music blasted through her ears again, and the lights swirled around her. It seemed there were less students dancing now. Some were eating, some were standing off to the side, and some had left altogether.

Sarala didn't see any sign of Ren or Zyn anywhere, for which she was grateful. Mint had stopped dancing crazily, and was now stuffing their mouth full of magical food. She rolled her eyes and peered around the room, until she saw the black-and-white symbols on Ak-tu's robe.

Making her way towards him, she wished he wasn't standing right next to the loud speakers. He glanced up and waved at her as they made eye contact; she quickly motioned for him to come over. Ak-tu frowned and weaved between the remaining groups of dancing students easily, until he was level with her.

"What?" Ak-tu asked loudly.

Sarala grabbed Ak-tu much like Zyn had grabbed her earlier, and dragged him out the door.

"Ugh, I hate all that noise!" she complained, once they were outside.

Ak-tu raised one side of his unibrow.

"Sorry," she muttered. "But it's true. You can't hear anything in there."

"Did you have something to tell me?" Ak-tu asked. "Is Ren okay? Is Zyn?"

"I don't know. We didn't stay together very long," she said earnestly.

Ak-tu narrowed his eyes, and Sarala pressed on quickly before he could ask any further questions.

"I was in the garden, and I felt like something was out there. Then C3 came through and told me he thought he saw a spirit. He was trying to look for it."

"Did he say what the spirit looked like?" Ak-tu asked.

Sarala shook her head.

"Did he say if it dropped anything?"

"No, but I went looking in the garden for the past half-hour," she said. "I didn't see anything on the ground."

Ak-tu ran his fingers over his mustache. "Hmm…I wonder if it's the same spirit, or a different one…"

"Or if C3 just made it all up," Sarala grunted.

Ak-tu frowned, but said nothing in response to that. "Can you show me where it happened?" he asked.

Sarala nodded and led the way back to the garden, wishing she could go inside and get warmed up. But she could rest after she was done with her task. She pushed through the bushes until she found the bench she'd been sitting at. Then, she pointed at the spot where she saw C3, and motioned to the areas she checked.

Ak-tu nodded slowly. "You may go back inside. You look like you're freezing. I'll take over from here."

"But what are you going to do?" Sarala queried.

"Look for any objects this spirit might have dropped," he told her simply. "And see if the frogoyles noticed anything."

Sarala shrugged. "Good luck, then."

She was set on heading back to the tower, but her feet carried her to the Theatre. She had to tell Ren and Zyn what she saw. But what if Ren didn't want to talk to her? She stopped in her tracks a few feet from the door, her heart beating rapidly. After all, she had abandoned the very person she was determined to bring to the dance. *I have to find her…make this up to her somehow….*

She searched through the groups of students, but she didn't see Ren or Zyn anywhere. After circling around three times, Sarala gave up and stopped by a food table. She hadn't eaten dinner (as dinner hadn't been served, since there was food at the dance), so she was quite hungry. But at the same time, she felt too guilty to eat, her stomach twisting more the longer she stared at the food. She sighed and turned her back on the table.

I don't deserve to eat, she thought glumly. Sarala therefore left the Theatre, her knotted stomach growling. *Shut up,* she told it. *You've had it much worse before. One night without food isn't that bad. Be glad it isn't three days!*

Sarala soon reached the Tai Chi Studio and went inside. She walked to the tower door and knocked loudly, knowing it'd be locked. A moment later, Zyn opened the door for her.

"I was wondering when you'd turn up," Zyn said.

"Is Ren here too?"

"Obviously. Why?"

Sarala peered around the family room as she entered. But Ren wasn't there. *She must be in her room.*

"You going to answer, or are you just going to stand there like a statue?" Zyn asked sarcastically.

Sarala shot a glare at her, then headed for the stairs. She went up without a glance back, reaching Ren's bedroom and knocking on the door.

"Go away!"

Sarala sighed. "What if I was Zyn?" she asked. "Would you let me in then?"

The door opened and Ren glared out at her. Her eyes were a bit red, and it looked like she'd been crying. Sarala felt even more guilty for leaving her.

"What do you want?" Ren snapped. "You asked me out to the dance, just to leave me alone the entire time! What was the point of that?"

"I'm sorry. I couldn't stand the noise and all the people."

"And you couldn't just put up with it for five minutes?" Ren growled. "You said you'd do at least five minutes! I would have been happy with five minutes, or even two!"

"I'm sorry," Sarala repeated, shifting uneasily. "I did go back to look for you, for what it's worth… But that music was terrible, and all those people…"

Ren snorted in disbelief at that. "We eat around all those people—all the time!"

"But it was different, with all the loud noise and bright lights and…" Sarala shivered.

Ren's expression softened, but she did not reply.

Not knowing what else to say, Sarala grumbled, "I was out in the garden, and C3 came in claiming that he saw a spirit. So I thought there might have been another mirror shard lying around. I went to tell your dad about it, and he's searching the garden now."

Ren perked up at this, momentarily forgetting her anger with Sarala. "Another mirror shard? Hmm...I wonder what that would mean, if there was another one."

Sarala shrugged. "That's why I was gone so long. But I did plan on going back...to...*dance*...with you..."

Ren smiled. "Really?" Then, her face hardened. "Well, too bad you didn't come back sooner. It's too late."

"Ren—"

"I'm going to bed. I'll see you tomorrow," Ren said stiffly.

She closed the door in Sarala's face. Sarala sighed, knowing she deserved it. *I hope this doesn't come between us... Why am I such an idiot?*

CHAPTER 20: BREAKTHRU

Once the Moonlight Dance was over, many of the students went home the following day for the rest of winter break. The Moon Festival, celebrating the winter season, began on December 22. The Day of the Moon was the official winter holiday, but the students would be back in school by the time it arrived on January 22. Most families therefore celebrated the holiday during the Moon Festival instead.

Zyn and Ren were quite accustomed to being the only kids in the whole school during the summer and winter breaks. But now, they had Sarala with them too (once Ren got over her annoyance with Sarala, which took a few days until Sarala persuaded her to finish the game of YAT they'd started before the dance). The three girls had plenty of fun together, playing games or chatting. They even practiced martial arts, though Ak-tu refused to teach them any new moves.

December 28 was soon upon them, and Ak-tu woke Zyn very early. Zyn blinked in confusion for a moment, then remembered what this day meant.

"We're going to Graytor," Ak-tu whispered.

"I'm going to see the therapist today!" Zyn yelped.

"Shush!" Ak-tu ordered, though his eyes lit up in amusement. "Come on."

"What about breakfast?" Zyn queried.

"We'll make it on the way."

"Okay!"

Ak-tu left the room as Zyn got dressed in her typical stripy shirt and baggy pants. She threw on a robe with lightning bolts across it, then hurried after her father. She ran up the stairs, passing Sarala's room on the fifth floor and coming to a stop outside Ak-tu's room on the sixth. Ak-tu waited between two doors. One door led to his bedroom, while the other door led to a bridge that connected to the northeastern tower.

"Wear this," Ak-tu said, and he shoved a fuzzy hat on Zyn's head.

"Hey!" she complained as the hat went over her eyes.

"You can't beat me!" Ak-tu exclaimed, and he bolted out the door and across the bridge.

Zyn pushed the hat out of her eyes and took off after her father. She skidded to a stop after a few steps, almost forgetting to close the door; otherwise, the tower would be freezing. Once done, she hurried across the snowy bridge, but Ak-tu had already reached the opposite tower.

"No fair! You cheated!" Zyn scoffed. "*And* I bet you woke up everyone!"

Ak-tu shrugged. "It's winter break. They'll probably go back to sleep for hours anyway."

He unlocked the door he stood next to, and led the way inside the other tower. This tower was six floors tall as well, but there weren't any actual floors. The entire tower would have been empty, if there wasn't a giant ship sitting in it. Most people used small boats to get around, which were powered by magic. But Ak-tu traveled with the ship; the large vessels were most often seen at sea or in busy cities.

Ak-tu lifted his hand in front of him, and the whole place soon lit up. He then walked down two flights of stairs to a platform that sat parallel to the ship's deck. He hopped across the small gap and landed on the deck, then went to check the sails. Zyn followed him onto the deck and to the next level.

The ship was four floors in height, if the sails weren't being counted. The third floor, which Zyn was now on, contained the kitchen and several bedrooms. The kitchen was located at the very front of the ship, with a giant window instead of a wooden wall, so they could keep an eye on what was in front of them without being on the deck itself. Beyond the kitchen was a narrow hallway, with doors that led to various bedrooms.

The second floor was the fun floor. One side of the hallway was dedicated to a vast library. On the other side was a game room and a big training room (complete with orange mats and a long mirror, just as in the Kung Fu and Tai Chi Studios at the school).

The first floor wasn't meant for much beyond the engines, bathroom, and extra storage space. It also contained a large door that allowed them to get on and off the ship. The door had to be big to allow furniture and other enormous objects to get on board. Zyn remembered when Ak-tu ordered beds for the school; there wasn't enough space for the beds in the storage room, and they had to make multiple trips to Graytor. A weekend trip turned into a two-week-long project.

Zyn sat down at the square-shaped kitchen table, still feeling tired despite running in the frigid temperatures. She had no idea what time it was, but the sky wasn't even gray yet, so she assumed it was quite early.

Ak-tu came down the stairs. "Are you ready to fly, Zyn?" he asked cheerfully.

"Why are we going so early?"

"The appointment is at 9. Graytor is hours away, as you know," Ak-tu pointed out.

"Ugh."

"You can always go back to bed."

"Nah, I'm already up," Zyn said with a yawn. "Besides, the engines are always so loud—it takes forever to fall asleep when they're on."

Ak-tu shrugged. "Suit yourself," he said.

He walked away down the hall, where another set of stairs lay. After a few minutes, the loud engines roared to life, causing the whole ship to vibrate. Zyn went to one of the side windows and watched the engines come out from the first floor. There were four engines in total, two in the front and two in the back, on both sides of the ship.

Ak-tu soon returned, but he didn't stop at the kitchen. He walked up the stairs to return to the deck. Zyn trailed after him, always fascinated to see the ship take off.

Ak-tu now stood facing the tower wall, where the forest around the school lay on the other side. He lifted his hands in front of him, focusing entirely on the stone. After a few seconds, the rock began to shift and scrape to the sides. Several minutes passed, then there was a large gap in the tower wall. Zyn could now see the forest, full of pine and fuzzy trees.

Once the wall was open, Ak-tu moved to the steering wheel at the front of the ship. He hit a button, which made the ship fly in reverse, then steered it carefully through the aperture. After they were out of the tower, Ak-tu pushed another button, which made the vessel hover in midair. He then faced the tower, raised his hands, and the wall closed once more.

"Ready to go?" Ak-tu called to Zyn.

Zyn leaned against the railing and stared out at the school. "Definitely," she said, grinning.

The enchanted ship then raised higher into the sky until it was above the treetops. Ak-tu hit another button, and the ship went forward, heading west for the city.

Zyn was full of anxious energy as the ship got closer to Graytor hours later. What would the therapist do? Was she going to be able to keep taking the potions that Fern had given to her, which shrunk her chest?

"Please calm down," Ak-tu said, setting a dish of steaming pancakes on the kitchen table.

Zyn stopped tapping her foot and glanced over her shoulder at her father. "Sorry," she murmured.

She snatched a pancake from the plate, then decided she was too anxious to eat and merely held it as she continued to bounce. Would she be able to set up a permanent surgery? What about taking hormonal potions? What sort of process would she have to go through to be comfortable in her body?

Ak-tu walked over to Zyn, placing a hand on her shoulder. "Don't worry. From what I understand, this first meeting is just to get to know you. The therapist needs to make sure you're actually feeling dysphoria, then you'll start the process. It all depends on what you want to do with your body—which the therapist will go over."

Zyn fidgeted uneasily. "But what if I've had my realization too late? Will I not be able to take Fern's potions?"

"What do you mean, too late? It's never too late to figure out more about yourself, or make changes in your life. If *I* felt dysphoric at my age, I'd be able to go and chat with the therapist too."

Zyn chuckled lightly at the thought. "Okay, maybe not so much with age, but...does it matter if I didn't feel too dysphoric until a few weeks ago? I mean, I've been feeling like that for a while, but it took me a bit of time to *realize* what it was...."

"Ren told me you were very upset when you started puberty," Ak-tu said simply. "You started at what, thirteen? You've been feeling like this for over a year, then."

Zyn shrugged in return. "To be honest, ever since I was a kid, I've never felt comfortable about the idea of having..." She motioned to her thankfully-flat chest.

"I understand," Ak-tu assured her. "But if you start taking hormonal potions, you can get off those at any point if you decide this isn't for you. That is, if you *want* to take hormonal potions."

"I think I do," Zyn said. She suddenly grinned. "Then I can grow a nice long mustache, like you!"

Ak-tu stared at her blandly.

Zyn snapped her gaze to the window. "DAD!"

Ak-tu looked up, then dashed away to the deck for the wheel. They were only feet away from hitting the top of a building. Ak-tu managed to reach the wheel in time, and Zyn stared out the window to watch the mighty ship fly higher in the sky. She let out a sigh of relief, then hurried to the deck.

Ak-tu moved the ship to the outskirts of the city. Once the ship landed with a rumbling thud, the two went to the bottom floor of the ship. Ak-tu turned off the engines, and they went to the storage room. He opened the door with a quick hand wave, and they got off the ship, Ak-tu closing (and locking) it behind them.

Zyn suddenly didn't know what to say. She realized she was still holding the pancake and offered it to Ak-tu, who merely pocketed it.

They climbed up a small green slope, towards the heart of the city. Zyn stared at all the trees and plants, finding it hard to focus on the people milling about. Boats drove by on the cobblestone roads, their wooden wheels rattling and creaking as they went. Merchant stalls were set up on the sidewalks, selling food, clothes, jewelry, and more. The buildings were mostly made of stone rather than wood, and stood at least five floors tall with small plants growing on the roofs.

After several minutes of walking, they reached a building with "Graytor Gender Services" printed in large letters over the doorway. Ak-tu held open the door for Zyn, and she stepped inside.

They went up to the front desk, Ak-tu taking over the conversation as Zyn's mouth suddenly went dry. Ak-tu announced that they were there for an appointment at 9, filled out some paperwork for Zyn since her hands were too shaky, and the two went to sit in the waiting area. They had barely sat down when they heard their mispronounced names.

"Ock-too and Zinvus Kayhong?" a loud voice called.

The voice belonged to a tall person with angular eyes and blonde hair. They stood in a doorway off to the right of the front desk. Ak-tu and Zyn got to their feet and approached the person.

"Welcome to Graytor Gender Services!" the person said. "I am Dr. Yeong. Please verify your names and dates of birth."

"*Hyahk*-too Sigh-hong," Ak-tu pronounced slowly and loudly. "And Zin*ni*vus Sigh-hong. My birthday is March 17, 12 JE, and Zynivus is July 28, 40 JE."

The year was 54 JE (though it would soon be 55 JE). JE stood for Juniper Era. Each "era" lasted two-hundred years, and then another era would be listed with the next letter of the alphabet, starting the number cycle again. Every era had so far been named after a tree. The first era was the Aspen Era, and the eras following were named Birch, Cypress, Dragon, Elder, Fir, Gorse, Holly, and Ivy. Many titles derived from nature, especially first and last names.

"Right this way, then, Yak-too, Zynivus," the doctor said cheerfully.

Ak-tu rolled his eyes beside Zyn once Dr. Yeong had turned away. They then trailed the doctor down a small hall, soon turning into a room on the left. After the two entered, Dr. Yeong closed the door and sat down on a chair. Ak-tu and Zyn sat on a bouncy couch across from them.

"What brings you in today?" Dr. Yeong asked brightly.

"I hate my body," Zyn said bluntly.

For the next twenty minutes, she told the doctor how she had despised her body since she started puberty, that she had feared her body changing when she was younger. She told them how she had felt very dysphoric a mere two weeks prior to the appointment, and how she wanted to rip her chest off. She didn't mention anything about taking Fern's potions, as Ak-tu warned her not to.

"So what are you hoping for?" Dr. Yeong asked, after Zyn finished speaking. "What do you want to get out of coming to therapy?"

Zyn looked to Ak-tu for guidance.

"I know transgender people have to go to therapy first, in order to get a referral to healers that can help them change their bodies," Ak-tu said.

"So you want a referral? After one session?"

Ak-tu frowned. "I assume it's going to take more than one session."

"You thought correctly," the doctor said. "It takes at least three sessions before you can get a referral to any sort of healer. And no, the sessions cannot be in the same month."

Zyn's heart sunk at once. Fern said she wouldn't make more potions for Zyn if she didn't get permission. Was Zyn's chest going to grow again? What if it got even bigger than before?

"Why not?" Ak-tu asked. "If a person knows that they want to take potions—"

"Some people think that's what they want, but realize they don't want it after all," Dr. Yeong interrupted. "Zynivus is still going through puberty. The most we can do right now, between sessions, is give her a hormonal blocking potion. The potion will stop her body from changing any further, and basically put puberty on pause."

Zyn perked up at once.

"But...there is a downside to that. Stopping puberty will also stop magic, in most cases," Dr. Yeong said seriously.

Ak-tu stared at them. "Not...permanently?"

The doctor shook their head. "No, of course not. But if your body thinks it is pre-puberty again, then your body won't be able to unlock its magic—even if you've already accessed your magic. It's rare for people to still be able to do magic while on hormonal blocking potions."

Zyn sighed lightly.

"Well, what are the other options?" Ak-tu asked, frowning.

"Zyn doesn't take any potion while seeing me for therapy," they said promptly. "She can wait until she gets a referral for hormones. The hormone potions will have testosterone, which will make her body become more masculine, giving her facial hair and more muscle and stopping cycles. Her body will still be going through puberty, so she will still be able to access magic if she goes that route.

"If she doesn't want to take hormonal potions, she can get a referral to a surgeon to get a permanent surgery done for her chest. It sounds like her chest is the biggest cause of her dysphoria, and many people come in just to get the surgery done, without taking hormonal potions. However, as Zynivus is still so young, she will have to wait until she is sixteen before she can get surgery done."

"I want to have *both* done!" Zyn exclaimed. "I want to have the body of a male or intersex person, not a female. Do I start the hormonal potions after I see you three times?"

Dr. Yeong shook their head. "You have to be at least fifteen before taking hormonal potions. You can take hormonal *blocking* potions at any point between now and then, though. Your magic will just be blocked off during that time."

Zyn exchanged a glance with her father. *{What do I do?}*

{It's your decision, Zyn.} Ak-tu said, looking over at her. *{If you want to wait, your body will just go back to how it was before. You'd only have to wait seven months before you can get a referral for the hormonal potions. Or you can take the blocking potions until you turn fifteen...in which case your magic will be blocked off. But on the bright side, you'd have your magic by the next school year, once you're fifteen and on the hormonal potions.}*

Zyn had no idea what to do. On the one hand, she was horrified to think that her body would go through with puberty, that her chest would continue to grow. But on the other hand, she wanted to at least *try* to connect with her magic and stay enrolled in school for the spring semester.

"I...I don't know," she mumbled aloud.

"This is why it's so important to have multiple sessions of therapy," Dr. Yeong said with a small smile. "Therapy helps you clear away the fog and realize what decisions you want to make. But we are out of time for our first session. Would you like me to give you a prescription for the hormonal blocking potions? Or would you like to keep your body as it is until we next meet?"

Keep my body as it is... "No!" Zyn said, getting to her feet abruptly. "I don't want my body to stay that way! I want the blocking potions, please!"

Dr. Yeong grinned. "Consider it done," they said, grabbing a paper and scrawling across it. "There you go! That's enough for one cauldron-full of potions—which is roughly one month. Take it to the front desk, and they'll give you the potions. I'd like to see you in another month, once you've been taking the potion for a while. That way, if you want to stay on it, you can let me know in the next session. Of course, if you want to stop taking it, you can simply stop and dispose of the potions."

Zyn nodded numbly.

"See you soon!" Dr. Yeong said, waving them out the door.

Ak-tu led the way down the hall and back to the front desk. They reached the desk, Ak-tu taking the prescription from Zyn and handing it to the person waiting for them.

"We'll have this ready for you in about ten minutes," the person said. "We have so many of these stocked up, you know, but they've got to be enchanted. And when did the doctor want to see you back?"

"A month," Ak-tu said.

"January 28 fine? It's a Thorsday."

Ak-tu nodded.

"Okay, you're scheduled for that day, same time. You can sit in the waiting area until your potions come out."

"Do I need to pay?" Ak-tu asked.

"You will receive the bill through the air-mail address you provided on your paperwork."

Ak-tu and Zyn went to sit down in the waiting area. There were a few more people in the room now, and they were each called away to their appointments. After ten long and silent minutes, a door opened and another person brought them a large box of potion vials.

"You take one potion each day," the person told them. "It will reverse any changes puberty brought with it."

"Thanks," Zyn said.

Ak-tu took the wooden crate and they headed out the door. Once they were outside, Zyn looked at her father. His eyes were glistening.

"Dad?" Zyn mumbled.

"Come on," he said, leading the way to the main street.

"Are you mad at me?"

"No."

Zyn could feel tears pricking at her own eyes. "I'm sorry," she whispered.

"You don't have anything to be sorry about," Ak-tu said firmly, glancing over at her.

"I chose a potion...over *magic*," Zyn murmured. "How could I do that? How could I choose this over *you*? You're hurt by my decision, aren't you? You always wanted me to go to school and learn magic, and...now I'm doing the opposite..."

"No, you chose your body and your mental health over magic," Ak-tu said, putting a hand on her shoulder as he shifted the box to one arm. "Besides—you can't expect to learn magic if you aren't at home in your body. Once you are comfortable with yourself, you can focus on the world around you. Like that saying—you can only help others once you've helped yourself. In this case, magic is the others, and your body is what you need to help first."

"But I betrayed you," Zyn said hoarsely, unable to look into her father's eyes.

"You did not betray me in any way," Ak-tu growled. "Get that idea out of your head. Yes, I want you to learn magic—but not at the expense of your own health. You'll learn magic when you're ready to learn it. *You* come first, not magic."

Zyn sighed. "But now I won't learn magic until next year."

"You made the decision that will make you happier in the long run," Ak-tu said firmly. "I'd much rather have you late to learning magic than hurting yourself over being stuck in a body that makes you uncomfortable."

Zyn shifted uneasily, unable to meet her father's gaze. "But is this...going to...come between us?"

Ak-tu's eyes widened and he squeezed her shoulder. "No, of course not!"

Zyn knew she should trust her father. But she still felt she had caused a rift between them, by choosing herself over the path she should be taking.

"I'm *proud* of you, Zynivus," Ak-tu said. "I'm proud of you for taking the steps to be who you want to be…to be who you *are*. We all have our own paths in life, and this is *your* path you must take."

He pulled her into a tight, one-armed hug. Zyn was glad he couldn't see the tears streaking down her cheeks.

"Anyway, the good thing about taking you out of classes is that we can just blame the potion instead of cheating," Ak-tu said, patting his daughter's back.

"That'll still be an embarrassment," Zyn muttered.

"We've had a few students like that before. They'd leave the school and come back at a later date. That's why some students come to the school at fifteen or even sixteen, instead of fourteen. It's not that strange at all."

"Okay," Zyn muttered. "But you'll still let me take Kung Fu? And Art? And Magic Studies?"

Ak-tu nodded. "Of course." He pulled the pancake from his pocket and gave it to Zyn. "Hungry?"

CHAPTER 21: WILL SOON BE GONE

School was back in session January 11. And Ren couldn't believe that she wouldn't have her sister beside her—at least, not in all of the classes.

After Magic Studies class that Moonday morning, she waved goodbye to Zyn. She still remembered when Zyn had returned from Graytor with Ak-tu, carrying the large crate of hormonal blocking potions. At first, Ren had been happy for her sister. But then, when she'd learned that the potion would definitely block off magic, not even permitting Zyn to reach for her magic…

Ren sighed as she walked to the Magic Channeling classroom. *It's not like Zyn had magic in the first place,* she thought. *But she could have had it by now if she didn't get that potion, if she actually connected with herself. Now we're not doing school together….*

She luckily didn't have time to dwell on her thoughts. Khurshid had a small surprise for them when the twenty first-years entered the classroom.

"Today, you'll be using the magic from *within* you," he announced. "This is different from using the environment around you. Last semester, you used your magic to control what was around you, rather than *create* your element yourself. I am sure a few of you are wondering how this can be. How does an earth student create their own earth? How does someone with fire magic create—"

"I know how!" C3 said, raising his hand. "Earth is the basic molecules that we are made of (besides water, of course). The proteins, the fats, the DNA. Water is everywhere. It's in the cytoplasm and outside of the cells. Fire is the ATP—what powers the body to move and perform reactions. You can also see it as the electrical impulses in nerves, which control the body and monitor it. Air is, well, air. You need it for cellular respiration, which is how cells get energy. The body is a perfect combination of the elements."

Everyone stared at him, including the blind Khurshid.

C3 sighed in exasperation. "Earth is what makes your body. Water is what maintains your body. Fire is what controls your body. Air is what gives your body life. Is that simple enough for you fools?"

Ren frowned. "That still doesn't explain how an earth person can create a rock or something, though."

"I was getting to it, but you all looked helplessly lost," he retorted, sticking his nose in the air.

They continued to gaze at him, until Khurshid cleared his throat. "Thank you for explaining how the elements make up the body, C3. Now, how *does* an earth person create a stone?"

"Is it the wand?" Raimugi asked from the back of the class. "With the plant's magic, it can create things?"

Khurshid smiled. "A lot of people might think that, but how would a person use their inner magic if they're without a wand, using their body or hands instead?"

Nobody answered him.

"Your inner magic will take parts of the element from your *own* body," Khurshid said. "Parts that aren't overly necessary. For example, an earth magician can take excess fat or even a bit from muscles. But using the body for earth magic can be dangerous, especially if you're not taking breaks and giving your body time to recover. Your magic will replenish the parts of you taken, but—again—it takes time. This is why most earth magicians just control the earth around them. After all, there's plenty of earth.

"Fire magicians, on the other hand, don't often find their element around them. They therefore depend more on creating fire, which works when taking it from the electrical impulses in the nerves. These electrical impulses regenerate in milliseconds, so it's not a big deal. That's why fire magicians create their element more than control it.

"As for water and air, those are abundant for both control and creation. Water can be found around you, even in thick fog or plants if there aren't any rivers around. And air is clearly all around us. Bodies are made of water, and you definitely need air to survive. So both forms are plentiful.

"Raimugi, it *is* true that wands can help when you're creating your own magic," Khurshid went on. "The plant magic aids you, and you won't feel as worn out. It also helps replenish your own body, especially if you're an earth magician.

"But enough theory! You will each be trying to create your own element today. Earth magicians, you will only do the exercise half as many times as the other students. If you feel faint or dizzy, you are to stop immediately. The rest of you can have a bit more fun, but the same thing applies. Using your inner magic to create the element takes a lot of energy on the first attempts, wand or no wand."

"Do we still need to tell the element what to do?" Frost asked.

"Yes, that would be best," Khurshid said. "While it's not necessary, the more you tell your magic what to do, the more you can visualize it yourself and make it happen."

The students broke into their normal elemental groups—except that the air group was now a trio without Zyn. Ren sighed as she joined C3 and Mernao on the edge of the classroom.

"Where is Zynivus?" C3 asked Ren. "She was just here for Magic Studies."

"She won't be doing magic classes anymore," Ren said shortly.

"Why not?" Mernao asked, wide-eyed. "Did her magic block off?"

"Yes," Ren replied.

"How?" C3 queried.

Ren sighed. Zyn and Ak-tu had both told her that she could tell the truth about the hormonal blocking potions, but she wasn't sure she wanted everyone prying into Zyn's life like that.

"She's on a hormonal blocking potion," Ren muttered at last.

"Why would she do a silly thing like that?" C3 scoffed. "Does she *want* to wait until she is fifteen to learn magic? That's what I had to do, and it was not fun."

Ren scowled at him. "She's doing that because it's important to her. More important than magic." *More important than staying with me.*

The others did not press her further, as they started on the exercise set before them: creating their own element. Ren struggled with connecting to her magic, and though she ordered it to make her own wind, she could feel she was controlling the air around her instead. C3 was the first of the trio to create his own air, and Ren only managed it by the end of class. Mernao didn't get his magic to come at all.

"We'll be doing the same thing next week," Khurshid told them as the bell rang. "Once most of you get the hang of it, we'll have some fun!"

Not without Zyn, Ren thought.

She went to Plants class with the other first-years, barely talking to Sarala on the way. Ak-tu had been right when he said that the second semester would include more magic. Fern had the students using their own magic to determine how much magic was in a plant, before harvesting the magic from that plant.

Potions, meanwhile, saw the students doing more enchantments throughout the process of brewing a potion rather than simply at the end. They only had to do three enchantments as they brewed a sleeping potion (one halfway through, and two towards the end), but Fern promised they'd be doing up to twenty enchantments by the time the semester ended.

Ren was in a better mood by lunch when she saw Zyn sitting at a table. She hurried over to her sister eagerly.

"Hey, Ren!" Zyn said in a somewhat high voice, setting her spoon down in her bowl of soup. "How was class?"

She's trying to be happy for me... Ren realized. "Oh, you know...a bit boring," she lied.

"Oh, really?" Zyn queried. "That's too bad."

"So what did you do?" Ren asked, sitting down as Sarala walked on towards the counter.

Zyn shrugged. "Played a few games of YAT with Dad, then drew some pictures."

They fell into silence for a bit.

"I can't wait for Kung Fu," Ren said at last. *At least we'll both be able to do that!*

Zyn nodded. "Should be fun to learn new material again! You think we'll be able to get to blue sash before the end of the year?"

"Only if we work super hard," Ren replied.

"I wonder what Sarala's going to learn in her new Kung Fu class tomorrow," Zyn commented, glancing over at Sarala, who was now collecting food on two trays.

"I know there are weapons at the blue sash level, but I don't know what weapon or how many," Ren said. "I guess we'll just have to wait and see when she goes tomorrow! But she'll definitely be happy to learn some weapons at last, since she's interested in them."

By the time Sarala returned with the two trays, handing one to Ren, the three girls were chatting about martial arts like Zyn hadn't been absent from the morning classes. Once they finished eating, they went to the Kung Fu Studio together, as they typically did. But Sarala soon left them when the minute-bell rang.

Great. No Zyn in the morning, no Sarala in the afternoon, Ren thought glumly.

But with Zyn beside her, Ren didn't feel Sarala's absence terribly. She and Zyn learned their new green sash kicks from Ak-tu, as he didn't have to run any tests. In the combative class, the sisters partnered up for the grappling drills. They went to Tai Chi together and learned the beginning of the 40-Step, then played push hands in the next class, having fun as they pulled each other off-balance.

As the sisters crossed the snow-covered Courtyard to the Eating Hall together, Ren was feeling normal again. She beamed at her sister, who returned the smile.

"You know, I don't think this whole not-taking-classes thing will be too bad," Zyn commented. "I'm still taking a good amount of classes, after all."

"Yeah…" Ren murmured. "But the three classes you're *not* taking feel so different without you."

"You'll get through it," Zyn said. "Just like I will get through not going to them."

"But you're going to get so bored. Is Dad going to teach you anything at all?"

Zyn shrugged. "He didn't say anything about it today. I suppose it's because I'm still in some classes, that he doesn't feel he needs to homeschool me again."

"Ooh, I could show you what we went over in class, so you

can still learn something," Ren said excitedly.

"That would not be fair," said a loud voice behind them.

Ren and Zyn glanced over their shoulders to see C3. He was glaring at the sisters through his green-and-blue eyes as he trailed them to the Eating Hall.

"Why not?" Ren queried. "It's not like Zyn can *do* the magic, so why can't she just learn the concepts behind it? It'd be like doing research without doing the practical part."

"If Mr. Caihong took Zynivus out of the magic classes," C3 said pointedly, "he clearly thinks they are above her level. And he's right, isn't he? She can't do any of the stuff we did in classes today."

Ren rolled her eyes and faced back forward. She looked over at Zyn and smiled. "Let's ask Dad if you could come to the classes, to observe only! Or if I could at least show you what we did, and tell you how magic works. Like we harvested magic from plants today, and—"

"Are you just going to throw this magic knowledge out to any nonmagical person?" C3 scoffed, walking alongside Ren now, his feet crunching the snow loudly in his irritation.

"Zyn's magical!" Ren growled. "At least—she would be if she wasn't taking the potion. But she's still magical! She's still at the magical age!"

C3 frowned. "If she doesn't have magic now, then she shouldn't be enrolled in this school. It's not right that she still gets to learn about magic and do martial arts—even if martial arts isn't magical. Mr. Caihong said that the school turned away anyone without magic. So why does Zyn get to stay?"

"Because she *lives* here," Ren grunted sarcastically.

"I meant, in the *classes*," C3 said coldly. "If other students would be kicked out of *all* classes, then why does she get to stay? Just because she's the founder's kid?"

"Just leave her alone already!" Ren snapped. "Zyn—"

But Zyn was no longer beside Ren. She stopped in her tracks abruptly, spraying snow in all directions as she glanced around. Her sister was nowhere to be seen. C3 continued walking towards the Eating Hall, leaving Ren standing alone in the snow.

Ren looked back the way they'd come, and realized that there were tracks leading back to the Tai Chi Studio. She hurried over the icy ground (nearly slipping several times) until she was back in the classroom.

"Zyn?" she called as she opened the door.

Zyn's hand was on the knob of the tower door, ready to open it. She glanced over at Ren, then lowered her gaze guiltily.

"C3's wrong, you know," she said, not even sure how much of C3's words Zyn had heard. "He's just a jerk. We all know it."

Zyn sighed and dropped her hand from the knob. "Yeah, he can be, but…he *is* right, isn't he? It's not fair that I get to keep taking classes. And it wouldn't be right of you to show me everything you learned if I'm no longer in those classes. If you're willing to show a nonmagical person stuff about magic…wouldn't that just be hurting Dad by passing on his teachings to those who don't deserve to learn yet? There's a reason people have to pay for magical education. This stuff isn't just on the air-net, free for everyone and anyone to see."

"Zyn, that's not the point," Ren said sternly, walking over to her sister. "I wouldn't be putting this information on the air-net or teaching any random person I come across. I'd be teaching *you*."

"But we both know I'm nonmagical, with or without the potions. I never should have been enrolled this year. Which means that I never should have learned anything that I already did."

"Zyn—"

"I'm just gonna ask Dad to drop me from the rest of the classes," Zyn muttered, closing her eyes. "It's not fair to everyone else."

"But, Zyn—"

"I'm sorry, Ren. It looks like we won't be learning anything together, after all."

Zyn opened the door to the tower and went inside, locking it behind her. Of course, Ren had her own key and could easily unlock it, but she knew Zyn would be in her room by that point. Ren sighed and turned away from the tower, her heart aching as she felt more alone than at any other point that day.

She exited the Tai Chi Studio and stared at the snowy Courtyard. Kicking the ice beneath her feet, she let out another sigh. *I guess I better go have dinner…alone…*

But before she could take another step towards the Eating Hall, a flash of light caught her eye, reflected on the snow in front of her. She glanced up, trying to see where the light had come from.

"There!" she muttered under her breath, squinting up at the tower.

A bright light was shining from the fifth floor window. But it wasn't the regular ceiling light that was on. It was a beam of light, transitioning between bright and dim. The white light shined for several moments, then vanished. Ren frowned, wondering what Sarala could be doing in her room.

"Weird," she muttered.

As far as she knew, the only thing Sarala owned was a wand, a notebook, and a few clothes Ren had given her. None of those objects could possibly be causing the light—unless she was a fire magician using her wand to practice magic.

"But she's an earth magician," Ren uttered. "Unless she gained a second magic. Hmm…"

Ren turned back to the Tai Chi Studio and entered, hurrying over to the tower door. But she stopped at the sound of voices within. Zyn was talking to Ak-tu…about dropping classes…about leaving her…

Ren took a deep breath, though her body was still full of tension. She forced herself to relax after several more breaths, then turned and exited the studio. She didn't want to hear the conversation on the other side of the door.

"I'll just ask Sarala about it later," she uttered, trying to keep her mind off of Zyn.

She soon reached the Eating Hall, shooting a glare at C3 on the other side of the large room, where he sat alone. Ren went to the counter and grabbed a tray, collecting a small amount of food, as she suddenly lost her appetite despite the tasty aromas floating through the air. She saw Sarala sitting at a nearby table and joined her.

"You okay?" Sarala asked, glancing up at Ren as she sat down.

"I don't know," Ren moaned, shaking her head.

"Want to talk about it?"

"I don't know," Ren repeated, resting her pointed chin in her palm. Then, she frowned at Sarala. "Wait—have you been in here?"

"Yeah, I got in early before a line could form," Sarala said, pointing at her empty bowl. "Why?"

"I saw a weird light in your room," Ren said. "It was like…a bright white light. It flashed a few times before stopping."

Sarala frowned. "That's odd."

Ren nodded. "Especially if you weren't in there."

"You sure it wasn't the ceiling light?" Sarala queried.

Ren shook her head. "Those lights only turn on when they detect movement," she pointed out. "Unless a bug got in your room? Even so, there's no way that light was *that* bright."

"I better go check it out, then," Sarala growled, getting to her feet abruptly.

Ren grabbed her hand. "Please don't leave!"

Sarala stared down at her for a long moment, then muttered, "Just come with me."

"Oh—I guess I can," Ren muttered, blushing. "I just…I don't want to be alone. I feel like Zyn's pushing away from me… Is there something wrong with me?"

Sarala shook her head at once, leaning on the table. "Nothing is wrong with you."

Ren lowered her gaze to her small amount of food. "Yeah. Right," she murmured.

"If there was something wrong with you, I wouldn't be your friend," Sarala huffed.

Ren snorted. "That's a bit harsh."

"I don't make friends with jerks," Sarala said plainly. "Now let's go check out that weird light."

"Can I eat first?" Ren asked.

"Fine," Sarala grumbled, and she resumed her seat. "You have five minutes."

Ren leaned forward in her chair and scooped the smooth soup quickly into her mouth. Instantly warm, the feeling spread through her whole body and made her smile. She was glad to have Sarala with her.

She glanced out the window of the Eating Hall, to the snow beyond. An image came to her mind, from years before: Ren and Zyn throwing snowballs around as kids, and one of them striking Ak-tu in the face by accident. She smiled at the memory.

"Zyn and I always do everything together," she mused in a soft voice, still staring out the window with glazed eyes. "We have this little house. It was sort of our house before the school was built, at least when we were taking a break from traveling on the ship."

"You have a ship?" Sarala asked blankly.

Ren's eyes focused on her friend as she snorted in amusement. "How else would Dad have taken Zyn to her appointment in Graytor? That city is a few hours away, even by air!"

"Your ship flies?" Sarala pressed.

"Have you never seen a flying ship?"

"I saw a few flying boats once, but not a whole ship," Sarala said with a shrug. "I didn't venture into cities much, and I never liked being near boats. Though I wouldn't say no to having my own."

Ren chuckled lightly. "Well, we have a large ship," she said with a shrug. "Anyway, we haven't been to that little house in years. But I miss being there. I miss all the fun we had together…" She sighed, her smile turning into a frown. "I just…wish things didn't change."

"Unfortunately, everything changes," Sarala muttered darkly, her jaw clenching as she glared at the ground.

Ren glanced at her curiously, the small house fading from her mind. "You okay?"

"It's fine," Sarala grunted.

The two girls fell into silence for a moment, then Sarala got to her feet again. Ren swiftly finished her soup, then stood as well. She grabbed her tray and put it on top of the dirty trays near the door, taking her toast off and munching on it as she trailed Sarala to the northwestern tower.

Ren unlocked the door to the tower once she finished her second piece of toast, and the two girls entered. Ak-tu and Zyn were sitting at a small round table. They looked up at their arrival, falling quiet at once.

"Sorry!" Ren yelped.

She grabbed Sarala's arm and dashed towards the spiral stairs, the other girl stumbling along after her. They swiftly went up, Ren able to hear a low murmur of voices below them. She hoped Ak-tu wasn't dropping Zyn from school!

They reached the fifth floor, Sarala opening the door to her room. The ceiling light flashed on as they went in, but it wasn't as bright as the beams Ren had seen from outside.

"Definitely couldn't have been the ceiling light," Ren commented, glancing up at the metal rods.

Sarala scanned her bland room, containing a bed, wardrobe, and desk. She frowned, then glanced over her shoulder at Ren. "You sure you weren't hallucinating?"

Ren shrugged, glancing around the room as well. "Not that I know of!" she replied cheerfully. "I guess whatever it was must be gone now."

"Or it was never here to begin with," Sarala said.

"You don't believe me?"

Sarala clenched her jaw. "I'd like to see things for myself, thanks," she uttered.

Ren sighed. "Okay, well…it seems there's nothing here, after all. I'll see you tomorrow…"

She turned on the balls of her feet and left the room before Sarala could reply. Disappointment, irritation, and sadness were swirling through her as she walked down the stairs.

Why doesn't Sarala believe me? I thought we were friends! I thought she trusted me. But she's never going to trust me, is she? She's pushing away…just like Zyn…

Ren shook her head roughly as she reached the third floor and entered her own bedroom. *No, I can't think like that. Sarala's had a rough past…it'll take her time. That's all! She'll come to trust me. She is my friend!*

CHAPTER 22: PLAY THE GAME

"Absolutely not," Ak-tu said flatly.

"But, Dad, it's not fair to other students that I'm still taking classes," Zyn objected, tapping the round table in front of her impatiently.

Ak-tu smiled. "Well, I made this school, so I get the final say. Anyhow, I've got a *better* idea."

Zyn frowned. "A better idea? For what? You're not going to put me *back* in classes, are you? Even if it's just observing, that doesn't feel right. Besides, Ren said she would show me stuff, even though I told her—"

"No," Ak-tu said. "Though, to be fair, that's not a bad idea, either—Ren teaching you what she learned. I mean to say, if I don't know anything about it and never catch you at it..." He winked, then pressed on. "But no. Remember how I was originally going to make this a martial arts school?"

"Yeah, until you met Khurshid," Zyn said promptly. "Then you two decided to make the school be a magic school, since you saw the potential that'd have."

Ak-tu nodded. "But what if I opened the martial arts—and Art —to the nonmagical? Of course, the students would still have to be at least twelve or thirteen, and we'd cut off the age at about nineteen."

Zyn cocked her head, leaning forward in her seat. "You'd do that? Let nonmagical students in to learn martial arts early?"

Ak-tu shrugged. "Like I said, my plan was originally to make this place a small martial arts school. I would have taken in students of all ages, magical or not. So why not do something similar?"

"But why include Art?"

"Art is vital for a martial artist," Ak-tu said simply. "It teaches just as much discipline, focus, and meditation. It is proven that doing something creative makes people happier too, and therefore healthier."

Zyn shrugged. "I guess?"

"Well, this sounds like a good plan," Ak-tu said, smiling at Zyn. "I'm sure it'll bring in some more students too. Martial arts aren't overly common around Galia."

"But you can hardly get new students in the middle of the year," Zyn pointed out.

"I don't have to," Ak-tu said plainly. "You'll be the test student. So if anyone else bothers you about not belonging in classes or how it's unfair, you can tell them that you *are* allowed to be in certain classes, as the test student for next year's plan."

"O-kay."

"Don't worry about it, Zyn."

Just then, the door to the tower opened, and Ren and Sarala entered. The two girls hurried to the stairs and went up. Both Ak-tu and Zyn waited for their footsteps to fade away before they turned back to one another.

"Want to play a game of YAT?" Ak-tu asked.

Zyn blinked. "Sure!"

She pulled out a deck of cards, which she almost always had on her. She handed the cards to her father to shuffle, watching him without paying attention as she thought about learning magic again.

The two played several rounds of cards, then Ak-tu claimed he wanted to eat a (late) dinner. Zyn joined him, having not eaten yet.

After dinner, Zyn returned to the tower while Ak-tu went to "talk with a friend" elsewhere. She went straight to her room, as neither Ren nor Sarala were in the family room. She was about to place a blanket on the floor to sleep on, when her desk suddenly caught her attention.

Zyn walked over to the desk and picked up one of the objects sitting on top of it. She frowned thoughtfully. Her father said that she couldn't do classes with a magic object, and not to put too much faith in the objects since their enchantments wore off quickly. But what if Zyn made her own enchanted objects, which stayed enchanted for a long time? She could make objects do specific tasks for her!

"Ugh, I'm so dumb," she muttered, hitting her palm to her forehead. "How am I going to enchant them in the first place?"

The answer came quickly to her. "Dad, obviously. But would he do it for me? He didn't seem too keen about the idea... I guess I could always ask the other teachers."

But would they want you to have magic? asked a doubtful voice in Zyn's head. *You're nonmagical, after all. They wouldn't want you playing with anything magical... There's a reason enchanted objects are so expensive, that way kids don't get their hands on them...*

"*I* have magic objects," she uttered aloud. "And I'm not a kid, just because I'm reversing puberty. I can play with my magic objects all I want...."

However, she still doubted that the other teachers would enchant more objects for her—or re-enchant the objects she already had, if she used up the magic stored in them. She sighed, wondering who she could turn to for help.

Ren? No, she wouldn't know how to enchant an object. None of the first-years know that, not yet. But maybe a higher student? I wonder if Mint knows anything about it. I should ask them at the next club meeting!

Happy that she had somewhere to start, Zyn curled up on the floor with several blankets. After she fell still, the ceiling light turned off, plunging her room into darkness. She soon fell asleep, feeling more hopeful for the future....

On Trizday, Zyn told Ren about Ak-tu's plan. Ren was beyond delighted to hear this, and instantly showed Zyn what she learned in classes the previous day. Zyn took notes instead of doodling, paying close attention to Ren.

Ren demonstrated using magic to create an element, and explained how each of the elements took from the person's body. She then led Zyn to the Greenhouse (before Plants class started for the second-years), where she showed Zyn how to test a plant for its magic powers.

"The key is to get the plant to react to your magic," she told Zyn. "You basically have to annoy it. If it has a big reaction, it's got plenty of magic. If it has little to no reaction, its magic levels are low, like pine trees."

She demonstrated this by throwing wind at a spiky plant. The wind hit it, and the plant seemed to blow up. The red spikes shot off it in all directions, and the sisters had to jump behind trees to avoid getting hit.

"Whoops!" Ren yelped, pulling a spike out of her arm. "I guess I chose the wrong plant, huh?"

Zyn snorted in amusement. "And I guess *that's* a highly magical one." She walked over to Ren and frowned at the wound. "You should have Fern heal that. Who knows if it's poisonous?"

"Yeah, we haven't covered that plant yet," Ren said. "I'll just wait for Fern to show up here."

"But we might get in trouble if we stay."

"We were just taking a stroll in the Greenhouse," Ren said lightly. "We can go anywhere in the school, so long as it's not someone's room or there's a class inside. Or the Kitchen, I guess."

Zyn snorted. "Or the other towers, in general."

"Or the second and third floors in the southern building," Ren commented.

"You know, there's a lot of places we *can't* go."

"Yeah… But the point remains—we're allowed to be in the Greenhouse, so long as there's not a class inside! And there isn't. Not yet."

Almost as soon as the words left her mouth, the glass door to the Greenhouse opened and Fern led the way inside with the second-years. Ren and Zyn hurried over to her, as she raised her eyebrows in surprise at seeing them there.

"Hey, Fern!" Ren called. "Sorry—Ms. Oakley!"

Fern sighed. "I knew it was a bad idea for you to grow up calling teachers by first name."

Ren ignored this and held up her arm. "I got stabbed by a spiky plant. Is it poisonous? Am I going to die?"

Zyn snorted at how upbeat Ren sounded about potential death. Then again, there wouldn't be a deadly plant at the school, even if a few of the plants were poisonous. Fern was also an accomplished healer, able to stop plenty of deadly wounds.

"You'll be fine," Fern grumbled. She searched in her cloak

pocket and pulled out a vial. "Rub this over the wound, then come see me at lunch."

"Thanks!" Ren said, taking the vial. "Do you just carry around vials like that all the time? It's like you pull them out of thin air!"

"Mmhmm."

Zyn pulled Ren's uninjured arm. "Time to go!" *Before we annoy Fern even more...*

The sisters left the Greenhouse, waving to Mint and Moon as they passed. Mint waved, but Moon did not seem to recognize the sisters as being from the art club and had no response—or she had zoned out.

Once the twins made it back to the tower, Ren rubbed the potion over her wound. It was a thick paste the color of cantaloupe.

She then got back to telling Zyn how to harvest a plant's magic, which required the person to merely take off a small piece of the plant. It was easier said than done, as some plants were reluctant to let their wood or leaves be taken. They would curl in, bite, scratch, or even release a poisonous gas if they felt threatened. It was therefore best to speak to the plants in a soothing manner or even play music for them to relax. It was also important that not too much of the plant was stripped away, otherwise the nature spirits would get angry and attack.

"But that's just old stories, right?" Sarala interrupted Ren, entering the family room after being in her room all morning.

Ren shook her head. "It's true! If you hurt nature, nature will send spirits after you. That was a huge issue when people began building cities. They'd cut down forests and anger the spirits, then the spirits would destroy their buildings and supplies. Eventually, people and spirits came to a compromise, which holds true all around the world: Humans don't take too much, and they allow nature to thrive in their cities."

Sarala huffed. "Yeah, like I said—old stories."

"Why are you so against believing in spirits?" Ren inquired.

"Because I'm an adult."

"No, you're not," Zyn pointed out.

She shot her a glare. "I'm mature enough to be one."

Zyn knew it was better to hold her tongue on that point and so said nothing.

"Anyhow," Sarala continued, "I've never crossed any spirits in the wild. And I've hurt many plants along the way. I did what I had to, to survive. If that meant I cut down a few plants to light a fire for a warm meal, then so be it. And no spirits ever came after me."

Ren shrugged. "I think Fern was mostly referring to large plants, and the more magical ones. Not every plant has a lot of magic in it, after all. And if you're using the plants to survive, that still falls under the whole 'take what you need' thing."

"Whatever."

"What's it going to take for you to believe in spirits?" Zyn asked.

"A real spirit appearing in front of me," Sarala said flatly. "And not some hallucination, so don't you dare get your dad in on the joke to make the perfect spirit."

"Suit yourself, though it'd be funny," Zyn chuckled.

Lunch was soon upon them, and Ren went to get her wound checked out by Fern. Zyn and Sarala, meanwhile, went to the Eating Hall, promising to get a tray for Ren. They moved to stand in line, and, a moment later, Mint showed up behind them, dressed in his typical green sweater.

"Hey, Zyn! Hey, Sarala!" he said, waving; his bracelet was purple, signaling that he identified as a boy that day.

Ooo, now's my chance! Zyn thought. "Hey, Mint! I actually had a question."

Mint immediately looked nervous. He seemed to be remembering the last time Zyn had asked Mint a question, after the Moonlight Dance. Zyn had only asked if Mint enjoyed the dance, but Mint felt guilty for abandoning Zyn and started crying in response—even though it was *Zyn* who had left Mint. Many tissues later, Zyn learned that they *did* have fun at the dance, despite being alone.

"It's nothing bad—or good," Zyn said hastily. "It's, um, neutral?"

"Oh, okay. What is it?"

Zyn lowered her voice. "Do you know how to enchant objects?"

Mint blinked in surprise. "Sorta? I mean, we kinda learned the theory in Magic Studies last semester. But, um, I'm not the best with magic."

"Could you share your notes with me?" Zyn asked.

"What are you planning?" Sarala growled to Zyn.

"Yes, what *are* you planning?"

Zyn sighed and looked up to see C3 standing just behind Mint. He was glaring at Zyn, as if Zyn had just insulted him.

"None of your business," she snapped.

Mint was starting to look nervous. "Umm…well…I dunno what's going on here, so um…"

"Can you just bring your notes to the next art club meeting?" Zyn asked. "That's all!"

Mint shifted uneasily. "I dunno, Zyn…"

"Please?"

"O-okay," he stammered in a low voice.

C3 narrowed his eyes, but said nothing and walked away. Zyn stuck her tongue out at his back, hoping he wasn't about to tell a teacher.

But Zyn did not get told off by Ak-tu that night. None of the teachers approached her the rest of the week, either. Art classes went fine on Freday (apart from a few people asking Zyn why she was no longer taking magical classes), and Zyn reminded Mint at dinner to bring the enchantment notes the following day.

Zyn was excited to go to the Art Studio the next morning.

"You look happy," Ren scoffed lightly as they entered the studio together, breathing in the scents of paint and paper.

"Yep!" Zyn beamed.

The sisters were the first ones there. Sarala didn't feel like getting up early, and had barely made it to the Eating Hall in time before the food got put away. She was more interested in practicing martial arts than going to the club anyhow, as she was learning jump kicks at the blue sash level.

A few minutes later, C3 entered the room, keeping a close eye on Zyn. Zyn ignored him, waving at Raimugi and Mernao as they entered the classroom. Frost was not with them, as he had been avoiding Ren since the spring semester began. Moon walked in, ignoring everyone as she went to the corner of the room to start knitting a fuzzy hat. As everyone got out art supplies and set to work, Zyn was beginning to wonder if Mint wasn't going to show up.

But then Mint came charging through the door, panting heavily and looking flustered. "Sorry!" she gasped. "Woke up…late…"

"This isn't class, Mint!" Ren chuckled. "Calm down!"

Mint smiled meekly, wiping the sweat off her face. "Good point," she mumbled, and she took a seat near Zyn.

Before Zyn could ask anything though, Mint shook her head. Her large green eyes flicked towards C3 watching nearby, and Zyn shrugged almost imperceptibly. *Fine, we'll wait until the end,* she thought dismissively.

She pulled out her sketchbook, which she had placed in her leaf-patterned robe that morning. Turning to a blank page, she started doodling a flying ship.

The students chatted about their winter breaks as they worked. Mernao had gone to the state of Neu, where his extended family lived. The students were then talking about where they'd like to travel in the future, from states in Galia to other countries around the world. Zyn's heart ached as she yearned to travel again, hoping the Caihong family would go somewhere new for summer break.

Ren turned to Zyn and brought up fun memories they spent at their old home. Zyn snorted in laughter as Ren reminded her of the time they attempted to bake a cake for Ak-tu and nearly burned down the house. And how could she forget the time they got lost in the woods and asked the spirits to help them, and a small deer appeared to lead them back home?

Eventually, the students packed up their art supplies. Raimugi and Mernao left first, then Moon went. Zyn hoped C3 would go too, but he remained sitting at his desk, working on his watercolor painting.

"Oh, no!" Ren gasped. "Moon forgot her scarf! See you in the Eating Hall, Zyn!"

She grabbed the fluffy scarf and hurried from the room. Zyn watched her go, slipping her notebook back in her robe pocket. She then inched closer to Mint, who was flipping through a binder.

"Should we go outside?" Zyn whispered in the lowest voice she could manage.

Mint glanced meekly at C3. "I dunno," she replied, fumbling nervously through the papers. "It's easier to sit down."

"Then let's sit down outside," Zyn hissed.

"I'll still be watching you," C3 said loudly.

Zyn shot him a glare. "Why can't you mind your own business?"

C3 gave her a bland look. "I do not think you should be enrolled in classes, no matter what your father might be 'attempting to set up' next year. You do not deserve to be learning any sort of magic theory, and definitely not that of year two—or above."

"Yeah, yeah," Zyn muttered. "But like I said, it's none of your business."

"I'll get your father," C3 growled.

Zyn frowned at that. "If I tell you what I'm doing, will you leave me alone?"

C3 perked up at this. "Potentially," he said.

Zyn sighed, glancing towards Mint for her opinion. But Mint was staring determinedly at the floor, her mouth stretched wide like a frog's, leaving the decision entirely up to Zyn. Zyn looked back at C3.

"I'm trying to enchant objects, so I can use them as my form of magic," she said.

"How would you be able to enchant them if you don't have your magic? Or are you going to skip taking your hormonal potion for a day to enchant them then?"

"I was going to give the notes to Ren. She'd figure it out," Zyn said with a shrug.

"Second-year magic?" C3 murmured, rubbing his chin thoughtfully. "Let me see these notes."

"No!" Zyn growled at once.

"Or I tell your father," C3 said. "And I'm guessing you don't want that, otherwise you would have just asked him to enchant objects for you in the first place."

Zyn scowled at him. C3 smirked and got to his feet, stepping around the table and looking over Mint's shoulder. Mint sat in place, not sure whether to close her binder or leave it open. In the end, she merely continued to sit there and do nothing as sweat slid down her forehead as quickly as ice melting in hot sunlight.

C3 scanned her notes, flipped to the next page, and read on. After a few quiet minutes, he looked up.

"Had your fill?" Zyn scoffed.

"It seems simple enough, in theory," C3 replied. "That is, if these notes are reliable."

Mint made a small noise of fright, glancing at C3 quickly.

"Still, it would be interesting to try it out," C3 muttered to himself.

Suddenly, C3 snatched the pages of Mint's notes and ran out the door. Zyn was so taken aback by the action, that she blinked in confusion. Mint screamed in terror and hurled herself to the floor.

"Come back!" Zyn yelled, and she hurried after C3.

C3 was already on the elevator outside the eastern building. He sniggered at Zyn before flinging open the door on the third floor and darting inside. Zyn hurried after him, slipping on the snow. She nearly crashed into the wall.

"Elevator! Come down!" she yowled.

The stone seemed to take five minutes to lower itself to the ground again. Zyn swiftly hopped on and ordered it to go to the third floor, and it moved slowly once more. She didn't know if the enchantments needed to be redone, or if she was just being impatient.

She opened the door as soon as the front railing lowered, and darted inside. The door opened onto a long hall, with a bathroom directly across from it. The rest of the hall was dedicated to student rooms.

Great. How am I supposed to know which door is his? Zyn thought irritably.

But the first door she glanced at had Raimugi's name on it. She looked at the other doors, and they were all labelled with student names too.

"Oh. That's convenient."

In the time she lived at the school, she never had the need to go up to the student quarters. When she *did* dart down the halls on those rare occasions, it was during the summer or winter breaks, when there weren't any students around. The doors had been blank, as far as she remembered.

Zyn hurried down the hall, glancing from left to right and right to left. She reached the end of the hall, and the very last door on the left read "C3" in large letters. It looked like the students were allowed to put preferred names on the doors, if they didn't want to go by their legal ones.

She tried opening the door, but it was locked. She pounded on it loudly, a jolt running up her arm at how hard she was hitting. "C3! Open up!"

But C3 was hardly going to open the door, not after stealing the notes.

"C3!" Zyn shouted, knocking on the door harder. "Don't make me break down this door!"

"You'd be in serious trouble if you did," C3 sneered, his voice muffled.

Zyn frowned. He had a point. How would she explain to her father that she broke down his door just because he took Mint's notes? And—knowing C3—he'd probably hide the notes away someplace like he'd never done anything wrong. In addition to that, Mint was hardly going to be a good witness, as she always avoided conflict wherever she could, simply listening to what others told her to do.

"I thought you said that we weren't allowed to learn second-year magic?" Zyn growled, lowering her voice.

"I said *you*, specifically," C3 said. "Anyhow, I am fifteen and my magical education has been put off for far too long. I should rightfully be in my second or third year now, not my first. I very much would like to try this out."

"Then try it out with *me*," Zyn pleaded. "We can enchant objects—together!"

"And allow you to take these objects for yourself? No, thanks," C3 said. "Now, leave me alone."

"But—"

"You can run to your father if you'd like, but then you'd have to tell him your plans. Wouldn't want that, now would you?"

Zyn was shaking in fury. She was tempted to take a step back and slam the door down with one of the heel thrust kicks she'd learned in Kung Fu. But she forced her temper down, taking deep, rattling breaths.

"You can't do anything, so run along now," C3 said briskly.

Zyn didn't know what else to do. Her sister would certainly be wondering where she'd gotten, and what was the point of telling her about this disaster if Zyn didn't get the notes? Sighing, she turned away from the door, walking to the opposite end of the hall.

She reached the door and opened it, poking her head out to see where the platform was. It sat in front of the second floor door, so the railing was up in front of Zyn to prevent her from falling out. She called the elevator to her in a dejected voice, got on, and told it to go to the ground level. She then crossed the Courtyard to the Art Studio, poking her head in to see if Mint was still there. She wasn't.

Zyn therefore headed to the Eating Hall glumly, telling Ren that she had stayed behind to chat with Mint, then went to the bathroom. Ren didn't seem to notice as she talked to Sarala about astrology, leaving Zyn alone to her thoughts.

What do I do now? Find a different second-year student to question? Hmm...maybe Moon? No. I doubt she pays any attention in class, and she probably wouldn't know who I am if I asked.

But Zyn didn't know too many students outside of the first year. Of course, she chatted with some in the more laidback Art classes, but she wouldn't even call them acquaintances. They'd probably tell Ak-tu or the other teachers too.

I don't think asking someone else will work. I'll just have to get those notes back from C3...somehow.

CHAPTER 23: BIJOU

On January 22, all Art classes were cancelled for the Day of the Moon. Though many of the students had celebrated the holiday early with their families during winter break, they still got the day off to celebrate on the holiday itself.

Sarala left her room that morning just as a snowball hit her window. She jumped in fright, but quickly recomposed herself and went to glare out the window at whoever had thrown the snowball. It was Zyn or Ren—of course. Only they would be brave enough to throw a snowball at the Caihong tower, and at *her* window specifically. She scowled at them, then realized that students were flinging snowballs all over the place.

"Maybe I'll just stay inside," she uttered.

She went down the stairs to the family room and was surprised to see decorations all over. There were dazzling lights strung around the room, of gold and blue. A few clippings of pine and holly branches were strewn about the tables, adding green and red to the mix. Several tall candles stood on the largest round table, each of them sparkling whether they were white, black, or blue; they released smells of cinnamon and spruce. Snowflakes floated in the air, probably a result of Ak-tu's magic.

"O-kay," she murmured as she poked a chilly snowflake and sent it flying across the room. "Must be for the holiday."

Ak-tu was sitting at one of the small tables, dressed in a blue sweater and fuzzy hat. He glanced up at her and smiled. "It's indeed for the holiday," he said. "Our family has yet to celebrate the holiday itself, since we didn't celebrate the Moon Festival over winter break."

"Why is the holiday even during school time?" Sarala asked.

"While each of the festivals take place in the beginning of the season, each of the holidays are halfway through their respective seasons," Ak-tu explained. "Winter begins in December, and lasts until the end of February. Its holiday would therefore be in January."

"Well, why not have it sooner?" Sarala grumbled. "Why not have it on the first of the month, when we were on break?"

"The seasonal holidays and the minor holidays switch between eleven and twenty-two. Double numbers are important in Galia. Anyhow, it's not like I can change the country's holidays."

Sarala rolled her eyes, then frowned. "Wait—minor holidays? There are more than the seasonal holidays?"

"Oh, yes," Ak-tu said with a nod. "The major holidays are the Day of the Moon, the Day of Nature, the Day of the Sun, and the Day of Spirits. Each of those are seasonal holidays. The other holidays are scattered throughout the rest of the months. These holidays would be those celebrating the elements, plants, crystals, and planets. Not too many people celebrate them these days, but they're still noted on calendars."

Sarala frowned. "So there's like…an Earth Day?"

"Yep. That's on March 22," Ak-tu said promptly.

"So only earth magicians would celebrate that day, right?"

"No. Anyone is free to celebrate it. I personally celebrate each holiday as it comes, even if it's with a small meditation focused on thanking nature and the spirits for the element or season. But, for the most part, yes. Mostly earth magicians would celebrate that day, and not be keen on celebrating Air Day or Water Day, for example."

Sarala twirled her hair around her finger thoughtfully. "I kind of understand why we have holidays for the elements, and the sun and the moon. But why the planets? And plants and crystals?"

"Plants and crystals are the source of natural magic, and plants especially make up a large part of our magic. They make the wands we use, they're in the potions we brew, they're a part of enchantment magic, they help heal. And, of course, we eat plants and rely on them for clothing. Plants are very important to Sater. Crystals are also a source of magic, and aid us in enchantments and healing.

"As for the planets, it's more of an astrology-based holiday. Our sun and moon signs determine which elemental magic we are born with, after all. A good handful of people celebrate the holiday by appreciating the planets, even if it's mostly just the sun and moon which determine our magic."

"Do the other planets play a role in determining our magic?"

Ak-tu chuckled. "I can see you've already forgotten last term's lectures."

Sarala scowled.

"Yes, the other planets play a small role in determining a person's magic. Mostly if the person is born at dawn or dusk, when the sun or moon are both out. But I won't bore you with all the details. Why don't you run along outside, and join Ren and Zyn in a nice snowball fight?"

Sarala snorted. "No, thanks," she said plainly.

"Or you can stay in and hide with me," Ak-tu said with a shrug. "Care to join me for a game of checkers?"

She really didn't want to, feeling suddenly awkward as she stood there. But she already said she didn't want to go outside, and how would it look if she denied Ak-tu's invitation? Sitting down across from him, she realized the board was already set. Had he been expecting her to play?

"I was waiting for Zyn to come back in," he explained as she eyed the game. "We always play games on this day. Well, on any holiday, actually."

"Do you do anything else for the holidays?"

Ak-tu nodded. "Just before or after lunch, we go on a walk in nature. We show our appreciation of the seasons and the natural forces at work in our world, and we show our gratitude to the spirits. We then hold a meditation in a spiritual region. When we return to the tower, we often play games and music together, showing our appreciation of one another. We also share gifts, which is an annual tradition most families take part in. On this particular holiday, we do one more meditation at nightfall, as close to the moon as we can get."

Just then, the door to the tower opened and the twins stepped in. They chuckled as they threw snowballs at Ak-tu and Sarala.

"What was that for?" Sarala snarled, barely able to block the snowball before it hit her face.

"Oh, lighten up!" Ren laughed. "You didn't come out to join us, so we thought we'd join you!"

"Is it game time?" Zyn asked excitedly.

"Sorry, but I'm already playing with Sarala," Ak-tu said, and he quickly moved his game piece forward with one hand, using his other hand to make the water from the snowballs turn into more floating snowflakes.

"But—"

"You two were too busy playing outside. Why don't you get changed into warmer clothes? We'll go on our morning walk soon," Ak-tu said.

"Okay!" the twins said in very different voices, and they bounded away up the stairs.

Sarala and Ak-tu managed to play several quiet games of checkers before the sisters returned, Sarala winning each match. Zyn was dressed in the white robe covered in rainbow stars that she had "stolen" from the Theatre. She wore a gray-and-white stripy shirt and baggy blue pants underneath.

"Zyn, did you steal my pants again?" Ak-tu asked in pretend exasperation.

"No… Maybe… Don't worry about it," Zyn said, trying not to laugh as she waved her hand carelessly.

But Sarala wasn't focused on Zyn. Her eyes were glued on Ren, who looked similar to how she did for the dance. She was dressed in a brilliant blue robe, with moon patterns all over it. Beneath the robe, she wasn't wearing her usual sports shirt or sweatpants, but a collared shirt and dress pants. She also wore a crystal moon necklace, which reflected the blue and gold lights of the room. Her purple hair was pulled back in a tail, leaving a fringe of hair nearly falling over her left eye. Throughout the entire semester, Ren had never pulled her hair back. She typically had a sloppy look about her, which matched her energetic personality. But now, she was an impressive sight to behold.

Sarala felt her mouth suddenly go dry and she shifted uneasily in her chair. "Umm…if we're supposed to dress all fancy," she said to Ak-tu, "I don't have anything."

"Sure you do," Ak-tu said. "Zyn will get that Theatre costume you wore at the dance."

Sarala really did not want to wear those clothes again, not after what had happened—or didn't happen—at the dance. But before she could protest, Zyn hurried away to do as her father asked. Sarala felt an uncomfortable knot twisting in her stomach.

Zyn soon returned with the purple dress Sarala had worn. She took it from Zyn, not bothering to thank her, then went up to the bathroom to get changed. When she entered the family room again moments later, Ak-tu was gone.

"Where'd your dad go?" Sarala asked blankly.

"He went to get a nicer robe too," Ren said. "He felt under-dressed next to us three!"

A few minutes later, Ak-tu came down the stairs, dressed in a royal blue robe with a large moon on the back, much like the robe Ren had worn to the dance. He also had a crescent moon necklace, similar to Ren's. He would have looked well-dressed if it wasn't for the fuzzy hat he still had covering his head.

"Ready to go?" Ak-tu asked.

"Yep!"

"Okay. Let's meet up with Khurshid, Aster, and Fern."

Sarala stared at Ak-tu in dismay. The other teachers were joining them too? Why?

"Now, considering what happened for the Day of Spirits," Ak-tu said, looking at Ren, "we will be going on a walk in the Greenhouse instead of the forest. Not to mention, we can't have all of the teachers leave the school when students are here."

"Are we not having breakfast?" Sarala asked.

Ak-tu considered her for a moment. "We already ate breakfast, and it's put away by now."

Sarala sighed. Sometimes, she really hated sleeping in.

The four left the tower and crossed the freezing Courtyard, many students yowling and laughing as they held snowball fights. They stumbled through the garden outside the Greenhouse, then entered to see that the other three teachers were already there. The teachers were dressed in clothing made from the thick substance found on fuzzy trees (which was a common material in clothing, especially in colder regions).

It wasn't as chilly in the Greenhouse as it was outside, but it was still cooler than what Sarala was used to. They walked along the bottom floor as best as they could, pushing through the thick undergrowth of purple leaves and spotted flowers. The plants were making lots of shrieking and sucking noises, seeming louder than usual.

Sarala didn't speak much to her friends as they went. Zyn was chatting with Ren, who was taking pictures of the plants with the family mirror. Sarala soon dropped back, feeling that it was a bit pointless to be walking with them if she wasn't saying anything.

The teachers were just behind the students. Sarala tried to fall in step beside Ak-tu, wondering if she could strike up a conversation with him. But he was talking to Khurshid and Fern. The only one who seemed left out was Aster.

Sarala found herself next to the librarian, feeling awkward. She knew he was friendly and upbeat from the one class she took with him, but she couldn't say she knew him more than her fellow first-years. After all, Fashion was more of a laidback club where the students chatted with each other while designing clothing, and Aster didn't take too active a role in teaching them. She therefore tried to fall behind a bit more by staring at a spinning bush. To her dismay, Aster joined her.

"It's a very interesting plant, isn't it?" he commented.

Sarala shrugged. "I guess," she said. "I've seen plenty of these before."

Aster nodded. "Yes... You lived in the wild, didn't you? Those who come from cities are always a bit surprised to see plants like this. Cities are certainly not the most magical places."

"But magic is in everything," Sarala said bluntly. "So cities have to be magical places, don't they?"

Aster shrugged, combing his hand through his blonde hair. "I suppose that's true, in a way. But in terms of environments... there's not much magic to cities, now is there? You can *feel* it."

Sarala frowned, but didn't know what to say. She therefore hurried to catch up to the other teachers, wondering if Ak-tu or even Khurshid were free to talk instead.

Zyn and Ren, who were leading the group, came to a stop beside what looked to be an ancient tree covered in squishy moss. They had now climbed to the second floor, where the tree's uppermost branches reached. Sarala waited in the back, wondering why they had paused. It was soon apparent, as Ak-tu approached the tree with his arms spread in front of him.

"Nature, we thank you for the season of winter. We thank you for allowing us to get through the past year, facing challenges that made us grow. We thank you for the balance and peace you bring, and appreciate the storms and turmoil you throw at us that challenge us to grow.

"Spirits, we thank you for the guidance and lessons you teach us. We thank you for showing us how to merge with our own inner spirits. We thank you for the moments of fun and of hardships, knowing both are necessary."

Sarala shifted uneasily. She knew Ak-tu had mentioned something about spirits and praising nature, but this seemed a bit ridiculous. Who was he even speaking to?

Zyn and Ren stepped closer to the tree, their arms out on either side of them too. They started speaking, saying similar things of following nature and maintaining balance. Sarala tuned them out.

"Not liking it?" Aster asked her quietly.

Sarala stiffened.

"It's quite fine, if you don't," he continued, his gaze amused. "I don't care for it, either."

She frowned, glancing up at him.

"I've told Ak-tu many times now that praising the spirits does no good. Nobody listens...or...hardly anybody does. And they certainly don't care. Spirits are selfish beings. They do not worry about others, particularly those in the physical realm. They do not care if they've impacted someone's life in a good way or not. The majority of spirits are just there...existing...not caring what's going on beyond their noses."

Sarala did not know how to reply. She still refused to believe in spirits until she saw one. But she had mostly heard good things about spirits from the Caihong family. It seemed spirits only acted badly if nature was destroyed or the spirits were disrespected. Aster was making it sound like all spirits were bad, no matter what —if they existed, that was.

"So you...still believe that spirits exist...despite not liking them?" Sarala asked in a whisper, as Ren continued praising the spirits.

Aster nodded. "Oh, yes. I've seen plenty of spirits, and I've lived in the spirit realm myself."

Sarala stared at him.

"It's not a lie," he said, inspecting one of his painted nails. "I used to be connected very much to the spirits. But now..." He shrugged. "My connection to the spirit realm has long since vanished."

Sarala wondered why that was. Didn't spiritual people, who claimed to make a connection to not only the spirit realm but also spirit magic, want to *keep* that connection? Who would suddenly choose to become un-spiritual, if being spiritual was such a highly sought-after state of mind? If it was the key to a great and powerful life?

The praising was soon over, with Khurshid and Fern adding a few words themselves. Ak-tu then led the group onwards, walking with his hands on his children's shoulders. Sarala and Aster followed at the back of the group, several paces away.

"It's a bit difficult being here sometimes," Aster told her. "You know—at this school, with the Caihong family, all the spiritual stuff. There's nothing wrong if you don't fit in with the rest of that lot." He nodded at the group in front of them. "There's nothing wrong with being an outsider."

An outsider? Sarala wondered. *Is that what I am? Is it so obvious that I...don't belong here?*

"Of course, I don't have a problem with Ak-tu or his family, or any of the other teachers," Aster persisted. "I'd just rather not get involved in all this spirit stuff."

"Then why are you here?" Sarala grumbled.

"Because I want to spend time with my friends."

"Even though you're such an outsider to them?" Sarala asked pointedly.

Aster shrugged. "I could have a conversation with them easily if I chose to. But I'm talking with *you*, now aren't I? Anyway, I always promise to do at least one of these holiday traditions with Ak-tu. I know how much it means to him."

Sarala frowned, but made no response. *Is that what I'm doing? Just going along with it to make them happy?*

Ak-tu brought them to a halt on the third floor, beside another ancient tree that smelled like sweet berries. The tree had long drapes of blue moss-looking leaves, appearing like a tall stick with blankets covering it. Ak-tu sat down on the walkway as close to the tree as he could get. He then closed his eyes, sitting upright. Zyn and Ren followed his lead, Khurshid and Fern soon joining.

"We don't have to do the meditation," Aster told her softly, and he nodded to the stairs behind them. "Let's wait downstairs."

The two therefore proceeded back down the spiraling wooden steps, until they reached the ground floor. Sarala could not see the tree that the group was meditating around, as the undergrowth was so thick and the plants constantly moved. Though she still wasn't sure what to make of Aster, she was grateful he allowed her to get away from the weird meditation.

Aster continued to make small chat, talking about school and classes, and how he was already planning his finals. Sarala ignored him, only making small noises every now and then to pretend she was listening. She wasn't sure how long the two stood there, but eventually, Ak-tu and the others returned. She sighed in relief, glad that they could get on with the day and hopefully put all these spirit rituals behind them.

"Who's ready for some games?" Zyn yowled, bounding forward.

"And music!" Ren said excitedly.

"Gotta love the family traditions," Aster said, his eyes sparking in amusement.

Sarala glanced up at him, frowning. *Family traditions…is that what all of this is? Is that why Ren and Zyn are so excited?*

Did my family have traditions? Would I be so excited for them too? What if…what if my family was spiritual? That'd be so weird… What if I was some sort of version of Ren? Ugh, that'd be the weirdest *thing! I can't imagine ever being like her.*

Sarala followed the others back into the Courtyard. It had started to snow again, and the students throwing snowballs had mostly vanished indoors to escape the creeping cold. *I wonder…was my family ever a family? Did I have a family before I became an orphan? What would it have been like?*

The image of a person in red appeared in her mind's eye. Sarala shut her eyes tightly. *No. You're not family. You never were, not after what you did,* she thought dismissively. *Leave me alone!*

Sarala joined the Caihong family for games until lunch. After eating, Ak-tu announced they'd be doing the traditional gift exchange. Sarala instantly retreated to her room without a word. She didn't know if she was supposed to get anything for the family (not that she had anything to give), and she didn't want to receive anything from them. She therefore practiced martial arts alone, trying to do her jump kicks properly. It was such a struggle to propel herself up, and she didn't want to land too hard and jolt her knees.

She gave up after several attempts, due to the wood floor being a bad surface to jump upon. She practiced the three techniques she'd learned in the previous class, but soon grew bored. She wanted to do something else…she wanted to play with weapons!

But I have *weapons,* she remembered.

She went over to the large desk on one side of her room, and pulled open a drawer. Two knives sat within, thick and curved. The dual butterfly knives had been her only possessions when she arrived at the school. She had kept the knives in her robe at the start of classes, but didn't want to be found with them. She therefore stashed them away at the beginning of the fall semester.

And I've forgotten about them since, she thought dismally. *I'm so sorry. I'll make it up to you!*

She pulled out the knives and began practicing with them. She had played with knives a lot when she lived in the wild, as it was something to do to pass the time when she wasn't traveling or looking for food. By the time she had reached the school, she had admittedly grown a little weary with the weapons, so doing Kung Fu was new and more interesting.

At first, Sarala would just play games with the knives and didn't know how to use them. But she taught herself different techniques, practicing on the plants around her. Now that she knew Kung Fu, she could apply different stances to these techniques and refine her movements.

She was practicing with the knives for so long that she was only made aware of the time when the bell rang for dinner. *I'll go in a bit,* she thought, as she wanted to finish the technique she was putting together. But she soon forgot that the bell had even rung, and continued working on her form, wishing she had a mirror to check that her stances were low enough and her knee wasn't poking too far over her toes.

A knock sounded loudly on her door, and she whirled around, clutching her weapons more tightly.

"Sarala? You in there?" Ren's voice called.

"Yeah," Sarala replied.

"You coming for dinner?"

"In a moment."

"What are you up to? Martial arts?"

"Yeah."

"Ooh, are you doing your jump kicks? Can I see?"

Before Sarala could protest, Ren opened the door and poked her head in. She froze when she saw the knives in Sarala's hands, which Sarala failed to hide behind her back quickly enough. The two girls stared at one another, Sarala uncertain and Ren's face unreadable.

"What are you doing with those knives?" Ren finally asked in a low voice, stepping in and closing the door behind her. "Did you take them from the Kung Fu Studio?"

Sarala shook her head. "You have butterfly knives here?" she queried.

"Well, I saw Dad with them before," Ren said. "But what are you doing with them? Where did you get them?"

"I've had them for a while," Sarala said plainly.

"Wait—you had them when you came to the school?" Ren asked in surprise. "But we didn't see them on you. Dad would have confiscated them right away."

"They were in my robe," Sarala said in exasperation.

Ren frowned. "Well…you're not allowed to have weapons of your own. All weapons have to be in the Kung Fu Studio, and weapon training has to be under Dad's supervision—or Khurshid's, I guess. But either way, you can't have those."

"Oh, like *you* didn't break the rules with getting Zyn enrolled and leaving the school to help a nonexistent animal," Sarala scoffed. "They're *my* knives, and I'm keeping them."

"I understand they're one of your few possessions—"

"They're my only possessions."

"—but it's a really important rule that everyone has to follow,"

Ren said, a bit apologetically. "Weapons can be dangerous."

"It's not like I'd use them on anyone! Besides, we have *wands*. Aren't those weapons too? You don't even have to use them for magic. You can just stab someone with them. Same with a pencil. Anything can be a weapon."

Ren snorted. "Sarala, you know what I mean! Bladed weapons aren't allowed, unless they were fake, perhaps. But those are clearly *not* fake."

"I'm not giving them up," Sarala hissed. *They mean too much to me...even though they shouldn't...should they? Ugh, I was better off just leaving them in the drawer and forgetting all about them!*

Ren bit her bottom lip, looking apprehensive.

Well, even if I feel uncertain about them... Sarala shook her thoughts away and declared, "I made them myself. I'm not losing them."

"You made them?" Ren asked in surprise.

Sarala nodded once.

"You're a blacksmith?"

"I suppose," she grumbled.

"But I thought you lived in the wild?"

"I did."

"Then how did you—"

"You said it was time for dinner, right? We'd better hurry if we're going to eat, then," Sarala said abruptly.

She walked over to her desk, opened one of the drawers, and placed her knives in the very back. Taking a notebook sitting on the top of the desk, she threw it in front of the knives, so they'd at least be somewhat concealed. Sarala then pushed past Ren, opened the door, and led the way down the stairs. Ren trailed after her a bit hesitantly once closing the door, much to Sarala's relief.

"Why don't you ever want to talk about your past?" Ren asked.

"Why would I?" Sarala grunted.

"You know, there's no shame in being an orphan. I know it's terrible, as you don't know your real family—or maybe you do, if you grew up with them, and then that'd be even worse to end up as an orphan, but—"

Sarala whipped around angrily. "Just because you're apparently an orphan doesn't mean you get to speak for other orphans—or other children who've had rough lives!" she sneered. "You've had a family your whole life, blood-kin or not! You've lived in a mighty school, always protected and looked after! You didn't have to fight to survive, or attempt to steal food without being caught. You didn't have to face the wrath of nature, or the dangerous wildlife. You don't know what it's like out there!"

She turned and stomped down the stairs, the image of the red-clad woman appearing in her mind's eye again. Her jaw clenched. *I'm better off alone. I've always been better off alone…*

Sarala and Ren did not speak much that night, despite Ren joining Sarala for dinner and apologizing several times. Sarala did her best to ignore the other girl, even when Ren brought her the last sweet chocolate roll for dessert. But by the time they returned to the tower and Ren gave Sarala a book about weapons as a gift for the Day of the Moon, Sarala was more willing to forgive her words. She therefore shrugged it off, thanked Ren, and hoped to sleep off their small fight.

The next day, Sarala woke up in a better mood. She was a bit hesitant to see Ren at first, but when Ren was overjoyed to see her, she realized that she had nothing to worry about. Feeling a little guilty for how she'd snapped at Ren, Sarala agreed to go to the art club meeting that morning. But it seemed her bad mood had transferred to Ren when Ren learned Zyn didn't want to go too.

As soon as the door to the Art Studio closed behind the two girls, Ren started whispering to Sarala. "Why do you think Zyn didn't want to come today?"

"How should I know?" Sarala replied gruffly, not in the mood to talk.

"Did she mention anything to you?"

Sarala grabbed a piece of paper from a cabinet on the far side of the room. She returned to her seat, nodded to Mint as she entered, then faced Ren. "No, she didn't say anything."

The door opened again as Raimugi and Mernao entered. Sarala smirked in satisfaction as she saw Frost was not with them.

Ren lowered her voice further. "You know how Zyn's next

therapy appointment is coming up?"

"Yeah. It's next Thorsday, isn't it?"

"Well, she was talking to me a bit last night, before we had our...well, when we were doing the family gift exchange...and she..." Ren took a deep breath, then whispered so faintly Sarala had to strain to hear her, "she wants to go by he/him pronouns and identify as a boy."

"Okay," Sarala said. "So why are you referring to him as a girl still?"

"She's—he's—pushing away from me!" Ren hissed. "Can't you see that? He no longer wants to be twins!"

Sarala stared at the purple-haired girl for a long moment, glad that she wasn't the only one to overreact. "Ren, you're such an idiot," she finally grunted. "You and Zyn will always be twins."

"But we do everything together, and now she—he—no longer wants to!" Ren cried softly, taking off her glasses to rub at her watery eyes. "I feel like this whole gender crisis is just making him push away from me even more..."

"Twins aren't supposed to be the same person," Sarala pointed out, propping her elbow on her desk as the door opened to admit C3. "Just because Zyn no longer wants to be a girl doesn't mean he no longer wants to be your twin. You two share a special connection...unlike any I've ever seen."

"But even regardless of the gender thing, Zyn doesn't want to spend time with me. Or maybe it's because of it."

"Just because he literally didn't come to *one* art club meeting?" Sarala scoffed. "Ren, you're being ridiculous."

Ren glared at her for a long moment, then sighed. "Yeah...but I still feel like...there's something Zyn isn't telling me."

"Zyn just needs time to figure things out for himself," Sarala said with a shrug.

The two fell quiet for a while, both of them staring down at their blank pieces of paper. Raimugi and Mernao were talking in low voices on the other side of the room, while Mint hummed softly to herself as she colored at the desk across from them. Nobody seemed to have heard their quiet conversation.

"What are you going to draw today?" Sarala asked Ren, changing the topic so Ren would stop worrying.

Ren glanced down at her paper, as if noticing it for the first time. "Oh! Umm…I don't know."

"How about a cat?"

Ren glanced over her shoulder at C3, who sat at the desk behind her. He was focused entirely on sketching a castle lightly with his pencil. Sarala frowned, not even noticing he had entered the room.

"A cat?" Ren said thoughtfully.

"Oooh, did you say cat?" Mint asked eagerly, glancing up. "Cats are so cool!"

"Cats are scary," Sarala muttered, remembering the time a large tiger had been stalking her in the jungle. She shivered and added, "I hate cats."

Mint pulled out her mirror from her backpack (nearly dropping it as she did so) and unlocked it. She tapped along its surface, then turned the mirror for Sarala and Ren to see. There was a photo of a small cat with spots.

"Cats are really cute!" Mint said, beaming at Sarala.

Sarala squinted closer. "That's…tiny."

"It's a farm cat," Mint said promptly. "Little cats that hang around farms!"

"They don't kill the farmers?" Sarala queried.

Mint looked horrified and nearly dropped her mirror again. "*Kill* them? No! Why would you think that?"

"Because big cats kill people all the time," C3 said, still concentrated on his sketch.

Sarala nodded. "That's too true," she growled in a low voice.

He looked up at her, seeming surprised that she agreed with him. His lips twitched slightly, but then he returned to his drawing without a word.

"I guess I'll draw a farm cat, then!" Ren declared, and she leaned forward to draw. "I saw a farm cat a few months ago, and it was so cute!"

Sarala shifted uneasily. "It's not that cute," she said.

"I doubt you find anything cute," C3 commented.

Sarala turned in her chair to glare at him. "Oh, and *you* do? What do you find cute?"

C3 froze, his pencil hovering over the paper in front of him.

"That's what I thought," Sarala replied, smirking lightly.

"But there are so many cute things in the world!" Mint said, her voice shrill as she glanced from Sarala to C3 and back again. "Have you ever seen a screaming bush? It's so tiny and its screams are like melodies! I wish they'd call it the singing bush instead."

C3 snorted derisively. "Only a fool would enjoy the wails of a plant," he said.

"Stop being a jerk!" Sarala growled, clenching her jaw as Mint's eyes grew watery.

C3 huffed. "I'm just pointing out a fact. It's called a screaming bush for a reason. It does *not* sound like it's singing."

"Maybe not to you, but to Mint, it does," Ren said, offering Mint a smile. "She sees things from a unique perspective!"

"And not a box," Sarala said bluntly.

"I wouldn't talk if I were you," C3 sneered.

Sarala's jaw clenched harder.

"Why don't we just get back to drawing?" Mint asked, her voice high and tense. "Please?"

"That sounds great!" Ren agreed, turning to her art again.

Sarala glared at C3, who returned her gaze steadily. But then he went back to his castle sketch, pushing his pencil down so strongly that the tip began to wobble as he darkened the lines. Sarala turned around and stared down at her own blank paper.

Am I as narrow-minded as C3? she wondered, sighing heavily. She glanced at Ren, who was now adding wings to her cat. *I guess I can be. I sure don't care about all that spirit stuff…not at all….*

Sarala began sketching absentmindedly as she thought. She wasn't even aware of what she had been drawing, until Ren glanced over.

"Ooh, who's that?" Ren asked, pointing.

Sarala looked down at her paper and froze. She swiftly crunched up the sketch, before C3 or Mint could take a good look at it.

"It's nobody," she hissed.

C3 snorted. "Looked like you, but with short hair. I don't think that's a very good look for you."

Ren shot a glare at C3. "I think Sarala would be *very* beautiful with short hair!" she snapped. "You just have no fashion sense!"

Sarala forced herself to relax. *They think it was just me... Good...*

C3 scowled at Ren; he seemed to be in a very bad mood, like an experiment he conducted did not go according to plan. He practically stabbed his pencil on his paper, causing the tip to snap. Grumbling in annoyance, he grabbed his artwork, got to his feet, and left the Art Studio.

"Good riddance," Sarala said in satisfaction.

"I wish he wasn't so mean," Mint moaned softly.

"He'll have to work a lot on himself first," Ren grumbled.

"Like *that* will happen," Sarala scoffed.

"People can change," Ren said, glancing at her in an odd fashion.

"Sure," Sarala muttered darkly, glaring at the ground. "People say they want to change, then never do. And I doubt C3 will ever want to."

Ren shrugged. "I believe people can change. Look at you."

"What about me?"

"You used to be really quiet and never wanted to be around people. But now you've opened up with me—and Zyn and even Dad! And you're in an art club, spending time with other students," Ren pointed out.

Sarala felt like her jaw would break from how taut it was. She glared at Ren for a long moment, then got to her feet and exited the studio as well. She nearly crashed into Zyn outside.

"Hey, is C3 in there?" Zyn queried.

Sarala frowned. "C3? He just left a bit ago. Why?"

Zyn shrugged. "I dunno," he murmured. "I didn't think he'd be there today."

"He's always at the meetings, isn't he?"

"Yeah. But last week..." Zyn let his sentence trail off.

"What happened last week?"

Zyn shrugged again. "He was just being a jerk to Mint after the club. I didn't think he'd show his face there again."

"Well, he's still a jerk, and I hope he doesn't come back," Sarala grumbled. "Anyway, you better go in and spend some time with Ren. She's driving me crazy!"

"About what?"

Sarala sighed. "Just go see her," she muttered.

"O-kay."

Sarala pushed past him. Her body was tense, a surge of irritation rising through her. She kept her fists clenched at her sides, still clutching the crunched-up paper in one hand. She just wanted to be left alone.

And free, she thought dismally. *I want to be free, from everyone else's problems, from myself, from…her….*

She sighed, heading for the garden, as she still didn't have a key to the Caihong family tower. She doubted very much that she'd ever be free again; her memories would always be tormenting her….

CHAPTER 24: REPRISE

Snow drifted from the dark blue-and-gray sky, twirling down peacefully to an icy pond. The frozen water gleamed in the moonlight peeking through the clouds, causing the wintery terrain to feel more tranquil. A light breeze swirled through, pushing snowflakes across the ice and off the pine trees before falling still.

Ak-tu breathed deeply, the frigid air piercing his lungs. He released his breath in a puff of fog, his stiff body relaxing a little. Violet eyes scanning the trees and pond in front of him, he bounced up and down on the balls of his feet to keep his body warm while he waited in the forest.

Any day now, he thought, wishing he had brought a metal bottle of hot cocoa.

The trees rustled as another light breeze swept through, causing Ak-tu to shiver and pull his fuzzy hat further down his head. Cold and bored, Ak-tu began practicing martial arts, starting with swinging punches to keep his blood flowing and tingling through his fingertips. He wasn't striking the air for too long when he saw a shadowy figure on the other side of the pond.

"Finally!" Ak-tu uttered under his breath, smiling as he recognized the broad-shouldered man.

He got out of his low stance and ran forward, his crunchy footsteps loud as he kicked up snow behind him. Once he reached the pond, Ak-tu hopped onto the ice, using a combination of water and air magic to propel him across: The water magic allowed his feet to glide on the ice without slipping, while the air magic made him move rapidly.

"Yo!" Jabali's voice rang out as the man stepped foot onto the ice as well, nearly slipping right away.

"Stay there!" Ak-tu called, trying to hold back a snort of amusement. "Don't fall!"

He thrust his palms behind him, creating more wind to jet him across the pond. Wind whizzing through his hair and stinging his eyes, Ak-tu could barely see Jabali and didn't realize how fast he was approaching. He lowered his arms to stop the magic, but it was too late.

Ak-tu crashed into Jabali, throwing them both to the ice with yelps of surprise. Dizzy and the air knocked from his lungs, Ak-tu found himself sprawled on top of Jabali, who groaned beneath him in a daze.

"Ya crazy dunderhead!" Jabali huffed, shoving Ak-tu off. "Wha' are ya doin'? Tryna break the ice and have us go for a midnight swim?"

Ak-tu groaned, feeling a bruise already forming on his side as he propped himself up to his knees. "Sorry, I didn't realize I was going so fast," he uttered earnestly, clutching his side.

Jabali raised his eyes to the sky in exasperation, then got to his feet. He brushed snow from his tangled hair and off his blue robe, then examined the top pocket. Frowning, he pulled out a crushed white-and-indigo plant.

"Look wha' ya did to my moon-shadow flower!" Jabali complained.

Ak-tu felt guilt course through him at once. "I'm sorry," he murmured, dipping his head to the ice. "I didn't mean to crash into you like that."

Jabali eyed him for a moment, then tossed the flower over his shoulder. "Eh, whatever. I've got more at home. Just thought I'd bring some decor with me to celebrate the Day o' the Moon tonight."

Ak-tu glanced up at him to see Jabali offering him a small smile. Beaming, Ak-tu sprung to his feet at once, only to slip on the ice. Jabali quickly grabbed hold of his arm and held him up.

"Clearly, someone wants t'go iceskating!" chuckled Jabali.

"I mean—"

Before Ak-tu could finish speaking, Jabali slid away, tugging the smaller man after him. Ak-tu let out a bewildered cry, which quickly turned into laughter that echoed through the still air. He used his water magic once again, allowing them both to glide more easily.

Jabali shifted his weight from one side to the other, Ak-tu following his lead as he pressed himself closer to the ice. The two men crisscrossed the pond in circular motions, twirling like the snowflakes dancing down from the sky. The clouds shifted aside, moonlight illuminating them as they made their way, back and forth and side to side, looping here and spinning there. Though the wind was frosty as it swirled across them, Ak-tu could only feel a warmth spreading from his chest to his fingertips and toes.

Eventually, they slowed to a stop at the other side of the pond, where Ak-tu had begun. Jabali nearly stumbled, and it was Ak-tu's turn to grab hold of him with both hands to keep him up.

"Clearly, somebody wanted to dance," Ak-tu mocked Jabali.

"Hey, y'know I like dancin' the night away!" Jabali chuckled, waving his arms about and nearly throwing Ak-tu over his shoulder.

Ak-tu released his grip before he could be tossed, his grin broadening. "Yeah, yeah!"

"So now tha' we've had our fun," Jabali huffed as he sat down on the ice, "was there any reason ya wanted t'meet up?"

"The Day of the Moon," Ak-tu said promptly, sitting down across from him.

"Yeah, 'n wha' else?"

"Why do you always think there's something else?"

"Has there been anythin' more going on with tha' mirror shard, or any spirits?"

Ak-tu shook his head.

"No more visions for Ren?"

"Nope."

"And no magic for Zyn?"

"Not since he started the potion."

"Ah-ha!" Jabali declared, pointing a large finger at Ak-tu. "So there *is* somethin' new!"

"Oh, yeah, Zyn's trying out identifying as a boy now," Ak-tu said, running his fingers over his mustache.

"Mmm, how's tha' going?"

"He just told us tonight," Ak-tu said with a shrug. "I'm glad he's trying things and getting it figured out."

"And how 'bout ya? You getting things figured out?"

Ak-tu blinked in confusion. *Figured out? About what?* he wondered. *The gender stuff? Never figured that out and don't care to at this point. Or is he asking about—*

"Have ya figured out wha' t'do with the school?" Jabali clarified as he saw Ak-tu's blank face.

Ak-tu raised one side of his unibrow. *It sounds like he's picking up from a conversation we left off at, but...* "What are you talking about?" he asked aloud.

Jabali brushed his curly hair out of his eyes and said, "Now tha' Zyn can't do magic school 'til next year, tha' means you gotta have the school longer. And don't ya wanna get back t'traveling?"

"We've already been over this," Ak-tu uttered, flicking his fingers to create a small twirl of wind floating in front of him. "I'm content with the school. We'll travel after…"

"After what?"

"After my kids are done with school," Ak-tu said, his eyes glazing over. "It's just a few years."

"But wha' about after? They gonna go to university?"

"I'm not sure. It's up to them," Ak-tu replied.

"So you're gonna be travelin' alone?"

Ak-tu sighed lightly, the spiraling wind vanishing as he let his hand drop to his side. "Well, maybe. I'm sure we'll have one more big trip before they go to universities…if they do. Again, I'm not sure what either kid wants to do…as I don't think they know themselves just yet."

"Eh, good point," Jabali uttered. "Most people tha' age don't know wha' to try out."

"Anyhow, that's years from now," Ak-tu went on, shifting into a more comfortable position as the ice was hurting his tailbone. "I try to live in the present moment…. The future is too uncertain, and so many things could change…"

Before Jabali could respond, a loud cry split the air, a chill trickling down Ak-tu's spine like freezing water. He and Jabali hopped to their feet, struggling to maintain their balance.

"There!" Jabali yelled, pointing at the trees to their left.

Ak-tu squinted, catching sight of a small shadow darting through the snow-covered bushes. The creature shrieked again, a high-pitched yet short noise that almost sounded like a bird.

"What is that?" Jabali grumbled.

"Let's find out," Ak-tu murmured.

Without warning, he hopped off the ice and returned to the snow, landing with a soft crunch up to his knees. The cold crystals soaked through his pants and immediately froze his legs, but he paid no attention to this as he pulled his feet free and sprinted after the shadow. He could hear Jabali's heavy footsteps behind him, and hear his light huffs as he tried to catch up.

The figure was now skittering between bushes, its long tail flicking snow off branches and not allowing Ak-tu to make out its features. At one point, the shadow even pulled a twig back, then released it, throwing snow at Ak-tu and blinding him momentarily. Staggering after it, Ak-tu knew this was no animal they were dealing with.

{I think they're a spirit!} Ak-tu called telepathically, not wanting to alert the creature. *{It might be the spirit who's been reaching out to Ren, or the one who got into the school! We have to catch them!}*

Jabali did not respond, having never mastered telepathy.

Ak-tu forced his legs to keep pushing him across the snow and through the plants, glad that he had only been sitting for a few minutes. Ducking beneath a low-hanging branch and dodging around a hopping bush, he managed to catch up relatively quickly to the spirit.

Gotchya now! Ak-tu thought, springing off his toes with a burst of wind as he threw himself at the creature.

But it vanished.

His hands clutched empty air, and his momentum carried him right into a tree. Wincing as he slammed into the rough bark, he swiftly lifted his hands to prevent the tree's snow from dropping all over him. Successful, he staggered to his feet in a daze and stumbled backwards, keeping his arms up until he determined he was far enough away from the floating heap of snow. He then lowered his arms, the snow plopping down with a crunchy thud.

Jabali skidded to a stop beside him, throwing snow in all directions that Ak-tu might as well have allowed the frozen stuff to fall on his head. Rolling his eyes as he wiped the snow off of him, he continued speaking to Jabali by mind.

{Did you see that spirit pop out anywhere?}

"No," Jabali murmured in a low voice. "I thought it went invisible."

{If they had turned invisible, I would've been able to grab them still. No, they teleported away someplace…} Ak-tu shook his head in disappointment. *{We better keep looking for them…}*

Jabali grunted lightly beside him.

Ak-tu led the way through the forest, the pond now far out of sight as the trees thickened. This region was much darker since it was harder for the moon's light to pierce through the undergrowth, especially as clouds continuously passed by. They kept their ears pricked for any footsteps padding across the snow. Ak-tu kept his fingers and wrists flitting about, trying to feel movement in the still air. Jabali kept his head turning, scanning for any spirit magic in use.

The men had been walking for almost half-an-hour, yet nothing seemed to exist in the snowy forest. Eventually, Ak-tu came to a stop in his tracks, sitting down abruptly in a lotus position next to a bush.

{I think the spirit is gone, but I'll try to reach out with my energy.} He told Jabali as he closed his eyes.

Ak-tu took a deep breath, then released it to relax his sore body. He imagined crawling through the bushes and floating through the tallest trees, covering the length of the forest like a giant blanket. Yet all he could detect were low buzzes, the tiniest sparks of energy coming from animals or plants. The biggest presence he could feel was Jabali standing beside him like a guard. The spirit had truly gone.

Ak-tu opened his eyes and looked up at his friend, shaking his head. "They're gone," he said aloud.

"Well, that was bound t'happen," Jabali murmured, holding a large hand out to Ak-tu.

Ak-tu grabbed the calloused hand, allowing Jabali to tug him to his feet as his energy seeped away like snowflakes in a breeze.

"Did you recognize the sound tha' spirit made?"

"I don't think so. Did you see any spirit magic?"

"Nope."

"Then we're no closer to figuring *anything* out," Ak-tu uttered with a sigh, his shoulders slumping.

"We'll get there, don't ya worry!" Jabali encouraged, slapping Ak-tu hard on the back and knocking him back to the snow. "Whoops." Helping him up again, Jabali added, "We now know there's definitely a spirit trailin' ya 'round, right?"

"But are they?" Ak-tu wondered, running his fingers over his mustache. "What if they're the one reaching out to Ren?"

"Then I guess they're reachin' out to ya both," Jabali said with a shrug.

"Do you think they're trying to warn us of something? Or guide us?"

Jabali raised his eyes to the sky. "Always optimistic 'bout them spirits, aren't ya? I think it's more likely tha' spirit is a threat."

Ak-tu frowned. "Maybe…but maybe they've just been trying to get in contact with me, and I've been too busy to notice, so they tried reaching out to Ren, and then they saw me out here and—"

"Please, Ak-tu, keep your guard up!" Jabali growled, grabbing Ak-tu by the shoulders and shaking him a few times. "I don't trust tha' spirit to be 'good' or even 'neutral'! I think some spirit is after ya, maybe your whole family!"

The hair prickled on the back of Ak-tu's neck, his eyes widening and a lump forming in his throat. He gazed up at his friend, not knowing what to say for a long moment.

Finally, he swallowed the lump away and murmured, "I will be upping the security at the school…and looking for more mirror shards myself…. I'll try to figure out what's going on…why this spirit's hanging around…how they might have gotten in…"

Jabali nodded curtly, releasing his hold on Ak-tu. "Good. And call me with any updates, ya hear? I'll be with ya in an instant to check out anythin' tha' might be goin' on, m'kay?"

Nodding wordlessly, Ak-tu stepped forward and hugged his friend. "Thank you, Jabali," he whispered. "You've been too helpful…"

"Hey, I don't want anything to happen to your family," Jabali said seriously. "And I don't want anything to happen to you. Ya hear?"

"Loud and clear," Ak-tu said, pulling away from him. "Anyhow, I'd better get back to the school…. Are you fine going home alone, or would you like to stay?"

"Gotta get back to my shop," Jabali replied, pulling out his mirror. "It's late, and I gotta be there soon enough. But call me if anything changes."

"I will," Ak-tu promised. "You'll be the first to know."

Jabali nodded curtly, hugged Ak-tu one more time, then left without another word. Ak-tu watched him go until he vanished into the shadows.

After his friend had gone, he pulled his own mirror out of his pocket, glad to see it hadn't broken with all the action it'd been through. He opened the map app, blinking in surprise that he was closer to the school than he'd thought. Once he ensured he was going in the right direction, he pocketed the object again and started walking.

My kids might be in danger...I have to get this puzzle figured out... Who is the spirit, and what do they want with us?

CHAPTER 25: WAS IT ALL WORTH IT

Classes were starting to keep all of the students busy once more. Even Zyn, taking less classes, was finding himself doing extra schoolwork during his free time. He was so focused on doing martial arts outside of class, that he was now practicing with Sarala on a regular basis. Ren joined at times, but she often had other homework to do; she didn't like to skip it, even if Sarala didn't mind turning in sloppy work.

Ren also had the feeling that her family was keeping secrets. Zyn always left the tower without telling Ren where he was going, and Ren was bogged down by too much work to pursue him. Ak-tu also never seemed to be around, apologizing to his kids at least once a week as he claimed he was too busy grading homework and trying to practice martial arts. When Ren asked if he'd found more mirror shards, he would shake his head but never expand on it; Ren had a feeling something was going on behind the scenes, but she was clearly not supposed to inquire about it. Saddened by all the secrecy, Ren stopped asking questions and focused on her copious homework.

She was luckily still able to enjoy her birthday when February 12 rolled around, her family acting normal for the day.

Ren celebrated turning fifteen by having fun in the Art classes. Zyn made her day extra special, creating something for her in each of the classes, from a funny-looking hat in Fashion to a bad attempt at a song in Choir. Ren appreciated the efforts and began to feel more hopeful that her brother *wasn't* pushing away from her, after all.

Ak-tu, meanwhile, was busy teaching classes, that he only had the evening to spend with Ren. The two meditated together after dinner, then he gave her a new mossy plant that Ren squealed about in delight. She began to feel more hopeful that her father was getting things figured out, and would be back to normal soon.

This definitely seemed to be the case as Ak-tu seemed less distracted in classes as time went on. February soon ended, her father at ease as the snow melted away with the arrival of spring. The forest was once more blooming with flowers, and Ren was happy to catch sight of the farm cat weaving between blossoming plants on occasion.

The first-years had finally finished the basic exercises of producing their own elements in Magic Channeling. Their first creative homework assignment appeared in March, when the students had to come up with a practical every-day use of what they could use their elemental magic for.

"I hope I do my magic okay," Ren said, biting her lip nervously over breakfast that Moonday morning.

Sarala stared at her. "You're one of the best magicians in the class," she said bluntly.

"But what if I do it wrong?"

Sarala rolled her eyes. "Quit your worrying and eat your muffin—before I steal it."

Ren stuck her tongue out at Sarala, snatching up her apple cinnamon muffin before her friend could take it.

"I wish I could do that assignment," Zyn said, looking a bit glum for a moment. But he quickly brightened up. "I guess I will next year!"

The minute-bell soon rang for class, and they went to the Magic Studies room together. Khurshid lectured the class about different ways that magic could be used in day-to-day lives, as if giving the first-years ideas for their homework in the following class, if they still had yet to come up with something. Once the lecture was over, Zyn waved to Ren and Sarala, then left in the direction of the Theatre.

"Where's he going?" Ren asked Sarala.

"No clue," Sarala said simply.

The girls crossed the short distance to the Magic Channeling classroom. Ren was tempted to trail Zyn, as it looked like he was heading for the elevator that would bring him up to the student quarters. But that couldn't be right. Why would Zyn have to go up there?

"Does Zyn have a new friend he's not telling us about?" Ren asked Sarala in a low tone as the students went to stand by their elemental cauldrons.

"How should I know?" Sarala asked gruffly, clearly weary of Ren asking the same questions for weeks.

Ren shrugged. But she couldn't think of any other reason why Zyn would go to the student quarters, if he was indeed heading to the platform.

"I hope you're all ready to show off your unique magic!" Khurshid said, once the final bell finished ringing. "Who'd like to go first?"

It came as no surprise that C3 raised his hand quickly. Khurshid seemed to expect this, and called for him to move to the front of the classroom. C3 took a few books from his bag and set these on Khurshid's desk, then moved to the side and raised his wand in front of him.

"Books, come to me!" C3 ordered briskly, waving his wand.

A line of air streamed from the end of C3's wand. When creating one's own element, the element came directly out of the wand (or directly out of the body, if the body was channeling the magic instead). This was different from when the students had controlled the elements around them, as their surroundings would move in accordance to the wand. C3's wind wrapped around the books on the desk and carried them over to him. He caught them and smiled lightly.

"I would like to think that this bit of magic would come in handy with carrying homework to you."

Nobody seemed impressed with his magic. After all, the air magicians had already used their magic to shove objects around the room. Carrying an object was just an extra step. C3 glared around at their bland faces, before returning to the air cauldron at the back of the room.

"Nicely done," Khurshid said with a nod. "Who's next?"

"Me!" Ren said, and she skipped forward.

She had props as well, which she'd stuffed in her backpack from dinner the previous night. She took out an onion and a big chopping knife that she had permission to use from the Kitchen.

She pointed her wand at her head and said, "Make an air bubble around my head, so I do not cry while cutting this onion."

Her magic complied, the wand producing a large bubble around her entire head. She then proceeded to chop the onion on the front desk, careful that she didn't slam the knife too hard into the wood.

When she had finished, the students nearest the front were wiping at their crying eyes. Ren, however, was perfectly fine. She beamed around at her classmates as they applauded her.

"That's genius!" Raimugi called out with a sniffle.

"Quite so," Khurshid agreed. "Well done, Ren. You actually did more advanced magic than I was expecting of the class. You set your wand down and yet your magic continued to hold tight. Good job."

Ren beamed at him. She scooped up the cut onions and knife, and returned to the cauldron. She set the knife in her bag, where she'd return it to the Kitchen at lunch, then munched on the onion pieces. She offered some to the other two air students, but only Mernao took a tiny handful. C3 glared at her, probably angry that she had gotten praise when he did not.

The class proceeded to watch presentations. Some of the first-years did the same as C3, just adding an extra step to the basic exercises they'd already done in class.

After about half of the students went, Sarala decided to go. She walked over to the obstacle course that took up most of the room, where the ground was completely made of stone. Most of the fire magicians had demonstrated at the obstacle course too, where their fire wouldn't burn any of their fellow students.

Sarala lifted her wand and focused on the ground for a long time. Then, she took a deep breath and commanded sharply, "Lift the ground and make it bumpy, so nobody can tread over it easily!"

The floor in front of her vibrated a bit, then several stones spiked up. They were so pointy, that Ren would hate to step on them. Some other parts of the ground shifted slightly, giving them a rolled look. Sarala turned back to face Khurshid, who was frowning.

"You used your wand to control the ground, not to create your *own* ground," he said. "Put the ground back and try again."

Sarala whipped back to the stone floor and growled, "Make the ground completely smooth!"

The rock shifted back into position, flattening out as if it had never changed in the first place. She then lifted her wand in front of her, but didn't move for a long moment. Ren was beginning to wonder if she had forgotten what she was supposed to be doing, but then she spoke.

"Make the ground bumpy!" she ordered.

This time, a substance appeared from the wand and hardened as it dropped to the floor with a squelching-turned-clattering thud. It became a single spiky stone. As Khurshid had explained many times to the earth magicians, creating their own element would be very difficult to manage and the effect was usually the opposite of grand.

"Better," Khurshid said, as Sarala wiped sweat from her forehead. "May I ask, how was making the ground bumpy an everyday task?"

Sarala reddened. "It wasn't what I was going to do. I originally planned to make the ground smooth, so people with injuries or in wheelchairs could get across it more easily. But the ground was already too flat, so I raised it."

"That is considerate of you," Khurshid said.

They continued to watch the presentations until the end of class.

"Good efforts today!" Khurshid exclaimed as the bell rang. "There won't be any homework this week. Keep up the good work. Class dismissed!"

Ren was relieved they weren't assigned any homework. She and Sarala exited the classroom, making their way towards the Greenhouse with the other first-years. Now that it was spring, the glass house windows were wide open, allowing noisy birds and insects in again.

Before she and Sarala could enter the garden leading to the Greenhouse, Ren glanced over her shoulder towards the eastern building. She half-expected to see Zyn coming down on the stone platform from the student quarters. But there was nobody there.

Maybe I just imagined Zyn going that way, she thought dully. *I just wish I knew where he was always wandering off to...*

The weeks pressed on as March turned into April. Ren was trying to keep a closer eye on Zyn, and had even tried to confront him about where he was going. But Zyn said he was just bored, and went around the school to get some fresh air after being cooped up in the tower. Ren wasn't sure if she believed this answer. But finals were only a little over a month away, and she didn't want to deal with whatever other trouble Zyn might be getting into.

On April 6, Ren and Zyn celebrated Sarala's sixteenth birthday, but soon had to bid her farewell as she went to her Kung Fu class after lunch. She was still a blue sash, much to their surprise. Whether she tried to test for the purple sash or not, they didn't know, as she hardly spoke about the class to the twins.

"Have you noticed that she's been more...closed recently?" Zyn commented to Ren, as the two made their way to the Tai Chi Studio to work on their own martial arts.

"Sarala?"

"Who else doesn't like to tell anything of their past?" Zyn pointed out.

You, Ren thought. *Though you're more silent about the present, not the past...*

"She speaks less and less each time I see her," Zyn continued. "Did something happen between you two again?"

Ren raised an eyebrow at her brother. "Umm...no? Why are you blaming *me* for Sarala's moods?"

"I dunno," Zyn said with a shrug, opening the door to the Tai Chi Studio. "I just thought—"

But whatever Zyn might have thought, Ren didn't find out. She collapsed to the floor, screaming in pain as her head hurt more than ever before, ready to burst like a tomato in a hot pot. She was having another vision...

Focus! she tried to tell herself. *FOCUS!*

There was that shiny object again... That wasn't water rushing towards her, but some sort of magic swirl... The purple thing looked almost like a face... And there were more images Ren was able to focus on! Something transparent...something large...something cracked....

Ren panted as the pain vanished almost as quickly as it had come. She was left with a small headache, but she ignored it as she sat up in a daze. Zyn was sitting beside her, his face concerned.

"There was more to it this time!" Ren said, and she quickly told him what she'd seen before she could forget.

"What did the shiny thing look like?"

"I couldn't tell, it was blinding."

"What about the water? How do you know it's magic? I mean, was it water magic? Is Mint going to flood the school or something?"

Ren snorted. "Stop being silly, Zyn! It just...I could *feel* that it was magic, you know?"

"No."

"Well, anyway, it was like a...a big wave."

"But it wasn't water?"

"No."

"O-kay. Well, what was the large thing?"

"I couldn't tell. I could only see it was something massive."

"That's not helpful. And the cracked thing?"

"I don't know," Ren muttered. She sighed. "These visions are useless. I was hoping I'd be done with them."

Zyn shrugged. "It seems like you're not," he pointed out. "Should we go tell Dad?"

"Dad's in the middle of class, or the middle of a test for all we know," Ren pointed out.

"But this is important," Zyn said.

"I promise I'll tell him before dinner," Ren muttered. "I think I'm going to lay down for a while."

She got to her feet shakily and unlocked the tower door. Zyn trailed after her, looking uncertain.

"Do you need me to get Fern or anything?" Zyn asked.

"No," Ren said, taking several steps before plopping on the couch. "I just need some rest."

She closed her eyes, hoping to fall into a dreamless sleep. But she soon found herself in the blackest space she'd ever seen, with no distinguishable walls or floor... She was surrounded by purple faces, peering down at her from all angles… A wave of magic overcame her, locking her in place… Something large was headed for her…

Ren's eyes flew open and the nightmare ended. Zyn was sitting on the armchair nearby, watching her anxiously. Sighing, she turned away before he could ask if she was okay. She closed her eyes, but did her best not to fall asleep again.

Eventually, she heard the tower door open. She looked up to see Ak-tu entering the family room.

"You're back!" Zyn yelped, and he hurried over to Ak-tu. "Ren had another vision!"

"Another vision?" Ak-tu asked, his calm face instantly concerned. He hurried to the couch as Ren sat up, taking a seat beside her. "Are you okay?"

Ren groaned lightly. *Great. He was just getting back to normal. Now he's going to be all stressed and distant again…*

"Ren?"

"I'm fine," she said, forcing herself to sound cheerful.

The upbeat tone gradually faded from her voice as she told him what she'd seen, though she did her best to keep a smile plastered to her face.

"How long has it been since your last vision?" Ak-tu asked her when she finished. "Months, right?"

"Yeah."

"Hmm…" He fingered his mustache, staring at the ground in deep thought. Finally, he glanced over at her. "I think the vision might be coming true soon."

"Really?" Ren mumbled.

"You've had the same vision three times now, and you're seeing more with each one," Ak-tu explained. "The more vivid it gets, the closer it is to happening. I think. I will check with Aster on that one. Plus, it's been months since anything of note has happened…"

"Anything of note?" Zyn questioned, cocking his head.

Ak-tu ignored him and asked Ren, "Do you have any idea of where you were in the vision, or if these things were happening to you or around you? You, specifically, not someone else?"

Ren frowned. "I'm not sure," she admitted, trying to think

back. "I couldn't really make out my surroundings… I was focused on the things I saw—or, trying to, anyway."

"If you have the vision again, I'd like you to try focusing on the surroundings," Ak-tu said.

Ren sighed and rested her chin on top of her open palm. "I *hope* I don't have it again," she muttered.

Ak-tu put his hand on her shoulder and rubbed it soothingly. "We all hope that," he said. "But you might not have a choice."

"It felt bad, though," Ren murmured. "Not just getting the vision, with my head feeling like it'd explode. But the vision itself. It felt…dangerous."

Ak-tu stood up abruptly. "I'll look more into this. It's not much to go off of, but I'll do my best. And I will protect you from whatever might be coming. Both of you," he added, glancing at Zyn still lingering nearby.

Without another word, Ak-tu left the tower. The twins watched him go, then Ren slumped back down on the couch. She wished she had seen more to help her father. What was the point of the visions if she couldn't see everything going on? How were they ever going to warn her of anything? And why did it hurt so much?

Hold on…that bright light, she realized suddenly, sitting upright again. *It was like that bright light I saw from Sarala's room!*

"Are you okay?" Zyn asked, staring at her for her sudden movement.

"Yes," Ren said after a small pause. "I just need some water. Do you think you could get some for me?"

"You got it!" Zyn said at once, and he raced away.

Ren was off the couch the moment the tower door closed, hurrying up the stairs to Sarala's room.

But Sarala doesn't have anything that could make that bright light, Ren thought, panting as she reached the fifth floor at last. *Unless…what if it's her knives? I didn't know she had knives when I saw the light…. Is it possible they're enchanted?*

Ren opened the door, glad Sarala hadn't locked it. She looked in at the plain room, empty apart from the furniture. *No, that's just silly. How could it be the knives? She can't enchant objects, and she said she made them herself. Besides, she clearly hides them away, so how would I able to see their light from outside?*

She walked over to the desk and opened the drawer. The knives were hidden in the back, where Sarala had placed them the last time Ren had been in the room; clearly, she had not practiced with the weapons since she'd been caught.

"Definitely can't be the knives," Ren uttered. "So stupid of me to think that."

She sighed and walked down the stairs. As she reached the third floor, she heard Zyn's voice call for her in the family room below. Ren quietly opened the door to her bedroom and went to sit down on her bed, in position by the time Zyn darted through the gaping doorway.

"There you are!" Zyn said, holding a cup of water. "I was worried when I didn't see you."

"I think I just want to go to bed," Ren lied. "Thanks for the water."

Zyn gave her the cup and left the room, pausing only once to glance over his shoulder uneasily. Ren stared down at the water in her cup, a knot twisting in her stomach. What if it *was* the knives that were causing the bright light? Should she tell Ak-tu about it?

I can't... Sarala made those knives herself. They're the only things she owns... I can't have Dad confiscate them, just because they might *have glowed for a few seconds. And it's such a slim chance that they did, anyway. Sarala can't enchant them, and doesn't seem interested in enchanting....* Ren sighed and sipped at her water. *I just won't say anything...not unless I have proof...*

Besides, Dad's clearly been trying to figure out my visions and the mirror shard all these months. He seemed to calm down, so maybe he figured something else out that he's just not telling me...

Yet even as she had that thought, she doubted it. *He said nothing of note has been happening, so he probably hasn't figured out anything...*

Grumbling in discontent, Ren placed her cup on the nightstand and lay back on her bed. *But I can't tell him about Sarala's knives...they've got nothing to do with what's going on...they won't help him....*

She rolled onto her side, ignoring the glasses jabbing into her skin as she closed her eyes.

We'll figure it out. We have to.

CHAPTER 26: MASTER- STROKE

Zyn patted the magical objects in his robe pockets, hoping they wouldn't be too noticeable. He took a deep breath and released it.

I have to do this. C3 needs to hand over those notes. I don't know where he's keeping them, but he better give them to me…

Zyn had tried getting into C3's room on numerous occasions during the spring term. But the lock couldn't be picked, even after Zyn searched lock-picking tutorials on the air-net. Only specific keys could open the doors, and there was no way Zyn would be able to snatch C3's key from him. He therefore gave up on that idea, as the only other option would be to kick down the door—which was not a good idea in the slightest.

He had tried following C3 around, but that plan quickly failed too. C3 only seemed to go to classrooms and the Eating Hall. A few times, he saw C3 go to different clubs during the week, but Zyn would always be in the middle of something and unable to trail him.

Zyn was starting to lose patience. He had already played around with his few enchanted objects, trying to test out the magic in them. As a result, the magic within them weakened. Zyn had stopped using them, wanting to conserve the remaining magic.

But Zyn wanted to be able to enchant any object, even if it was Ren enchanting them for him. He could spend all summer playing with the objects, that way he wasn't a stranger to magic the next school year. In fact, Zyn was hoping he'd be able to learn magic over the summer and be placed in the second-year classes by the next school year, where he'd be with Ren again.

Yet if Zyn was unable to work with any enchanted objects,

how would he ever be able to catch up? He had to get those notes!

He left his room, glad that his robe was patterned in leaves, which would hopefully hide the lumps formed by the objects. Reaching the family room, he was happy to see Ren wasn't there yet. Zyn then left the tower and headed towards the eastern building, the only student who seemed to be awake that morning. He breathed in the morning air, floral scents mingling with the dampness.

But soon after Zyn thought he was the only one up and about, the door to the Art Studio creaked opened. Zyn jumped in fright, then smiled as he saw the very person he was looking for.

"C3!" Zyn said joyfully. "What are you doing up at this time?"

C3 frowned, pausing in the doorway with his hand still on the wooden knob. He had stopped showing up to the art club, clearly trying to avoid Zyn wherever he could.

"What, not going to say hi?" Zyn scoffed, keeping his tone light.

"What are *you* doing up?" C3 queried instead.

Zyn shrugged. "I'm always up early."

"You're never in the Courtyard at this hour, though," C3 said suspiciously.

Zyn raised an eyebrow. "What—are you keeping track of my movements?"

"Only because you've been keeping track of mine," C3 replied.

He knows, Zyn thought. "Well, you *did* steal my friend's notes," he pointed out. "I want them back."

"I don't have them," C3 said shortly.

"Of course you do. You stole them, and you know it."

"I have no idea what you're talking about," the boy said slyly.

Zyn's lip curled back. It was just like C3 to deny he'd ever done anything wrong! Zyn was quivering in anger, but tried to keep his temper down.

"Well, I'll see you later," C3 said with a shrug.

"I challenge you to a duel!" Zyn growled, stepping forward quickly before C3 could make his escape.

C3 paused in his tracks and looked back at Zyn, an odd look

on his face. "A duel? A magical duel? A magical duel that's against the rules?"

Zyn nodded once, pursing his lips.

"You *must* be desperate for those notes," C3 sneered.

"If I win, you hand them over," Zyn said.

"And when I win, you stop pestering me about the notes and following me," C3 said.

"Don't you mean, *if*?"

C3 shrugged carelessly. "You don't have your magic. And even if you didn't take your potion today, so you could potentially reach your magic, you've not been practicing. So I doubt you have much chance of winning."

That's what you think, Zyn thought angrily. "Whatever. Nobody hears about this duel. Are we in agreement?"

C3 nodded. "Quite so. Let's go to the Kung Fu Studio."

He closed the door to the Art Studio and walked towards the Kung Fu Studio. Zyn followed right after him, his feet scuffing against the stone.

"What were you doing in the Art Studio?" Zyn asked, not bothering to keep the accusing tone from his voice.

"None of your business. And no, I will not tell you if you somehow win."

Zyn scowled.

They entered the Kung Fu Studio, the lights turning on as the door opened. Closing the door behind them, they pulled the blinds over the front window overlooking the Courtyard. The two then took off their shoes and stepped on the mat (outside shoes weren't allowed on the mats), taking their places in the center about six feet apart.

C3 pulled out his wand almost lazily. "You ready? I'll give the order to go."

Zyn nodded, not bothering to take out any of his objects just yet. He didn't bring his useless wand with him and therefore didn't pull out anything.

"No wand?" C3 scoffed. "You could at least go into a duel somewhat prepared, even if your magic is pathetic. Especially since you *wanted* this duel."

Zyn shrugged quietly, trying to appear more confident than he felt.

"Go!" C3 ordered.

Before C3 could demand his wand to throw any magic, Zyn pulled out the first object in his pocket. He didn't need to look at it to know that it was a small stone, the smoothest rock he had ever touched. He squeezed the stone twice before throwing it at C3. The rock released a cloud of smoke, which covered C3 and made him cough.

Zyn smiled and pulled out his next object, which was a cube with rounded edges. He tapped each side of the box in a specific order, which awoke the enchantments; this was why he needed the smoke to delay C3's attack. Once the cube was glowing in Zyn's hand, he threw that towards C3 too. The cube opened up as it was thrown, growing in size at the same time. A large cage soon stood before Zyn, the top of it visible over the smoke.

"Clear this smoke!" C3 ordered.

A waft of air flung the smoke aside, and Zyn saw with delight that C3 was successfully captured in the box. And he looked furious.

"You can't do that! You're cheating!" C3 growled.

Zyn chuckled. "No, I'm not, actually. I looked up all the rules on the air-net, and a magic duel surprisingly has few rules. There was nothing against enchanted objects in there. The only requirement pertaining to magic was that both people use magic, and they don't kill or seriously wound each other. Obviously."

C3 frowned. He seemed to be thinking this over in his head for a moment, then he sneered at Zyn. "This doesn't mean you've won! You don't win until I'm knocked off my feet. I can still fight from in here. Knock Zynivus over!" he ordered his wand.

Air hit Zyn at once, trying to force him down. He lowered his body to be more stable, and luckily did not fall over.

"Are you out of magic tricks?" C3 jeered, sounding delighted as he stopped the slamming winds.

"Funny that you mention magic tricks," Zyn said, and he pulled another box from his pocket.

"What is that?" C3 asked, squinting to see it better.

Zyn got to his feet and approached the cage, but made sure not to get too close. He then opened the box and pulled out a card.

"Magic cards?" C3 asked, his eyes widening.

"A whole box of magic," Zyn said cheerfully. "I've been working with them throughout the semester. They each do different things. It's quite fun!"

"You wouldn't," C3 hissed.

"Oh, yeah?"

Zyn glanced at the card in his hand, which had a circle drawn on it. Zyn used the card to make a circle in the air, then slashed the card through it. Drawing the circle triggered the enchantment, and slashing the card a certain way sent the card's magic in that particular direction.

This card was labeled "Plant" and, sure enough, a plant appeared directly in front of C3. The deck of magic cards was probably the most expensive item Zyn owned, as the enchantments were stronger than other enchanted objects. Ak-tu had come up with the idea himself, and this was the only deck he had ever made.

The plant was tall and slimy, with a large mouth that snapped towards C3 in the cage. C3 yelped in fright and staggered to the back of his prison, lifting his wand in front of him. Then, he smiled at Zyn from around the plant as he pocketed his wand. He slid the gold ring from his elbow, allowing his left sleeve to fall down.

"Did you think I wasn't able to enchant any objects myself?" he sneered.

He shook the ring several times, then threw it out the cage. It sliced the plant in half, causing the biting plant to die and vanish. The ring returned to C3's hand like a boomerang.

Zyn frowned. Why didn't he consider that C3 would have enchanted objects of his own? *No matter...I still have more than him! I hope...*

He pulled another card from his deck, drawing a spiral in the air this time. As he slashed the card, sending a wave of water towards C3, C3 threw his ring again.

The water pummeled C3 at the same time that C3's ring smacked Zyn. C3 was knocked to the ground, the water vanishing as it hit the floor. Zyn fell down, the ring slamming into him with the force of a thrown couch. They both sat on the ground, staring at one another as C3's ring returned to him.

"It's a draw," Zyn muttered at last.

They both sprang to their feet at the same time, as if whoever was on their feet first would win.

"I guess neither of us has to do anything," C3 said snootily, pointing his nose in the air.

Zyn shook his head. "Or both of us win, and we both get what we want. If you give me the notes, then I'll no longer bother you. It's a win-win!"

C3 snorted. "Like that'll happen."

"Come *on*, C3! Just give me the notes!"

"It seems like you already know how to enchant objects—or your sister does, anyway."

"These are objects I got from our travels around the world," Zyn said, motioning to the box and stone. "I want to be able to enchant my own. I need those notes."

"Just wait until next year. Your sister will learn how," C3 said.

"Please, C3!"

"I don't have them!" C3 shouted.

"You're lying!"

"No, I'm not," he muttered. "I destroyed them."

"You…destroyed them?" Zyn mumbled. *"Why?"*

C3 sighed and held up the ring. "I didn't actually enchant this. I was not able to enchant a single thing. Those notes are either fake, or there's something that was missing. So I ripped them to bits when I got frustrated."

Zyn frowned. "Then…who enchanted the ring for you?"

"I got it when we were traveling around Galia," C3 said, shoving it back on his elbow to hold up his sleeve.

"But…I thought your family was…well…"

"Poor?" C3 spat. "Yeah, we are. I received this as a gift from a stranger."

Zyn wasn't sure he believed that. Who would give an enchanted (and expensive) object to a complete stranger?

The box holding C3 fell away, returning to the form of a small cube. Zyn glared at the cube and stone on the ground. They were useless now, their magic entirely gone.

C3 kicked the cube away from him, as if frightened that it'd cage him again. He then approached Zyn, a smug smile on his face.

"It appears I've won, then," he said.

"What makes you say that?"

"I don't have any notes to give you, so you'll leave me alone," C3 pointed out.

Zyn snorted, his hands clenching. "I won't leave you alone. I know how to be annoying, and I'll annoy you *every* day."

"But there's no reason to do so," C3 argued. "I don't have anything to give to you. I cannot help you."

"What if we looked up ways to enchant objects—together?" Zyn asked. "I couldn't find anything in the Library, but I was probably looking in all the wrong sections, or skipped some tiny paragraph when I was flipping through books. And the air-net has nothing on this stuff, unless you know someone who can get you in a group forum. We can be a team!"

C3 shook his head. "I think not," he said as he walked towards the door, pausing to place his shoes back on.

Zyn sighed, then saw a small object lying on the floor. "Hey— you dropped something!" he said, pointing at the place where C3 had just been.

C3 glanced back, then his mismatched eyes widened. He hurried over, but not before Zyn had picked up the object.

"Hey—that's a mirror shard!" Zyn yelped.

"Give it back, it's mine!" C3 growled, snatching it from his grasp quickly.

"No, it's not!"

"Yeah, it is," C3 hissed, pocketing the shard.

"Sarala found one of those ages ago," Zyn said, his lip curling back as he glared at C3.

C3 narrowed his eyes, but made no response.

"Those things are dangerous. Dad said so!"

"Are you certain he said that?"

"Yeah?"

C3 snorted. "You sound doubtful."

"Let's bring it to him right away," Zyn urged, stepping closer to C3.

C3 moved back a pace. "Mr. Caihong is not here right now. He left the school."

"What? No, he didn't!"

"Yes, he did," C3 grunted. "I saw a giant ship fly out of the northeastern tower this morning, when I was going to the Art Studio. Since the only way into that tower is from the bridge connected to *your* tower, I'm going to assume your father was the one flying it. Unless Ren or Sarala know how to, which I seriously doubt."

Zyn's heartbeat quickened. *Why did Dad leave the school? Did something else happen with Ren's visions? What's with all these mirror shards?*

"Farewell."

C3 abruptly left the Kung Fu Studio, Zyn gaping after him. Zyn shook his head roughly, grabbed his cube and rock from the ground, and hurried towards the door. He stopped only to stuff the objects in his pockets and pull on his shoes, then flung the door open and hurried after C3. C3 was already on the elevator going up to the third floor of the eastern building.

"C3! Wait up!" Zyn called.

A few students glanced as he ran past them. The sun was higher in the sky, and the bell had already rung for breakfast. Zyn must have missed it when he and C3 had been dueling.

"Zyn! There you are!"

Zyn skidded to a stop as he reached the eastern building. He glanced over his shoulder to see Ren headed towards him, Sarala on her heel. A door closed above him, telling Zyn that C3 had already darted inside the building.

"Elevator!" Zyn called, before he turned to his sister.

"Where are you going?" Ren asked. "We've been looking for you everywhere! I thought you were sick since you didn't yell out your greeting."

"Your lack of a greeting woke me up," Sarala added grumpily.

"I was just practicing martial arts," Zyn said hurriedly. "See you at breakfast!" He hurried onto the platform, shouting, "Third floor!"

But Ren and Sarala soon hopped on board, just before the railings came up and the elevator lifted into the air.

"Where are you going?" Ren repeated.

"You're right, Ren—he *is* hiding something!" Sarala muttered in an accusing voice.

Zyn ignored them and flung the door open to the third floor of the student quarters. He hurried to the end of the hall and came to a stop outside C3's door. Knocking on the door loudly, several students opened their doors and told him to stop the noise. Luckily, the students quickly went to breakfast, leaving Zyn, Ren, and Sarala alone in the hallway.

"C3! Open up!" Zyn shouted, rattling the door so much he was surprised it didn't already fall off its hinges. "Or I'll kick down your door!"

"Zyn!" Ren yelped in alarm. "You can't do that!"

Zyn sighed. "C3 has a mirror shard!"

"The same type of shard I found?" Sarala asked.

"Yes! He doesn't realize that it could be dangerous!"

"C3, please open up!" Ren said loudly, knocking on his door too.

"Leave me alone! I will file a complaint with Mr. Caihong when he gets back. Or with Mr. Jihan, if your father gives you special treatment again," C3's muffled voice growled through the door.

"That mirror shard is dangerous, though!" Ren said. "At least—I think it is. What are you doing with it?"

"I'm putting them together," C3 said eagerly. "There's still some missing pieces, but it's a puzzle, isn't it? So I'll put the puzzle together—make the mirror whole again!"

Zyn and Ren exchanged a glance, Zyn's heart beating in his throat.

"He has more than one?" Ren asked.

"Sounds like it," Zyn muttered.

"Oh, just *move*!" Sarala grunted, and she shoved the twins aside before they could move themselves.

In the next moment, Sarala lifted her leg and thrust her heel at the door. The door smashed inwards as the wood splintered and the hinges broke, falling to the ground with a loud thud.

"Sarala!" Ren squeaked, covering her mouth with her hand. "You're going to be in *so* much trouble!"

"If these mirror shards are a threat—"

But Sarala couldn't finish her words. As the trio stumbled into C3's room, they were blinded by a bright light. Zyn shielded his eyes with his hand, then squinted through his fingers to see what was happening.

The shards sat on the ground, making up a cracked mirror almost the length of a door. C3 didn't just find a few shards—but *most* of them! There were only about six or seven missing pieces. Yet each mirror shard lit up, and the holes were concealed by the blinding white glow.

The light swirled all around the four students, creating a whooshing wind as it got faster and faster. Then, quite suddenly, it stopped and the room fell into darkness.

Zyn blinked several times, his eyes slow to adjust. It took him a moment to realize that there were transparent figures all around the room—which soon solidified. Zyn and Ren exchanged another glance, Zyn able to see his own petrified face reflected in Ren's glasses.

"Spirits!"

CHAPTER 27: COOL CAT

Ak-tu breathed in the fresh morning air, watching the sun climb into the sky as his indigo robe flapped about his ankles in the cool wind. He glanced over his shoulder at Jabali, who now had his curly hair styled as a messy tail that sat on top of his head. The two men had just departed Jabali's house, and it was still quite early in the day.

"We're making good time," Ak-tu said, scanning the rainbow-colored trees below the flying ship. "We should make it to the school soon..."

Jabali crossed the deck to Ak-tu's side, his feet thudding loudly against the wood. He peered down at the forest too, a frown on his bearded face. "So wha' were you wantin' to tell me? All ya said on the call was tha' there was a new development and ya needed me at once. But why haven't ya told me anythin'?"

Ak-tu switched to telepathy at once. {*I don't want anyone overhearing, and I had to wait to be in-range for telepathy.*}

"Did you figure out Ren's *images*?" Jabali asked in a whisper.

{*Not quite... I was just doing some qigong in the family room this morning when I looked out the window and saw...a cat.*}

"What?" Jabali yelped, his eyes widening as he took a step back.

{*Shush!*} Ak-tu ordered, glancing all around them before setting his eyes back on Jabali. {*I saw a farm cat, but I don't know if it's actually them. The cat ran off before I could get a good look. But with what's been going on the past few months...*}

"You think they're back," Jabali muttered solemnly.

{*Yes. And I want us to find them before—*}

"Your pocket!" Jabali suddenly gasped. "There's spirit magic in your pocket!"

The shard!

Ak-tu reached for the mirror shard in his robe, but it was blazing hot when he tried to grasp it. Wincing in pain, he grabbed it and dropped it as soon as it was out. The shard was glowing brightly as it hit the ground, and both men raised their hands to cover their eyes.

After a moment, the shard stopped glowing. Ak-tu blinked several times, then detected a movement to his left. He whirled about, but it was only the sail flapping in the wind.

"Ak-tu!" Jabali yelled. "Behind you!"

Ak-tu dived for the floor and rolled towards Jabali, not wasting time to see what Jabali was pointing at. Once he was beside Jabali, he turned around. His violet eyes landed on a small creature at the front of the ship.

"Chaocat," Ak-tu uttered.

The cat looked up at him and grinned widely, their pupil-less eyes and jagged mouth outlined in bright red. They didn't have a nose, and none of their toes could be seen, their body jet black.

"Hello, Ak-tu," the spirit said. "Ah, it's been *so* long!"

Ak-tu frowned as he got to his feet, numbness tingling through his fingertips. "I thought you were dead. I thought you had perished, all those years ago!"

The cat's form changed. They now appeared almost like a farm cat. Their thick coat was solid red, and each of their toes could be seen. Their face was no longer so creepy, and appeared almost-normal with a nose and whiskers. But their eyes were now pitch black, and the slitted pupils were neon red; Ak-tu knew these pupils always remained in slits, no matter how much light hit (or didn't hit) them. The cat wore a blue crescent moon necklace.

"I hate it when that cat does that," Jabali muttered from beside Ak-tu.

"Don't be such a critic, Bluebeard," Chaocat said, still smiling broadly.

Jabali's teeth gritted. "What are you doing here? Didn't you die?"

"Ah, of course I didn't die! How silly of you to assume such a ridiculous thing!" Chaocat chuckled, swishing their long tail.

"Then what happened to you? Where have you been all these years?" Ak-tu pressed, his body tense.

"And what are you doing here *now*?" Jabali repeated, his lip curling back.

Chaocat snorted. "What, you really think I'd answer any of your questions?"

"Yes!" Ak-tu said, forcing his body to relax and his glare to soften. "Please, Chaocat. Tell me what happened on the island."

"No, thanks."

"Tell us!" Jabali growled. "You *have* t'tell us!"

"No, I don't," Chaocat sneered, their claws unsheathing and digging into the wood. "I'm the one in control here, not you."

"*You're* not in control!" Jabali growled, jabbing a broad finger in the cat's direction. "There's two of us, and we're more than ready for whatever ya throw at us!"

"Are you, really?" Chaocat chuckled.

Their fur turned orange as they shifted into a different form. Ak-tu recalled the cat switching between colors in the blink of an eye: red, orange, yellow, green, blue, purple.

Once they'd changed, Chaocat hopped onto the wheel at the front of ship and turned it abruptly to one side. The vessel groaned as it swiveled, Ak-tu and Jabali staggering off-balance.

"Stop!" Ak-tu growled, falling to the floor.

"No, I don't think I will!" Chaocat laughed, sitting easily on top of the spinning wheel.

"You're gonna make us crash!" Jabali shouted, before the air was knocked out of him when he slammed into the railing.

"Don't give them any ideas!" Ak-tu retorted.

Chaocat chuckled. "Ah, that idea's mine entirely!"

"What do you want?" Ak-tu seethed. "Why are you doing this?"

"It's in the name, darling. In case you've forgotten, I'm the bringer of chaos."

And with that, Chaocat turned purple before vanishing on the spot. Their maniacal laughter could be heard on the rushing wind.

"Where'd they go?" Jabali snarled, his hands curling into fists at his sides.

"Never mind that, we have to stop the ship before—"

But it was too late.

The ship smashed into the colorful trees that had been below it just minutes before, bumping through branches and splintering wood. Ak-tu and Jabali were tossed about like dolls, helpless to do anything as the vessel descended. The engines groaned loudly as they scraped trees and struggled to keep the ship in the air. Smoke surrounded them—something was burning.

"Get to the wheel!" Ak-tu shouted, trying to propel himself forward before Jabali could be tossed into him again.

A second later, the world seemed to explode.

CHAPTER 28: FIGHT FROM THE INSIDE

Sarala hurried to the mirror pieces lying on the ground. She stomped on the glass, kicking the tiny shards all over the place. But it was too late. The spirits—or whatever they were—were still in the room. And they gazed upon her with hatred.

"Stop what you're doing!" shrieked one of the figures, which looked like a large pumpkin with legs and antlers.

"It doesn't matter," another creature growled, this one with the appearance of a tiger. It flicked its club tail, smashing it into C3's bed. "We won't need the mirror any longer. We're finally in the school, and that's all that matters."

Sarala's heart was beating more rapidly than at any other point in her life. So *these* were spirits? These odd-looking creatures that just came out of the mirror? How was that possible? And why did there have to be a tiger, the very same creature that had stalked her in the jungle only months before? She still had nightmares about that….

"Humans, stay here," the tiger spirit commanded.

Ren raised her hand shakily, as if they were in class. "Umm… spirit…what's going on? Is there anything we can help you with?"

Sarala could have gladly knocked Ren out to make her shut up. Why would she offer to help these beasts? The tiger seemed to take Sarala's point of view, and glared upon Ren suspiciously.

"What are you going on about?" the tiger snarled, its ears flattening.

Ren lowered herself to the ground and bowed her head, careful to avoid any shattered glass. "We are here to serve you," she said. "We praise the spirits."

The tiger's lips curled back. Sarala's heart skipped a beat as it advanced towards Ren, its club tail sliding along C3's bed and tearing the cotton sheets. But it did not strike at her exposed neck. It instead glared down at her for a long moment, then hopped over her and entered the hallway. The other spirits—the pumpkin with antlers, a twig, a moss-covered lizard-bird, a feathered armadillo-turtle creature, a shadowy figure with five tails, and an eel-looking griffin—followed it soundlessly.

"What do we *do*?" Sarala hissed in a dazed whisper.

Ren got to her feet, biting her bottom lip. "I'm not sure," she replied. "My vision *felt* bad, but those spirits didn't seem too mean."

Sarala stared at Ren incredulously. Several thoughts were swimming around her head like frenzied fish, each of them flashing danger. But she was too astonished to form words, her mouth moving pointlessly as she struggled to speak.

"Those spirits didn't look too friendly," Zyn murmured. "We have to warn the teachers."

"Yes! Let's do that!" Sarala said.

She left the room with the twins behind her, ignoring C3, who sat on the ground in a daze.

"Do you think they're in range for telepathy?" Ren asked.

Zyn shrugged. "It's worth a try. Let's just be as loud as we can."

Sarala glanced back at them for a moment, frowning at their focused faces. She had a suspicion throughout the year that the twins held silent conversations, but she didn't realize they were doing *telepathy*—or that it was possible.

After a moment, Zyn and Ren looked up at each other, their eyes no longer so glazed.

"Khurshid heard me," Zyn said.

"And Fern heard me," Ren replied.

"So…they've been warned?" Sarala asked, as they reached the door at the end of the hallway. "Elevator!"

The platform came back from the ground level outside, and the railing in front of the door lowered once the stone was level with it. The three got on the elevator, just as Khurshid's voice rang through the school.

"Students, stay exactly where you are. There is a potential threat in this school. Remain calm as we handle it. We will tell you when it is safe. In the meantime, all doors will be locked for your safety. If you are outdoors, please go to the Theatre; the door is unlocked."

As soon as he finished speaking, the door behind the trio closed—right in C3's face as he hurried to catch up to them. They could hear a small yelp of surprise, but no matter how much he rattled the door knob, it wouldn't open.

"We better get to the Theatre, then," Ren mumbled. "Ground floor!" she ordered the elevator.

"Look!" Sarala said, pointing.

The group of seven spirits was wandering the Courtyard near the pond. They seemed almost confused about what they were doing, or where they were going. Movement caught her eye, and she quickly looked to see Khurshid, Fern, and Aster exiting the Library.

The elevator reached the ground, and the teens got off. They hurried to the garden for cover, then peered around the sweet-scented bushes. Behind them, two students entered the Theatre rapidly, the door slamming after they were in.

Cowards, Sarala thought, clenching her jaw. She focused her attention forward again, watching as Fern hurried to the spirits.

"Greetings, spirits," Fern said loudly, her voice echoing around the Courtyard. "May I ask what business you have here?"

The spirits remained silent as they watched her. Then, they simply turned and headed for the front of the school. Fern hurried after them, keeping several meters away.

"If you are looking for Ak-tu Caihong, he is not here," Fern went on briskly. "May I show you to a waiting room?"

The spirits ignored her, coming to a stop outside of the southern building.

"Please answer me," Fern called. "Otherwise, I will have to remove you from the school. What are you doing here?"

The tiger turned around to face Fern, sharp spikes appearing on its back as it bristled. "You will not remove us from this school!" it snarled.

"Then please tell me why you are here," Fern repeated.

But the tiger had swiveled away from her and stared up at the sky. Sarala followed its gaze. She gasped lightly at what she saw.

Purple lines appeared in the sky, zigzagging all around the school.

"Are those the protection enchantments?" Zyn asked Ren in a whisper.

"I think so," Ren replied quietly, her voice quavering. "I only saw Dad put them up once, but they were a bunch of purple lines like that."

"They're taking down our defenses," Sarala muttered, pulling her wand from her yellow robe.

Ren grabbed her arm quickly. "Sarala, no!"

"What—are we supposed to sit here and wait for the defenses to come down?" Sarala snapped. "You do realize they're probably lowering the protections for something *else* to come in, right?"

"Yeah, something *bigger*," Zyn said, emphasizing the word to Ren. "Which could be from your vision."

Ren shifted uneasily. "But what can *we* do against the spirits? They're—"

She broke off at the commotion across from them. Fern had jumped forward, her tattoos and spiral necklace glowing a vibrant green. She had no use for a wand as she flicked her wrists, causing plants to rise out of the ground.

"How's she doing that?" Sarala breathed.

The plants grew quickly, slick vines spreading towards the spirits. But the spirits were faster. They jumped out of the way or used their claws to slash the vines. The tiger lunged towards Fern, diving between the plants that tried to grab it.

"We have to help her!" Sarala growled, shoving Ren's hands off her.

"No!"

But before any of them could move, a huge wave of air smashed into the tiger and sent it flying backwards. Khurshid had arrived just behind Fern, his palms striking forward as he leaned into his low stance. Aster had joined them as well, holding up his wand at the ready, though he looked quite nervous judging by his stiff body.

The large winds stopped as Khurshid straightened up. The spirits were now lying on their sides in a grumbling dismay, after being thrown several meters away. The eel-griffin had even landed in the pond, and swam out.

"Leave the school," Khurshid ordered the spirits. "You are not welcome here!"

"Attack!" the tiger yowled, swinging its club tail.

"No!" Sarala hissed, and she raced forward, wishing she had her knives on her.

Nobody saw the three students approach, locked in battle by the time they arrived. Khurshid was using Kung Fu to slam the creatures with air strikes. Fern continued to use her plant powers, using vines like tentacles as she snatched spirits and threw them about. Aster waved his wand, using the water from the pond to hit the spirits. Even purple-eyed frogoyles had hopped forward, the stone statues jumping at the spirits with fangs ready to chomp down on them.

"What do we do?" Ren asked, holding her wand hesitantly in front of her. "I don't want to fight the spirits!"

"Then go hide," Sarala grumbled in annoyance.

She plunged into the battle, commanding her magic like she never had before. "Imprison the spirits in the stone! Make the ground sharp! Stab them!"

The earth listened to her orders. She trapped the stick spirit as the ground lifted around it, locking it in place. The stone then rose up in sharp spikes, poking the rest of the spirits' feet and sending them backwards. But just as she was making good progress, the twig trapped in the rock broke free, chunks of stone clattering to the ground.

Sarala glared at the stick and growled, "Trap this spirit, do not let it go!"

The twig darted away from the earth as the ground reached for it again. Floating without a care in the world, the spirit laughed down at her with its long arms crossed in front of its skinny chest.

"I got this!" Zyn said, and he jumped forward with a card in his hand.

Sarala watched in amazement as he made a triangle in the air in front of him, then flicked the card towards the spirit. A burst of fire shot forward, hitting the creature and setting it ablaze. The stick-looking spirit seemed to be made out of wood, as it burned quickly. Screaming in agony, it fell into the pond, putting out the fire at once—or had the fire vanished before it hit the water?

Sarala and Zyn watched tentatively as it crawled out of the pond, looking angry. It stood up, and suddenly, it was much larger than before. Its form had changed into that of a giant walking tree. Hadn't Sarala seen a walking tree outside the school, just months ago?

"Try that fire thing again," Sarala told Zyn, backing up quickly as her mouth went dry.

But Zyn shook his head. "I don't think that'll work! Come on!"

Zyn grabbed Sarala's arm and pulled her away. The two darted through screaming spirits and slimy plants and clunky frogoyles and whooshing magic bursts until they slid to a stop beside Aster.

"What are you kids doing out here?" he asked in a stern voice. "Get in the Library! Hurry!"

"Plants, to me!" Fern yowled loudly nearby.

Before either of them could reply to Aster's words, there was a loud shatter of glass. Everyone looked towards the Greenhouse, where the highly-magical plants were now crawling from holes in the glass panels. The dancing trees seemed to glide across the ground, while the spiky plants hopped forward with difficulty. Soon enough, Fern had an army of plants at her back.

"Get inside!" Aster growled, and he grabbed Sarala and Zyn by the scruff of their robes and shoved them towards the western building.

"But we can help!" Zyn protested, holding out his box of magic cards.

"No, get inside!"

"Wait—where's Ren?" Zyn yelped, glancing all around.

Sarala's heart skipped a beat, and she returned her gaze to the thicket of yowling spirits and humans. She couldn't see Ren's purple hair anywhere.

"Ren!" Sarala screamed. "Ren! Where are you?"

Zyn closed his eyes beside her, clearly trying to reach out to her through his thoughts. After a moment, he opened his eyes, appearing more worried than before.

"Where is she?" Sarala asked hastily. "Tell me where she is!"

Zyn shook his head. "I dunno," he mumbled. "She wasn't responding!"

"No!" Sarala hissed.

She hurried forward, ignoring Aster as he tried to grab her. Lifting her wand, she screamed, "Bring Ren to me!"

The ground shuddered violently, knocking down everyone but Sarala (including the plants). The battle was paused as the earth continued to shake. A large stone slid forward rapidly, coming to a sudden stop in front of Sarala. Ren was lying on it, shrieking in pain and writhing. A plant clung to the stone, shooting its red spikes in all directions but somehow missing Ren beside it.

Sarala lowered her wand and ended her magic, allowing the fight to continue. The spiky bramble hopped off to rejoin the chaos. Sarala bent down beside Ren, Zyn appearing at her side.

"Help me lift her!" Sarala growled.

"Dad!" Ren shrieked, tears running down her freckled cheeks. "No! Dad!"

Zyn's whole body froze and their eyes widened. "Ren? What are you seeing? What's happening to Dad?"

But Ren couldn't hear him as she continued to cry out in agony, her hands tense at her sides.

"YES!"

Sarala and Zyn glanced up in alarm at the triumphant scream. The spirits were gazing at the sky again, and Sarala realized that some of the purple lines had vanished. The creatures faced Fern and Khurshid with menacing smiles.

"Keep flinging your magic at us," the tiger growled. "We'll have the defenses down in no time!"

Fern replied by punching her hand forward, causing a large vine to wrap around the tiger's scruffy neck and drag it towards her.

"You are leaving!" she bellowed.

Fern lifted the tiger into the air, the vine circling several times as it picked up speed. She then threw the spirit over the school wall and into the forest beyond, the animal shrieking the entire way.

However, the action seemed to take lots of energy from Fern, as the vines became smaller and her tattoos glowed weaker. Even the plant army seemed to slow down as their leader got worn out.

We can't keep this up for long, Sarala thought. *Why did they have to lock away all those other students? The more advanced students could be out here, helping us!*

"Ren, what's going on with Dad?" Zyn pressed, as Ren had stopped screaming at last.

Ren was unusually pale as she sat up, her angular eyes dazed. "That large thing—it was the ship! Oh, Zyn, the ship's *crashed*!"

"No!" Zyn choked out, tears springing to his eyes at once.

"Focus!" Sarala snapped at them, though fear flooded her whole body at Ren's words. "We don't know that he was on it, now do we? He could have jumped off, or survived, or maybe it hasn't happened yet."

"Everything else has happened," Ren moaned, taking her glasses off to rub at her wet eyes. "The shiny mirror, the magic, the transparent spirits, the cracked enchantments… Dad was on that ship, I know it!"

"Focus!" Sarala repeated, clenching her jaw. "We have to help the teachers before they run out of energy. Come on!"

But neither of the twins moved. Sarala glared down at them, then rose to her feet and hurried to Khurshid's side. He was now commanding a small tornado, which had managed to pick up the tree and the lizard-bird. The spirits were flung from the school, just like the tiger.

There were now four spirits remaining, making the fight more even, at least. But Khurshid was panting heavily and Fern had stopped glowing. Aster was busy trying to get the twins to go inside.

It's not an even fight at all, Sarala realized.

The spirits glared at their foes, but did not attack again. The antlered pumpkin and the armadillo-turtle stepped forward, while the five-tailed creature and the eel-griffin moved behind them. The ones in the back looked up at the cracking defenses, and began throwing bright balls of magic towards the sky.

"We are taking your protection away," growled the pumpkin in front.

"No, you aren't!" snarled a voice beside Sarala.

She glanced over to see Ren and Zyn had joined her. Ren's face was a mask of fury, unlike anything Sarala had ever seen. Zyn's lip was curled back as he held his box of magic cards in front of him.

Without warning, Ren jumped into a square stance and punched the air, causing a large gust of wind to strike the two guards over; Sarala almost got tugged away by the whooshing wind as it flew past her. Shoving her long hair out of her eyes, she nearly missed Ren's next move as she hopped onto an air slide, which carried her and Zyn behind the spirits taking down the defenses. Zyn whipped out another card, drew a square in the air with it, and ice flew at the shadowy figure. It screamed in agony and lost its concentration as the points hit its flank.

Sarala stopped watching the twins and ran forward. She slashed her wand through the air, pointing it at the earth. "Trap the spirits!" she ordered the stone again.

The earth listened to her commands, spikes shooting up beneath each spirits' arms and legs. They were now unable to move so easily, and therefore unable to break down the defenses.

"Throw them out of here!" Sarala shouted.

Hard earth and whooshing air combined to send the creatures flying away in a yowling mess. Sarala's magic propelled them up, while Ren's air blasts cast them over the wall.

"We did it!" Aster yelled, dancing in the background.

Sarala shot him a glare. "You barely did anything," she growled. *I bet the other students would have done more than you…besides those cowards in the Theatre, that is.*

"Hey—I did the water stuff!" Aster protested.

Before she could bicker any further though, Ren and Zyn were beside her once more. She glanced at the twins in concern.

"Was there anything else you saw in your vision, Ren?" Zyn asked his sister.

"No," Ren muttered. "I don't know what happened to Dad…"

"What?" Khurshid asked, limping over.

"His ship crashed," Zyn told him. "Ren saw it in her vision."

Khurshid tensed as he turned to Fern. "We have to find him."

"We have to get these defenses back up, more likely," Fern said sternly. "Come on. We'll find him after."

"Do you know where he was going?" Ren asked, her voice desperate.

"He said he was getting his friend to help him with—"

"I can't do this alone, Khurshid!" Fern hissed.

"Coming!"

And Khurshid hurried to follow Fern into the Entrance Hall, leaving the three students alone with Aster. Silence surrounded them for a long moment, the dust still settling around the Courtyard.

"I'm sure he's fine," Sarala finally murmured. "Your dad is strong…and powerful…"

Ren hugged her twin and closed her eyes. "He *has* to be okay…"

CHAPTER 29: CLING TOGETHER

Ak-tu staggered to his feet, the world spinning around him. He blinked several times, trying to get his bearings. The ship had crashed…he had used his spirit magic to teleport himself off the deck just in time… But what about Jabali? He had to find him!

Ignoring his aching body, he forced his feet to carry him through the purple bushes and rugged trees. He reached his hands out in front of him, prepared to catch himself if he should stumble. Ak-tu had no idea where he was going, where he had ended up…

But I will find you, Jabali, he promised.

Ak-tu lifted his head and sniffed the air. Was that smoke? It had to be. He couldn't have teleported too far away, otherwise he'd be completely out of energy—or worse. He hurried in the direction of the burning smell, the scent growing stronger as he reached a clearing. The trees parted, allowing him to see the sky more clearly. A thick plume of smoke was coming from several hundred meters ahead.

I'm coming, Jabali, he thought as he pushed onwards. *I'm coming…*

The pain in his body began to subside, and he was soon feeling his energy return. He still went at a slow pace, knowing he'd need to conserve his energy to save his friend—and potentially more. But as Ak-tu got nearer, he couldn't hold himself back any longer and rushed ahead, shoving brittle twigs and poofy flowers out of the way.

Stumbling into another clearing—this one made from the falling ship—he realized that the ship didn't look as bad as he thought it would. He was expecting the entire thing to be up in flames, the wood splintered far beyond repair. But only one engine had blown up, and that large chunk was sitting on the ground, burning itself out. The rest of the ship was scratched and splintered, but luckily not on fire.

"Jabali! Jabali! Are you here?"

"'bout time you showed up."

Ak-tu turned towards the voice and let out a sigh of relief to see his friend sitting nearby, in the shade of a tree. He hurried over, looking Jabali over. His pale blue shirt had been torn and scorched in multiple places, and blood trickled down his shoulder from a wound on his back.

"I'm fine," Jabali said, rising to his feet and brushing off his dusty pants. "Thanks for teleporting me outta there."

Ak-tu's heart ached with guilt at once. "I'm sorry, it was more out of instinct that I did it in the first place, but I would've grabbed you if you were closer and—"

Jabali laughed and waved his hand, his solemn expression clearing at once. "I'm just messin' with ya! I know teleporting takes a ridiculous amount of energy outta you. You'd hardly be able to take me along for the ride, especially since it all happened so fast."

"I still wish I saved you," Ak-tu murmured, lowering his eyes.

"Eh, I saved myself," Jabali replied carelessly.

"Are you okay, though?" Ak-tu pressed, hurrying behind his friend to observe the blood on his back.

"Chaocat did tha' to me. Jumped on my back when I was off the ship, then ran off. It don't hurt too much, at least," Jabali said.

Ak-tu frowned, pulling the collar of Jabali's shirt down to see several scratch marks, result of the cat's sharp claws. The smeared blood glistened on his black skin.

"We best get that cleaned up soon," Ak-tu murmured. "Any sign of Chaocat since then?"

Jabali shook his head. "I haven't seen any spirit magic in use," he reported.

"Hmm… I'm not sure if that's a good thing or not," Ak-tu muttered under his breath. "Come on. Let's try to get this ship up and running."

"No need," Jabali said.

He stomped on the ground, and a large stone rose up beneath him. Holding his hand out to Ak-tu, he helped the smaller man clamber up beside him.

"Do you know the way to the school?" Ak-tu asked, grabbing the rough edges of the boulder.

"More than you," Jabali chuckled.

"What's that supposed to mean?" Ak-tu scoffed.

"We all know you have a *terrible* sense of direction and rely on that map app," Jabali chuckled.

Ak-tu rolled his eyes.

Jabali slammed his fist on the front of the stone, and it suddenly shot forward, smashing through plants and bumping along the uneven ground. Ak-tu flattened himself out, holding on as tightly as he could, his hair and mustache flying behind him. The wind seemed to sear through his eyes and nose, blinding him. He hated going on these rock rides with Jabali!

But it's the most efficient way to get to the school, he told himself, over and over as he felt more dizzy from how quickly they were going.

It seemed to take ages and yet no time at all when the stone slid to a stop near the school. Ak-tu sat up, but wasn't quite ready to get off the rock, light-headed and nauseous. He remained seated for some time, even when Jabali made the stone sink into the ground once more.

"Come on," Jabali said gruffly, and he pulled Ak-tu reluctantly to his feet.

They had made it to the western side of the school, noticeable by the glass paneling of the Greenhouse. Jabali led the way to the wall, keeping a firm grasp on Ak-tu's arm as his shaky legs stumbled along beneath him. By the time they reached the front of the school, Ak-tu's legs were beginning to feel normal again, and he was able to walk on his own. He only took a few steps when Jabali came to a sudden stop.

"Spirits!" Jabali whispered.

There were seven figures farther away, next to the southeastern tower. They each seemed to be limping as they paced to and fro, their frustration clear even from a distance. Ak-tu and Jabali slunk behind the western wall again, before the spirits could see them.

"They're trying t'take down the defenses," Jabali muttered to Ak-tu.

"They are?" Ak-tu asked, his heartbeat quickening.

Jabali nodded, then peered around the corner and narrowed his eyes. He was quiet for a long time, evaluating the situation, seeing what the spirit magic was doing. Then, he smiled and said, "But they ain't having any success from the outside."

Ak-tu let out a small sigh of relief. "That's the good thing about putting the defenses on the inside. Not that they've been tested before, so I'm glad to see my strategy worked…. But why are they injured?"

"Magic backfire?" Jabali suggested.

Ak-tu shrugged. "Let's just get inside. We'll have to find a way around them though…"

Jabali shrugged carelessly. "Easy enough!"

He stepped out from behind the tower, creating a rock in his hand. Once he had a stone the size of his fist, he threw it over the spirits' heads and into the forest beyond. Ak-tu could hear the loud thud as the rock hit the ground.

"What was that?" one of the spirits—an eel-griffin-looking creature—snarled. "Chaocat?"

"Come on," Ak-tu muttered.

He led the way towards the front doors, keeping his footsteps soft. The spirits hurried in the opposite direction, skittering across the dirt ground and vanishing from sight, allowing Ak-tu and Jabali to sneak up to the double-doors.

Ak-tu took a key from his robe pocket and unlocked the door as quietly as he could. He then opened it and hurried inside, Jabali at his heel. Ak-tu locked the door once more, though it didn't truly matter. There was a spirit-repelling enchantment that would keep most spirits out. The locked door was more for if a human stumbled upon the school.

"Well, we're here," Jabali said. "And we know Chaocat is back, and the one who led 'em spirits here. Now wha'?"

"Let's make sure the school is secure," Ak-tu said. "It'll be best if you stick with me."

"Yeah, ain't nobody here knows who I am," Jabali remarked.

"My kids will soon," Ak-tu reassured him. "And my teachers know of you, so they won't be alarmed."

He opened the door to the Courtyard and stopped in his tracks again. Jabali halted behind him, the two men staring in surprise at the destruction.

There were plants everywhere, some of them torn and dead, while others crawled about. A few were returning to the Greenhouse, where some of the panels had been broken. Water lay in puddles across the stone ground, and there were twigs and leaves floating in the pond. The ground was cracked in some areas, and completely pointy in others. At least two frogoyles had crumbled, barely distinguishable from the stone ground.

"DAD!"

Ak-tu whipped his head around, then grinned and hurried forward to greet his kids. Ren and Zyn looked exhausted, their clothes torn in places and their eyes red. But they bounded to their father eagerly, until all three were hugging tightly.

"You're safe!" Ak-tu exclaimed. "You're safe, thank the spirits!"

"Don't thank the spirits!" Zyn said sharply, pulling away. "They just attacked us!"

"Yeah, they came out of the mirror!" Ren added, looking concerned. "Fern tried to make them leave, but then they attacked. They were trying to take down the defenses!"

"But Fern and Khurshid got them back up now," Zyn said. "We watched the whole time."

Jabali nodded beside Ak-tu. "Them defenses look strong to me," he commented, staring up at the blue sky where he undoubtedly saw the magic circling the school.

Zyn and Ren glanced curiously at Jabali.

"Why did the spirits do that?" Ren queried, returning her gaze to Ak-tu. "The spirits are supposed to be our friends, aren't they? Or at least, you know, neutral? But why'd they come here and just totally attack us?"

Ak-tu sighed, not knowing how to respond.

"Who's that?" Zyn asked, pointing at Jabali.

"That's Jabali Kenyada," Ak-tu said, glad he could answer one of their questions. "He's my best friend."

"Your best friend?" Ren and Zyn asked in unison.

"But you've never mentioned him," Ren added.

"Yeah, we didn't think you had any friends—besides the teachers, that is," Zyn said.

"Yo, kids!" Jabali called, holding out his hand for them to

shake. "Nice to finally meet ya."

Sarala stood nearby, watching with wary eyes. Ak-tu beckoned her over, so she could meet Jabali too.

"Let's go inside," Ak-tu told them, once they were all done shaking hands. "I think there'll be a bit of explaining to do. Are the students okay?"

"Yes," came a brisk voice.

Ak-tu turned to see Fern and Khurshid coming out of the Healing room.

"The students are all accounted for," Khurshid told him. "Aster took attendance for all of the years. We also sent out an announcement that the danger has passed and the enchantments are back up. Of course, you will probably want to add your own protections again, Ak-tu, but for now, the spirits are out."

"Did a small cat attack at all?" Ak-tu asked.

"There was a big cat," Zyn said, his eyes puzzled. "It was a tiger, but with a club tail and spikes on its back."

Ak-tu sighed in relief. *Chaocat didn't get in, then.* "Fern, can you check the students and give them soothing potions if any of them are anxious?"

Ren opened her mouth, as if to say something, but she quickly closed it again as Fern answered.

"Already done," Fern said briskly.

"We currently have all students gathered in the Theatre with Aster," Khurshid added.

"Okay, I'll be sure to speak to them all after we're done with our meeting," murmured Ak-tu. "Come on, let's get inside to talk."

Ak-tu led the way to the Entrance Hall, then went down the hall leading to the Admin Office. Khurshid, Fern, Jabali, Ren, Zyn, and Sarala trailed him. Once they were inside the wood-scented room, he sat at the desk in the center of the space, signaling for the others to pull up chairs in front of him.

"So how did all of this start?" Ak-tu asked simply.

"It was C3!" Zyn growled. "He had a mirror shard! I told him we had to bring it to you, but then he said you were gone. And then he just ran back to his room, and when Sarala broke down the door, we saw he had like, *all* of the mirror shards!"

Ak-tu blinked. "Sarala broke down the door?" He glanced over at her. "Why'd you do that for?"

"He had a potentially dangerous mirror shard," Sarala pointed out. "And he wouldn't open up. It's a good thing we went in, though, don't you think?"

Ak-tu nodded. "What happened next?"

His kids launched into how the spirits had come out of the mirror and the fight began. They talked about different points in the battle, with Ren's vision and how the spirits tried to take down the defenses.

"Why were they doing that, Dad?" Zyn asked.

"How did you survive the ship crash?" Ren added.

"And how did Ms. Oakley control those plants?" Sarala queried.

Ak-tu sighed, not even knowing where to begin. He sat in silence for a long minute, the others not pressing him to speak as he thought. Finally, he stirred, looking up at his kids.

"I didn't realize what was going on until this morning, when I saw a small cat outside the school. A cat who I believed to be dead all these years… A spirit by the name of Chaocat."

"Kay-oh-cat?" Zyn mumbled, cocking his head.

"Like chaos cat or chaotic cat," Jabali offered.

"Oh!" Zyn snorted. "Weird."

"Anyhow," Ak-tu continued, "Chaocat is a powerful spirit. And though I didn't know if they still lived, I always made enchantments to keep them away wherever we went: the little house, the ship, the school… So it wasn't *actually* Chaocat who got into the school to place all these mirror shards. But they *were* the one behind the plan.

"And from what I can gather, their plan was to have someone set the shards inside the school and put together a mirror, which would then teleport their spirit friends when complete. The spirits would then be able to dismantle the enchantments from the inside, which would allow Chaocat into the school."

"Dad," Ren murmured, her eyes on the floor, "I saw a cat outside the school a few times…"

"You did? When?" he asked in alarm. *Has Chaocat really been under my nose this whole time?*

"One time last semester, and a few times this semester," Ren said, blushing. "I thought it was just a normal cat, not a spirit!"

Ak-tu sighed and closed his eyes. "It's my fault. I should have told you about Chaocat ages ago, so you'd know what to watch out for. It's just, all these years, I truly thought they had died... I never saw them while you kids have been alive, until today..."

Ren looked up at him again, the redness fading from her cheeks. "Why was Chaocat trying to get into the school?"

Ak-tu knew the question would come. But... "I don't have an answer," he uttered. "Yet it must be for more than just causing chaos for the fun of it, if they've been present all year...."

"Are we ever going to be able to leave the school again?" Zyn asked.

"Of course," Ak-tu said. "I'll just have to put enchantments on the ship when we travel...once it's back up and running, that is."

"How did the ship crash?" Ren asked.

"Chaocat," Ak-tu replied simply. "They came out of the mirror and got inside the enchantments."

"Plus them enchantments were barely existing on the ship in the first place," Jabali cut in.

Ak-tu nodded. "It's been a moment since I updated them, so Chaocat had an easy time getting on and crashing us. Anyhow, we found each other again and got back here as quickly as we could. Only one engine blew out, but it'll take a long time to get that ship repaired. We likely won't be traveling this summer...."

Nobody spoke for several long minutes. Ak-tu ran a hand through his hair, Zyn bounced his leg up and down, Ren chewed her bottom lip, Sarala stared at the floor, Jabali glanced around the table, Khurshid rubbed his large nose, Fern inspected her tattooed hand...

"So how does Ms. Oakley control the plants?" Sarala finally asked. "Is that some sort of extension of earth magic? Or is that plant magic?"

Fern sighed. "I'm a spirit," she muttered.

"You're a spirit?" Sarala growled.

"And so is Aster, though he'll deny it," she grunted. "You better not tell anyone. Especially after today, the students might not see spirits in a good light again."

"I do," Ren said firmly, beaming at Fern. "Not all spirits are evil. They're just like us, after all."

Ak-tu smiled. "Well said, Ren. I sincerely hope our students don't hate spirits after this, though...."

A small silence followed.

"Ooo, Dad, are we gonna get a reward for saving the school?" Zyn asked eagerly, his leg bouncing more rapidly.

Ak-tu chuckled lightly. "You kids did good. I'll think about it."

"Can I get a cool magic sword?"

"No."

Zyn moaned in disappointment. "But if Chaocat's still out there, shouldn't we get cool weapons to defend ourselves? It's not like I have magic."

Sarala snorted at that. "You have magic, Zyn—at least, with those objects you used in the fight."

"Yeah, but weapons would still be cool!"

Ak-tu sighed lightly. "I do suppose I'd better start teaching you two more martial arts... I don't want you to be locked up in the school forever. So you will learn more self-defense. You too, Sarala," he added, looking over at her.

She smiled lightly, then frowned. She seemed suddenly small in her seat.

"Is something wrong?" Ak-tu queried.

Sarala glanced at him briefly, then lowered her eyes. "I...need to tell you something..."

"What is it?"

Sarala clenched her jaw as everyone turned to stare at her. "I wasn't telling you the truth, when I said I'd been surviving in the wild alone. Because I wasn't alone. Not entirely..."

CHAPTER 30: MOTHER LOVE

Sarala took a deep breath. *I have to tell them. They deserve to know the truth…* She released her breath, trying to calm down though her heart was pounding in her ears.

"I grew up in the orphanage, but I ran away early on. In the beginning, I stayed in the same city. I learned how to get food on my own, climbing trees for fruits or stealing from others if I wanted a treat. But I was bored, so I eventually left the city behind and ventured out.

"I definitely wasn't prepared for surviving in the wild. There were so many animals that scared me…and maybe some spirits too, for all I know. They weren't exactly transparent today, were they?"

She sighed. "Anyway, I managed to make it to a town, where I stayed for a little bit. But the people there tried to put me in another orphanage, so I left. I didn't want to be stuck inside all day, feeling unwanted and…unloved…"

Sarala was a bit surprised that nobody interrupted her, telling her that a family would have adopted her if she'd stayed. She was glad, as she didn't want to expand on how much of a troublemaker she was, that *nobody* had wanted her. She didn't want to admit that she'd been adopted on two occasions, and sent back both times.

"I left that place, and went from town to town, sticking to the main road. But then I came across this traveling blacksmith… Her name is Mimiteh Donoma."

Ak-tu's eyes narrowed, but Sarala couldn't tell if he recognized the name or was merely making note of it.

"I was always interested in weapons and fighting," she admitted. "I never got along with other kids when I had been in school, since I'd always pick fights."

"I'm glad you didn't do that here," Ak-tu said.

Sarala shrugged. "Anyway, when I saw the weapons that she was selling along the road, I just had to take one for myself."

"So you stole your knives?" Ren asked. "I thought you made them?"

"Knives?" Ak-tu asked in surprise. "You have knives?"

"Yes, I have knives, but no, I didn't steal them," Sarala grumbled. "I tried to steal a sword, but it didn't work out. Mimiteh caught me by my wrist and threatened to get me arrested. But then she suddenly claimed that I'd be her new apprentice. I don't know why, honestly. Maybe she realized how young I was, or knew I was an orphan with nowhere to go. Either way, she took me under her wing and taught me all about blacksmithing. I was with her for a long time. She…she was almost like a…mother…to me."

Sarala could feel tears stinging the corners of her eyes, but she forced them away again. Taking a shaky breath, she pressed on in a hoarse voice, the words feeling scratchy in her throat.

"One day, she told me that she wanted me to learn magic. She gave me the butterfly knives I'd made, some food, and a pamphlet. Then, she just dumped me on the side of the road and took off in her boat. Like I didn't matter."

Sarala was unable to hold back the tears now. They dripped down her hooked nose and onto her shaking hands. A bitter rage swelled inside of her, and she almost forgot that she was talking to the others. She felt a warm hand on hers and looked up into Ren's reassuring eyes, but didn't feel any comfort.

"The pamphlet was for *this* school," Sarala said. "That's why I didn't know how to say 'Caihong' properly. Anyway, I lost the pamphlet ages ago, but I never forgot the name of this place. I made my way through the wild, as Mimiteh taught me survival skills too. It was still…scary…being out there, all alone, looking for some magic school.

"I don't know why I honestly bothered searching. There were days where I hated her so much, where I didn't want to do anything she told me to do. There were days I almost threw out my knives, since they were a connection to *her*. But I didn't. I kept the knives to ensure my survival, and when I discovered my magic, I wanted to learn. She told me that this school would take me in, if I managed to find it. So I searched, until I finally came across this place. But even then, I was still skeptical anyone would ever want to take me in...."

"Oh, Sarala!" Ren murmured, and she reached across the chair to hug her.

Sarala remained quiet, wishing her friend's hug could soothe her mingled anger and sorrow. As she said nothing more, Ren spoke up.

"Dad, I kinda have a confession too..." Ren whispered, lowering her eyes.

"What is it?"

"I think Sarala's knives might have something to do with everything," she said a bit hesitantly, glancing sidelong at Sarala, who clenched her jaw. "One night, I saw a bright light coming from Sarala's room. I asked her about it, and we checked out her room, but there was nothing inside. At the time, I didn't know she had knives. But that bright light I saw was very much like the light coming from the mirror when it'd been assembled, and the spirits came through."

"You think Mimiteh put a spirit in my *knives*?" Sarala gasped, realizing what Ren was saying.

Ak-tu inclined his head. "It's definitely possible a spirit is possessing your knives," he murmured. "That would explain how a spirit got past the enchantments to place the mirror shards in the school, as I don't think I made any enchantment against spirit-possessed objects... And if the spirit was in your knives, it'd make sense why Mimiteh wanted you to come to *this* school. And if she's working with Chaocat, that'd further explain how she knew I'd take you in...."

"But why wouldn't the spirit in her knives take down the enchantments?" Zyn asked, frowning at Sarala in confusion. "Why would it just drop mirror shards around the school?"

"It was dropping mirror shards," Fern spoke up, "so C3 could assemble the mirror and bring in more spirits. After all, spirits who possess things wouldn't have much power to do anything else, so the spirit probably needed help with getting the mirror together."

"Do you think C3 was working *with* the spirit? Or was he possessed too?" Khurshid inquired.

Ak-tu shook his head. "I'm not sure," he admitted. "I'll look more into the situation. But first, Sarala, could you show me your knives? If there's a spirit in there, we'll have to get rid of them."

Sarala got to her feet. "I'll happily get rid of the knives," she uttered. "I don't want any connection to them anymore."

"But, Sarala, you said you loved your knives," Ren reminded her.

"They're still a connection to Mimiteh," Sarala pointed out darkly. "Who knows what other enchantments she might have put on them?"

"Oh, oh, oh!" Zyn yelped, flapping his arms about. "I just remembered! C3 said that he got his elbow ring thingy from a stranger. It's enchanted. Do you think it was Mimiteh who made and enchanted it? I mean, who would just give some random kid an enchanted object?"

Sarala stomped her foot angrily. "Yes! That's it! She has rings just like that! I knew it looked familiar, but I couldn't place it…. It's been months since I saw her," she explained. *Still not a good reason to not recognize the same exact golden ring she wore on her wrists….*

"Khurshid and Fern, I'd like you to bring C3 to the Counseling Office and keep an eye on him until I get there," Ak-tu said heavily. "He could have been working with Mimiteh to get the spirits into the school. But I'll take a look at Sarala's knives now."

"Yes, Ak-tu," Khurshid said, and he and Fern left the Admin Office at once.

"Now, let's see those knives," Ak-tu groaned, getting to his feet and stretching.

Sarala stood and led the way across the Courtyard to the Tai Chi Studio, the Caihong family and Jabali following. They were soon climbing up the stone steps to Sarala's room on the fifth floor. She opened the door and went straight to her desk, grabbing the cold knives from her drawer and handing them to Ak-tu.

Ak-tu held the knives up to the light, inspecting them closely. "Ah, yes, I can feel a small source of energy here…. This spirit definitely would have been too weak to put the mirror together on their own. They barely seem to exist…."

"What are you gonna do with the spirit?" Zyn asked.

"Bring the knives outside the school and knock the spirit out," Ak-tu said with a shrug. "I don't care where they go, so long as they aren't inside the school."

"So you're not going to kill them?" Ren asked.

Ak-tu shook his head. "Why would I do that? Killing is wrong."

"*Can* spirits die? How does that work?" Zyn pressed.

Jabali placed a hand on his shoulder, causing him to jump in surprise. "Tha' can be a little complicated t'explain, and I'm sure your dad's worn out right now."

"I can give you spirit lessons later," agreed Ak-tu. "I have other matters to attend to."

He then slipped out the door, Jabali following quickly after him. Sarala glanced at the twins, nobody speaking for a long moment until Zyn's stomach growled loudly.

"Do you think lunch is ready?" he asked.

Ren snorted. "I guess we better check. You coming, Sarala?"

"In a bit," Sarala sighed, staring down at her feet.

"What's wrong?" Ren asked, stepping closer to her friend and placing a hand on her arm.

Sarala sighed again. "I'd just rather be alone..."

Ren exchanged a glance with her twin, then looked back to Sarala and nodded. "I understand," she whispered. "It must be hard for you, to relive all of that... We'll be in the Eating Hall, okay? We're here for you, whenever you need us."

"Thanks," grunted Sarala.

She moved to her window as the twins exited the room, their footsteps echoing in the stairwell until they faded entirely. Eyes glazed, she stared down at the Courtyard, watching mindlessly as students exited the Theatre and made for the Eating Hall as well. They stared at the destruction as they went, but the three teachers kept the students moving. Ren and Zyn soon exited the tower and hurried to join the group.

Is this why Mimiteh got rid of me? Sarala wondered, gazing at the destruction she had contributed to. *Is it all because she was using me, to get the spirits in the school? Or did she actually care and want me to learn magic? What did she want with me? From me? For me?*

Her gaze focused on her reflection on the glass. She looked

much the same when she had first come to the school: Her hair was a tangled mess, her robe was torn in places, and she was coated in dirt.

Would she have been proud of me for fighting the spirits off? Or angry that I did?

"I guess I'll never know…" She took a deep breath, then released it. "Goodbye, Mimiteh Donoma."

And she turned her back on her reflection.

CHAPTER 31: THE LOSER IN THE END

The Counseling Office could be entered from both the Courtyard and the small administration hallway. The lemon-scented office was dedicated to a small waiting area and two private rooms. A frogoyle was always stationed in the waiting room, to set up appointments if students needed counseling.

Ak-tu wished that he had received an appointment request from C3 at any point during the year. The boy was now sitting across from him in one of the private rooms, the door closed.

"So…you had a mirror shard," Ak-tu said, watching C3 closely.

C3 made no response, but stared at his black shoes.

"You had *plenty* of mirror shards. You've been putting them together all semester, to make the mirror whole again," Ak-tu went on. "Why didn't you tell me you had found mirror shards?"

C3 remained silent.

Ak-tu sighed. "C3, you're making this very difficult for me to figure out what happened. I've heard my children's accounts of how you put together the mirror. I just want to understand *why*. If you do not speak, I'm afraid I will have to expel you from this school, under suspicion of working with the spirits willingly."

C3's eyes widened as he flicked his gaze up to Ak-tu at last.

"If you tell me what happened—even if you were working with the spirits—I will not expel you," Ak-tu went on. "I will help you with whatever problem you might be facing. I will see this from your point of view. But if you do not tell me anything, I cannot help you, and I cannot trust you to remain at this school."

C3 nodded slowly, straightened his white collared shirt, then took a deep breath. "I'm…sorry…Mr. Caihong. I just…"

"We all make mistakes, C3. I'm not going to be angry with you for telling the truth, for admitting your mistakes."

"Okay," C3 said in a very small voice.

Ak-tu sat back in his wooden chair, allowing C3 to take over the conversation once he felt ready. C3 waited a few more moments, clearly trying to gather his thoughts. Then, he began, his mismatched eyes looking anywhere but at Ak-tu.

"I first found out about the spirits during the Moonlight Dance. I wanted a break, so I went outside for some fresh air. But then I saw something in the garden. I went to take a look. It was a spirit—but it didn't stick around long enough for me to get closer. Sarala saw me looking for it, and I thought she might have seen the spirit too. I was…hoping she'd want to help me look for it."

"Why?" Ak-tu asked, frowning.

C3 twiddled his thumbs together and stared at his feet. "I thought maybe we could be friends," he said in a low voice. "I haven't had a friend this entire semester."

"I believe people tend to be turned off by your blunt words," Ak-tu said.

C3 fidgeted uneasily.

"What happened next?" Ak-tu pressed. "You saw the spirit, but they left. Right?"

C3 nodded. "I left the garden, but then I saw it again. It was transparent and glowing. It was in the form of fog—or, at least, that's how it appeared. I watched it float up to your tower, to the fifth floor. It went right through the window.

"I didn't have my wand on me, since wands were not permitted at the dance. So I went back to my room to grab it, and by the time I was outside again, there weren't too many students around. They had either left the dance completely or went back inside. But nobody was watching, so I used my wand to lift me into the air. I was right outside the window. It was a bit difficult to open the window and hold my magic at the same time, but I managed to do it."

"Did you find the spirit when you trespassed into Sarala's room?" Ak-tu asked, stressing the fact that C3 had certainly broken a rule.

C3 noticed this and narrowed his eyes as he looked up at Ak-tu. "Sarala broke down my door and trespassed into my room. I'd say we're even."

"She was aware of a security issue," Ak-tu said.

"If the mirror shards were such a matter of importance—so dangerous—then why did you not alert the students? If I knew they were dangerous—"

"I did not want to alarm anybody since only the one had been found, and nothing had happened with it for months. Please continue with your story," Ak-tu interrupted.

C3 sighed. "Fine," he muttered, pushing his left sleeve up his arm, though it was still tucked away in the golden ring—the ring that apparently held enchantments.

"I didn't find the spirit. I tried calling to it, telling it that I wasn't going to hurt it. I told it that I wanted to meet it. The next day, right before we were all allowed to go home to our families for winter break, I found a mirror shard in my room."

"Your room?" Ak-tu asked with a frown. *I only had the fro-goyles check the public spaces...not the student quarters... No wonder they didn't find anything, then....*

C3 nodded. "I thought it had to be connected to the spirit. I asked aloud if it *was* the spirit's, and the fog-looking thing appeared. It told me in such a weak voice that it needed my help to assemble the mirror shards."

"Why would they ask this of you?" Ak-tu queried, fingering his mustache.

"It told me that it was stuck in that fog-looking form if I didn't get the mirror together," C3 said. "I told it I would help. It was pathetically fragile. It clearly needed some assistance. And since I've always wanted to see a spirit—"

Ak-tu nodded. "You'd do anything to keep them under your eye for research purposes," he said. "So the spirit continued to give you mirror shards?"

C3 shrugged. "Yes and no," he replied. "It *tried* to give me the mirror shards. But when it pulled them out from wherever it had them...or created them...or however it obtained them...the mirror shards wouldn't always end up in my room. There'd be pieces all over the school, which I'd need to locate. Once I attained the pieces, I brought them to my room and put them together, like a puzzle. It was a bit hard at first, but once I got more pieces, I was able to figure it out."

"The spirit never said where these mirror shards came from?" Ak-tu pressed, leaning forward.

C3 shook his head. "I assumed they were coming from somewhere else, though. If the spirit was creating them itself, how would it have lost them all over the school?"

They could have been doing that on purpose, to see how loyal you'd be, Ak-tu thought grimly.

"The last mirror shard I took—the one Zynivus saw and Sarala broke down my door over—was in the Art Studio."

"And how did you get the spirits to come through?"

"I did not know that was going to happen," admitted C3, looking Ak-tu in the eye. "I swear, I did not know. The spirit never told me that would happen. The spirit wasn't even in my room when I had followed its last instructions. It was sleeping in the object it claimed to be possessing—which I assumed was in Sarala's room, since that's where I saw it go."

"What 'last instructions' were these?" Ak-tu asked, his violet eyes narrowing.

"The spirit told me that once I had most or all of the mirror together, I had to shake my elbow ring several times," C3 said, taking his ring off. "I told the spirit it was enchanted to be heavy and come back to me, like a boomerang. But the spirit said there was another enchantment on it, from the blacksmith who made it."

Ak-tu frowned deeply. *So Mimiteh Donoma is behind this… she* did *help Chaocat and the other spirits.* "How did you get that ring?" he asked.

"I got it as a gift…from a stranger…" C3 murmured.

"How?" Ak-tu pressed.

C3 shrugged. "I was almost to the school when this person in a hood came out of the bushes. They gave me the ring, said it was enchanted, and just…left. It was odd, I admit, but how could I turn away an enchanted object? My family isn't well-off," he added in a bitter tone.

C3 waited a moment, then said, "Anyway, I did what the spirit told me to do, once the mirror was mostly assembled. I did not want your children and Sarala to interfere, not when I'd come so far with putting the mirror together, not after promising to help the spirit. But when I did that, all of those spirits appeared. I realized that I had been lied to."

Ak-tu nodded slowly. "The spirit used you."

"Yeah," C3 muttered, his lip curling back a bit.

"Very well," Ak-tu said with a sigh. "Is there anything else that you feel you need to tell me? Whether it relates to the mirror shards and spirits or not...."

C3 slumped in his chair, then said, "I stole Mint's notes on enchanting objects."

"Why?"

"I wanted to see how to do it, and Mint presented the perfect opportunity. So I took the notes; they were useless. Even the spirit I was trying to help did not guide me."

"So you did not learn how to enchant objects?"

"No," C3 said dully. "I wish I had."

"I once more admire your eagerness to learn, C3, but stealing from other students is not the way to go about it. Nor is helping unknown spirits," Ak-tu said seriously.

C3 nodded.

"Now, as I said, I will not expel you," Ak-tu went on, sitting up in his chair. "I'm glad to hear you weren't *actually* trying to get those dangerous spirits into the school. I'm going to let you off with a very serious warning, C3."

C3 nodded quietly.

"I would also like you to serve meditation sessions with me for the remainder of the school year, on both Saterday and Sunday, to reflect what you've done."

C3 nodded again.

"Next time, if you see anything weird, I want you to report it to me at once," Ak-tu went on. "Understand?"

"Yes, Mr. Caihong," C3 murmured.

"Very well."

Ak-tu got to his feet and walked the short distance to C3. He put a hand on the boy's shoulder. After a moment, C3 looked up at him, and Ak-tu offered him a small smile.

"I understand none of this was intentional," Ak-tu said. "I understand we all make mistakes. Don't let this define who you are.

You've learned the lesson."

C3 nodded.

"You may leave."

C3 got to his feet and moved towards the door.

"Just give me that elbow ring of yours," Ak-tu added, before he could open the door.

The boy hesitated, then reluctantly handed the ring to Ak-tu. He exited the room, leaving the door gaping wide behind him.

Ak-tu inspected the golden ring, frowning.

Chaocat, Mimiteh, and that possession spirit were working together, to bring in those other spirits, to take down the defenses…. But why? Why does Chaocat want to get in? Why would Mimiteh work with them? How do they know each other? And who was the possession spirit?

When Ak-tu had managed to shake the spirit out of Sarala's knives, the spirit had been in its fog-looking form, just as C3 had said. The phantom had quickly headed for the forest, leaving the knives plain again. Once sure the knives weren't further enchanted, Ak-tu had merely added them to the Kung Fu Studio; there was no point in getting rid of perfectly crafted knives, after all.

Ak-tu sighed deeply and sat back down, turning the ring over in his hands. *What does Chaocat want?*

A knock sounded on the door, and he looked up to see Jabali peering down at him. Ak-tu offered his friend a small smile.

"We gotta talk," Jabali murmured. "Admin Office work for ya?"

Ak-tu nodded wordlessly. He got to his feet and trailed Jabali out of the Counseling Office, down the Admin Hall, and to the Admin Office once more. After entering, he closed the door behind them and sat on the floor in a lotus position, his legs aching after sitting in the chair.

"What's on your mind?" Ak-tu asked.

Jabali remained standing for a moment, then sat down across from him with a sigh. "Y'know them students likely took pictures 'n videos o' the spirit attack, right?"

Ak-tu nodded.

"Word's gonna get out. This school could get shut down by the gov. You could be seen as a criminal, for allowing this t'happen."

"It wasn't my fault, and nobody was harmed," Ak-tu said.

"Well, apart from the teachers, and I'm sure my kids were a little scuffed up. But there was nothing serious. And we'll have the Courtyard cleaned up in no time."

"Tha' don't matter when it comes to the gov. You *know* that, Ak-tu," Jabali murmured seriously.

Ak-tu groaned and raked both of his hands through his soft hair. "Yeah…I know," he uttered. "But they can't shut down the school if everything is fine. The most they can do is inspect it. And we can say the spirit attack was…an illusion, a magic show!"

Jabali looked doubtful. "Maybe it's time you shut down the school, and get back t'traveling. Whatever Chaocat might want, it can't be good. You and your family would be safer if you leave this place."

"But the ship is damaged."

"I'll pay for the repairs."

"But we still need to get it to a shop, and by the time we get it there, it'll probably be summer," Ak-tu pointed out. "And by the time it's all fixed up, school will be back in session. Besides, I can't shut down the school on all of these students."

"Transfer the ownership to Khurshid," Jabali said with a careless wave of his hand.

Ak-tu crossed his arms over his chest. "Wouldn't that just make me look *more* like a guilty criminal? To leave the school and run away with my kids?"

Jabali sighed. "I suppose you're right…"

Ak-tu's gaze softened and he reached his hand out to his friend's arm, feeling a scratch on his smooth skin. "Jabali, I understand your concerns. I really do. I'm worried that the government will come too. But I'm confident I can keep this place open. I'll make the school take three years instead of four, that way we're outta here sooner. And when my kids are done, I'll give Khurshid the school. He's the one who wanted a magic school, after all…so he can have it.…"

"Why not give it to him now?"

Ak-tu shook his head. "I'm not running from these problems. I'm standing my ground. Besides—I'm the one who teaches the advanced magic classes, and the martial arts, and most of the art classes. The students need me."

Jabali eyed him for a long moment, then placed his large hand over Ak-tu's. "Why d'ya gotta be so stubborn?"

Ak-tu stuck his tongue out at his friend. "Why do you always want to run away?"

Jabali's gaze darkened and he shoved Ak-tu's hand away as he shifted his position. "I know when it's best to move on."

"And I'll move on when it's time to move on," Ak-tu said gently, surprised at Jabali's sullen tone. "But it's not time yet. Soon. But not yet."

Jabali sighed. "Well, ya would know best…"

"Besides, what would I do with Sarala?" Ak-tu pointed out. "I can't leave her at the school alone, especially after she's made friends with my kids. And I don't know if she'd want to go with us…if she views us as family yet."

"Why not ask?"

Ak-tu shook his head. "Not yet," he murmured. "She's been through a lot, and bringing up that stuff with Mimiteh is likely to leave her in a poor headspace. I don't want her choice to be tainted by memories of Mimiteh."

Jabali nodded his understanding. "Makes sense to give her more time. Ya think one more year of the school before you travel again?"

"Probably two."

"And do ya know wha' Chaocat wants? Why they'd find you all these years later?"

Ak-tu shook his head. "No…but I'm sure we'll figure it out soon…."

CHAPTER 32: SON AND DAUGHTER

Ren was happy to see that the school was back to normal in no time.

Ak-tu told his children that C3 had been working with the possessive spirit, but that he had been used. He made it clear that the twins were not to discuss the matter, especially in public. Of course, Zyn couldn't resist telling Sarala, but the siblings otherwise kept their promise to their father and did not speak of it to anyone else. C3 now avoided the twins and Sarala, refusing to talk to them in classes or outside them. He stopped making rude remarks and asking so many questions, staying quiet in class after his near-expulsion.

The other students were terrified at what had happened with the spirits, and a lot of them felt anger towards spirits after. Fern told the students that she was a spirit to quell their bitter feelings, which surprisingly worked. A good number of students had their wounds healed by Fern, and every student had taken her Plants and Potions classes for their first year (at the very least). Ak-tu reminded the students that not all spirits were bad-tempered, and that plenty of kind spirits like Fern existed.

He also requested that the students did not share any pictures or videos they might have taken with anyone. Of course, a few students had already told their families or friends, but luckily there wasn't a public sharing platform on the air-net for the files to spread even further.

Ak-tu added enchantments to the school's defenses in broad daylight, for all of the students to be reassured that they were indeed protected again. He further told the students to tell him of any suspicious activity, especially if there were weird objects lying around. He gave the students a brief version of how the spirits got in and why they had attacked, but left out all names.

Once the Courtyard was back together, classes resumed the following week. It was almost like nothing had happened at all, though the students spoke eagerly about the events like it had been a thrilling story and not a dangerous situation. Most of the students had watched from the windows as Ren, Zyn, and Sarala battled the spirits, so the trio was continuously pestered to relive the fight. Sarala eventually threatened to use her magic against the students if they kept asking questions, so the requests finally stopped.

Ak-tu, Jabali, and Khurshid went back for the broken ship and brought it to the school, which took quite some time. Ak-tu was confident it was salvageable, but Ren wasn't quite so sure.

Afterwards, Jabali left, barely saying a word to the twins. They still didn't know what to make of their father's friend, and they did not understand why Ak-tu had kept him hidden their whole lives. The twins pondered Jabali's role in the mess as the semester went on.

Ren assumed that Jabali knew something about Chaocat, while Zyn made a mad guess that Jabali ran a secret anti-spirit organization ("Dad would never associate with someone like that," Ren had pointed out in exasperation). Sarala gave no input, remaining tight-lipped after she had revealed her own background.

Whenever passing the open windows, Ren would glance outside for any sign of Chaocat or other spirits. But no cats or walking trees lingered outside—at least, for as far as Ren could see.

By the time May 10 arrived for the first day of finals, it was like nothing had happened at all.

Ren, Zyn, and Sarala hurried to their Magic Studies class after they finished breakfast. They took their seats at the front of the classroom, arriving early to get some last-minute study time in.

"I'm still a bit confused by how magic works in boats," Zyn commented, checking the study guide Ren had made on the family mirror.

"Zyn, you have a flying ship and you don't know how it works?" Sarala scoffed.

"*Dad* has a flying ship, and it's not like it's doing much flying right now," Zyn pointed out. "But, um, yeah…I'm not the best with all the mechanical stuff, and I don't get how the magic works with it. Is it like enchanted objects?"

"No, boats aren't enchanted at all," Ren said. "People use their magic to move the boats around, typically using the environment around them. But some boats have mechanisms in them—like our ship—which are meant to be triggered by certain types of magic, like fire."

"But *how* does it work?" Zyn pressed.

He didn't get an answer, as Khurshid entered the room. The teacher smiled over at them, gazing a bit past Sarala's head.

"Hello, you three," he greeted. "Ready for your finals?"

"Yep!" Ren said confidently, as Zyn and Sarala quickly agreed.

"Good. Because the bell's about to ring."

And the bell rang.

The Magic Studies final was a lot longer than the test they had taken the previous semester. It was a written test once more, but with more essay answers than multiple choice ones. The test covered both semesters' worth of learning, from the difference between magicians and wielders to how magic helped progress society. By the time the class was over, the students were dreading the coming tests, more out of exhaustion than worry.

Zyn waved farewell as the first-years went to the Magic Channeling room. Khurshid ushered the students to their elemental cauldrons and told them to sit down. He then had each student go up to the in-class obstacle course one at a time, where the student had to make it through using both the elements around them and the elements within them. The obstacle course was ridiculously easy for Ren and Sarala, considering they were in a real obstacle course of a battle only weeks before.

The students moved to the Greenhouse for Plants. The glass paneling had not been restored, as the plants seemed to like the gaping holes. Ak-tu was willing to leave the panels broken, at least until it got cold. The students had gained a new appreciation for the plants, after watching them battle at Fern's command.

Fern had the students go up to different plants, one at a time. They had to name the plant, describe its properties, test how much magic it had, and harvest a piece of it.

Ren was quite pleased that she got the spiky plant, which had stabbed her with one of its spikes at the beginning of the spring semester. She now knew all about the plant, and was extra fond of it for shielding her against the spirits when she had collapsed to her vision.

"This is a bristled bramble, which has highly defensive properties. A lot of wands are made from its branches—or spikes—and its leaves have healing properties, particularly for fighting off infections. This plant is even used as a fence around someone's house! Umm…Ms. Oakley, do I have to show off how to detect its magical level? I mean, we all know it's very magical, one of the most magical plants there are, due to its ability to move and shoot spikes."

Fern smiled softly. "Quite true. I'd rather not get struck down by a spike, so you can have a pass on that one. Please harvest a piece of it."

Ren nodded and walked up to the plant, her wand raised at the ready to make an air shield if necessary. Reaching her hand out and smiling at the bramble, she hummed softly to it, imagining the energy around her glowing with joy. It made her hum more loudly and feel calm, which the plant felt in turn. It crooned and quivered its branches, its spikes shrinking a bit in size. Ren then stretched her hand out, running it over the smooth bits of plant she could find, before pulling one of the spikes. She continued humming as she did it, and even as she moved away.

"Excellent!" Fern praised.

The students had to make a very complicated brew for Potions—and they had to do it alone, much to Sarala's relief (she sent Frost a glare from across the room, which made him trip over a cauldron). There were luckily few ingredients, which were pre-chopped. The most difficult part was coming up with all the rhymes for the enchantments. But Ren completed her brew successfully, getting a dark green potion by the end.

The girls went to the Eating Hall, ecstatic that they were done with their toughest tests.

"Ready for Kung Fu?" Zyn asked them during lunch.

"I hope I pass my test tomorrow," Sarala grunted; she'd been trying to test for her purple sash, but no matter how many times she tested, Ak-tu wouldn't pass her.

"I mean, at least if you don't, you'll have all summer to make your martial arts better," Ren pointed out cheerfully.

Sarala cast her a glum look.

"Yeah, if you get your purple sash, you'll be bored all summer, unable to learn anything of the next level," Zyn added.

"But didn't your father say he'd teach us more Kung Fu?" Sarala asked.

"Maybe he will, maybe he won't," Zyn said with a shrug.

Sarala looked like she was ready to pummel him.

They went to Kung Fu class, Sarala leaving them at the door. Most of the class was made of green sashes now, though there were two yellow sashes.

"I'm testing you all today!" Ak-tu called. "Yellow sashes, you're up first. Green sashes, get ready. My goal is to get you to your next sash before the year ends."

"Can you imagine still being a yellow sash?" Zyn asked Ren. "Even if we got green, we'd still be stuck in this first-level class next year."

Ren shrugged. "I guess we'd better practice hard, so we make it to blue. It's not a guarantee that we'll get it, even if we test. Just look at Sarala."

The twins therefore moved to the far side of the mat, leaving a good amount of space for the two testing students, Frost and Ayl. The siblings practiced shuffling kicks and forms, moving almost in unison.

Once the yellow sash students earned their green sashes, Ak-tu took four students at a time to test for blue. It took a long time to test everyone, that they went overtime into the Kung Fu 1B class.

Ren and Zyn were part of the last group to test. They performed the green sash kicks, some self-defense techniques, the form exercise, the yellow sash kicks, the rest of the techniques, and the white sash kicks. They ended with a grappling match, Ren and Zyn able to partner up. Ren beat Zyn by a few points, but it was an even match; Zyn's grappling skills had definitely improved over the semester.

Ak-tu gave them feedback once they were dressed in their white uniform tops again. He then passed each of them to the blue sash, beaming at his children for a long moment before ruffling both of their heads fondly (the other students laughed while Ren blushed in embarrassment and Zyn shoved Ak-tu's hand away).

For the rest of the second Kung Fu class, they did some light matches for fun. Once class was over, Ren, Zyn, and C3 went to the Tai Chi Studio.

"We'll just do the test and be done with class for the day," Ak-tu told them. "Perform the 40-Step."

The students positioned themselves around the room, then began their form once they were sure they wouldn't bump into one another. Ren moved her bare feet slowly across the ground, making sure she shifted her weight properly.

Heel, toe, then go, she repeated in her mind as she went. *Toe, heel, then peel…*

Once they finished the slow-moving form, which took about ten minutes, the students teamed up to do push hands. Ren and Zyn did a match, in which Ren won easily. Zyn and C3 then went together, the match more of a challenge that C3 just barely managed to win, much to Zyn's annoyance. Ren and C3 went last, Ren avenging Zyn as she sent C3 staggering several paces back and won by ten points.

Ak-tu gave them all feedback once more, then passed them all to their blue fringes. They tied the new fringes around their waists, each of them smiling proudly, including the quiet C3.

"Next year, you'll be in the Tai Chi 2 classes!" Ak-tu said. "You'll learn how to use a sword. Should be fun!"

"We *do* get magic swords!" Zyn yowled, causing C3 to wince.

Ak-tu stared at Zyn, then said, "No."

Ren and Zyn had a break for the rest of the week. Sarala managed to pass to her purple sash in Kung Fu on Trizday, and the three celebrated by playing plenty of games in the brightly lit Courtyard. None of them worried about their Art finals; even Theatre wouldn't be too difficult, as both Ren and Zyn wouldn't be taking to the stage this time.

They were right not to lose sleep over the Art tests. The students had to do the same thing the previous semester, showing off their work and performing their art. The Theatre production, which was a story about two lovers, was a joy for the school to watch. Ren and Zyn had the lighting and sound effects on point.

"We're done!" Zyn yowled as they left the Theatre that afternoon. "We're done with the first year!"

"Now we can forget everything we learned!" Ren added.

"Don't forget *everything*!" Ak-tu scolded, coming up behind them and placing his hands on their shoulders.

"Okay, we'll remember exactly five percent!" promised Ren.

Ak-tu rolled his eyes. "I was actually hoping to talk to you two, now that you don't have to worry so much about learning and tests. Let's get inside."

"But it's time for dinner," Zyn complained.

"Come on!"

Sarala hurried towards the Eating Hall as Ak-tu steered his children towards the Tai Chi Studio. They entered the tower, where Ak-tu locked the door behind them. He ushered the twins to sit down at the round table, though he remained standing on the woven rug.

"There's a little more I need to tell you," Ak-tu began. "And I'm sure you still have questions. Let's start with those."

"Who's Jabali?" Zyn asked. "Besides your best friend?"

"We grew up together at the martial arts school where I was raised," Ak-tu said. "We eventually traveled together, looking for spirits."

"You were spirit seekers?" Zyn gasped.

"In a way," Ak-tu murmured. "We sought spirits and tried to lay traps to capture them a few times, in order to study them. But then we stopped, as we realized what we were doing was wrong—not that any of our traps were ever successful, and the spirits always got away."

"Is that why you never told us about him?" Ren inquired. "Because you didn't want us thinking you harmed spirits?"

"We didn't," Ak-tu said earnestly. "But...yes, I suppose that's why I was reluctant to tell you all these years...plus it'd mean bringing up Chaocat, and...other things.... I just wasn't ready. But now I am."

He cleared his throat and continued. "Anyhow, Jabali was still traveling with me when I first got you kids. But we later went our separate ways, as he wanted to open some businesses and get started with his life. We've stayed in touch, and I'd reach out on occasion to see if he ever seen or heard anything of Chaocat. But he never did."

"Who *is* Chaocat? And what would be at the school that they want?" Zyn asked. "It can't be you, right? So is it your enchanted objects? Like the deck of cards you gave me?"

Ak-tu sighed. "Chaocat is complicated. One moment, they might act like your friend. And the next, they can be your enemy. If we ever have the bad luck of running into Chaocat again—which, I daresay we will, since they've found the school—I warn you two to keep your guard up. Chaocat is an excellent actor. They will pull you in close, then—" Ak-tu clapped his hands together abruptly, the sound sharp and causing all three to wince.

"It seems like you really know this spirit," Ren observed.

"We used to be friends," Ak-tu admitted.

"Friends?" gasped Ren.

"Like I said…they're a great actor," he said darkly. "Jabali and I used to travel with them, and they taught me a lot of the spirit magic I know… But that was a long time ago… Just watch your step around them. There's no telling what they might do to get whatever it is they want."

"And you really have no idea what that might be?" Zyn asked.

"Did you *do* something, to end your friendship?" Ren asked quietly. "To make Chaocat hate you?"

Ak-tu turned away from them, facing the back of the couch. "We fought. Long and hard. And that's when…" He glanced over his shoulder at her, his eyes gleaming. "That's when you appeared, Ren."

Ren stared at him, wide-eyed. "W-what do you mean, I 'appeared'?"

"After we fought, there was a terrible storm," Ak-tu murmured, sitting on the top of the couch. "And I looked for Chaocat. But I found you instead."

"I thought you said you adopted us? From an orphanage?" Ren queried.

"Yeah, and then you changed our names and left the country, so you wouldn't have to deal with the adoption agency bothering you all the time, checking up on us and all that. Right?" Zyn added.

Ak-tu shifted uneasily. "That's true for *you*, Zyn. But it's not true of Ren. Ren, there's a reason I gave you the middle name of 'Arashi'—storm. It was in that storm that I found you."

"Where were my parents?" Ren questioned as she leaned forward, intrigued.

"That's the thing. There's no way you could have been on that island, Ren," Ak-tu murmured. "The island was tiny and deserted. There was never any form of civilization on that rock."

"Then…where did I come from?" Ren mumbled.

"I can't say for certain, but I think you were a gift from the spirits themselves," Ak-tu said, staring into her eyes. "I think they gave you to me."

Ren gaped at him. "But…does that mean…am I a spirit? Is that why I have visions?"

Ak-tu shook his head. "No. I don't believe you are. A majority of spirits do not appear human in the slightest, unless they know how to shapeshift and choose a human form as their second form —which is something a baby would not be able to do."

"What about Fern and Aster? They look human," Ren pointed out.

Ak-tu nodded. "Fern is a faery, noticeable by all those tattoos on her body. Aster is actually in a second form, as his first form was far from human. Anyhow, I don't know where you came from, Ren, but I think it was the spirits that gave you to me."

"What if Chaocat gave me to you? And now they want me back?" Ren gasped, her hands twisting nervously in her lap as her heart began beating in her throat.

Ak-tu dipped his head. "That was another point I've been considering. They were the one who told me spirits would gift humans children. And before meeting on that island, we had still been friends…. It was only after the storm that I remembered we had fought…that they had turned on me… And I thought they had perished in that battle, or in the storm that followed."

His eyes were glazed over by now, his mind clearly far away. Ren and Zyn exchanged a glance, but neither said anything. It was several minutes before Ak-tu shook his head roughly and pulled himself from his stupor.

"I just want you two to be *very* careful. You understand?" he asked seriously.

They both nodded, Ren feeling quite dazed.

"Good. Now, if you don't have any further questions, we should go have some dinner."

Ak-tu unlocked the door of the tower and left, not bothering to lock it behind him. Ren turned to Zyn, her eyes still wide in shock.

"What if you *are* a spirit?" Zyn whispered.

Ren shook her head. "I-I dunno," she mumbled. "I mean, I think Dad's right. I'm not that different, am I?"

"You're different in that you're *you*," Zyn said, offering her a smile. "There's only one you, and you'll always be special, spirit or human or poky bush."

Ren snorted in laughter. "Well, I've got elemental magic, and very few spirits possess that, so that pretty much settles it!"

"Then let's get some food!"

The twins got to their feet, Ren feeling discontent as they went. All she could hear were Ak-tu's words running through her head...

What if Chaocat *did* drop her off on the island, for Ak-tu to find? Was she being used in some way, like Mimiteh had likely used Sarala? What would that mean? Was she some sort of secret weapon to get to Ak-tu? But why would Chaocat need her for that?

"By the way, I don't think I care for the whole he/him pronouns," Zyn commented as they crossed the Courtyard to catch up with their father.

"Oh?" Ren mumbled, blinking several times as she registered what Zyn said.

"I wanna try out they/them!" Zyn said eagerly. "I think I like that. It's kinda like I can be both genders that way—a mix, you know? A balance of each."

"Well, whatever you choose," Ren said, smiling at her twin, "there will only ever be one you too."